**Praise for th**

T0085798

"The grim title should serve as a warning. This psychological thriller has some fine language and a strong narrative pull that keeps the pages turning, but the series of crimes that occur are unnerving. As *Head Wounds* rolls to its clever, crazy gothic conclusion, no one could accuse Mr. Palumbo of being flat."

—*Pittsburgh Post-Gazette*

"The author gets maximum suspense out of the buildup to each killing, taking us along on a child kidnapping and grave robbing, until we get to an ending that has something to do with a Warren Zevon song. Yes, it makes a kind of sense, but it's the compelling craziness of the story that keeps us reading."

—*Booklist*

"A spectacular ride."

—Thomas Perry, *New York Times* bestselling author

"This is a book that'll make you lock your doors and check your computer's security settings."

—Joseph Finder, *New York Times* bestselling author

*Phantom Limb*

"He serves as the perfect point of view character, central to the action without needing to clamor for attention as Daniel's personal story continues to evolve."

—*Publishers Weekly*

"Pittsburgh psychologist and police consultant Daniel Rinaldi is the refreshingly low-key and unassuming protagonist appearing in this fourth in the series of crime novels. Yet as a former Golden Gloves boxer, he's willing and able to throw down in situations that warrant a good right cross to the jaw."

—*Pittsburgh Post-Gazette*

## *Night Terrors*

"Answers prove elusive as the murders begin to pile up. Palumbo ratchets up the stakes in this psychological thriller but maintains the emotional complexity."

—*Publishers Weekly*

"Palumbo's thrillers are strictly for late at night and for readers who have no pressing engagements early the next day."

—*Kirkus Reviews*

"Palumbo, an award-winning Hollywood screenwriter turned psychotherapist, uses all his professional experience to craft short, action- and tension-filled chapters and insightful sketches of people traumatized by violence."

—*Booklist*

"Complications abound, but Rinaldi—and Mr. Palumbo—resolve them in ways both plausible and compelling."

—*Pittsburgh Post-Gazette*

*Fever Dream*

"Palumbo's exciting second mystery featuring Pittsburgh psychologist Daniel Rinaldi takes the reader into the seamy side of the Steel City, chock-full of corruption and crime, love and loss."

—*Publishers Weekly*

"In this fine novel. . . Rinaldi's methods are as much Columbo as shrink: he notices details that don't fit and picks at them until the whole psychodrama comes clear. A smart, strong read."

—*Booklist*

"A smoking hot trail of dirty money, dirtier politicians, and wholesale killing. . . Daniel Rinaldi keeps his cool and his edge, Jack Reacher with a psychology degree."

—*Kirkus Reviews*

"A high-octane police procedural. Lots of action makes for a roller-coaster read."

—*Library Journal*

"Running at a fever pitch, Palumbo's second novel featuring Pittsburgh psychologist Dan Rinaldi opens with the trauma expert called to the scene of a bank robbery and hostage situation. Multiple twists attest to the fact that Palumbo, a therapist himself, got his chops in Hollywood."

—*Ellery Queen's Mystery Magazine*

"A high-adrenaline action thriller with some clever deductive reasoning to show whodunit. Highly recommended."

—*San Francisco/Sacramento Review*

"The brisk pace and intelligent writing about the adventurous and heroic psychologist will leave the reader wanting more."

—*Portland Book Review*

*Mirror Image*

"Using his background as a licensed psychotherapist to good advantage, Palumbo infuses his fast-moving, suspenseful story with fascinating texture, interesting characters, and the twists, turns, and surprises of a mind-bending mystery. Very impressive."

—Stephen J. Cannell, writer/creator of *The Rockford Files* and *New York Times* bestselling mystery author

**Also by Dennis Palumbo**

The Daniel Rinaldi Thrillers

*Mirror Image*

*Fever Dream*

*Night Terrors*

*Phantom Limb*

*Head Wounds*

Nonfiction

*Writing from the Inside Out: Transforming Your Psychological Blocks to Release the Writer Within*

# PANIC ATTACK

# PANIC ATTACK

A DANIEL RINALDI THRILLER

DENNIS PALUMBO

Poisoned Pen Press

Copyright © 2021 by Dennis Palumbo
Cover and internal design © 2021 by Sourcebooks
Cover design by The BookDesigners
Cover images © Joseph Sohm/Shutterstock, Lincoln Beddoe/Shutterstock, Rattanapon Ninlapoom/Shutterstock, FOTOKITA/Shutterstock

Sourcebooks, Poisoned Pen Press, and the colophon are registered trademarks of Sourcebooks.

All rights reserved. No part of this book may be reproduced in any form or by any electronic or mechanical means including information storage and retrieval systems—except in the case of brief quotations embodied in critical articles or reviews—without permission in writing from its publisher, Sourcebooks.

The characters and events portrayed in this book are fictitious or are used fictitiously. Any similarity to real persons, living or dead, is purely coincidental and not intended by the author.

All brand names and product names used in this book are trademarks, registered trademarks, or trade names of their respective holders. Sourcebooks is not associated with any product or vendor in this book.

Published by Poisoned Pen Press, an imprint of Sourcebooks
P.O. Box 4410, Naperville, Illinois 60567-4410
(630) 961-3900
sourcebooks.com

Library of Congress Cataloging-in-Publication Data

Names: Palumbo, Dennis, author.
Title: Panic attack : a Daniel Rinaldi thriller / Dennis Palumbo.
Description: Naperville, Illinois : Poisoned Pen Press, [2021] | Series: Daniel Rinaldi thrillers ; book 6
Identifiers: LCCN 2020056420 (print) | LCCN 2020056421 (ebook) | (trade paperback) | (epub)
Subjects: GSAFD: Suspense fiction.
Classification: LCC PS3566.A5535 P36 2021 (print) | LCC PS3566.A5535 (ebook) | DDC 813/.54--dc23
LC record available at https://lccn.loc.gov/2020056420
LC ebook record available at https://lccn.loc.gov/2020056421

Printed and bound in the United States of America.
SB 10 9 8 7 6 5 4 3 2 1

*To Daniel, for whom Dr. Rinaldi is named, with love—*

*"Never say you know the last word about the human heart."*

—HENRY JAMES

# Chapter One

On a bitterly cold afternoon in late October, I was one of twenty thousand witnesses to a murder.

Not ten minutes before, I was sitting next to Martin Hobbs, dean of Teasdale College, sipping spiked cider from a thermos, my head sunk low in the collar of my winter coat.

Above, enormous white clouds loomed like a chain of floating islands, backlit by a wan sun whose diffused light crowned the trees still boasting autumnal colors. Beyond, a carpet of crisp, freeze-dried grass stretched to meet the ancient Allegheny Mountains. A typical fall landscape in Western Pennsylvania, yet less than twenty miles from downtown Pittsburgh, in a small, formerly thriving farming community called Lockhart.

"Isn't this great, Dr. Rinaldi?" Dean Hobbs rubbed his gloved hands in excitement. "Perfect football weather, eh?"

I nodded, shivering. We were in the cushioned VIP seats, right on the fifty-yard line in the small private college's new football stadium. I'm more of an NFL fan, especially when it comes to the Steelers, and hadn't been to a college game since my undergraduate days at Pitt. But when the dean asked me to join him for Saturday's matchup against the team's division rivals, I didn't see how I could refuse.

The evening before, I'd given the commencement address in the Reynolds Auditorium, another newly built facility on the rural campus, a gift of billionaire alum William Reynolds. Having amassed a fortune in real estate, the late philanthropist had earmarked the funds for the stately building in his will.

Now, with kickoff only a few minutes away, I let my attention drift from Dean Hobbs' relentless boosterism and replayed my speech from the night before. It had gone reasonably well, though both the school's faculty and its graduating class were perplexed by the phalanx of print, online, and broadcast journalists who rushed me as soon as I'd finished.

I couldn't believe I was still news, now more than eight months after the Sebastian Maddox case. Although I'd done my best to keep a low profile, the media wouldn't let the story go. Just last month, I was approached by a cable news producer who said they were planning a special about the crimes, and asked if I'd agree to be a participant in the program.

Naturally, I refused. Not that they needed my onscreen presence, anyway. There was enough news footage from that period—the various bloody crime scenes, the smoking remains of the fire that had raged through the psychiatric clinic; there'd even been coverage of the last victim's funeral. After all, the mayor himself—never one to pass up a photo op—had attended that gaudy affair.

To me, this proposed "special" was nothing but a particularly gratuitous exploitation of a real tragedy. It's what my late wife used to call "murder porn," and I was having none of it. Those horrific days left psychic scars on me as fresh as when they'd first been inflicted—not to mention what had happened to friends, colleagues, and patients. Eight months of therapy later, and I still barely slept at night.

But the Maddox case, following numerous high-profile investigations I'd been involved with in recent years, had cemented my reputation as both a psychologist and consultant to the Pittsburgh Police Department (officially the Pittsburgh Bureau of Police, though no one calls it that). While I hadn't exactly become a household name, a good number of people knew who I was. A PR guy even called, offering to help me enhance my "brand." I couldn't hang up fast enough.

Nowadays, unlike in those earlier cases, and especially in recent months, I made sure to stay out of the public eye. No more interviews with the *Post-Gazette*, no more "expert" commentary on CNN about the possible motives behind the latest mass shooting or new string of serial killings. Like the victims of violent crimes I specialized in treating, I needed time and therapeutic support to address my own traumatic reaction to what Maddox had put me through. Lately, other than a few intimate meals with close friends and my ongoing clinical practice, I'd kept mostly to myself.

So, when the invitation came to speak at Teasdale College, a modest private institution east of the city, my initial reaction was to politely decline. Then I mentioned it to my own therapist, who suggested it might aid in my recovery to, in his words, "return to the land of the living."

That's how I ended up cupping a thermos of not-quite-spiked-enough cider and smiling as attentively as I could while Dean Hobbs prattled on about his school. In his late fifties, reed-thin and balding, his neck swathed in a scarf emblazoned with Teasdale's colors, the dean had finally taken a breath and glanced at his watch. His small, inoffensive eyes gleamed merrily.

"Almost time for the tiger."

"What tiger?"

"The Teasdale Tiger. Our team mascot. The fans love him. Especially the kids."

He nodded at the home team's sidelines, where in addition to legendary local coach George Pulaski and his heavily jacked players, a two-legged tiger was doing deep knee bends.

It was a full-body costume, complete with a head cover with an appropriately tiger-ish dark, whiskered snout and muff collar. There were also impressive-looking claws on the furry hands and feet, and a floppy tail. For a moment, I wondered how the guy inside the costume could breathe. On the other hand, he was probably warmer than anyone else in the stadium.

Dean Hobbs nudged me. "Know who's in the tiger costume?"

"No."

A conspiratorial chuckle. "Neither does anyone else. Only Coach Pulaski and I know. It's an idea we borrowed from Pitt. Their Pitt Panther mascot."

Of course I knew what he was talking about. For years, my alma mater, the University of Pittsburgh, kept the identity of its similarly costumed football mascot, the Pitt Panther, a secret. All anybody knew was that it was one of four undergrads who rotated in the job, all of whom had been sworn to secrecy. Even after they graduated, they kept their promise not to reveal that they'd worn the fabled costume. Only the university's provost and football coach knew their names.

Hobbs took a sip of hot chocolate from his own thermos, embossed with the school's logo. The guy was a walking advertisement for the campus store.

"Now in *our* case, Doc," he said casually, "we only have one student per year who dresses as the Tiger. This year it's a sophomore bio major named Jason Graham. Great kid. Really likes to put on a show for the crowd." A worried frown creased his brow. "I assume you'll keep that information to yourself."

"I'm a psychologist, Martin. I keep secrets for a living."

He breathed a sigh of relief as my eyes swept the tiers of seats all around the stadium.

Since many of the fans were returning alumni of Teasdale, I found myself wondering which, if any, had once worn the tiger outfit. And who, many years later, having weathered the pains and indignities of life, now looked down at the energetic student doing push-ups on the sidelines and recalled the carefree days of his youth?

Or maybe I was thinking about myself, and all the unexpected twists and turns of my own life since my early years at Pitt. The long, complicated journey that's led to where I am now.

Suddenly, my reverie was broken by a tremendous uproar from the crowd. No surprise why. The Teasdale Tiger had taken to the field, doing cartwheels on his way to the middle of the artificial turf.

Dean Hobbs had joined the rest of the fans in jumping to his feet, whistling and shouting. I hauled myself out of my seat as well.

I had to admit, it felt good being enveloped by the enthusiastic energy of the crowd. After all these somber, halting months, obsessed with what Sebastian Maddox—in his fury at me—had done to those closest to me. The grief, the guilt. But now something about that lunatic mascot cavorting on the field, leading the fans in a protracted "tiger roar," gave my spirits a lift.

Until a few seconds later, when, as the crowd noise lessened, it was replaced by another sound. A loud, booming crack, like a tree branch breaking in a storm.

A gunshot. From somewhere above and behind where Hobbs and I stood.

I whipped my head around, eyes sweeping the mass of people behind me, some of whom had themselves frozen in place.

Then another sound, a massive collective groan from the stands, brought my gaze back to midfield.

It was the mascot. The Teasdale Tiger.

On the ground. Motionless.

—

Chaos. There's no other word for it.

People yelling, screaming, crying. Some were so stunned they stood rooted at their seats, others scrambled over seat backs and down the slanted aisles toward the field.

Given our VIP seats, Hobbs and I had been among the first to reach the fallen student, though the dean had just as quickly backstepped away, hand on his mouth. Meanwhile, the entire team had poured from the sidelines and stood, wide-eyed, stricken, in a loose semicircle around the body. One of them bent and retched, while others cried out or moaned in terror. By then one of the campus security guards had reached the body and, shouting and waving his arms, began pushing the student athletes back.

Only Coach Pulaski, his face old and cracked as drying clay, refused to move, merely staring down at the costumed body at his feet. His beefy frame slumped, as though having collapsed in on itself. Mouth chewing air, trying to form words.

"Jesus Christ." His anguished whisper over my shoulder echoed my own horror as I crouched by the body, forcing myself to look.

Almost immediately, I turned away, the bile rising in my throat. Willing myself, I swallowed a couple huge breaths, trying to tamp down my fear, my revulsion. Then I caught sight of another security guard and motioned him to my side.

"Bend down across from me." I managed to gesture across the body. "Help me shield him from onlookers."

The man's face was white as a paper plate, but he nodded and scrambled to the other side of the body. Keeping his own eyes averted from the fallen boy, he unzipped his coat and spread it wide behind him, like sheltering wings.

Steeling myself, I reached with both hands and gingerly peeled the torn, bloodied hood from the victim's head. What came away with the ragged strips of cloth and plastic was a horrible mixture of brain, fleshy pulp, and jagged shards of bone.

Gulping more frigid air, I struggled to comprehend what I was seeing and what I was holding in my cupped, trembling hands.

Seeping through the shredded cloth, dripping bright red droplets to the ground, was the shattered top of the victim's head, literally sheared off. Exposing a scalloped divot of scorched brain tissue, swimming in blood...

By now, more security had arrived. A quick backward glance revealed that they were having a hard time keeping the fans at a distance. A throng of people, varsity hand banners drooping at their sides, breath misting in the biting cold, moved like a living thing toward the scene. I knew the overwhelmed guards wouldn't be able to contain them for long.

Meanwhile, his own breathing quick and shallow, Dean Hobbs had finally joined me, falling to his knees beside the body.

"Poor kid. This will kill his parents. This will—"

His voice caught as he stared down at the dead boy. For the first time, I, too, registered the victim's white, nondescript features and received another shock.

It was perhaps the most horrific thing of all. A grotesque joke. A final, nightmarish touch.

Below the severed skull cap, rivulets of blood ran down

the sides of an impossibly unmarred face. Like a mannequin's molded visage, the victim's smooth, clean-shaven features looked essentially undisturbed. Frozen, lifeless, but obscenely intact. Lips slightly parted, as though about to speak. Eyes wide open, staring up at Hobbs and me.

I took another deep breath to steady myself. The victim looked to be about the same age as the players. What was the kid's name again? Jason Something...?

Then the Dean made a strange, garbled sound. Peering down at the still, achingly young face, he blinked in confusion.

"What is it?" I gripped his arm.

He turned, aiming that same bewildered stare at me.

"This... I don't know who it is..."

"What do you mean?"

"I mean, this boy... He *isn't* Jason Graham."

# Chapter Two

"Anybody know the poor bastard's name?"

Lockhart's veteran sheriff Roy Gibson—a lapel pin on his weathered olive-green jacket proclaimed his ten years on the force—stood on the Teasdale team's sidelines. He was as tall as me, sturdily built, and boasting a full head of silver hair with a matching mustache. Hands behind his back, feet planted wide, he affected a kind of paramilitary stance as his flinty gaze went from one frightened, confused player to another. Each student athlete claimed not to know the identity of the victim. Nor did George Pulaski or any of this coaching staff.

Dean Hobbs and I stood behind Sheriff Gibson, just inside the crime-scene tape that surrounded a wide swath of stadium field. In its center a medical tent had been erected, shielding the work of the hastily called medical examiner from prying eyes. In this case, twenty thousand pairs of prying eyes.

Though Gibson's officers had quickly secured the scene and had—via the stadium loudspeaker—instructed those of the onlookers who'd left their seats to return to them, this didn't prevent dozens of fans from recording the proceedings on their cell phones. In fact, I was sure video of the tragic event—perhaps of the shooting itself—was already coursing through the internet's bloodstream. Going viral. Other observers were no doubt tweeting about it or sharing real-time images on Facebook.

Which meant the media wouldn't be far behind.

Meanwhile, Martin Hobbs had drifted from my side and was leaning against one of the city's patrol cars. Head down, he was muttering to himself. I went over to join him.

"It's a disaster." He didn't bother to look up. "I can't imagine what this will mean for Teasdale. The harm it will do."

"It hasn't been a fun day for the victim, either, Martin."

This brought his face up, eyes absent their former peering benevolence. "I don't mean it that way, Doctor. But this kind of scandal can ruin a small school like ours. We'll be assailed by worried parents, our donors might disappear, students may leave. Not to mention whatever legal or financial liability this leaves us vulnerable to."

I nodded as sympathetically as I could. In the short time I'd been in his company, it had been clear to me that the long-divorced, childless academic derived his entire sense of being from his position as college dean. His job, his reputation, was the glue that held his self-concept in place. So while it was easy, under the circumstances, to dismiss his concerns as callous, I also had to acknowledge how potentially devastating this crisis could be to the only thing that mattered to him.

With that in mind, I gripped his slender shoulder and offered a reassuring squeeze, which he seemed to ignore.

I felt my throat tighten. The sight of my red, roughened knuckles reminded me of how my hands, only a short time before, had been spackled with the victim's blood and brains. And how thoroughly—almost compulsively—I'd washed them in one of the stadium's restrooms. Lathering soap up to my elbows, scrubbing so hard my skin burned.

Afterward, I just stood there for countless minutes, regarding my haggard face in the smudged mirror, letting my hands dry in the concrete cold of the windowless room. Thinking of old horrors, other murders. Wondering if I was fated for the rest of my days to be followed by sudden, violent death...

—

In the single hour since the shooting, a gunmetal-gray dusk had descended, bringing deeper shadows and an even more ear-biting chill. I noted the half dozen uniformed officers scurrying about, stiff-legged and red-cheeked from the cold now seeping into their bones. They ignored the seemingly perplexed security guards standing in twos and threes, stamping their feet and blowing into their cupped hands.

When I turned to look, I saw Sheriff Gibson finally dismissing the coach, his players, and staff, and sending them back to the team locker room with a police officer as escort. Then, after a few words with another of his men, Gibson came back over to Dean Hobbs and me.

"Nobody we've talked to can identify the victim. That stupid tiger suit doesn't have pockets, so there's no wallet or student ID on him. But Coach Pulaski told me they use an old basement storage closet for changing into the suit. This way the wearer stays anonymous. So I'm hoping our vic left his personal effects inside after he changed. Coach gave me the key, and I've just sent one of my men to check it out."

"Are you even sure he's a student here?" Hobbs asked.

"At this point, Marty, we're not sure of a damned thing. Other than we got a dead male, Caucasian, early twenties, with the top of his head blown off." Gibson looked at me. "You're positive the shot came from behind you?"

"Yes. Behind and above. Up in the bleacher seats."

He registered this, then turned again to Hobbs.

"You said the vic wasn't the one supposed to be in the tiger outfit. So who the hell *was,* Marty?"

"A sophomore here at Teasdale named Jason Graham. He's been our Tiger mascot the whole season."

"So where is he? Do you have his number? His email? We need to get in touch with him. Get some answers. Like maybe why this other guy was wearing the suit."

"Give me some credit, will you, Roy? Soon as it happened, I called Dr. Bishara, our assistant dean. She'll have that information for you." He peered past the sheriff's shoulder. "In fact, there she is."

I followed his gaze to the opening of a narrow tunnel that ran beneath the stands, where a slender, dark-haired woman was giving each of the athletes a brief hug as they passed on their way to the locker room. Then she turned in response to a wave from Hobbs and headed over to us.

As she neared, bundled in a heavy coat and boots, her smooth, pretty features framed by severe glasses, she reached out to Hobbs with her hands spread wide. The two colleagues folded into a long, warm embrace.

Gently extricating himself, the dean introduced her to Gibson and me. After a quick nod at the sheriff, she offered me an oddly penetrating look, her red lips tilted up in a sad smile.

Up close, she looked to be in her late thirties, with a determined set to her chin and not a hair out of place. The quintessential no-nonsense administrator.

"I'm sorry to meet you at such a tragic time, Dr. Rinaldi. I've wanted to do so for ages and was pleased to learn you were giving the commencement address. Which I greatly enjoyed."

"Thank you, Dr. Bishara. Nice to meet you, too, though I agree about the circumstances."

"Please call me Indra. I'm not one for formalities, as Martin here will gladly tell you."

The dean gave her an indulgent look. "Dr. Bishara was born in New Delhi but came here to Lockhart with her family as a little girl. Even went to Teasdale for her undergraduate work."

"Yes, and then came right back after Princeton. Though it wasn't to the Lockhart I grew up in."

Hobbs winced. "Oh, please, Dr. Rinaldi. Don't get her started on Big Ag and the destruction of family farms."

Her eyes narrowed. "It's wiped out an entire way of life, Martin. As you well know. Local people once had jobs, pride, hope for the future. But now..."

I knew what she was talking about. On the drive here Friday evening from my office in Oakland, I had become fully aware of the community's depressed conditions the moment I crossed the town limits. Boarded-up storefronts, abandoned farms. Kids gathered in small, joyless clusters in a mini-mall parking lot. Vaping. Earbuds glued on. Giving passing cars the finger.

Whatever small-town charm Lockhart once enjoyed had faded into a palpable, weary resignation. Now the place was just another American small town on life support.

Sheriff Gibson's sharp tone interrupted my reverie. "Look, folks, I'm dealing with a murder here. This isn't the time for a social studies debate. Especially not *that* old one."

Indra Bishara looked appropriately rebuked. "I'm sorry, Sheriff. It was wrong of me. As my daughter will tell you, I've got a one-track mind where the issue is concerned."

"Maybe, but what I need from you now is info about this Jason Graham. What can you give me?"

"Not much, I'm afraid. Admissions gave me both a cell

number and email address. I tried the number and got Jason's outgoing message. And there was no answer to my text. Nor my email."

"Did you check social media?"

"Of course. No posts in recent days on either his Facebook or Twitter account. I don't think he's on Instagram."

Hobbs said, "I'm thinking we should consider calling Jason's parents. They might know where he is."

The sheriff shot him a sidelong glance. "Give *me* some credit, okay, Marty? Already figured on doing that. Though I'm worried it might freak them out. 'Hey, folks, it's the cops. Any idea where your kid is?'"

I spoke up. "Why not let Dean Hobbs call them? He can say he has a question about a class Jason took."

Gibson grunted his assent. "Good idea. For all we know, Jason could be at his girlfriend's place right now, getting laid. With no idea about what's just happened." He stirred suddenly. "There's a thought. Assuming he lives on campus, does Jason have a roommate?"

"Yes," Dr. Bishara said. "Vincent LaSala. I have a call in to him as well but haven't heard back."

"Okay. Give me that address, and I'll send one of my guys over to check out the dorm room. Might be something there that could help us locate Jason." He massaged his chin. "Hell, this LaSala kid could be right here, too. In the stands. Along with the killer, by the way. Unless he made his escape between the time of the shooting and the lockdown."

Hobbs very deliberately cleared his throat. "About that, Roy. When are you going to let all these people leave? You can't hold them here forever."

"Not planning to. But we need to check each one of them as they exit. Their IDs, personal items. Bags, backpacks."

I surveyed the area encircled by the crime-scene tape and counted heads. "You only have six or seven uniforms on-site, Sheriff. And a handful of security guards who look like they got the job yesterday. How do you plan to do a stop-and-frisk with twenty thousand people?"

"Good question, Doctor. Luckily, there's a National Guard unit doing maneuvers less than five miles away. I've already contacted the C.O., and he's volunteered to send his people over to help."

He sighed heavily. "Which still leaves us with no idea who the shooter is or why he did what he did. I mean, maybe this was a random act. By some whack-job. Unless he was *targeting* the Graham kid. In which case, he got the wrong guy."

Dr. Bishara removed her glasses and pointed them at the sheriff. "It's also possible the killer knew that Jason *wasn't* in the tiger suit. That the poor soul who was murdered was the target all along."

"About the murder victim," Hobbs said quietly. "Like I said, it seems we're all assuming he's a student here at Teasdale. But what if he isn't? Shouldn't we determine that?"

"Way ahead of you, Marty," said the sheriff. "I asked Dr. Sable—" He glanced at me. "He's the county coroner. I asked him to take a good photo of the vic while he's on the table and send it to me. Then we do a computer check with all the registered students at Teasdale. Even compare the picture with yearbook photos going back a while. See if we can get a hit. Get us a name to go with the face."

"I assume the lab will take his prints as well," I said.

"Of course. We'll run 'em through the national database, including ViCAP. Just in case. You never know. Still, I'm betting we find his ID in that storage closet."

I had another thought. "Did your men find the bullet?"

"Doc Sable figures it's still in the vic. We'll know exactly what kind after the autopsy. But it had to be heavy-duty to get through that thick hood."

Indra Bishara carefully replaced her glasses. "You're getting a *photo,* Sheriff? But the boy was shot. His face… I can't even imagine how it looks."

Gibson's sudden grin was decidedly unpleasant.

"No worries, lady. It's kinda weird. Kid practically got scalped, but everything below that looks fine. Pretty as a picture."

# Chapter Three

"We found the gun."

Sheriff Gibson bent to speak to Hobbs and me through the inch-wide opening in the driver's side window of the dean's late-model Chevy.

Without asking, Gibson opened the back door and slid inside, trailing a gust of stinging cold behind him.

It was almost two hours since the murder, yet Gibson's few officers, a half dozen security personnel, and the press-ganged National Guard troops hadn't finished taking the names of fans exiting the stadium and checking them for weapons.

Once we'd retreated to the warmth of his car, I sat beside Martin Hobbs in the front seat as he called Jason Graham's parents. To my surprise, he kept his voice calm and professional as he asked to speak to their son about an issue concerning one of his classes. But the boy wasn't there. After assuring them that it wasn't anything serious, he asked that if Jason showed up there, they'd have him call back. Hobbs then gave them his private cell number, since it was a Saturday and the college office would be closed.

After he'd clicked off, I asked if he thought they bought his story. He nodded but didn't speak. Couldn't. Instead, his teeth had started chattering.

I realized then that he was probably suffering a delayed reaction to the day's events. He was so visibly shaken that he popped a Xanax, gulping it down with the last of his thermos' hot chocolate.

At his request, I'd stayed with him, providing a kind of psychological triage for the agitated man. Gloved hands twisting on his lap, head shaking, he kept repeating that the small college would be rocked by the scandal.

"I can't cope," he'd said at one point. "My therapist says my ego is too porous for extreme stress. I decompensate."

*Great,* I thought. Like so many therapy patients, Hobbs had already learned the jargon. I worried that he used the clinical terms to distance himself from his actual feelings, turning his experience into mere data.

"Have you called your therapist?"

"Yes. And left a message. But she hasn't called back." He darted his eyes at me. "What is it with you people? Don't you work on the weekends? Maybe I should take another Xanax..."

"Not for eight more hours, Martin. You know that."

He gave a quick, miserable nod, and then returned to listing his concerns about the small private college's future.

His worries were exacerbated by the appearance of the media not an hour after the shooting. Wedged in between the coroner's van and a half dozen patrol cars were TV trucks from both KDKA and WTAE, as well as a few stringers from the *Post-Gazette* and some wannabe media pundit from a local true-crime podcast. Above, a CNN affiliate station's helicopter swooped back and forth against the darkening sky.

Hobbs put his face in his hands. "Here it comes. The media circus. Good Lord."

Having some familiarity with what happens when that particular circus comes to town, I suggested he leave any statements to the press to Teasdale's media spokesperson.

"But how did they find out about this?" Face still buried in his hands.

"How could they not? Soon as it happened, hundreds of people in the stands probably took video of the victim on their cells. Or tweeted about it to their followers. We all live in an instant news cycle now, Martin."

I slipped my own cell out of my pocket and went online. As I'd feared, the story was already going viral.

It was then that the sheriff had shown up, breath coming in frosty puffs as he trotted across the parking lot gravel.

Now, leaning forward across the front-seat back, head swiveling from Hobbs to me as he spoke, he filled us in about what his men had found.

It was obvious from their previous conversation that he and Hobbs were well acquainted since the sheriff was sharing information about the case with a civilian. Very unlike how, in my experience, law enforcement usually operated. But I also knew that small rural communities had their own set of rules about things like this.

"Looks like a hunting rifle," Gibson was saying. "Long range. Had some kind of scope. Anyway, we went ahead and sent it to a private lab we use sometimes. But I'm betting there won't be any forensics. Prints, fibers, whatever."

"Where was it?" Hobbs asked.

"We found it in a trash can in one of the stadium men's rooms. Up in the cheap seats. One of my officers is kind of a gun nut, and he says it's not the most sophisticated rifle of its kind. But it did the job. My guy says it's a ghost gun."

I turned in my seat. "What's that?"

"Basically a mutt. Pieces of different weapons, assembled in a matter of minutes. That's probably how it was brought in. Unassembled. In a picnic basket or backpack."

"I don't understand. Doesn't the stadium have security?"

"You mean like metal detectors and experienced personnel going through each fan's pockets and beer coolers? Checking each and every purse? Ask Marty here about that."

Dean Hobbs offered me a rueful shrug. "We're a small college, Dr. Rinaldi, with limited resources. Truth be told, most of us aren't used to having such a nice, new stadium like this. All of our procedures, security and otherwise, aren't really up to speed yet."

He regarded Gibson. "Not that anyone could have imagined such a thing. Not at this school. Not in this town."

"Tell me about it." Gibson shook his head. "We're especially small-town when it comes to law enforcement. Not exactly a high-crime area, unless you count the meth labs."

Now the sheriff glanced knowingly at me. "We don't have the manpower, resources, or expertise to deal with something like this. That's why I asked Pittsburgh PD to come lend a hand. You know all about them, right, Doc? Since you work with them."

"Sometimes. As a consultant."

"Yeah, I've seen you on the news. I just hope to Christ they send somebody good. And soon."

Just then, a tall, broad-shouldered black man in a full-length overcoat approached the car, walking with a slight limp. He was somewhere in his sixties, with close-cropped iron-gray hair and a penetrating gaze. Climbing out of the car, Sheriff Gibson gave him a brisk nod, then introduced him.

"This is Dr. Max Sable. Doc, meet Daniel Rinaldi."

The older man reached past the sheriff so we could shake hands. His grip managed to be firm and warm at the same time.

"Sheriff Gibson mentioned you," I said. "The coroner."

"That's right. For the whole county. 'Course, I know who *you* are, too. Most folks do."

As always, I was slightly embarrassed by the remark. Like it or not, I guess I did have something of a "brand."

Sable turned back to Gibson, then broadened his gaze to include Hobbs and me. Professional courtesy, I figured.

"I'll know more when I get the poor boy on the table, Roy, but it looks like what it looks like: a very powerful long-range rifle shot. I found a high-caliber bullet, full metal jacket, lodged in the cranial cap that had separated from the skull."

Hobbs groaned audibly, which brought a somber nod from the coroner. Like practically everyone I'd met in Lockhart, the two men appeared to know each other.

"I know, Martin." Sable's eyes softened. "It's a grievous injury. Horrible. Saw a lot like it overseas."

The sheriff stirred. "Max here did two tours in Iraq and Afghanistan. Decorated medic. Wounded in combat. We're all damn proud of him here in town."

Sable gave Gibson a quick, wary look, as though unsure whether or not the sheriff was being condescending. Then, just as quickly, the look faded. Replaced by the doctor's previous solemn demeanor.

"Over there," he went on, "we saw sniper bullets like this go straight through infantry helmets. The slug would rattle around the interior casing, ripping the soldier's brain to shreds. In this case, the deceased's hood was just made from cloth and molded plastic, and so there wasn't a similar pattern. The bullet essentially tore straight through the skull, the impact shearing off the upper cranial structure."

He smiled ruefully. "It's not like they show on TV and movies, where a head shot leaves a nice, round hole in the middle of the forehead. Maybe up close it happens, but not from a considerable distance. And certainly not from such a bullet. One manufactured for maximum impact."

"I wonder if that was the point," I said.

The sheriff shrugged. "If so, we may be talking about terrorism. Which is way above my pay grade."

He offered a weak smile at this last comment before turning to go. Then he paused, looking back into the car.

"Oh, I forgot. More bad news. My officer searched the whole storage closet, where we're assuming the kid changed into the tiger suit. Nothing. No wallet, watch, car keys."

"Maybe he changed somewhere else," I said.

"Maybe. Anyway, I'm gonna have a tech dust the closet for prints. Compare them to what we get from the vic. At least then we'll know if he did change clothes in there." A thick pause. "Could take a while to get a tech over here, though. We hire 'em on a case-by-case basis from some private outfit over in McKeesport. And it's a damn Saturday."

The sheriff shot me a pointed look.

"Small-town policing, Doc. Like the kids say, it is what it is. Guess I've learned to live with it."

# Chapter Four

Gibson and Sable had no sooner departed than Dr. Bishara came up and tapped at the driver's side window. Despite the cold, Hobbs slid the window all the way down.

"I have to go pick up my daughter, Martin. Ballet class."

"Must you, Indra? Send one of the admin staff. Half of them are already here for the game. Call somebody."

"I'd rather get Becky myself. I want to see her, give her a hug. After what's happened today."

He nodded. "I understand completely. And please make sure to give her my love."

"Will do." Then she looked past Hobbs, eyes finding mine.

"Maybe sometime later we can have a real conversation, Dr. Rinaldi. I'd very much like that."

"Of course. Martin here can give you my contact info."

Again, I was aware of her frank, searching stare before she turned and headed across the lot to her own car, heeled boots clicking sharply against the gravel.

After Hobbs rolled up the window and adjusted the Chevy's heater, he offered me a thin, wry smile.

"You're wondering about Dr. Bishara. Those looks she keeps giving you."

"As a matter of fact, yes."

"You needn't be surprised. Pretty much everyone knows about your work with the Pittsburgh Police, treating crime victims."

"Has Dr. Bishara been involved in a violent crime?"

"You could say that. Her ex-husband tried to kill her."

I took a few moments to digest this.

"What happened?" I said at last.

"When she was young—right out of Teasdale, in fact—Indra married a man named William Reynolds. The Third. Or, as he liked to be called, Billy Three."

"You mean, as in the Reynolds Auditorium? Where I spoke last night?"

"Yes, he's our benefactor's grandson. And, from all accounts, a nasty, entitled jerk. He lived with his father and mother in the massive estate his grandfather had built on the outskirts of town. People around here say that having all that family money curdled him. Young Billy never had to work a day in his life. Not something that's admired in a community like this."

"It must have surprised everyone when Indra married him."

"I wouldn't say they were surprised. More like envious. Billy was handsome, rich, and very popular with all our young ladies. Some parents were outraged."

"I'm not following you."

He sighed wearily. "Remember, this was a good many years ago. Lockhart may have seemed like the ideal Norman Rockwell community from the outside, but the people were primarily white and steadfastly conservative. Still are. When the Bishara family moved to town, they weren't exactly met with open arms."

I rubbed my trim beard. "I get it. They were tolerated, because they had to be, but were always made to feel like outsiders. So when the rich kid decides to marry the pretty Indian girl instead of one of their own…"

"And there's the irony, of course. Because marriage to him was a nightmare for Indra, almost from the first. According to those who knew the couple, Billy was quite controlling, as well as prone to angry outbursts. Things only got worse after their daughter, Rebecca, was born. Finally, Indra kicked him out of their house and filed for divorce."

"A gutsy move, given the circumstances."

"Quite so. Here's a young woman, alienated from most of the community, and with a three-year old, up against a wealthy and powerful man whose family had given so much to the town. The family patriarch, Billy's grandfather, was a revered figure."

He drew a long breath. "His pride hurt, her husband fought the divorce. Then, one night, he broke into the house and tried to strangle her. Right in front of their daughter. In the struggle, a lamp overturned and the hot glass bulb shattered on the little girl's face."

"Jesus Christ."

"Even Billy was horrified by what had happened and ran out of the house. And apparently he left town, because he hasn't been seen since."

"Surely his own parents must know where he is."

"They claimed at the time not to have any idea. Then, not long afterward, they sold the Reynolds estate to some high-tech billionaire from New York and left for Europe. Nobody's seen *them* again, either."

"What happened to Rebecca?"

"She ended up in the hospital, requiring surgery. They say she's completely recovered and seems relatively well-adjusted—she was in therapy for a couple years—but she's been left with permanent scars on one side of her face. Pretty difficult for a girl entering her teens."

I considered this.

"Both Becky and her mother no doubt suffered significant trauma," I said. "Now I see why Dr. Bishara seems so intent on meeting up with me."

"Yes. I assume she wants to consult with you about her daughter. Or perhaps even herself."

A melancholy tinge shadowed the dean's face, and I wondered if his concern for Indra Bishara was merely collegial.

"Anyway," he went on, "not long afterward, Indra got a scholarship to Princeton and left town with Becky in tow. It couldn't have been easy, a single mother in a strange city, getting her PhD while raising a daughter. Working side jobs to pay for childcare and to keep a roof over their heads."

"I'm not that surprised. From what I can tell, she seems to be quite a capable woman."

A measured pause. "Believe me, Doctor, you don't know the half of it."

I was tempted to ask what he meant, since talking about Indra Bishara seemed to distract him momentarily from his concerns about the shooting. Normally, with patients, I tend to lean into their pain, to guide them through the difficult process of self-knowledge and acceptance, but in this case I opted to allow him the solace of distraction. For one thing, the horror of the situation seemed to warrant it. For another, Martin Hobbs was not my patient.

I never had the opportunity to explore whatever else he might want to share about Dr. Bishara. A sudden squeal of tires on the tightly packed gravel announced the arrival of someone new on the scene. Swiveling in my seat, I peered out through the Chevy's rear window to get a good look at the newcomer.

I could hardly believe it. It had been many months since I'd seen him, but there was no mistaking the unapologetic beer belly, the wrinkled, off-the-rack suit. And even in what had become the charred-black fullness of night, the glare of his headlights revealed the florid drinker's face.

Seeing Sheriff Gibson walk across the lot to greet our new arrival, I said a quick goodbye to Hobbs and got out of his car. Gibson had wanted an experienced detective to assist on the case, and Pittsburgh PD had obliged.

I headed over to join the sheriff in greeting Sergeant Harry Polk.

# Chapter Five

"Jesus Fucking Christ." Polk was in mid-handshake with Gibson when I stepped into the glow of his headlights. His acknowledgment of me came with his familiar throaty growl. "What the fuck are *you* doin' here, Rinaldi?"

"Good to see you, too, Harry."

Which brought a guarded smile to the sheriff's face.

"So you two *do* know each other." He folded his arms across his strong chest. "I figured you guys might've met before this, working on one of the Department's cases."

Polk regarded me warily. "Doc here ain't on the job, Sheriff. He's what they call a consultant and I call a huge pain in the ass."

"That's only when he's sober," I explained to Gibson. "When Harry and I knock back a few, we're goddamn BFFs. And you should hear him sing karaoke."

"Give it a rest, will ya, Rinaldi?" A scowl creased his weather-beaten face. "Ya know, I almost forgot how good life's been since you stopped pokin' your nose where it don't belong. How the hell did ya get mixed up in this shit anyway?"

"Pure chance, Harry. Dean Hobbs invited me to watch today's game. Think of me as just another innocent bystander."

"Innocent, my ass. I swear, God must be punishin' me for my sins." He turned back to Gibson. "You don't need this jagoff here, do ya?"

"Not really. He's been keeping Dean Hobbs company, that's all. Poor Marty's pretty shook up about the killing."

"Yeah, well, my heart fuckin' bleeds. Okay with ya if we send the Doc packin'? You an' me got *real* police work to do."

Sheriff Gibson took a quick breath. "Look, Sergeant, we really appreciate Pittsburgh PD sending you to help. But you have to understand the kind of place Lockhart is. Mostly older folks and pretty religious. We've got more churches per square mile than practically any town our size in the state."

"So what's your point?"

"My point is, people around here aren't that comfortable with some of the language you're using. I mean, we all say 'hell' and 'damn,' we're not angels. But still..."

"Like I give a flying fuck." A derisive sniff. "Are all the cops around here so sensitive or what?"

The other man's voice hardened. "It's not about me, Sergeant. Or how we talk back at the station. But if you're going to help in this investigation, if you're going to assist in talking to witnesses, or asking city officials for aid in cutting any red tape, you're gonna have to keep your 'fucks' to yourself. Am I clear?"

It was easy to see the internal struggle going on inside Sergeant Harry Polk. For a moment, I thought he'd tell Gibson *and* his candy-ass constituents to go to hell, after which he'd get back in his car and return to town. But, luckily, his sense of professional duty—as strong in him as his various gripes and prejudices—won out and he offered a crooked smile.

"All right, Sheriff, I'll try to clean up my act. I mean, when in Rome, right?"

As if to punctuate his words, Polk unwrapped a stick of gum

and popped it into his mouth, where it joined another wad he'd been vigorously chewing.

I peered at him. "What's with the gum, Harry? Usually you sublimate your infantile aggression with unfiltered Camels."

"I'm tryin' to quit, okay, Rinaldi? Doctor's orders. From a *real* doc, not some asshole headshrinker, like someone I could mention." He glanced at Gibson, unable to hide his sarcasm. "Is 'asshole' okay, pal?"

The sheriff grinned. "Fine with me. Lockhart's full of them. Pretty much anyone in a suit and tie."

Polk grunted, then mumbled something to himself.

Now I understood the bad attitude. Even for Harry, it was more antagonistic than usual. Polk had to quit smoking, and the whole world was going to pay the price for it.

Meanwhile, as if to reward Polk for his acquiescence to local sensibilities, Gibson turned to me.

"Look, Dr. Rinaldi, I appreciate how you've helped out Dean Hobbs, but now it's time for Marty to pull himself together."

"I think he knows that, Sheriff."

"Maybe. But the thing is, he and Dr. Bishara are gonna have a brutal day tomorrow, dealing with the press and wrangling freaked-out students. So I'm going to tell him to go home and get some sleep. And I think it's time for you to do the same."

"Ya heard the man, Doc." Leaning in, Polk showed me a sloppy grin. I could also smell the alcohol on his breath. Even Polk didn't drink on duty. Something was going on with the veteran cop that had nothing to do with quitting smoking.

"Ya feelin' me, Rinaldi? Sheriff here's in charge, and he just off-loaded ya. Did it all nice and friendly, too. So do us both a favor and hit the road, okay?"

I raised my palms in mock surrender, then turned to shake Roy Gibson's hand.

"Good luck with the case, Sheriff. Polk's a real piece of work, but he's good at his job. He'll do his best to help."

Polk blinked a few times in confusion at the unexpected compliment, but I ignored him. Then I headed back to Hobbs' car. He rolled down his window.

"I've been dismissed, Martin." I reached in to shake his hand as well. "But if you need anything, or just want to talk, give me a call."

"I will. And I'll be sure to email Indra your contact information, too. I know you'll be hearing from her. If so, I'm counting on you to do right by her."

An odd remark, I thought. For which I didn't have a reply.

Instead, I merely nodded and trotted across the gravel to where my own car was parked. The green reconditioned '65 Mustang had gotten detailed the week before, and its shiny skin gleamed under the parking lot lights.

I had to admit, it was weird seeing Harry Polk again. Though we'd known each other for almost five years, ever since meeting during the Wingfield investigation, we'd never gotten past a grudging respect for each other.

And despite my joking about it, it was true that the only time he and I felt anything like friendship was when we'd gone for a drink, usually at the end of a case. Whether at the Spent Cartridge, the venerable cop bar, or somewhere else where Iron City Beer was on tap and the Jack Daniel's wasn't watered down in the back room.

The problem was, thinking about Harry brought to mind his former partner, Detective Eleanor Lowrey. We had met during that same investigation and had worked in tandem on numerous cases since. Having grown from being colleagues to wary friends and then even more wary lovers, we hadn't seen each other—or even spoken on the phone—in over a year. Her sabbatical from the force had been lengthened due to her sister's continued need for Eleanor's assistance in dealing with her drug-addicted son and two other smaller children.

Of course, there was that other thing, too. Eleanor's relationship with her former lover, still doing time in prison upstate, had created a kind of chasm between us.

All of this left me totally confused about what the hell I was doing with Special Agent Gloria Reese, FBI, with whom I'd been emotionally and sexually involved, on and off, since the Sebastian Maddox case. Thrown together by the horrors of that series of events, we'd had a hard time since then figuring out what exactly we meant to each other.

*Jesus,* I thought. *My life sounds like a goddamn soap opera.*

Though as I knew from my years in private practice, so did most people's lives. Unfortunately, it was cold comfort.

Behind the wheel of the Mustang, I started the engine. I knew I'd better give the old chariot some time to get its slumbering parts awake and moving, so I lay back against the seat and closed my eyes.

Immediately, to my dismay, I saw once again the stark image of the Tigers mascot lying midfield, on his back and bleeding into the artificial turf.

Which brought back all the same questions. *Was* the shooting a random event, anonymous revenge on society by some deluded individual for perceived personal slights or misplaced political animus? Had Jason Graham, a second-year bio major at Teasdale College, been the intended target? If so, how did the unknown victim end up in the tiger mascot costume instead of Jason?

Sitting up, I rubbed my temples. Maybe Gibson was right. Given the tragedy that had unfolded today, a good night's sleep might be the best remedy. And a few extra sessions with my own therapist wouldn't be such a bad idea, either.

But neither sleep nor therapeutic support was going to come my way any time soon...

—

In the glow of my headlights, I spotted Sheriff Gibson running toward my car, Harry Polk lumbering after him. Rousing myself, I swung open my door and stepped out to meet them.

Gasping, Gibson held up a cell phone.

"I just got a call, rerouted from dispatch. It's Jason Graham."

"Jason—?"

"Yeah. He called the station house, and, Christ, he sounds like he's coming apart. Like he can't catch his breath. Can barely speak."

"Where is he, Sheriff?"

"No idea."

"Did you tell him to come in? Go to your office?"

"That's just it. He won't tell us where he's calling from, and he won't talk to us. He says he'll only talk to you."

"What?"

Polk chimed in. "It's true, Rinaldi. The crazy bastard says he'll only talk to you! So get on the damn phone!"

I put the cell to my ear but heard only a staccato string of short, gasping breaths.

"Jason? This is Dan Rinaldi. Are you—"

His words were sharp, anguished rasps.

"Starlight Motel...Greentree...just you..."

Then he clicked off.

# Chapter Six

After repeating Jason's words to Gibson and Polk, I took out my own cell and Googled the Starlight Motel.

"What are you doing?" Gibson grabbed my arm. I shrugged him off.

"Getting directions to the motel."

Polk stiffened. "Ya ain't goin' nowhere, Rinaldi."

"Yes, I am. I know a panic attack when I hear one."

I opened the driver's side door of my Mustang.

"A panic attack?" Gibson frowned.

"Yes. Think about it. Jason hears on the news that the Teasdale mascot has been shot and killed. Wearing the outfit that he, Jason, usually wears. He has to assume *he* was the intended target. No wonder he's panicking."

As I said this, I swung behind the wheel. By now, the idling car's engine had warmed up.

A moment later, Polk was opening the passenger side door.

"If you're goin', I'm comin' with ya."

"Bad idea, Harry. He sounds like he's on the edge. And he wants me to come alone."

"I don't give a shit what he wants. This is police business."

"I agree. But if he looks out the window of his motel room and sees two guys in my car, instead of just me, he'll feel betrayed. Which will only increase his panic. He'll bolt."

"Maybe. I'll take that chance."

"I won't. He's in distress. He believes himself the target of some killer. Panicked people don't always make the best decisions. And I don't want anything bad to happen on my watch."

"How the hell did this get to be on your watch?"

"Personal choice. I'm funny that way. Guy in crisis calls me, I gotta do my best to show up for him." I gunned the engine. "Listen, Harry, why don't you follow me in your unmarked? I'll meet with Jason, try to calm him down. Then you can come in."

"I got a better idea. Let's see if somebody in this hayseed PD has the tech skills to trace the kid's phone. Off the cell towers or however the fuck they do it. That'll tell us where he is."

"Unless he's using a burner phone, which he could've smashed to pieces or thrown down a sewer by now. You want to stay here and find a tech, be my guest. But I'm going now. You following or not?"

I knew Polk didn't like the plan, but I also knew he was aware that time was ticking by. With an aggrieved sigh, he climbed out of the passenger seat, slammed the door, and headed for his unmarked sedan.

As I put the car in gear, I heard him shout to Gibson that it was best if the sheriff stayed here, in charge at the scene. And that Polk would call when he had Graham.

Pulling out of the lot, I caught sight of Sheriff Gibson's face in my rearview mirror. That was one pissed-off lawman.

I didn't blame him. He'd wanted Pittsburgh PD's help. What he didn't want was to find himself taking orders from them.

Despite his earlier deprecating comments about the Lockhart Police force, I could tell that Gibson liked being a big fish in a small pond. Which made me wonder how his working relationship with Harry Polk was going to pan out.

—

I drove down the parkway approaching the Point, then headed west on US 376 toward Greentree, under a vast canopy of ebony sky. What few stars there were shone coldly from between thin, drifting splotches of leaden clouds.

Behind me, a more exalted array of lights outlined the new, towering structures dominating the triangle of cityscape formed by the Three Rivers. Glittering buildings of silver and glass represented the Steel City's uneasy transition from a blue-collar, industrial town into a trendy white-collar hub of advanced technology and medicine. This left the city—as well as myself—with one foot in the old Pittsburgh of smoke-belching steel mills and factories, the other in a shining new digital metropolis.

Every time I crossed one of the many bridges leading to and from Pittsburgh, I reflected on how the city had changed, primarily for the better, and yet simultaneously struggled to reconcile these changes with its venerable past. A time of coal-bearing tugboats and cobblestone streets, of rattling streetcars and bustling produce yards, of ethnically diverse neighborhoods whose hundred-year-old houses had sheltered multiple generations of the same family. Many of those families had since been displaced by burgeoning gentrification.

Pushing these all-too-familiar thoughts out of my head, I glanced in my rearview mirror and noted Polk's unmarked sedan keeping its steady pace behind me.

The Greentree exit was up ahead, and as I headed down the ramp, I checked my GPS for the route to the Starlight Motel. It only took a few minutes to arrive at the single-story, mid-century building whose name was spelled out in bright neon letters on wooden stilts above the roof—one of hundreds of such places fronting lonely streets throughout the country.

A dozen cars were parked in the lot facing a row of scuffed, paint-flecked doors. Jason hadn't mentioned a room number, but when I saw a window curtain hurriedly parted and then closed again, I figured I'd found him. After pulling into an open spot near the room, I texted Polk, whose own vehicle was just entering the lot: Give me ten minutes with him first.

He texted back: Make it five.

I didn't want to waste time arguing with him, so I got out of the Mustang and went up to knock on the motel room door.

It opened before my fist could make contact, and a slender, dark-haired kid in a gray hoodie stood in the doorway, body jangling like a live wire. He looked to be about twenty, as I'd imagined, wearing rimless glasses that magnified the fear burrowed deep in his moist blue eyes.

His breath coming in short, hurried gasps, he ushered me inside and slammed the door behind me. Hands trembling, he struggled to throw the safety bolt.

Then, before either of us could speak, he backstepped into the room until his legs collided with the bed. The old mattress springs creaked as he sat on the wrinkled sheets, body bent forward, hands clutching his chest. Rocking back and forth.

"Oh, God, I'm dying..." His words mere puffs of air, faint as ghosts.

The room was small, squalid, with a smell like damp wool. A weary, sorrowful room, as if from decades spent absorbing the forlorn loneliness of the people who'd occupied it.

Keeping my demeanor calm and relaxed, I sat beside Jason and put my arm around his shoulders and felt his whole body shaking uncontrollably.

"No, Jason...you're not..."

"I'm having a heart attack, I know it!"

"No, it just feels like that. I promise."

"But my chest is killing me. Like it's gonna burst! And I'm dizzy. I'm gonna faint."

I gripped his shoulders more tightly, my voice still quiet.

"Listen to me, Jason. Just close your eyes and listen, all right? Close your eyes."

As terrified as he was, Jason managed to close his eyes.

"Now I want you to breathe with me. Breathe in, deeply, and then slowly exhale."

"But I..." Eyes popping open again.

"Try to keep your eyes closed. It really helps. And breathe with me. Deep inhalations, then let it out."

Eyes shut once more, he mirrored the deliberate breathing pattern I'd begun.

"Again, Jason. Deep breaths, like I'm doing. Match what I'm doing."

The effort to focus on his breathing, to keep its rhythm in tandem with mine, was lessening his tremors. Two more deep breaths and his rocking slowed.

"You're doing great, Jason. Now keep your eyes closed and continue breathing like you're doing, okay?"

He didn't reply. Kept clutching at his chest.

"You're having a panic attack, and your body is reacting to it. But the more you concentrate on your breathing, the better you'll feel. And soon."

With my arm still holding him, Jason began to calm himself and to feel he'd regained some measure of control.

We sat like that for another few minutes, enveloped in a heavy silence broken only by his deep, measured breaths.

Finally, he spoke again, his voice a tentative whisper.

"A panic attack, huh? Shit, man, I thought I was dying."

"Common reaction to severe panic. Along with dizziness, sweating, or chills."

"I had those, too. Right before you got here."

"How about now? How are you feeling?"

"Still pretty shaky."

He took another couple long breaths, as though to assure himself he was able to. Then he glanced at me through his wire rims, offering a feeble, slightly embarrassed smile.

"I think you can let go of me now, Dr. Rinaldi."

I returned his smile and did as he asked.

He shook his arms out, sniffed heartily, and slowly got to his feet. I watched as he crossed the room and took a seat on the lone cushioned chair. The harsh light from the lamp table beside him threw his slim shadow against the faded, peeling wallpaper.

Sitting forward, elbows on his knees, he spoke clearly and deliberately. Striving again to center himself, regain control.

"Thanks so much for coming, Dr. Rinaldi."

"I did wonder why you asked for me, specifically."

"I was at the commencement ceremony last night and got to hear your speech. I liked it, and liked you, too. You didn't come across like a dick."

"I try not to."

"Anyway, when I started coming apart, your name flashed through my mind. So I reached out. It was the only thing I could think of."

"I'm glad you did." I let a brief silence pass. "I'm assuming you heard on the news about what happened at the game today. I'm also guessing it triggered the panic attack."

He swallowed hard.

"I couldn't believe it. That could've been me, Doctor. It was *supposed* to be me, right?"

"We don't know that for sure, Jason. There's every chance it could've been random. Someone wanting to create fear and panic for his own unknown purposes."

"Well, it sure as hell worked. On me."

Again, that tepid, unconvincing smile.

"Besides," I said, "nobody knows you're the guy in the tiger suit, right? Besides Dean Hobbs and Coach Pulaski?"

"Theoretically, yeah."

"What does that mean?"

"It means somehow my identity leaked. Some kids at school. I just found out about it last week and…"

He hesitated, licking his lips.

"It leaked?" I said quickly. "How? To whom?"

"Doesn't matter."

"Yes, it does, Jason."

"Not to me. All that matters is that somebody's trying to kill me. And it got poor Lucas killed instead."

"Lucas? Was he the boy in the suit?"

His face reddened, a mask of shame. A slow nod.

"He's…his name's Lucas Hartley. 'Bout the same age as me. We met in high school, but he dropped out. Does odd jobs around town, but mostly sells weed. His girlfriend, Vicki, goes to Teasdale, though, and when it got out about me being the mascot… Well, she must've heard about it and told him, 'cause Lucas came to me right after and offered me five hundred bucks to let him take my place in the suit for just one game. I'm always short on cash, so I figured, why not? Nobody'd know."

"Why did he want to do it? Did he say?"

"Yeah. Vicki comes to the games sometimes with her friends and told Lucas she'd get a kick out of him being the mascot. Dared him to do it. Promised that if he did, she'd go along with the three-way he'd always wanted to do with a girlfriend of hers. It was messed up, man."

"So you let him switch with you today. Change into the mascot suit."

"Yeah. He'd been on his high school gymnastics team, so he knew how to copy the kinda moves I do on the field."

He shook his head mournfully. "I mean, Vicki was in the stands today. She knew it was Lucas in the suit. She must be totally wrecked, wigging out… Hell, Doc, I can't even *imagine* what she's feeling…"

"Look, I'm sorry about Lucas. But the police are still trying to identify him. We'll have to tell them."

"Yeah. If Vicki hasn't told them already…"

Jason looked off for a long moment. "I feel like shit about Lucas, I really do…but it doesn't change anything. The killer must've thought it was me in the damned suit. And once he finds out he got the wrong guy…"

A tinge of despair in his voice. I let another silence fill the space between us. He merely stared at me, his breathing clipped, shallow. Softer this time, but I could read the signs. The panic cycle starting again.

Then, without glancing down at his hands, he began repeatedly flexing them. I doubted he was even aware of this.

I reacted quickly. "Right now, I think we should concentrate on keeping you calm. We can deal with the police later. We need to get you out of here, maybe get you home to your parents..."

By now, his breathing had become more labored, and he continued flexing his fingers. Numbness or tingling in the hands and fingers is a pronounced panic symptom.

Then, to my surprise, he suddenly offered me a grave, doubtful smile.

"I appreciate what you're doing, Dr. Rinaldi. It isn't working, but I appreciate it."

"If you feel it starting up again, do what calmed you down before. Close your eyes and—"

The mirthless smile faded, to be replaced by a stern, unyielding set to his jaw. He pressed his hands on his temples.

"Jason, you have to—"

His voice crackled with sudden anger. "Are you serious, man? Don't you understand? Somebody out there wants to fucking *kill* me!"

Suddenly he leapt out of the chair and began spasmodically pacing, spitting out words between choked, anguished sobs.

"They're gonna try again! I *know* it!"

With every second, his voice rose more sharply. I got to my feet and tried to grab him, stop the pacing. But the eyes that met mine were wide with a kind of hopeless terror.

"Leave me alone! I'm going to die!"

"Jason—listen! It's happening again. Like before. You know what to do..."

"What, you mean breathe? Try to stay calm? How does that stop somebody from putting a goddamn bullet in my brain? Huh?"

He mimed pointing a gun to his head with his forefinger.

"It's gonna happen, I fucking *know* it! I can *feel* it!"

I'd seen all this before, early in my clinical training. Intense, unreasoning feelings of impending doom. Maybe the most agonizing symptom of severe panic attacks.

"Jason! Please! This is just your panic talking—"

Oblivious, he pushed me aside and headed for the door.

"I gotta get out of here! They could be on their way now to kill me! I thought no one could find me here. I'd just heard on the car radio about the shooting when I saw the motel's sign up ahead, so I—"

"Listen to me! You're right! Nobody knows you're here. You're safe—"

Jason's trembling hands were pawing at the dead bolt, and his panic had become ungovernable. Words were useless.

I crossed the room in two steps, but before I could reach him he'd managed to slide the bolt and pull open the door.

Only to find Harry Polk, a hulking, shadowy figure bathed in an eerie neon glow, standing in his path. Like death itself.

Jason cried out, stumbling backward, right into my arms.

"They're here! They're—"

His words had become hoarse, guttural, as he collapsed in my embrace, his body shaking with fear.

"Holy shit." Polk stepped across the threshold and stared at the pitiable boy. "Fucker's really lost it, eh?"

"Shut up and help me with him, Harry."

"Sorry, Doc, I left the straitjacket in my other car."

He must have sensed the rage boiling up in my throat, because he took a step back and spread his hands.

"Okay, okay. So what do ya want me to do?"

"Call Pittsburgh Memorial. Tell them we're bringing in a patient with acute panic symptoms and possible dehydration. *Do it,* Harry! Now!"

While Harry fumbled in his jacket pocket for his cell, I shifted position so that I had one arm around Jason's waist. His breathing had become even more hurried, short. With my free hand, I felt his neck for his pulse. It was dangerously fast.

There was no time to lose. I heard Polk talking urgently to the hospital on his cell as I half-walked, half-dragged Jason out of the room. By now he was incoherent, sputtering, in a voice thick with tears.

The night air was meat-locker cold, so I did my best to hustle us quickly across the lot and into my parked car.

Polk had finished his call and walked past me just as I was buckling a semiconscious Jason Graham into the passenger seat.

"I'll follow you to the hospital." He had to shout through my closed driver's-side window. "I wanna talk to this Graham mook as soon as they'll let me. He's got some explainin' to do."

I merely nodded and put my Mustang in gear. In moments I was pulling out of the motel parking lot and racing back to the parkway on-ramp. A glance in my rearview mirror confirmed that Polk was following right behind.

Crossing the Fort Pitt Bridge, I took the downtown exit and, given the Saturday night traffic, had to pull some risky lane-changing maneuvers to make it over to Grant Street. Luckily, Pittsburgh Memorial was less than two miles away.

Meanwhile, I kept my eye on my passenger, his body slumped against the seat belt's constraint. Eyelids fluttering behind his rimless glasses, Jason seemed to be drifting in and out of consciousness—the psyche's natural defense against intense, overwhelming panic.

Suddenly, my cell rang. I'd clipped it to the dashboard holder, so had to reach to answer. It was Polk.

"Change o' plans, Rinaldi. I just got taken off the Lockhart case. Captain wants me down in Shadyside."

"Why? What happened?"

"Another goddamn shooting, that's what." I heard the weariness in his throaty rasp. "Looks like our sniper's havin' himself a busy night."

# Chapter Seven

Before I could even respond, Polk went on.

"At least this time we know who the victim is. Had her license and credit cards in her purse. Woman in her sixties named Harriet Parr. Waitin' at the bus stop on Maple. Another head shot. Uniforms on the scene figure it came from the building across the street."

"When did this happen?"

"'Bout a half hour ago, accordin' to the witness. Some CMU student standin' right next to her. Had those fuckin' earbuds on, so all he heard was a muffled sound, then he saw the vic spin around and hit the pavement. 'Course, the kid totally lost his shit but got it together enough to call 911."

"You figure it's the same shooter from this afternoon?"

"Who the hell knows? Biegler thinks it might be. For once, I gotta agree with him. Similar M.O." A former lieutenant and Polk's boss at Robbery/Homicide, Stu Biegler had recently been promoted to captain. "But if it *is* the same perp..."

I could guess where he was going with this.

"Then that means the shooter *is* picking targets at random," I said. "In which case it doesn't matter who was in the Teasdale mascot suit. Not to the shooter. He just wanted to make a big splash with his first victim. Killing someone in such a public way, in front of thousands, to make sure it had maximum impact."

Polk gave a hoarse, derisive laugh. "Don't start with the theories already, okay, Rinaldi? At this point, we don't know nothin'. Hell, it might not even *be* the same perp, and—"

"Bullshit, Harry. You and I both know it is. But did they find the gun? Remember, the shooter had to get hold of another rifle. The one used in the Lockhart shooting is being examined at some lab somewhere."

"Tell me somethin' I *don't* know. Besides, I got no idea if they found the weapon, and I wouldn't tell ya if I did. 'Cause in case you forgot, none o' this is your business. You just take care o' the Graham kid." Another sour laugh. "Panic attack, my ass. Do me a favor, will ya, Doc? Help the gutless chooch find where he left his balls so we can question him."

"Look, Harry—"

But he'd already clicked off.

—

The ER at Pittsburgh Memorial on a Saturday night was filled with the usual suspects: wailing, angry walk-in patients presenting with car accident injuries, drunken brawl bruises, and finger-severing kitchen knife disasters.

However, thanks to my visiting privileges, as well as Polk's earlier call, I was able to get Jason Graham a bed in a room in a side corridor off the main reception area. Within minutes, and at my urging, a duty nurse had put him on an IV saline drip.

I stood by the bed railing and gently put my palm on Jason's forehead. He blinked a few times at the glare from the ceiling fluorescents, then came more fully awake. Although shallow, his breathing was relatively calm and regular.

"Where am I?"

I told him.

"Sorry I've been so much trouble, Dr. Rinaldi."

"No problem, Jason. I'm just glad you're here, where you can get the care you need. Though you should probably call your parents. They might be worried."

His swallowed. "Jesus, you're right. Especially if they saw the news...they'd think—"

He sat up abruptly, face gone ashen, and reached for the wall phone next to him. To give him some privacy, I started to leave the room, but he shook his head as he dialed.

As he feared, his parents had indeed seen the story on the news about the murder of the Teasdale mascot and assumed the worst. Luckily, after frantically calling the police, they'd been informed that the victim—whose name the cops didn't disclose—was in fact *not* their son. And that Jason had been located and was being attended to.

Regardless, I could tell from Jason's end of the conversation that his parents had been desperate to hear from him. Though obviously relieved, they planned to drive down to the hospital right away to see him.

Jason had just hung up when the physician on call stepped into the room. She was small, almost swallowed up in her hospital scrubs, and had her hair pulled back in a ponytail. I'd met Dr. Jennifer Chang a few times, and had been impressed by her cool professionalism and warm bedside manner, which belied her relative youth. Not the usual combination in most medicos I knew, and certainly rare on the ER night shift.

I filled her in about her new patient, and she quickly checked his vitals. Satisfied, she folded her arms.

"I'm going to have the nurse give you one of the benzodiazepines," she said to Jason. "They slow down the central nervous system by targeting particular receptors in the brain, which will help you relax. That and some serious R&R should do the trick."

He nodded and thanked her, but I could see the worried strain edging his puffy, red-rimmed eyes. No amount of physical or psychological exhaustion had diminished his fear.

So, right after Dr. Chang left the room, I made a decision which I doubted Pittsburgh PD would be too happy about. Not that this was exactly a first in my uneasy relationship with the Department.

"Listen, Jason, I think you should know. There's been another shooting, so it appears the sniper is targeting people at random. Unless you have some kind of connection to the latest victim. A woman named Harriet Parr."

"Never heard of her."

"I figured as much. This means that you hadn't been the sniper's intended victim. Whoever happened to be in the tiger suit today was, unfortunately, the target."

I watched his pale face as he slowly registered the news. For the first time, his eyes lost that pinched, haunted cast.

"I wonder how Vicki is taking it," he said after a long moment. "She's the one who put Lucas up to it."

"I've been wondering about that myself. I'll check in with the Lockhart police and get an update. I'm sure they've made contact with her by now."

He rubbed his forehead. "I guess somebody better talk to Vinny, too."

"Your dorm roommate, right?"

"Yeah, Vincent LaSala. He was at the game, too, so he probably thinks—I'll call his cell."

With that, he reached for the phone again.

Jason had just finished assuring his worried roommate that he was alive and well when the duty nurse returned with the medicine ordered by Dr. Chang.

I took that as my cue to leave.

"You get some rest." I handed him my card. "I know your parents will be here soon, but feel free to call me anytime, okay? If you want to talk."

"I will, Dr. Rinaldi. And thanks again. For everything."

—

In an alcove down the hall from Jason's room, I found a vending machine and a lone plastic chair, both of which were old, scuffed, and pockmarked, as if they'd been here since the hospital was founded. Which didn't stop me from shoving a few coins in the dented machine and getting some undrinkable but badly needed coffee. Black.

I choked down half of it in a single gulp, then called Sheriff Roy Gibson on my cell. After updating him about Jason Graham's condition and current whereabouts, I asked about Lucas Hartley.

"Yeah, we know now the vic was this Hartley kid. His girlfriend, Vicki Morrison, identified herself to one of my officers as he was doing the exit checks. She was pretty hysterical when we questioned her, though. Took half an hour to get the story out of her."

"That she dared her boyfriend, Lucas, to take Jason's place in the tiger suit."

"Yeah, she admitted to putting Lucas up to it. But she did more than that. She was with him in that storage closet when he changed into the suit."

"That's why his keys and ID weren't there when your people searched it."

"Right. Vicki took them away with her. Then she joined her friends in the stands to watch the game. And Lucas." He sighed. "Anyway, one of the EMTs still on-site gave her a sedative and I had someone drive her to her dorm. Her parents are in Philly, but she has a roommate who can help take care of her. Don't take a shrink to figure she feels guilty as hell."

I didn't reply. Instead, I said, "Anything new from the coroner's office?"

"Not much. They still haven't officially finished the autopsy. Although Doc Sable did tell me ballistics confirm that Lucas Hartley was killed by a .338 Lapua Mag, a large-caliber bullet favored by military snipers."

"Just as he'd guessed. By the way, Jason called his parents and his roommate, Vincent LaSala, to let them know he's okay. At least, physically."

"Probably some guilt there as well. On his part."

Again, I didn't respond.

"Listen, Sheriff, I heard from Sergeant Polk that he's been pulled off the Lockhart shooting."

"Yeah." As I'd expected, Gibson didn't sound too broken up about it. "Looks like the shooter took out another vic, over in your neck of the woods. Some woman waiting for a bus."

"That's right. And Jason has no knowledge of her. The cops assume the sniper is targeting people at random."

"Yep. Like I feared. Some nutjob. On the plus side, our shooting here gets folded in with Pittsburgh PD. And the Feds, probably. So it's not our headache anymore."

"Tell that to Martin Hobbs and Dr. Bishara."

Gibson gave a dark chuckle. "Oh, yeah. From a PR standpoint this sucks for Teasdale. Again, not my headache."

At first, I was struck by Gibson's attitude. Surely he had to know that Pittsburgh PD's investigation would still require his cooperation. There'd be witnesses to interview, especially Vicki Morrison. Maybe even Coach Pulaski and Vincent LaSala.

Plus, there'd be crime techs, city and federal, crawling all over the stadium, trying to determine from which location the sniper fired. Not to mention any additional evidence that might be gleaned from that storage closet where Lucas changed into the tiger suit.

That's why Gibson's seeming indifference had caught me off guard, coming from a cop whose jurisdiction was a small town in which practically everyone knew everyone else. People he'd have to answer to.

Then I remembered the sheriff's angry face in my rearview mirror, right after Polk had told him to stay behind while we went after Jason Graham. I realized now that his feigned indifference masked a bitter resentment. A major case—probably one of the few he'd have the chance to work in a town like Lockhart—was being taken out of his hands, and bumped up to Pittsburgh PD and, as he'd surmised, probably the FBI.

"I think I understand, Sheriff," I said. "It's tough to get back-benched on a case like this. Especially when it involves your own community."

A long, heavy pause. "I don't know what you're talkin' about, Doc."

I silently cursed myself for the blunder. Gibson wasn't the kind to own up to his feelings, especially not when they involved his response to being reduced to a supporting role in the case. And certainly not to someone he barely knew, who was associated with the Pittsburgh Police.

"Look, I better go," he said quickly. "We're still wrapping things up here, and everybody wants to go home. Thanks for the info on the Graham boy."

I heard the impatience in his voice, so I put us both out of his misery and ended the call.

—

As I passed the reception desk, I glanced up at the TV monitor bolted to the wall just above and behind it. A report on Harriet Parr, the second victim of the sniper, led the late newscast on KDKA-TV. Video from the scene earlier that night, showing a cordoned-off street corner swarming with cops and EMTs, was accompanied by the anchor's voice-over.

"Police say that Harriet Parr, a widow and mother of two grown children, was waiting for a bus after having dinner with a colleague when she was fatally shot by an unknown assailant. Ms. Parr was a bookkeeper at Hayes and Company, and, according to that colleague—who spoke exclusively with KDKA—she was liked and respected by all her coworkers." The station then cut back to the anchor at his desk.

"Though Pittsburgh Police have been reluctant to release many details, it appears that Ms. Parr was the victim of a sniper, possibly shooting from the roof of a building across the street. Coming just hours after the similar shooting of a young man named Lucas Hartley in Lockhart, it seems likely that the two murders are connected, and the work of the same killer. The police, however, have declined to comment further, since both investigations are in their early stages."

As it turned out, it was a busy news night. The sniper story was followed by a report out of Oregon, where a state senator, a leading fiscal conservative, had been caught by a hidden video camera accepting what looked to be a payout from a well-known lobbyist. Denials and accusations had begun flying from both sides of the aisle, while calls for the politician's resignation kept escalating.

Meanwhile, during a press conference taped earlier that day in Washington, DC, a Justice Department spokesman detailed plans for a new investigation into the rise of violence attributed to a variety of white supremacist groups.

"These heinous acts stemming from racism and anti-Semitism do not in any way reflect the values of this country," he read from a prepared statement, "and will not be tolerated."

*Good luck with that,* I thought, and immediately chastised myself for my easy cynicism—the intellectual cushion against appropriate, though wearily familiar, outrage.

This brief segment led to another potentially tragic report featuring video of a hurricane gathering strength off the coast of Haiti. It was accompanied by live footage of locals piling sandbags where the storm was expected to make landfall, while others were seen boarding up their homes and businesses.

More reports followed, detailing the usual litany of armed robberies, suspicious fires, and fatal car crashes. By then, I'd had more than enough of the news—as worrisome and disheartening as ever—so I turned and headed down the corridor.

Still, the lead story occupied my thoughts. While I knew enough about how the police operated to understand their reluctance to link the two sniper attacks, there was no way the public would see it any other way. It had all the earmarks of some crazed shooter picking targets at random.

And should there be a third…

I'd no sooner had that thought when I literally ran into Dr. Chang, coming from around a corner. Recovering, we exchanged awkward smiles.

"Oh, Dr. Rinaldi. I just heard that someone you know found out you were here and wants to see you."

"Friend or foe?"

"My money's on friend. Her name's Angela Villanova."

"She's here?"

"Up in rehab. Fourth floor."

I thanked her, apologized for nearly knocking her over, and went looking for the elevator.

Angie and I were distantly related, and I'd known her since I was a kid. Now in her late fifties, she'd joined Pittsburgh PD right out of school and had worked her way up to chief community liaison officer.

Angie was the one who usually referred traumatized crime victims to me for treatment. She also chided me on a regular basis whenever my ego morphed into what she perceived as arrogance.

And, truth to tell, she was often right.

It was also Angie who led the charge among my friends and colleagues in calling my involvement in certain criminal cases a death wish. Or the residual effects of my survival guilt, having lived through a violent shooting many years before that cost my wife her life while mine, by sheer luck, was spared.

On the other hand, it was often Angie's influence in the Department that kept the brass from canceling my consultant's contract. It was such a recurrent threat over the years that it had almost become a joke between the two of us.

Now, approaching the rehab center, I paused to take a long breath. I hadn't seen Angie in a few weeks, since I'd visited her bedside at the home she shared with her husband, Sonny. She was on medical leave from the Department, still partially paralyzed on her left side—though as the result of her fierce determination and hard work, her speech had improved in recent months.

The discomfort I'd felt on this last visit was intensified by Sonny's usual bitter, angry glare. I couldn't blame him. It was because of me that his wife of thirty years had suffered a stroke.

She'd been one of Sebastian Maddox's victims, simply because of her connection to me.

Entering the spacious rehab facility, I was surprised to see about a half dozen patients being guided through their physical therapy by two young staffers, a man and a woman. Given the hour, I'd assumed the place would be pretty much deserted.

The man, catching my eye and reading my look, smiled knowingly.

"Rehab times are at a premium, sir," he said, "so patients grab whatever slots they can."

"Must be hard on you. It's late."

"Not so hard when I think of the overtime."

Another, slightly slurred voice came from a corner of the room. The words came slowly, haltingly, but with their characteristic insistence.

"Well, are you gonna stand there…shooting the shit with the help…or come say hi…to your Cousin Angie?"

"Do I have a choice?"

"Hell, no."

As I went to join her, she made the effort to sit up straighter in her wheelchair. In oversized jeans and a Pirates sweatshirt, she looked as thin and frail as when I'd seen her at the house. Given how stout and formidable she'd always seemed, I was struck once more by how the stroke had diminished her.

But her cloud of hair was as lacquered and stiff as always, and the wry, knowing look in her eyes remained undimmed.

I bent to kiss her cheek. "How's it coming, Angie?"

"Great. I'm training…for the next…marathon. How the hell…do you think…it's coming?"

"Well, your speech keeps improving. God help us."

"Funny man. You still moping around…like the walking wounded?"

Though her speech was getting appreciably better, it was obvious that the act of speaking was quite laborious.

"I'm still sorry about what happened to you, if that's what you mean."

"Yeah, well…your guilt about it…don't mean squat. I'm not mad at you… It's on that lunatic Maddox…not you. Besides… guilt…is the thief of life."

I nodded. It was a sentiment I often tried to impart to my patients. With limited success.

"Now," she went on, "what's all this…about a sniper? I may be…out of commission…but I still hear things. From friends… down at headquarters."

"Then you probably know more than I do. Looks like it's a random thing."

She stirred with difficulty in the wheelchair, her left side stubbornly stiff and unyielding.

"If it is…I hope my lame-ass replacement…as community liaison…knows what he's doing."

"What do you mean?"

"I mean… He's supposed to get together…with the Department's media hacks…to make sure…the public doesn't panic. Two murders on a Saturday… That's business as usual. But a lunatic out there…shooting people at random…" Her words died in her throat. I could also see how fatigued she was from even our brief conversation.

"I guess I should get out of your hair," I said. "You're not staying here tonight, are you?"

"In this place…? There are sick people here… Thank Christ, I only do rehab…three times a week. Anyway… Sonny'll be here any minute…to pick me up."

I smiled. "Then I sure as hell better take off."

"Lord knows…*I* would…"

I gave her another kiss and turned to go.

"And, Danny." Her voice now only a whisper. "You ain't gonna get involved...in this sniper thing...right?"

"Of course not, Angie. It's got nothing to do with me."

# Chapter Eight

I repeated as much to Gloria Reese when she called my cell as I was driving home.

"Not what I heard." The weary amusement in her tone was tinged with concern.

"How could you have heard anything?"

"We have field agents on both crime scenes now. Our guy in Lockhart says the local cops mentioned your name."

"Yeah?"

"To quote my colleague there, 'Hey, Gloria, I heard your boyfriend was at the stadium when the sniper struck.'"

"That's a direct quote, eh?"

"Yep. Which has me confused as hell, Danny."

"About what I was doing there?"

"No, about you being my boyfriend. Is that what you are?"

I let out a long breath, which she heard.

"Is that a sigh, Rinaldi? Are you giving me 'the sigh'?"

"No. I mean, yes. I mean, I thought we've been pretty discreet. How did this jerk find out?"

"We're FBI, Danny. We find out things. Besides, our downtown office is Gossip Central. Maybe somebody spotted my satisfied glow one morning after a torrid night together."

Her soft chuckle warmed me and made me suddenly anxious to see her. It'd been a few weeks.

"Now you're just screwing with me," I said.

"Hmm. If you're interested, that can be arranged."

After some back-and-forth, we made a date to see each other on Monday night and clicked off.

---

It was after midnight by the time I drove up the hill to Mt. Washington and my house on Grandview Avenue, with some mellow Chet Baker on the CD as background music.

Over the years, I'd become pretty much a creature of habit.

A timer had turned on the lamps in the front room, so I had no trouble navigating my way to the kitchen. After grabbing a Rolling Rock from the fridge, I carried the beer through the sliding glass door out to my rear deck. It was my favorite place in the house, even with an icy cold prickling the air.

I stood at the railing, sipping the beer and reflecting on the long day's events. Far below me, beyond the sloping hill behind my house, were the glittering lights of the Point, where the famed Three Rivers converged. The Monongahela and the Allegheny, their flanks dotted with gentrified housing and trendy night spots, joining to form the mighty Ohio.

How different from what I remembered from my childhood, when the rivers were choked with freight haulers and coal barges, the haunting foghorn of a tugboat echoing regularly throughout the night. When miles and miles of steel mills fronted those black, sluggish waters.

Today, though there was still considerable river traffic, the disappearance of Pittsburgh's industrial life had greatly reduced the stream of working seacraft. Now you were just as likely to see pleasure skiffs and tourist boats.

I finished my beer and went inside to my bedroom, changing into sweats and a Steelers T-shirt. But after lying in bed for twenty minutes, staring up at the ceiling, I accepted that sleep wouldn't come. My mind was a jumble of disconnected thoughts.

Finally, I got up and went downstairs to my makeshift gym. Though the panel-lined basement barely qualified for the term. Just a hanging bag and a few barbells, as well as a weight bench that had seen better days.

I quickly taped up my knuckles and slipped on the training gloves. I spent the next fifteen minutes working the heavy bag, the welcomed sweat sheening my bare arms and forehead and stinging my eyes. The exertion reminding me once again that the body has its own wisdom.

I'd done some amateur boxing in my late teens and had even made the ranks: Golden Gloves, Pan Am Games. But that was many years—and what seemed like a lifetime—ago. Now I just fooled around down here with weights and the bag to keep in shape.

As I'd hoped, the workout was helping to clear my head and to quiet what the Buddhists call "the chattering monkey mind." And after what I'd witnessed at the football stadium, I needed all the mental quieting I could get.

Unfortunately, it wasn't going to last long.

---

Eight a.m. I'd no sooner showered and made a fresh pot of coffee when my cell rang. I was sitting at the kitchen table, watching the cold morning light stream through the bay window, and debating whether or not to let the call go to voicemail.

As usual, it was a debate I invariably lost. I picked up.

It was Harry Polk. "Get your ass up, Rinaldi."

"No worries. Already on my second cup of coffee."

"Great. I'm gonna text you an address. You need to come down here ASAP."

"What is it?" I blinked myself more fully awake.

"For once, just hurry up and do what I'm askin'. Earn a little o' what the Department's overpayin' you for, okay?"

"Well, since you asked so nicely..."

He clicked off. Moments later, he texted an address in a tony area in the Squirrel Hill district.

I could only assume it was another shooting. But if so, why did Harry Polk, of all people, just invite my help?

—

The murdered man's wife crouched beside his prone body, her hand clutching his, her clothes soaked in his blood. Her body was rigid, as if made of stone.

But it was her eyes that told the deeper story: frozen in a kind of dull, uncomprehending stare. Her gaze never left her husband's equally frozen, contorted face.

A young uniformed cop, whose name tag read "Bronski," was standing a few feet away, arms folded across his gym-thickened chest. Trying to look sympathetic, his broad features betrayed mostly annoyance.

The same was true for Harry Polk, who greeted me on the sidewalk with his customary chagrined squint. In addition to his unmarked sedan, two patrol cars, blue lights flashing, blocked the street. No sign of the ME's wagon.

"She's been like this since I got here." Polk motioned with his chin in the direction of the stricken woman.

*Here* was the spacious front lawn of a house in an exclusive area of Squirrel Hill, one of dozens of similarly high-end homes set well back from the street. Despite the dawn chill, a cluster of neighbors, bundled into coats or tightly clasped robes, leaned against the warning tape barricading the scene, peering in the wintry sunlight at the silent, unmoving tableau.

"Where's the ME? Or ambulance?" I asked.

"Dispatch says they're comin'." Polk was curt. "But I hear it was crazy last night. Couple bar fights and some kinda brawl at a big outdoor wedding. An' ya know how it is nowadays, everybody's got guns. Probably includin' the bride and groom. Which means a lotta stiffs cloggin' up the city morgue. Still bein' processed."

I ignored his wolfish grin.

"Waitin' on CSU, too," he went on, "but Bronski an' me figger the shooter took position on the roof o' the house across the street. We're guessin' same kinda distance and angle as the others. Got uniforms canvassin' the area, but I'm gonna talk to whoever lives in that house myself. Maybe they heard somebody outside the house, climbin' up on the roof or whatever."

"Any idea when it happened?"

Officer Bronski answered. "Next-door neighbor heard a gunshot and we got the call in my ride. My partner's getting the neighbor's full statement now, but she says she heard the shot about an hour ago. Probably the same time as the wife did."

Polk sniffed. "Guy's in a suit, so we assume he was headin' to work or some meetin'. Wife was inside and ran out to him."

I noted the woman's silken robe and bare feet. But the man's suit was puzzling.

"Going to work? Today's Sunday."

"Some of us work on Sundays, Rinaldi. *Un*like you."

Before I could reply, Bronski spoke up again.

"The neighbor says the vic's name is Peter Steinman, a partner in a law firm downtown. The wife's name is Laura."

"Bronski says she hasn't budged since *he* got here, either," said Polk, "an' that was ten minutes before me."

The younger cop regarded me. "When my partner and I arrived, we found the lady on the ground next to the vic, holding his hand. Just like now."

"And she hasn't moved? Said anything?"

"No and no. Some kinda shock thing, right, Doc?"

"Maybe. Perhaps a catatonic state. Shock can do that."

I'd answered distractedly as I approached the woman, my focus on her rigid limbs and unblinking gaze. Her hand was dead-white from its iron grip on that of her husband.

He was a smallish, thick-waisted man who looked to be in his midfifties. In contrast, Laura Steinman was almost dangerously thin, with pale-blue eyes and streaked blond hair. She was maybe ten years younger than her husband.

By now, the blood pooling beneath the victim's head had spread, blackening the perfectly trimmed green grass. A quick glance at the house itself and surrounding grounds gave the unmistakable impression of wealth, which had spared neither the man nor his wife this unspeakable horror.

Without saying a word, I crouched on the other side of the body. As with Lucas Hartley, his scalp had been sheared off, revealing tendrils of blood and flesh. Bits of bone dotted the ground around his head like a grotesque halo.

I risked looking across the dead man at his wife. Without a full clinical examination, my idea about catatonia was little more than a guess. I knew nothing about this woman, her medical history, her possible substance use, her neurological state.

But I'd worked with traumatized patients long enough to trust my instincts. Her unblinking stare, her death grip on her late husband's hand, the muscle rigidity in her unwavering posture all presented as a severe catatonic reaction to an event that her psyche felt was literally intolerable.

It was the ultimate irony. The horror of her husband's brutal murder kept her inescapably in the present, and yet that very horror caused her to dissociate, effectively removing her, at the deepest psychological level, from her experience.

I would have to tread carefully. What she needed was immediate medical treatment, which generally meant antipsychotics in a hospital setting. But while I waited for an ambulance, I had to try anything to help free her from the prison of her own mind.

"Laura." I spoke softly, without any urgency in my voice. "Can you hear me, Laura?"

She was unresponsive. This didn't mean she hadn't heard me, but she might have been unable to speak. Mutism is one of the hallmarks of severe catatonia.

I said her name a couple more times but received only silence in response.

Then I had an idea.

"May I hold your other hand, Laura?"

Without waiting for an answer, I reached across her husband's body and took hold of her free hand. Unlike her right, which maintained its grip on the dead man's hand, her left merely lay at her side on the grass. When I closed my fingers around it, I thought I felt some movement.

I paused. Was it just a reflexive response, her body's autonomic nervous system reacting? Or was it consciousness of another hand squeezing hers?

Since there was no way to know, I kept slowly squeezing and then releasing.

I heard Polk's abrupt bark from somewhere behind me.

"What the hell ya doin', Rinaldi?"

"No idea." My reply was as much to myself as to him.

I squeezed Laura's hand again, a bit harder this time. And, suddenly, she squeezed back. Softly, tentatively.

*She's in there,* I thought. Maybe trying to get out—or inwardly screaming for me to leave her alone.

"Can you hear me, Laura?" I tried again. "I'm right here, right next to you. Can you hear my voice?"

Her head was still bowed, locked in its gaze at her husband, but I could see that she'd blinked. Once, twice. Until, finally, her chin lifted and she made eye contact with me.

I couldn't tell if she was actually seeing me, but her eyes stayed riveted on mine, blinking quickly, repeatedly.

Just then, a squeal of tires drew my gaze from hers, and I looked out at the curb. A city ambulance, lights flashing, had screeched to a halt. The engine had barely been shut off when two EMTs rushed from the vehicle, one carrying a litter.

After a moment's consultation with Polk, the two medics were at my side. As succinctly as I could, I explained the situation, adding that they needed to get Laura Steinman to the hospital ASAP.

It took some effort, but we managed to pry her hand free of its grip on her husband's, and then to slowly bring her to her feet. While the convulsive rigidity of her muscles had lessened, she was still verbally and physically unresponsive.

Within moments the EMTs had her on the litter and were carrying her to the rear of the ambulance. I walked alongside, until they transferred Laura to a wheeled gurney and slid her into the ambulance. I told her I'd check in later to see how she was doing. She merely blinked.

As the ambulance pulled from the curb, I looked back at what had once been a man named Peter Steinman. His arms were akimbo, legs twisted under him from the body's spin as the bullet exploded in his skull.

*Three deaths.* Just as I'd feared.

And my gut told me there'd be more...

# Chapter Nine

When I rejoined Polk, he informed me that he'd sent Officer Bronski to assist the other uniforms in canvassing the block. While we were speaking, the coroner's wagon rumbled to a stop behind the ambulance. At almost the same time, the CSU van arrived, depositing the squad's blue-suited crime scene techs onto the crowded front lawn.

Polk grimaced. "Looks like the gang's all here. Took 'em long enough. Meanwhile, Biegler's bustin' my balls about givin' him a report. In person. Him and the assistant chief are waitin' for me downtown."

"I don't envy you that little coffee klatch, Harry."

"Tell me about it. After they bag the vic and get him to the morgue, and I light a fire under CSU, I'm outta here. Soon as my lame-ass partner shows up."

"You're still working with Banks?"

His answer was a sour grunt. Jerry Banks, promoted last year to detective, second grade, had been assigned to Polk as his temporary partner while Eleanor Lowrey was on leave. In his late twenties, he was both inexperienced and supremely self-confident. Not the best combination in a homicide detective.

"Where is the Boy Wonder, anyway?"

"Says he's still at the morgue, on the Parr murder."

"Does that mean the ME's found something?"

"You mean, somethin' new? Who the hell knows? I *do* know that when they took the bullet outta the lady, it was the same make and caliber as the Hartley shootin'."

"I'm not surprised. Did they ever find the rifle the shooter used for Parr?"

"No. Guess he didn't need to have a weapon he could build from parts, like what he used to get it into the stadium. Probably left it there because he didn't wanna risk it bein' found durin' the exit checks."

I considered this. "Sure. He had to assume that, after the shooting, security personnel would do a much more thorough job searching people leaving the stadium. Speaking of which, weren't there surveillance cameras at the stadium? Maybe they caught something."

"There were and they didn't. Not that they had enough of 'em in place. Security there is a fuckin' joke."

"What about in Shadyside? The Parr shooting?"

"We got nice footage o' the lady gettin' her brains splattered all over the pavement. But that's about it."

"Nothing from the reverse angle? Maybe of somebody entering the building across the street? If the sniper *did* shoot from up on the roof, he—"

"Christ, Rinaldi!" Polk frowned suddenly, regarding me with suspicion. "How the fuck do ya *do* that?"

"Do what, Harry?"

"Get me talkin' to ya 'bout an open case." A heavy sigh. "Since you've been missin' in action lately, I forgot how much it pisses me off."

"Then you ought to thank me for jogging your memory."

This didn't help.

"I'm not fuckin' around 'bout this, wiseass."

To my surprise, his anger rose, along with the decibel level. Out of the corner of my eye I saw one of the morgue guys looking over at us.

"Jesus, Harry. Get a grip. Besides, you've given me this speech a hundred times before. I practically know it by heart."

"Yeah? Then how come it ain't stuck? You're a goddamn civilian, Rinaldi! Remember? The only reason I called ya down here was 'cause I figgered ya could help with the Steinman woman. That's done now, so get the hell outta here!"

I merely stared at his flushed, darkened face. Then, finally, I gave him a mock salute and turned away.

As I approached my car, I had two thoughts about this latest exchange with Polk. First, it was clear that his rage was over the top, even for Harry. As I'd surmised earlier, something was definitely eating him. Something that had nothing to do with me or this case.

The other thing I noticed was that Harry was half in the bag. Upright, functioning, but drunk on duty. I had my issues with Polk—as he'd with me—but this had never been one of them.

Pulling away from the curb, I glanced back at the crime scene and noticed Polk gulping a large paper cup of steaming coffee one of the officers had brought him.

I hoped he'd have another. The last thing Harry needed was his tight-assed captain, let alone the assistant chief, smelling liquor on his breath as he made his report.

I'd just turned the corner when I spotted the same two TV camera trucks I'd seen the day before now racing to the Steinman home. Obviously, print and internet journos wouldn't be far behind. Meanwhile, from high overhead, came the familiar, thundering pulse of a helicopter's rotors.

As I'd expected, the media frenzy, initially ignited by the shooting at Teasdale College, was gathering momentum. Soon, on TV and online, it would have a hurtling life of its own,with ludicrous conspiracy theories, wild speculation by various pundits, and urgent calls for calm by the authorities.

I'd seen it all before. But somehow, knowing it was coming didn't do much to allay my concerns about the inevitable tsunami of public outrage…

Followed by a growing panic.

—

It was worse than I thought.

I'd made myself a ham sandwich in the kitchen, then taken a beer into the front room. My head ached and my limbs throbbed with fatigue. Since I'd barely slept the night before, I figured I'd crash on the sofa, maybe grab a couple winks.

But my curiosity got the better of me, so I reached for the remote and turned on the TV. The shootings were the lead story on both the local and network news programs.

The coverage on CNN included a timeline—represented with a graphic depicting Pittsburgh and environs—of each of the three murders. Given the respective distances between Lockhart, Shadyside, and Squirrel Hill, and the travel time from one to the other, it wouldn't have been difficult for a lone sniper to hit all three targets.

Multiple cell phone videos from the Teasdale College shooting, sent to the media from fans who'd captured images of the fallen mascot from various spots in the stadium, accompanied the report of the first incident. There was also an on-scene reporter, microphone in hand, asking those having just been released from the exit checks to express their feelings.

The coverage of Harriet Parr's death not only featured news footage from the scene, but an interview with one of her adult children, an engineering student at Carnegie Mellon. Voice choked with emotion, she described her mother as a kind, God-fearing woman who volunteered at her church and loved her poodles Buddy and Sally.

Most striking of all were the video images of the latest death, that of Peter Steinman. There were shots of police and forensics techs swarming the manicured front lawn, as well as of a swelling crowd of onlookers behind the crime scene tape. Then, under the TV anchor's description of Laura Steinman's agonized response to her husband's death, helicopter footage showed her being loaded into the back of an ambulance.

From the video, the station cut to a live shot from Pittsburgh Memorial of a woman identified as the distraught woman's sister, Mary Anne North. She looked to be somewhat older than Laura but with similar features, including wispy blond hair, though her face understandably reflected a deep strain.

"This is a tragedy for the entire North family," she said into an upraised microphone. "But especially, of course, for my poor sister, Laura. We ask that you please respect her privacy, and ours, in this difficult time."

There was a sharp, wary tone to her voice, as though she didn't relish the job of family spokesperson. Certainly the guarded looks she gave to the reporters gathered around her signaled her distrust of the media–and, I suspected, her disdain for the feigned empathy and concern that disguised their more blatant, self-serving interests.

Not that I blamed her.

"If it bleeds, it leads," goes the well-known phrase about the priorities of the news business. Short of actual physical mayhem, getting up-close-and-personal interviews with grieving family members was the next best thing.

I clicked off the TV and swallowed the rest of my beer. Then I scooped up my cell and called Jason Graham at the same hospital from which Mary Anne North was speaking for the cameras.

When I reached him in his room, he told me that his parents had arrived and were talking with a doctor about his condition.

"Dr. Chang?" I said.

He hesitated for a moment. "Uh, no... My dad said he wanted to speak with somebody older. More experienced. White, to be honest. So the nurse introduced him to a guy named Rogers."

"I'm surprised Rogers was willing to poach a colleague's patient. No matter what your father said."

"Apparently Dr. Rogers spoke with Dr. Chang about it, and she was cool." He offered a weak chuckle. "My dad's pretty old-school. I give him shit about it all the time."

"Might be a generational thing. What does your father do?"

"He's got his own plumbing business. My mom's a retired elementary school teacher. Your classic blue-collar family. Pretty much like yours, right, Doc? Like you mentioned in your commencement speech the other day."

*Not exactly*, I thought. Not with my beat cop of a father, who raised me from childhood after my mother's early death, along with various aunts and uncles. A bitter alcoholic, my father was initially proud that his son was the first in the family to go to college, to wear a jacket and tie. That pride turned to something else when my choice to become a psychologist seemed irreconcilable with his hard-won common sense and the lessons he'd learned patrolling the harsher streets and alleys of the Steel City. Only crazy people went to see therapists, and even crazier people chose clinical work as a profession.

It was a position he maintained till the day he died.

"Still, I'm glad my parents are here," Jason was saying. "Though if you tell 'em I said that, I'll deny it."

"Well, one thing's for sure—you sound much better."

A real laugh this time. "I think it's the drugs, Dr. Rinaldi. Hell, even weed doesn't mellow me out like this."

"When are they discharging you?"

"Probably tonight. But they said I should probably see someone about my panic attacks."

"Attacks? Plural?"

"Yeah. See, I've had 'em on and off for years. Since high school. I mean, I didn't know what to call 'em before, but now I know what they were."

"And you didn't see someone? A professional?"

"For wiggin' out once in a while? Try sellin' *that* to my old man. Hell, if Dr. Rogers hadn't suggested it..."

"You're of legal age now, Jason. You can make a decision like that for yourself."

"I know. In fact, I'm hoping that you'll see me."

"That'd be fine. Call my office once you're discharged and we'll make an appointment."

—

I'd no sooner ended the call than my cell rang. It was Sam Weiss, a feature writer for the *Pittsburgh Post-Gazette*. Smart, funny, and irreverent, he'd managed to survive both the staff cutbacks and change of ownership at the city's main paper.

Sam and I had been friends since he'd referred his teenage sister, Amy, to me many years ago. She'd been assaulted and raped, and though I felt my work with her was fruitful, to this day Sam credits me with "saving her sanity." While I've always thought

Amy herself was primarily responsible for that, I've never been able to convince him.

"What's up, Sam?"

"You're kidding, right, Danny? I assume you've been watching the news."

"As much as I can stand."

"Then you know about the sniper attacks."

I paused. Apparently, Sam hadn't yet discovered that I'd had some involvement with two of the murders. But knowing him, it wouldn't take him long to find out.

"So, what can I do for you, Sam, and how badly am I going to regret it?"

"What do you think? I want a statement about the shootings from Pittsburgh's favorite psychologist."

"They're horrible. And you can quote me."

"Very funny. Not for nothing, but you sound a helluva lot more eloquent on CNN. You use the big words and everything."

"Sure. The pay is better."

"Seriously, Danny. What's the clinical take on these killings? What's behind all this?"

"At this point, Sam, I'd bet you know more than I do."

"Not much more, but we sure as hell will. We're doing background checks on all three victims. Interviewing friends, family, colleagues."

"You *and* the cops. Find anything interesting?"

"If you mean some kind of connection among the three of them, the answer's no. We think the cops are right and these are random hits."

"Probably. And, off the record, I fear there'll be more."

A beat of silence from his end.

"Okay, then, *on* the record… Any words of wisdom? C'mon, give me *something*, Danny. I'm on deadline here."

"Sorry, Sam. But you know as well as anyone that I'm on sabbatical from the pundit business. Ever since Maddox."

He grunted. "Jesus, when are you gonna stop beating yourself up about that?"

"When *you* stop trying to get quotes from me that end up landing me in deep shit with Pittsburgh PD. Besides, I thought you were on deadline. Find yourself another clinical know-it-all. I can text you the number of the American Psychological Association. They got tons of them."

—

Dinner was some leftover chili, after which I poured myself a Jack Daniel's, neat, and went out on the rear deck. I had a Thelonious Monk CD playing in the front room, at a high enough volume that the familiar urgency of his music pulsed through my house and easily reached my ears.

The autumnal darkness had settled like a damp shroud over the Point, though lights from the downtown office buildings were like a hundred pinpricks puncturing the gloom. The night's insistent chill raised goose bumps on my arms, even under the sleeves of my venerable Pitt sweatshirt. But the cold was bracing and, as it usually did, helped clear my head.

I don't recall how long I stood out there, elbows on the deck railing, sipping my whiskey. Yet at some point I realized it was getting late, so I figured I'd better hit the sack.

I returned to the front room and dutifully did the evening check of my office voicemail. There was only one message, delivered in a soft, plaintive voice.

"This is Indra, Dr. Rinaldi. Indra Bishara. I got your number from Martin Hobbs and was hoping we could set a time to meet. Not in your office. I don't want to enter treatment with you. But it would mean a great deal to me if you could spare an hour or so to talk. It's about..."

Here her tone changed, as if she were suddenly embarrassed.

"I'm sorry, Doctor. At the risk of sounding mysterious, it's not something I feel comfortable leaving on a message machine. Well, okay, that *did* sound mysterious. I hope I haven't just scared you off."

Then she left her phone number and said goodbye.

I stood there, staring down at the phone in my hand, reflecting on her message. Personal yet vague, it all but guaranteed that I'd return her call, which I did intend to do. But not at this hour.

Suddenly, my cell pinged. Earlier that day I'd set it to alert me whenever CNN aired breaking news.

A stark headline filled the small screen:

PITTSBURGH SNIPER STRIKES AGAIN

# Chapter Ten

I spent the next day, Monday, seeing my regular schedule of patients. As often happens, the tragic events over the weekend reverberated like a dull, background hum to whatever personal issues an individual might be dealing with. This was especially true for patients whose treatment involved their struggle with the traumatic aftereffects of a violent act.

As it happened, I had one patient who'd been hijacked weeks earlier, as well as another who was a teller at a bank that had been robbed by armed men. A third was still reeling from the hit-and-run death of her brother months before.

To these patients, the recent shootings had the potential to re-traumatize them. To send them spiraling back into the maelstrom of fears, real and imagined, that made daytime hours barely tolerable and a night's sleep impossible.

Like most trauma victims, they tended toward hypervigilance, and the randomness of the murders only reinforced that, deepening an inchoate dread about what horrors might await them in an unknown future.

This meant we spent significant time in therapy discussing such dubious options as never leaving the house, changing their names, buying a gun. One even said she was seriously considering moving out of town.

Dealing with these patients required that I both empathize with and relate to their concerns, and yet at the same time, help them gain the psychological tools to manage them. Depending on the day and the circumstances, I was usually able to make some progress.

On this particular day, however, and in these particular circumstances, I failed as often as I succeeded.

But, for a therapist, sometimes that has to be enough.

—

By now, thanks to the growing media firestorm, the unknown assailant had been given a name. The Steel City Sniper.

I'd learned this—as well as other details of the fourth shooting—from the all-news radio station on my drive down to work that morning. The victim had been identified as a physician, Dr. Francis Mapes, who was killed at around eleven p.m. on his way out of a restaurant in Station Square. Apparently, he'd been having dinner and drinks with his brother from out of town. Fifty-five years of age, a husband and father of three, Mapes lived with his family in Edgewood.

When pressed, the Department's media spokesperson admitted that the police assumed this was the work of the same person, and that the murders appeared to be random attacks, carried out by the killer from a safe distance.

As I pulled into my building's parking garage, it struck me how quickly the sniper was accumulating victims. If these were indeed random attacks, designed to instill terror in the city's residents, it seemed to me that putting some time between the shootings would be more effective. The public's fears would be more sharply inflamed if the murders were intermittently spaced. The irregularity of the shootings would intensify people's unease, leaving them wondering whether another attack might occur.

And yet, if I had any doubt as to the extent of the rising panic, it was dispelled by another news report. Police stations throughout the tristate area were being inundated with calls and emails from a terrified populace.

Local politicians also were reporting hundreds of calls from frightened constituents, demanding action. More police on the streets, better surveillance in public areas.

On my lunch break between patient appointments, I watched additional news footage on my cell. At a hastily convened news conference, the mayor and Police Chief Logan struggled to deal with an onslaught of reporters' questions for which they had no real answers.

Then some local TV stations aired man-on-the-street interviews with people at various locations throughout the city. Unsurprisingly, every person questioned described a growing level of fear and paranoia, with a few using their momentary platforms to decry the escalation of moral chaos and godless violence in society. Cell phone video from viewers captured people huddling at a bus stop, looking anxiously about them, and commuters running from their parked cars to the safety of their office buildings. One image was of a popular diner, whose owner had brought the front sidewalk's chairs and tables inside. A sign in the window read "Patio dining closed."

In essence, the city itself was having a panic attack.

—

My last patient of the day, a twelve-year-old boy, couldn't wait for his session to be over. Although it had slipped my mind until he'd mentioned it, tonight was Halloween, and he was anxious to get home, get into his Iron Man costume, and hit the streets for candy. That's when it occurred to me that I hadn't left any treats out on my front porch. I hoped to hell the house wouldn't get egged or TP'd as a result.

After escorting the excited boy out to the waiting room where his mother sat peering at her cellphone, I went back in my office and returned Indra Bishara's call.

This time, it was I who was forced to leave a message. I told her I'd try her again the next day.

The sun set even earlier now that October 31 had arrived, and the sullen night brought a chill so intense I could feel it through my office window when I put my palm against the glass. As I slipped into my coat, I reminded myself to pick up a bottle of wine to take to Gloria Reese's apartment tonight. The thought suddenly made me anxious to see her.

So, naturally, my cell phone rang.

"Dr. Rinaldi? This is Sharon Cale, in District Attorney Sinclair's office. He's wondering if it would be convenient for you to come here as soon as possible."

"You mean, tonight?"

"Right now, actually. Mr. Sinclair needs to see you on a matter of some urgency."

I paused. "Do I have a choice?"

Her tone sharpened. "Would you like me to ask him?"

"No, don't bother. I'll head over there now."

"Great, Doctor. I'll tell him to expect you."

We hung up. I'd known Leland Sinclair for many years, having met during the same investigation that introduced me to Harry Polk and Eleanor Lowrey. We became even more involved when he ran, unsuccessfully, for governor some time later. Sinclair was WASP-y, country-club handsome; also smart, articulate, and extremely ambitious. A totally unconflicted political animal.

We'd had no reason to be in contact in recent years, so I was surprised to be summoned to his office. Ours had always been a wary, distant relationship, personally *and* professionally. Yet, unlike the brass at Pittsburgh PD, Sinclair didn't have a problem with my consultant's contract with the Department, as long as it suited his interests. I was well aware, however, that the day it no longer did so, he'd side with his colleagues in blue.

Nevertheless, whatever Sinclair's plans were for me this evening, they messed up my own with Gloria. Sighing, I punched in her number. Before she could utter two words, I told her about the DA's unexpected call.

The silence on her end conveyed her disappointment, but, with wry humor, she rallied.

"Okay, Rinaldi. If you'd rather hook up with Sinclair than me, that's your problem. Meanwhile, what I'm I supposed to do with the can of whipped cream I bought for the occasion?"

"You have a fridge in that FBI-approved apartment of yours, don't you? It'll keep till later."

"So you *do* plan on showing up sometime tonight?"

"Soon as I can get through this meeting with Sinclair."

"All right, then I forgive you. But don't make it *too* late, okay, Danny? I'd hate to start without you."

---

The district attorney's office was in a new civic complex downtown, close to the Old City-County Building, headquarters of Pittsburgh PD. The sleek, four-story structure's construction was so recent that a number of floors still awaited final completion. The same was true of the adjacent parking garage, which meant finding a place to park on the street a few blocks away.

Passing a row of shops and restaurants festooned with Halloween decorations, I slipped through sparse weeknight traffic until I found a side street. Though well-lit by a single lamp high overhead, it was more alley than street, and ran between two squat, older buildings that had yet to fall victim to gentrification.

As I parked and locked the Mustang, I felt a nostalgic twinge for the similar brown-bricked buildings of my youth, when a trip downtown to Kaufmann's Department Store for school clothes with one of my aunts guaranteed ice cream as reward. It was a time when the clang of streetcars rumbling over cobblestone streets mixed with the bleat of car horns protesting rush-hour traffic, when block-long newsstands stood under fringed awnings, when cops actually did help old ladies across the street, and when everybody wore a hat.

I tightened my coat collar against the night's unremitting cold as I made my way to the half-finished civic complex. A drowsing guard nodded me into the expansive though as-yet undecorated lobby, and then directed me to the elevator. The district attorney's office was on the top floor.

Given the lateness of the hour, the corridor leading to the polished double doors was deserted, with that somber hush unique to office buildings after the workday's done. Yet when I stepped into the spacious reception area, I was enveloped by gleaming overhead track lighting, and met by an equally gleaming young woman, who introduced herself as Sharon Cale, Sinclair's executive assistant. She was young, attractive, and briskly efficient.

"Thanks for coming so promptly, Doctor. As I said on the phone, Leland is quite anxious to see you."

I wasn't surprised to hear that she and Sinclair were on a

first-name basis. From what I remembered about the DA's choice in women, she certainly fit his type: blond, leggy, smart.

After giving his office door a quick knock, she ushered me inside. She hadn't finished closing the door behind me when Sinclair was rising from behind his massive desk to greet me.

Despite the hour, his designer-label suit looked freshly pressed. His handshake was as firm and unrelenting as I remembered. And with his perfectly groomed hair having gone a distinguished silver, blue eyes possessing their usual glint of feigned intimacy, he looked as camera-ready as the day we'd met.

"Good to see you again, Dr. Rinaldi. Danny." He moved to the wet bar set discreetly against the near wall. "Can I get you something to drink? God knows *I* could use something."

"Whatever you're having, Lee."

He nodded and poured us each a whiskey, his with ice, mine without. I realized as he handed me my drink that I was supposed to notice that he remembered how I took it.

"You have a good memory," I said.

He shrugged. "For some things or, should I say, for some people."

He motioned me to a cushioned chair. His desk's polished surface was unadorned except for some framed family photos, a gold-plated penholder, and a neat stack of file folders. Gracing the wall behind him were portraits of the mayor, the governor, and the president, on either side of which stood the flags of the U.S. and the State of Pennsylvania.

"I like your new office." I glanced around the spacious, beautifully appointed room. Broad windows, high-end furniture. "It's probably what God would've done if He had the money."

Sinclair smiled, all teeth.

"Believe it or not, I had this somewhat ostentatious suite

forced on me. I was perfectly happy at City Hall, but the mayor felt it would lend some gravitas to the new complex if the district attorney's office was here."

I sipped my drink. "I think I understand. Show the taxpayers they were getting some bang for the buck. If Mr. Law and Order works here, it must be the real deal."

"Something like that." He leaned back in his chair. "Anyway, you're probably wondering why I called you here."

"Well, I figured it wasn't because you've missed my company. It's about these sniper attacks. Though I don't know how I can help you."

"To be candid, I called you because I wanted to talk to someone outside the Department. And not *inside* the city council. And certainly not some government expert." The smile widened. "In other words, someone I respected."

"More or less."

"Look, Danny, I know we've had some difficulties in the past, but I also know we're both pragmatic men. And, despite our differing professions and approaches, I'm sure we have the best interests of the city at heart."

"Listen, Lee, if you're looking for a running mate for your next political campaign—"

"Don't worry, it's nothing so dire. Or so desperate. Actually, you were right before. It's about these shootings."

"The Steel City Sniper. Catchy."

"Please. Don't get me started on the goddamn media. The pressure from the press about these murders has reached all the way to Harrisburg. That's why I have a strategy meeting later tonight with the mayor and Chief Logan. To figure out how we're going to deal with this, in terms of a public response."

"I saw the press conference."

"Yes. Boilerplate crisis management. Which buys us no more

than a day or two. Especially now that there's been a fourth victim. A doctor, for Christ's sake."

"Do the cops know anything more than they did before?"

He shook his head. "Not really. I just spoke to Captain Biegler, who's running the primaries on the case."

"Biegler's a jackass. In my clinical opinion."

"Maybe, but he's *our* jackass. At least I can control him. God knows what the FBI's going to do."

"I hear their field agents are already on the ground."

"They're not the problem. It's the assistant director I'm worried about. Chief Logan says he's flying in tomorrow from Quantico, and that he's supposedly a Grade-A prick."

Sinclair finished his whiskey in a single gulp, then rose and refilled his glass. "Another, Danny?"

I shook my head. "I'm good."

"Sure you are. You don't have to meet with His Honor and that blowhard Logan. Believe me, I need all the liquid fortification I can get."

Refreshed drink in hand, he sat on a corner of his desk, looking down at me. Collegial as hell.

"My point is, I want to have something to tell them. Something we can use."

"About the sniper?"

"Yes. Since you're on the city payroll, I figure why not pick your brain? Maybe you can give me some insight as to the kind of lunatic we're dealing with."

"You'd get better info from one of the FBI's profilers. They have all the data. In fact, I can refer you to one you've probably heard of. Lyle Barnes. We sort of worked together in the past. He's retired now, but knows more than—"

He shook his head.

"The Bureau's sending one of their own guys from Behavioral

Science. He's flying in with the assistant director. So I'll get an earful from them. But I wanted to know what *you* think."

"You mean, better the devil you know...?"

"Come on, Doctor. You've worked for the Pittsburgh Police for years. You know the politics, how the brass thinks. I'm hoping you can give me something I can share with them. That came from one of our own people. Because the last thing the cops want is to have to sit there while some FBI suit spouts statistics and starts making predictions."

I nodded. "Telling the cops how to do their jobs. Looking down its federal nose at them."

"Like it or not, that's how they see it. And they're not far wrong." Sinclair finished his drink. "So, Danny, what can you give me?"

"Well, from the few studies I've read, I've learned that most snipers *do* fit a particular profile. Unless they're using a spotter—which my gut says is not the case here—they like to work alone and pride themselves on being precision shots."

"That seems obvious."

"They also tend to be calm, calculated and, viewed from the outside, appear to be stable. Normal."

"And damn coldhearted, if they're willing to kill."

"But from afar, which usually means a lack of emotional connection to their victims. Those they kill are seen as targets, not people."

"So they're psychopaths?"

"Or at least classic narcissists, which can often underly psychopathology. If I were to guess, you're looking for someone who's highly aggressive when criticized, and is unwilling or even unable to admit flaws."

Sinclair laughed shortly. "Have you ever been to a City Council meeting?"

"Not on my bucket list, no." I drained my glass, suddenly

sorry that I'd refused another. "Seriously—and again, these studies are rare and varied—the data suggest a profoundly concrete, implacable self-image, coupled with an inability to relate to or empathize with the feelings of others. To such an extent that... Well, I'd bet that if you could monitor a sniper's vitals as he takes aim at his target, his heart rate and pulse would remain the same."

The district attorney grimaced. "My problem with what you're saying is that it demeans whole units of our military."

"Not necessarily. Snipers trained in the military may have some of these characteristics, but they're also motivated by other factors. Patriotism, concern for their fellow soldiers, respect for the chain of command. I'm not talking about people who feel they're doing their duty. It's more likely that our sniper is possessed of the required skills, no matter where he attained them, but is a rogue element. Unless..."

Sinclair stirred, uncomfortable. "Unless what?"

"Unless he thinks he *is* doing his duty."

Sinclair's shoulders slumped, and he once more stared down at the empty glass in his hand. As if looking for answers there.

Finally, he looked up. "So you're saying we might not just be looking for some whack-job, but a *dedicated* whack-job. On a goddamn mission from God or whatever."

"It's possible. But at this point, everything I said is simply conjecture. Same is true for the FBI profiler. We won't know for sure until the sniper's caught. *If* he's caught..."

Sinclair straightened up. "He sure as hell better be, Danny. Or somebody else is going to be sitting in this nice new office. For a good many of our fine citizens, the cops and the DA are joined at the hip."

There didn't seem much I could say in answer to that, and he didn't look like he expected a response. Smoothing his hair with the palm of his hand, he gave me an exaggerated shrug and went back to sit behind his desk. It took me a moment to realize that I'd just been dismissed.

I got out of my seat and headed out of the office. Then I turned at the door.

"I met Sharon, your new secretary."

"Executive assistant." He folded his hands on the desk.

"Well, she certainly seems competent. Sure of herself."

"You know me, Danny. I like strong, ambitious women." He let out a long, sad sigh. "Of course, she's no Casey Walters."

"No," I said. "But then again, who is?"

# Chapter Eleven

The night was cold, dark, and eerily still. Windless. The somber streets were nearly deserted, with only the neon glow of a distant restaurant or bar to indicate life at ground level. Myriad lights from the tall, sparkling buildings looming over the city's new urban core somehow made the concrete and glass landscape feel even more barren, rather than less.

I stood outside the lobby doors and buttoned my coat to the top. As often happened, my encounter with Sinclair had left me vaguely uneasy. Not least because of his comment about Casey Walters. His former assistant DA, she was brilliant, beautiful, and wildly unpredictable. She'd been his mistress for a while, before she and I began our own brief, ill-advised affair. This was years ago, during my involvement in the Wingfield investigation, when Sinclair and I had first met. It wasn't long after that that Casey left town for parts unknown.

Like a lot of career politicians, Sinclair maintained a picture-perfect life: appropriate, civic-minded wife; two appropriate, college-age children. Whether the seemingly devoted Mrs. Sinclair knew about his affairs—and, if so, even cared—was a closely guarded secret in the DA's office and at City Hall. They were among the dozens of other such secrets hiding in the nooks and crannies of any town's local government.

I hadn't gone half a block toward where I'd parked my car when my cell rang. Gloria Reese. Probably wondering where the hell I was.

I paused and looked at my watch. Just after nine p.m. I wasn't going to be *that* late…

I'd guessed wrong.

"Danny, bad news. We'll have to take a rain check on tonight's festivities."

"What's up?"

"The Bureau called me in to help with these shootings. They want all hands on deck."

"Well, I'm disappointed, but I can't say I'm surprised."

"That makes two of us, on both counts. You'll just have to keep that bad boy in your pants till we can reschedule."

"Looks like it. But now it's my turn to tell *you* to be careful. Nobody knows what the hell we're dealing with yet."

"Don't worry, I'll be fine. Small but mighty, remember?"

I did indeed.

—

After we hung up, I hurried along the sidewalk till I reached the mouth of the alley where I'd parked. As I turned the corner, I noticed two things.

The crunch of broken glass under my shoe.

And the fact that the alley was enveloped in complete and total darkness.

I froze where I stood. Something was wrong. Very wrong.

Clicking on my cell's flashlight, I aimed it up in the direction of the streetlamp overhead. The bulb was jagged, shattered. As if from something thrown at it.

Or shot at it.

Heart suddenly thumping in my chest, I lowered the cell's light and turned it toward the mouth of the alley. Given the poor illumination, all I saw was the vague outline of my Mustang, parked halfway down the narrow passage. There were other shapes hugging the alley's walls on either side, but they were blurred, indistinct. Thick, opaque shadows.

I took a step forward, hearing the snap of a glass shard under my foot. And no other sound.

Some part of me knew I should stop where I was and turn around. Get back to the street, to the safety of the new complex's lobby.

But some equally stubborn—or perverse—part of me forced me to keep walking. Keep heading down the length of the alley.

With only my cell's glow poking through the impenetrable darkness, I made my way far enough to see the outline of my car come into focus. My feeble light glinting off the front grille.

While the only sound in the profound, uncanny silence was the scrape of my footsteps on asphalt.

Something—some animal instinct—made me stop then. Hold my light waist-high, turning it in a short, swiveling arc.

A dark, hulking shape leapt into view. It was a large, industrial-gauge dumpster, standing against the right wall about a dozen feet ahead of me.

And then I heard it. The scrape of another shoe.

Someone was behind the dumpster. Crouched, hidden.

But it took me a second too long to register this. I'd no sooner cut the light than I saw the muzzle flash.

I hit the ground hard, my bones rattling against the cold,

unforgiving concrete at the same time the bullet pierced the air above me. Missing me by inches.

The echoing roar of the gunshot was still in my ears as I rolled against the near wall. I knew I had only seconds to crawl over to the safety of my car.

I'd just made it, huddling low behind the front grille, when I heard another gunshot. Followed by a sharp ping as the bullet grazed the exposed end of the fender.

Straining so hard to hear that I found myself squinting, I stayed where I was. There was no use debating my next move. I didn't have one.

Long, torturous moments went by, eaten up by a leaden, unremitting silence. Now the only sound was my own short, labored breathing.

Finally, I risked peering around the front of my car. My eyes now accustomed to the darkness, I could make out the near face of the dumpster. Paint-flecked, mottled. But I neither heard nor saw any sign of movement behind it.

I let another five minutes pass before I rose from behind my car and, turning on my cell's light again, slowly approached my unknown assailant's own hiding place. Holding my breath, I came around to the rear of the squat, rust-encrusted dumpster.

And found nothing.

Whoever had shot out the streetlamp before trying to do the same to me had vanished so stealthily that I hadn't even heard his retreating footsteps. A quick glance up to the other end of the alley revealed that it opened onto another street, with no gate or fence across it to bar an escape.

Letting myself breathe more easily, I surveyed the area from which my attacker had fired. I couldn't see any spent shells, which could mean he'd used a revolver or else had had the presence of mind to scoop them up before taking off.

Nor were there any footprints on the hard alley floor, either behind the dumpster or—as far as I could tell—indicating his path to or from the alley.

It suddenly occurred to me that I was pushing my luck hanging around that alley, so I got into my Mustang and pulled out onto the street. I drove a couple blocks, then parked at the curb.

To my surprise, my hands stayed glued to the steering wheel, in a kind of death grip.. Now that the adrenaline pulse was over—my fight-or-flight response quieted—I was left with the profound shock of having been shot at.

Closing my eyes, I began a series of long, slow, cleansing breaths. In minutes, I felt the pounding of my heart lessen, the muscles in my fingers loosening their hold on the wheel. Still, an important lesson. Given my own experience, and regardless of my clinical training, I had to accept that I was no more immune to the trauma of violence than any of my patients.

Meanwhile, as I slowly and methodically kept up my breathing, I also tried to think, to bring back into focus what I'd seen when the gunman fired. I'd had the distinct image of a hand, holding a gun. Not a rifle.

And while this didn't completely rule out my shooter as the sniper the cops were seeking, the MO was all wrong. My assailant hadn't positioned himself on a rooftop to take me out from a safe distance. Plus, his having shot out the streetlamp to give him the cover of darkness, making me more vulnerable to an attack, didn't fit the pattern, either.

And, finally, the most puzzling question of all: what made him stop shooting? I was unarmed, essentially helpless. Why hadn't he stepped out from behind the dumpster, come down to where I crouched behind my Mustang, and finish the job?

By now, I felt restored enough to function, so I got out my cell and called 911. As an employee of the Pittsburgh Police, as well as a reasonably civic-minded citizen, I was obligated to report the incident.

After giving the operator the specifics, I pulled away from the curb, made a U-turn, and headed back the way I'd come. Since I'd only driven a couple blocks from the alley, then parked to calm my nerves, I figured I'd arrive back there before the cops.

I did, and only had to wait ten minutes until the first cruiser showed up.

# Chapter Twelve

I spent the next hour standing at the entrance to the alley, describing what happened to the two uniforms who'd answered the dispatcher's call. The older of the two, a black woman with suspicious eyes whose name tag read "Sergeant Wills," merely nodded while her younger partner—a white male with a trim mustache—took notes.

Their patrol car, blue lights flashing, was parked at an angle to the curb. Ten minutes after it had arrived, a second police cruiser appeared. Sergeant Wills immediately sent its two uniformed occupants down the length of the alley, long regulation flashlights held like spears at their shoulders.

As I finished telling my story—for the third time—to the sergeant, one of the cops came back from the alley to join us. Ignoring me, he turned to her.

"Nothin', Sergeant. No shells. Some scuff marks on the concrete, but that don't mean nothin'."

I kept my attention on Wills. "What about the damage to the front of my car? You've seen it. That was from a bullet."

"Don't worry, Dr. Rinaldi. I believe you. It's fresh. Recent. Besides, we all know who you are, so I figure you wouldn't be jerkin' us around."

Her younger partner regarded me. "Ya want us to call for a medic? Give ya the once-over?"

I shook my head. "No need. I'm fine. But shouldn't you get a tech team to check out the alley?"

The sergeant gave a weary smile. "The whole force is stretched thin, Doctor. Now more than ever, due to these sniper attacks. I could make a request, but I don't think it'll have much traction. Especially since—"

"I'm not dead. Or wounded."

"Well, to be honest, yes."

The cop from the alley spoke up again. "Look, Sergeant, if yinz guys are finished, how 'bout we string up some crime scene tape and call it a night? It's fuckin' freezin' out here."

His superior smiled again, a brighter one this time.

"Excellent idea, Roberts. Go tell McGowan he can stop snooping around like Columbo down there."

As the cop trotted back along the alley to convey the news to his partner, Sergeant Wills' gaze met mine.

"You'll have to come downtown to make a statement, Doctor."

"I know the drill, Sergeant. But does it have to be now? Can't I come down and give my statement tomorrow? Before work?"

She scratched her chin. "Well, I guess we can extend you that courtesy. Just be sure you do. I'll have the incident report filed by then."

I shook hands with her and thanked her.

"Listen," she said coolly, "if it went down the way you say it did, I'd count myself lucky and go home."

As I drove away, glancing at Roberts stringing the crime scene tape across the mouth of the alley, I considered the sergeant's advice.

But I had another idea. Instead of heading toward the Fort

Pitt Bridge and home, I turned and drove down to Second Avenue, where it ran alongside the Monongahela River.

I needed a drink.

—

It was the first time I'd seen Noah Frye since the bandages had come off. He leaned forward, elbows on the bar, and slowly flexed his fingers. Though he winced slightly at the pain, he still managed to call up that sweet, goofy smile.

Another victim of Sebastian Maddox's vendetta against me, Noah suffered damage to his hands severe enough to require two surgeries and months of physical therapy. This was particularly devastating since he'd been a gifted jazz pianist and had been told at the outset of treatment that his recovery would be agonizingly slow—if it would even happen at all. And that, regardless, his days as a musician were probably over.

Noah was a paranoid schizophrenic whom I'd met many years before, when he was a patient at a private psychiatric clinic where I did my internship. Prone to severe persecutory delusions and hallucinations, yet possessing a unique intelligence and wit, he'd ultimately been released when his insurance ran out.

Since then, an informal collection of psychologists and psychiatrists had kept Noah supplied with the necessary meds to quell his more intense symptoms. We'd also enlisted the help of a compassionate retired steelworker, who'd sold us a former coal barge moored on the river at Second Avenue. The barge was converted into a floating bar, with Noah and his long-suffering girlfriend, Charlene, as live-in proprietors.

As I sipped my whiskey, I glanced around at the familiar surroundings. Though fitted out with leather booths, café tables, and a small corner stage at which jazz musicians played nightly, the bar still retained what Noah called its "nautical motif." Tar paper hung from the ceilings and portholes served as windows, while the ever-present sounds and smells of the Monongahela River provided an oddly comforting ambiance.

Like Angie Villanova, Noah's months-long medical ordeal had whittled away at his formerly thick, bearlike body. His typical attire of denim overalls and checkered work shirt hung loosely, his massive forearms reduced to sticks. Even his full beard seemed lessened, thinned by worry and strain.

But his eyes still held their telltale glint of shrewd, barely contained madness. Over the long years during which he ceased being my patient and had become a close friend, I'd seen those eyes reflect both the deepest despair and the heights of ecstatic joy. Particularly when it came to Charlene.

"Where is she?" I asked.

He jerked a thumb behind him. "Bustin' her butt in the kitchen. We got some damn college kids who came in lookin' hungry enough to eat the furniture. Charlene's makin' a fuck-load o' burgers for 'em."

I followed his gaze past my shoulder and spotted about a half dozen college-age kids talking, laughing, and drinking at adjoining booths along the far wall. Other than an older, more refined couple seated at one of the small tables, and a couple of typical barflies three stools down from me, the place was pretty empty. No surprise, as it was almost one a.m.

When I turned around again, I was met by Noah's stern look.

"Not for nothin', Danny, but ya ain't been in here for a while. Me an' Charlene have been discussin' it, and neither of us like it much. If I didn't know better, I might start takin' it personal."

"Yeah, well, it's just that I've been pretty busy and..."

"Bullshit." He stood back from the bar, arms folded. "We

both know what's goin' on. Ya feel guilty 'bout what happened to your crazy pal Noah. My hands an' shit."

I took a breath, then a deep swallow of my drink.

"Look, Noah, I know you and Charlene don't bear me any ill will about what Maddox did to you. But I still feel responsible. If you weren't my friend, none of this would've happened."

He shrugged. "What if I said it was a small price to pay for *bein'* your friend?"

"Then I'd say you were crazy."

A short laugh. "Hell, that's already been established. I got a medical file longer than my cock. Than *both* our cocks."

I finished my whiskey and tapped the bar with the glass.

With a rueful smile, Noah reached behind him for the bottle and gave me a refill.

"Ya think gettin' drunk's gonna help?" he said.

"No, I know better than that. But I've had a pretty shitty day, and watching how painful it was for you to flex your fingers didn't help."

"Nice job, Doc. Ya used sympathy for me, to justify your own self-pity. Not cool."

I nodded. "You ought to hang out a shingle, Noah. That was right on the money. Unfortunately. Sorry, my bad."

"Sure was."

A leaden silence filled the space between us, broken by a call from one of the barflies for another drink. Noah gave him a perfunctory wave and headed down the bar to deal with him.

I was still nursing this second drink when the outer door opened, letting in a blast of icy cold air and one Sergeant Harry Polk. His suit more wrinkled than I'd thought possible, he lumbered over to the bar and took the stool next to mine.

By this time, Noah had returned, giving Polk the narrow squint he reserved for police officers and bad musicians. I remembered how he'd complained once that the detective sergeant had become a regular, something with which Noah was extremely uncomfortable. Probably having to do with the times in his life when he'd been homeless, delusional, and hassled by the cops.

He sniffed noisily. "What'll it be, Sergeant?"

"Whatever ya got on tap. An' a Wild Turkey on ice. An' give the doc here another one o' whatever he's havin.'"

I shook my head. "No, thanks, Harry. I've had enough. From the looks of it, so have you."

He ignored me and motioned to Noah. "Just do what I said, okay? I don't need neither one o' ya bustin' my balls."

As Noah went away to fill the order, I turned to Polk.

"Not that it seems to matter lately, but are you off duty?"

"Fuck you, Rinaldi. I can handle my liquor. Besides, we're all workin' straight shifts 'cause o' this sniper asshole."

"Anything new on that front?"

"You mean, besides the brass turnin' up the heat and the feds comin' in tomorrow to piss on our turf? But it could be worse. I could be one o' those poor mooks down at the precinct, ridin' a desk and takin' tips from the public."

"Yes. I heard on the news that you're getting about a hundred tips a day."

"Yeah, an' all crap."

"What about surveillance cameras? They're practically everywhere. Hasn't anything shown up on tape?"

He scowled, and then managed a boozy chuckle.

"Ya know, Rinaldi, I gotta hand it to ya. No matter what I say, ya always gotta grill me about a case. I mean, Christ, can't a guy just drink in peace?"

"Point taken." I put down my half-finished whiskey. "But can I ask another question? Not about the case?"

"Depends. Is it gonna tick me off?"

"Probably."

"Then go ahead. I'm in the mood to punch somebody."

I looked him squarely in the eye. "What the hell's going on with you, Harry? You're acting more belligerent than normal, even for you. And I've never known you to drink on the job."

Polk stiffened. "Nothin's goin' on."

"I don't believe you. And it's not about this case."

He hesitated a moment, and then looked up expectantly as Noah returned with our drinks. Polk quickly downed half a mug of beer, then wiped his chin with the back of his hand.

I didn't make a move for the new whiskey Noah had brought me. Polk gave my full, untouched glass a reproachful scowl, then swallowed his own whiskey in one gulp.

I kept my gaze riveted on him. "I've got all night, Harry. At least until Noah closes up the joint. And you know how stubborn I am."

"That's for goddamn sure." Polk sighed heavily. "What the hell, might as well tell ya. Can't do nothin' 'bout it anyway."

He knocked back the rest of his beer and turned his rheumy eyes on mine. They were tinged with pain.

"It's Maddie, Doc."

"Your ex?"

"Yeah. She's gettin' married again, an' it's eatin' me up."

I nodded and risked putting my hand on his forearm. To my surprise, he didn't react.

I remembered Maddie, and how badly Polk had taken their divorce. He'd even stalked her for a while, and had chased off a guy she'd been dating who turned out to be a known con man. And despite her threats, her entreaties to him to leave her alone and accept that their marriage was over, Polk never got over it.

In fact, he still lived in one of those apartment buildings in Wilkinsburg where separated spouses often did, until they could find more permanent accommodations. And get on with their lives.

Polk never had.

"You should see the jagoff she's marryin', too." He shook his head. "Some kinda banker. Ugly as shit but he's got money."

"Maybe all she wants at this point in her life is security, Harry. A lot of people make that choice."

"I don't give a fuck what she wants."

I risked a smile. "Maybe that was one of the problems in your marriage."

He gave me a warning glance. "I might still punch your fuckin' lights out, Rinaldi."

"No, you won't, Harry. But drinking yourself to death won't change anything, either."

"Then what are *you* doin' here?"

"Visiting my old friend Noah. It's been too long."

He rubbed his bristled chin. "After what happened to him, I'm surprised he still speaks to ya."

"Luckily, he's a lot more evolved than I am. Than most people I know, actually."

"Maybe, but he's still batty as shit. Pours a good drink, though, I'll give him that."

He grew quiet, head bent over his glass, and I knew the conversation was over.

I said goodbye and slid off my stool, but not before offering to be a sympathetic ear should he want one. He waved me off, then reached for my untouched whiskey. Downed it.

Moving down to the end of the bar, where Noah was punching keys in the cash register, I offered him my goodbye as well.

"Tell Charlene I'm sorry I missed her."

"Ya wanna hang a few more minutes, I'm sure she'll be out of the kitchen soon."

"I'd like to, but I'd better go. I have a full day's work tomorrow, and I have to get up really early."

To make my statement to the cops about the attack in the alley, though I didn't want to burden Noah with that news.

"Okay, but wait..." He stepped over to where a coffee carafe bubbled on a hot plate. "Wouldn't hurt ya to take some java with ya. Keep ya from drivin' off the road."

Figuring I was probably more buzzed than I realized, I accepted the proffered paper cup and headed for the door.

"And Danny!" Noah called after me. "Like the man says, don't be a stranger."

---

Before pulling away from the curb, I sat behind the wheel, gingerly sipping the hot black coffee. Wondering why I hadn't told Polk about someone taking shots at me tonight. Especially since he'd no doubt find out about it soon enough.

Maybe it was as simple as not wanting to hear another lecture about how foolhardy I was. Going down that alley even when the streetlamp had been broken. Or, knowing Polk, he'd probably suggest that given how many people I'd pissed off over the years, tonight's incident was inevitable. And that the only surprise was that it hadn't happened already.

By the time I'd swallowed the last of the coffee, I felt sobered up enough to drive. Whether I actually was or not was a different matter. I decided to leave my car parked where it was and take a Lyft home.

Luckily, my driver wasn't talkative, so the ride up to Mt. Washington was relatively quiet. Due to the lateness of the hour, there were no trick-or-treaters roaming the streets. Even better, my house had apparently been unmolested by disappointed Halloween revelers during the long night.

The brief smile of relief this brought to my face vanished quickly. Unlocking my front door, I felt a sudden, unexpected jolt of nerves. Still spooked from the night's events, I instinctively turned on a few extra lights. I planned to keep them on while I slept.

I'd become convinced that the attempt on my life wasn't the work of the sniper. But if not, then who'd waited there in the dark for me?

Moreover, if he *had* wanted to kill me, why didn't he?

# Chapter Thirteen

The predawn chill drilled deep down into my bones as I stepped out of a second Lyft the next morning. On the plus side, my Mustang was not only parked where I'd left it, a half block from Noah's Ark, but it also still had its tires, bucket seats, and dash CD player. An All Saints' Day miracle.

Letting the engine warm up, I sipped the last of my thermos of coffee as Nina Simone's sonorous, bittersweet voice filled the car's interior. Troubles never sounded so achingly pure. Or unending.

Twenty minutes later, I was pulling into the lot at the Old City-County Building. As promised, I was here to give my statement to the police about the shooting in the alley the night before.

The detectives' suite of cubicles was on the fourth floor, and I'd just stepped off the elevator when I spotted someone I usually went out of my way to avoid. Lieutenant—now Captain—Stu Biegler, head of the division's Robbery/Homicide unit, was standing in an alcove in the hallway, pouring tar-thick black coffee from a bubbling carafe.

Before I could take evasive action, Biegler had glanced up,

his face tightening at the sight of me. Then he turned back to what he was doing.

"I know why you're here, Rinaldi." Deliberately keeping his eyes averted.

"Good for you, Stu. I guess you got the morning memo."

He sullenly poured a steady stream of sugar into a large ceramic mug. Even at this distance, I could see that it was personalized. His name emblazoned over the sepia-toned image of a police badge.

I kept walking until we were a few feet apart.

Biegler was tall and male-model thin, with a perpetually avid sheen to his narrow gaze. More bureaucrat than cop, he'd been steadily kissing the collective ass of the department higher-ups for as long as I'd known him. A strategy that worked, apparently, given his recent promotion to captain.

I had to give him one thing, though: early morning or dead of night, regardless of the circumstances, his suit was always pressed, his shoes shined, and his dark hair neatly in place. As though he refused to let the unpleasant realities of police work sully him.

"I'm just saying, wiseass, I heard about that shooting gallery you stumbled into last night. Nothing goes on that I don't end up hearing about. Even the trivial shit."

Now he looked up and straight at me. Casually stirring his morning's caffeine hit with a little plastic spoon.

I smiled. "Yeah? Luckily, he was a bad shot."

"Lucky for *you,* maybe. For the rest of us..." He offered an exaggerated shrug. "Hell, a guy can dream, can't he?"

"Look, just point me to the right cubicle and I'll let you go back to dreaming."

"I'm not finished, Rinaldi." He slowly, meaningfully stopped stirring. Tapped the rim of the mug. "I also learned that you were there at the stadium when the first sniper attack occurred. And were on-site for the third."

"Like you said, Stu, I'm lucky."

"And goddamn civic-minded, too, from what I hear. Helping out poor Mrs. Steinman. And that Jason Graham wuss. Something about a panic attack...?"

"Yes. Though I suspect Jason's been released from the hospital by now. Home with his parents."

"Whatever. We now come to my favorite part of this conversation. The part where I say stay the fuck outta this sniper thing, Rinaldi. From this point on, your bullshit services are no longer required."

"So you and Polk have made clear."

"Polk?" Biegler snorted. "Don't get me started on *that* loser. Some say he's getting to be an embarrassment to the department. That he might even be drinking on duty."

"Harry's a good cop. Just going through a hard time."

"Like I give a fuck. I've been thinking this might be the perfect opportunity to pension his fat ass outta here."

I took another step closer. His eyes fluttered.

"Then who'd be around to make you look good, Stu? Pretty thankless job, I figure, but somebody's got to do it."

Biegler made a show of swallowing a mouthful of coffee, but I could tell he was rattled by my crowding him. I had at least forty pounds on him, and he knew enough about my past to think twice about pushing things too far.

"You got a lotta balls talking to me like that." Feigning a bravado that wouldn't fool a potted plant. "If you were on the job, I'd bust you down to—"

"But I'm not, Stu. I'm a law-abiding citizen whose taxes pay your salary. A civilian under contract for the same brass you spend your days brownnosing. And the thing is, just enough of them like me—sort of—to keep me around. Like Chief Logan. And Lee Sinclair. Which you can't stand."

The captain's face turned the same color of burnt red I'd seen on bricks, as his eyes reduced down to black points.

"Maybe, Rinaldi, but don't push your luck. You don't have your cousin Angie Villanova around to always cover for you. How's the poor lady doing, by the way? She forgive you yet?"

I felt my fists ball up at my sides. But the last thing I wanted to do was let Biegler bait me.

Instead, I said, "Listen, Stu, fun as this is, shouldn't you be reporting to the Feds? The ones who're actually running this investigation?"

"They're *assisting*, dirtbag. *I'm* in charge of this thing."

"Then the city can sleep easy tonight. I know *I* will."

Without waiting for his response, I brushed past him and went the rest of the way down the corridor. I'd been told downstairs which cubicle I should seek out to make my statement.

I knew, as I felt the lance of his hatred piercing my back, that I'd probably pushed things too far with Biegler. From the beginning of my work with the Pittsburgh Police I'd taken an instant dislike to him, and he felt the same toward me. In my view, he oozed an unearned arrogance out of every pore, and as the son of a hard-working beat cop, I resented it.

Still, I had every reason to believe that what I said to him was going to come back at some point to bite me.

—

I'd finished giving my statement to a bored rookie and had just stepped outside the police station when I spotted Gloria Reese across the street. She was heading toward the entrance of another, smaller building. Boxy and unobtrusively wedged between two gleaming office towers, it housed the FBI's field station for the tristate area.

Hoping to catch Gloria before she went inside, I started after her. She wasn't alone, talking animatedly to a solidly built man in an off-the-rack gray suit. Both wore jackets that did little to hide the side holsters beneath.

"Hey, Special Agent Reese," I called out, approaching the pair as they went through the double-doored entrance.

After being momentarily startled, Gloria looked up at me and smiled. The man beside her barely managed a wary squint in my direction.

Like I cared. My gaze—and returning smile—were for Gloria, a smallish woman whose lovely face and slim figure were enhanced by her shrewd, knowing eyes. Like most female FBI agents, she wore a simple outfit of jacket, slacks, and low-heeled shoes. Her purse hung from her shoulder, and she carried a black briefcase.

"Nice to see you, Dr. Rinaldi." She let me breathe in her subtle perfume as she gave me a brisk, collegial hug. She then introduced me to her companion.

"Daniel Rinaldi, meet Hank Bowman. Hank's our station chief in the region, so he's leading the Bureau's team on these sniper attacks."

Shaking hands, I had the opportunity to give him a better look. Maybe forty, clean-shaven, reasonably good-looking. Gold wedding ring. American flag pin on his jacket lapel. The strength in his grip and the way his jacket sleeve bunched at his biceps gave the impression of a guy who spent way too much time at the gym. And though he managed a smile as he said hello, the suspicious glint in his eyes remained steady.

"We were just on our way to Hank's office," Gloria said.

"Whoa, don't let me interrupt." I backstepped a little.

"No worries," Bowman said. "I'm dying for an espresso. Why don't you join us? I make a killer cup."

Gloria gave a wry chuckle. "Yeah, life's rough for Chief Bowman here. Has an espresso machine in his office."

He spread his hands. "Hey, might as well have all the comforts of home. Especially since I'm never *there*."

I ignored the emphasis he'd placed on the word, and the domestic troubles at which it hinted. Instead, I merely smiled my assent and followed the pair through the lobby, across from which was a suite of offices. Bowman led us into his.

It was spacious, impressively appointed, and boasted a number of honorary plaques and framed citations on the walls. Though what drew the eye immediately was the espresso machine, a big, multi-levered silver-and-gold appliance fittingly accorded its own place of honor on a table in the corner.

Bowman motioned us to two cushioned seats opposite his massive mahogany desk, then stepped over to the machine and started pulling levers and pushing buttons.

Gloria's cell pinged the moment we both sat down, so while she read her text, I surveyed the rest of the room. Especially the bookshelf, volumes neatly organized. I glanced at the titles, quite an international array: *The Magus. The Seven Storey Mountain. Les Pleiades. Die Blechtrommel. Don Quixote.*

Glancing up from her cell, Gloria followed my gaze and smiled.

"In their original languages, too. Hank's either some kind of savant or a show-off. I can't make up my mind which."

"Hey, watch it, Reese," said Bowman. "Someone has to carry the torch for the Romance languages."

He came over to his desk, carrying a tray with three small steaming cups of aromatic espresso.

As Gloria and I lifted our cups, Bowman took his own and

went around to sit behind his desk. He took a sip, then gave me a steady look that was hard to read.

"You're that shrink on the police payroll, right, Dr. Rinaldi? I believe Captain Biegler's mentioned you a few times."

"For one thing, I'm a clinical psychologist, not a shrink. For another, when it comes to the captain's comments, I want thirty seconds for rebuttal."

Bowman gave a hollow laugh. "No worries, Doctor. I did my own due diligence on you. Not to mention Gloria's glowing reviews of your participation in some recent cases."

Gloria shrugged. "That said, I wouldn't count on Assistant Director Clemmons joining the Danny Rinaldi Fan Club. He flew in from Quantico in the middle of the night and immediately huddled with Captain Biegler. Seems like it was love at first sight."

"So this Clemmons is a tight-ass, too?" I said.

"Rumor has it," Gloria said. "Though I've never had the pleasure." Then, in mid-sip, she threw Bowman a guarded look. "With all due respect, of course. Tony Clemmons' impressive record at the Bureau speaks for itself."

"That's okay, Gloria." He gave her a quick, somewhat intimate wink. "You're not exactly alone in your feelings about Clemmons. I tend to steer clear of him as much as I can, myself."

"That won't be so easy today, Hank." She turned back to me. "We have an urgent meeting this morning at nine. Clemmons, Biegler, Chief Logan. And as many precinct captains and field agents as they can squeeze into a conference room. To get everyone up to speed on the case, especially—"

Bowman interrupted her. "Especially in light of some recent developments."

The sudden, abrupt tone of his voice didn't escape my notice. Nor did the significant look shared by the two agents.

"Sorry, Doctor." Bowman's voice quickly shifted gears. "Didn't mean to sound so dramatic. It's just that some new data's come in. Manna from heaven to the Behavioral Science techs Clemmons brought along with him. They're attending the meeting, too. To provide a psych profile of our guy."

I recalled my conversation with District Attorney Sinclair.

"I suggest your people not lay it on too thick with the cops," I said. "Theories are one thing, evidence is another."

"Better watch out, Danny," said Gloria. "You're starting to sound like a cop yourself."

"Don't let Biegler hear you say that."

Hank Bowman downed his coffee in one long swallow, then glanced at his watch, and got to his feet.

"Look, Gloria, I have a few calls to make before the meeting. See you up at the conference room, okay?"

"No problem, Hank." She put down her half-finished cup. "And thanks for the caffeine hit. It was delicious."

Gloria and I rose together, and I reached out my hand across his desk. Though Bowman smiled, responding to my outstretched hand with another viselike handshake, the steely glint had returned to his eyes. As if he'd only been cordial for Gloria's sake. As if, like Biegler and some of the other police brass, he was uneasy with my connection to the department.

Or at least any case that *he* was a part of.

---

Closing his door behind her, Gloria led me in the opposite direction to one of another series of offices. It was a small, windowless room containing just a steel desk and two hard-backed chairs on either side of it.

I looked around, confused.

"This isn't your office," I said.

"That's because I loaned mine to Assistant Director Clemmons. He needed someplace to work for the length of the investigation."

"And you don't mind?"

"Actually, I like being in here. Out of the line of fire, so to speak. Away from the Bureau's usual macho bullshit. Where I can hear myself think."

Sitting across from her, I watched as she opened her briefcase and took out her laptop and set it up in front of her.

As she did so, I leaned back in my seat.

"So," I said, "what about this Bowman guy?"

"Hank can be a tool, but he's okay. In small doses. He has a crush on me, so I figure I'll exploit the hell out of that."

"No kidding? Thanks for sharing."

"Cool it, all right? Jesus, men are idiots."

Looking up from her computer screen, her teasing smile softened, as did her voice.

"I missed seeing you last night."

"Same here. Any whipped cream left?"

"Sorry, big boy. I fed it to the cat."

"Then we'll just have to improvise the next time."

"If there *is* a next time." Her tone darkened. "This sniper thing… It could really turn into a nightmare. I mean, hell, Danny, we have nothing. Nothing."

"You're still thinking it's just one guy? A lone killer?"

"It's not about what *I* think. That's the preliminary judgment from Behavioral." She indicated the screen in front of her. "We all got an email from them in the middle of the night. Same profile as always. Single white male, early to midtwenties, disaffected. Probably a low-income job. Previous trouble with authority. The usual."

"Meaning…?"

"That's the same profile they came up with for the DC Sniper, remember? Except the single white male turned out to be two black guys, one older than the other. Working in tandem."

"But that was an anomaly, right?"

"I guess so. But these kinds of things always spook me. Unknown perp shooting people at random. I mean, c'mon. Give me something real, concrete. Something I can sink my teeth in."

A long pause. "It's just… Damn it, I hate chasing ghosts."

"I know what you mean. Sometimes I feel that way working with my patients. That what we're trying to reveal—and then lay to rest—are the ghosts of the past. And, believe me, they can be as elusive as they are destructive."

I watched her sharp eyes scan the laptop screen. "Meanwhile," I said, "anything you guys *do* know? Anything new?"

"That was in another email," she said. "Copied from what Pittsburgh PD has so far. All four bullets recovered from the victims are the same, a .338 Lapua Mag. No rifle found at any of the scenes except the first."

"What Sheriff Gibson said was called a ghost gun. Made up of separate parts of rifles."

"Yeah, but no forensics found on any of them. But that still leaves whatever weapon the sniper used for his next three targets. We have agents and however many uniforms the cops can spare canvassing all the area gun shops and weapons shows for recent purchases of high-velocity rifles. Without a make and model, though, this is laborious as hell and probably a waste of time. And manpower."

"What about the guy's targets? Last I heard, the cops believe there was no connection among the victims."

"Doesn't appear to be. Early statements from family, friends, and coworkers seem to indicate no cross-linking among all four.

"The only notable victim, in terms of public renown, is Dr. Mapes. One of those millionaire doctors you don't hear about anymore, though a background check revealed most of his wealth was inherited. But he was no player. Devoted husband, father, etcetera. And a real pillar of the community, on the boards of a dozen professional and charity organizations. High-value contributor to political and social causes. Everyone who knew him has praised this paragon of virtue to the skies."

"You mentioned financial contributions. There might be a connection there."

"Yeah, we flagged that, too. His widow gave us the names of a few charities she knew he supported. Usual stuff. Heart and cancer associations. Wildlife groups. Which made us hope that maybe Mapes shared his civic concerns with the other victims. But none of the charities to which he contributed also received funds from Lucas Hartley, Harriet Parr, or Peter Steinman. Of course, some charity organizations can be pretty stingy about releasing the names of their contributors."

"Plus, many donors prefer to remain anonymous."

"Still, as soon as we get permission to check all the victims' tax records, we may find some correlation. But the fact is, aside from maybe Steinman the law partner, neither a kid like Hartley nor Mrs. Parr run in the same circles as Mapes. Or have his kind of discretionary income. His tribe tends toward private jets and yacht clubs."

"Ah, yes. Exactly like my tribe."

She smiled again, shaking her head at my lame joke.

"I *am* curious about something else," I said carefully. "In Bowman's office, he said something about new developments..."

Gloria looked up, smile leaving her face.

I leaned in across the table. "It's important, isn't it? What he was talking about."

"Yes." A slow, pensive nod. "But, honestly, Danny, it's classified. At least for the moment."

"Hey, I get it. If you can't tell me, you can't..."

"It's just... I'm torn. I trust you, of course, but—" A hesitant breath. "And you would keep this strictly confidential? As if I were a patient revealing a secret?"

"Of course. But if it makes you uncomfortable..."

"No, I want to tell you. I mean, I know you're not officially involved, but..."

She lowered her chin, so that I couldn't see her eyes. "I...I really care about you, Danny. And when I share things with you...even related to a case...I feel closer. Like we're more than just...just two people who get together sometimes to...keep from being lonely."

She suddenly sat up straighter, rubbed her eyes.

"Christ, I sound like some high school twat at a slumber party. I'm a Bureau agent who can't wait to tell her boyfriend some classified intel. I mean, how fucked up is that?"

"I don't know, sounds pretty human to me. And I meant what I said, you don't have to tell me if—"

Suddenly, she blurted it out.

"We heard from him, Danny. The sniper. Late last night. He left a message."

"You...heard from him?"

"It came into Chief Logan's office. On his departmental computer. Though from God knows where. The chief shared the message with us, but our techs couldn't trace its source."

"What was the message? What did it say?"

She let out a breath, as though acknowledging that since she'd told me this much, there wasn't any sense in withholding anything now.

"Here. See for yourself."

She clicked a button on her keyboard and turned the laptop around, facing me.

On the screen, against a black background, was the eerie image of a dead-white, grinning skull. Above, in glowing, neon-bright letters, were the words:

HAPPY HALLOWEEN, BOYS AND GIRLS!

Then, in a raspy, metallic voice, came a single sentence:

*"This is only the beginning."*

After which, the suddenly animated skull began to laugh…

# Chapter Fourteen

The cackling, maniacal laugh was deliberately cartoonish. Exaggerated, over the top. Yet it still managed to unnerve me, so I hit the mute button.

Then, as another thought occurred to me, I felt the blood leave my face.

As though reading my mind, Gloria reached across and covered my hand with hers.

"It's nothing like what Sebastian Maddox did. Or would do. He was a tech genius, but it doesn't take one to do something like this. My teenage nephew could do it."

"Then that means anyone could've sent it. Some hacker looking for laughs. Maybe it isn't from the sniper at all..."

She shook her head and tapped the mute button again. The macabre metallic laugh still boomed from the laptop speaker.

"Keep watching till the end," she said quietly.

I did. In a few seconds, I saw something hurtle across from the right side of the screen. On a path to the grinning skull. Another oversized, cartoonish image. A bullet.

It hit the top of the skull's head, exploding it into pieces that cascaded out like a pinwheel. But the bullet froze where it had made impact, its markings ludicrously large and easily visible.

"A .338 Lapua Mag," I said.

"Yes." A sober nod. "The bullet that killed all our vics. Information that hasn't been released to the public."

"He's letting you know that the message is really from him. He *wants* you to know it's from him."

Gloria watched impassively while I kept my gaze riveted on the screen. As its final motionless image faded to black.

"That's it." Gloria took a long breath. "Our guy's playing games with us. For reasons of his own."

"I have some guesses, but that's all they are. Maybe the deliberately amateurish quality of the animation is his idea of a joke. Postmodern irony or something. On the other hand, maybe he saw something like it in a movie about serial killers. The ones who send messages to the cops or the press. And thought it would make him seem cool."

"In the end," she said, "all that matters is the message. 'This is just the beginning.' Christ."

She glanced at her watch, closed her laptop, and put it back in her briefcase. Then she got to her feet and straightened her jacket. "Almost nine. I have to move it, Danny."

Though we were in a windowless room with the door closed, we still hugged goodbye in an almost formal way. As though the bare, functional room—and the urgency of the case it represented—forbade a more personal, intimate embrace.

We'd each gone our separate ways when, as I headed back to where I'd parked, I decided to check my voicemail before driving across town to my office.

There were two messages. The first was from Indra Bishara, saying she had some business in the city today and asked if I could meet her for lunch.

The second was from Jason Graham, asking if I had any free patient hours in my schedule. He wanted to go into therapy with me.

---

As before, my morning patients paired whatever their usual personal issues were with concerns about the Steel City Sniper.

One woman, a widowed retired accountant who'd been mugged in East Liberty, had panicked as she drove to my office. Her route had taken her past Schenley Park, and she'd seen, hovering just above the trees, an ominous-looking drone.

"Do you think that's what the sniper uses, Dr. Rinaldi?" Her hands were welded together on her lap. "Maybe he shoots people from a drone. You know, like the military does now."

"I doubt it, Beverly. There are a lot of drones being flown nowadays, mostly for recreational use. Besides, from what little I've gleaned from watching the news, it seems like the police believe he targets his victims from a nearby roof."

She sniffed. "Oh, I don't trust what the cops say. Besides, you work for them. I bet you know more than what's on the news."

"I wish I did. Believe me, I don't."

Beverly gave me a dubious look. "Well, I suppose if you did, you couldn't tell me. You remind me of my late husband. I always suspected he knew a lot more about things than he ever let on. It was his way of controlling me."

I sat forward in my leather chair. "Is that what you think I'm doing with you? Trying to control you?"

She shrugged. "If so, it isn't working."

I smiled. "Glad to hear it. Neither of us would ever get anywhere if I tried to do so."

Beverly let me know by her wary expression that she was

unconvinced. Nevertheless, from my perspective our exchange had had significant importance. For the first time, she'd displayed a willingness to challenge me. To the extent she *did* see me as controlling, she certainly wasn't having any. Which was a crucial positive step away from her usual self-concept as a weak, vulnerable victim, a belief that had only been reinforced by the trauma of being mugged.

After she left, I made a point of calling Jason Graham back. I got his voicemail and left a few open therapy times when we might meet, as well as my office address on Forbes Avenue in Oakland. In case he hadn't Googled it already.

Beverly's had been the last session before my lunch break, so I pulled on my winter coat and headed for the parking garage. I'd returned Dr. Bishara's call earlier, and we'd agreed to meet at a small restaurant she liked in the newly gentrified South Side.

I found the place and, more surprisingly, also found a nearby parking spot. The restaurant itself was more like a café—small, intimate, and underlit. Most of the tables were occupied by college students, business execs, and a cluster of tourists. As expected, some generic world music played from the speakers, but thankfully the volume was low.

Dr. Bishara waved at me from a corner table, and I made my way over to her. She half-rose from her seat to take my hand. The Teasdale College administrator was without her glasses and dressed more informally than when we'd first met, wearing snug jeans and a silk blouse. The top three buttons were undone.

"Thanks so much for agreeing to meet." Her hand held its grip on mine a bit longer than seemed necessary.

"My pleasure, Dr. Bishara."

"Indra, please. No formalities, remember?"

I nodded and sat opposite her. She'd already started on a coffee, so I asked a passing waitress if I could have one, too.

It appeared within moments, after which Indra looked pointedly at me with the same intense gaze she'd leveled on me that day in Lockhart.

"I'm not hungry," she said matter-of-factly. "Are you?"

"Not particularly."

"Good. Then I'll get straight to the point."

I sipped my hot coffee and watched her root through the oversized bag on her lap till she found her cell. She clicked a couple buttons, then turned the screen toward me.

"This is my daughter. My Rebecca."

I leaned up and peered at the photo. It was a candid shot, taken at what looked like a dinner table, of a slender, flaxen-haired girl of perhaps fourteen or fifteen. She'd apparently been caught unawares by the camera, her stricken look a combination of embarrassment and irritation.

I could guess why. Running much of the length of her left cheek was a dark, rippling scar. Obviously, the result of that hot lamp bulb exploding on the side of her face. The lasting reminder of the terrible fight between her estranged mother and father. Indra and William Reynolds III. Billy Three.

Indra abruptly clicked off the image and returned the cell to her purse, her eyes meeting mine again.

"She's a pretty girl." I felt foolish the moment I heard the words come out of my mouth. But I could tell that Indra had neither misunderstood nor was she offended by the remark.

"Yes, she is. I certainly think so, and so do others."

"But she doesn't…?"

Indra shook her head. "It breaks my heart, but she's convinced she's ugly. That no one would ever find her attractive. She's even referred to herself as a freak show."

"I'm so sorry. I can imagine, as a teenage girl…"

"I can't tell you how hard it's been for her. Bullied and

belittled at school, shamed about her looks online. Thank God for her therapist. Dr. Neila Owens. I truly believe Becky might have taken her own life by now if it weren't for her. But Dr. Owens has retired and now Becky has no one..."

Suddenly, her eyes welled with tears.

"I...I need your help, Dr. Rinaldi. Daniel."

I took a guess.

"Do you need a referral to a new therapist for Becky? Or yourself? I'm sure Becky's struggles are equally hard on you."

Another slight shake of her head, strands of her dark hair falling on her forehead. "No. I need *your* help, Daniel. From everything I've read about you...and then when we met at the stadium... Call it intuition, call it wish fulfillment, but you were exactly as I'd hoped you'd be. Needed you to be."

"I appreciate the kind words, but I don't understand..."

"Becky needs a new therapist. Someone strong and capable. To help her see the mistake she's making."

"What are we talking about?"

"Billy. My ex." Now the tears flowed, and her voice quavered, began to quicken. "He...he wants sole custody of Becky. He wants to take her away from me."

"But he can't... Look, I don't know what your current custody arrangement is, but I'm sure if you and Becky stand before a judge and fight back—"

"That's just it!" She pushed the palms of her hands against her reddened eyes. "Becky...she doesn't want to fight it. She... wants to leave me. She wants to go with *him*!"

I admit, this stunned me. "She wants to be with the man who tried to hurt her mother? And then disfigured *her*? Why?"

She didn't answer. Instead, she said, "I assume you know that after what happened to Becky, after the accident, Billy disappeared. He never wrote, never got in contact with us."

"Yes. I understand even his parents didn't know where he'd gone. And then they moved out of their house. Went to Europe."

She nodded. "Once Becky was out of the hospital, and Billy's whereabouts were never established, I received sole legal and physical custody."

"Naturally."

"And now, all these years later... Suddenly, a few weeks ago, I hear from some fancy Pittsburgh law firm that they're representing Billy. That he's demanding a new custody hearing. That he wants full custody of Becky."

"But you haven't heard from Billy himself?"

"No, just the lawyers. As you can imagine, I freaked out. So I called them, and all I could get out of them was that Billy was back in the area. Somewhere in Pittsburgh."

"But I still don't understand. Why would Becky want to go live with her father?"

Indra gave me a plaintive look.

"It's not right, is it? She's only fourteen. Isn't she better off with me?"

It was obvious that she wanted me to agree, so I did. But I also had more questions.

"I assume you've retained an attorney yourself?"

"Yes. But he says that if Becky has no objection to going with her father, it will be hard to make a case otherwise."

"That's true. The primary concern in any court decision regarding custody is what's in the best interests of the child. And though Becky's a minor, most judges accede to the wishes of a child of fourteen. They're considered mature enough to decide for themselves with whom they want to live."

Indra's head dropped to her chest.

I spoke as gently as I could. "I'd be happy to see Becky, if she agrees. But it's obvious you need support, too. Even if it's just friends. People in your life who'd rally around you. There's Martin Hobbs, for example."

This actually drew a thin smile from her. "Marty's a sweet man. And I know he has feelings for me. But—forgive me for saying this—he's weak. Too easily cowed. I've seen it firsthand, working with him on college business."

"Then there must be others..."

"A few colleagues with whom I'm hardly close. And no one else in town. Ever since my family first moved to Lockhart, we've been treated with suspicion, if not outright hostility."

"Yes, so Martin told me, which had me wondering. Given how you and your family were treated, why did you come back to Lockhart after graduate school? Especially after what had happened here. The bitter divorce. Billy's assault on you. Becky's injury. You could've gone anywhere."

"That's true, but I guess it was just my pride. After doing well at Princeton, to return here for a big job at Teasdale, showed everyone they couldn't shame me anymore. That I'd come back to Lockhart with my head held high. Still, I suppose you wonder why I ever married Billy in the first place. I mean, it wasn't like I didn't know what he could be like. His moods, his temper."

"Then why marry?"

"The truth is, both Billy and I wanted to shove the town's nose in it. The rich, handsome grandson of the great William Reynolds marrying the dark-skinned foreigner. This way, he could give the finger to his parents—whom he hated, by the way—and I could do the same to all the white girls who'd made my life miserable growing up."

I said nothing.

She offered me a rueful smile. "Not the most noble of intentions, I know. But Billy and I *did* love each other. That part was true. Real. Until I had Becky, and Billy became…" A long sigh. "He changed. I mean, like I said, he'd always had a temper. He'd yell, throw things. But with every passing month he became more belligerent, more violent toward me. Then there was the drinking, the affairs…"

Indra grew quiet, dabbing at her eyes again. "But you know daughters and their daddies. I remember how much I loved my own father, and he was far from perfect. So I understand Becky's dismay when Billy and I broke up. Maybe I should've handled it better."

I let the silence stretch out between us, our two coffees growing cold in their mugs.

Finally, I said, "I can see what a blow this is, hearing from Billy after all this time. And it's obvious he has the financial resources to enlist big legal guns against you. But I still don't understand Becky's sudden desire to see him. To live with him…"

"It's because…"

She hesitated, eyes downcast. Unable or unwilling to make contact with my own.

"The thing is…everything's changed. After all these years, Becky's memory's coming back… She's remembering."

"What? You mean about that night she was injured?"

She nodded. "She was just a child when it happened. Dr. Owens told me Becky had been traumatized. Could barely recall the incident. All she had were vague fragments of memory… But now…in these past few months…"

Suddenly, her hands covered her face. And her voice fell to a choked whisper.

"Becky remembers now…she *knows*…"

"Knows what?"

"That it wasn't Billy who…who scarred her for life that night. *It was me.*"

# Chapter Fifteen

It was a full two minutes before she could let herself look up again. Her smooth cheeks were streaked with tears.

When she finally spoke, it was in a soft voice threaded with self-recrimination, audible only to me. In the public space of the café, it was as though she were in the confessional.

"I've replayed that horrible night a thousand times in my head since it happened. Almost to the point that I believed the story myself. The one that Marty Hobbs and everyone else believes. And that Becky thought was true, too. All her years growing up."

I kept my own voice quiet, measured. "You can tell me about it, Indra. Or not. It's up to you."

"I...I want to tell you. Need to tell you. Tell somebody."

Another long pause. Then, her voice still low:

"That night, when Billy broke into the house...he *did* attack me, tried to strangle me. Right in front of little Becky, who was screaming her lungs out. Billy and I struggled... It was terrible. Physically and emotionally. Him shouting curses at me, claiming I was ruining his life. How dare I leave him? He was a Reynolds, and I was embarrassing him. Plus, I was turning our daughter against him. He was drunk and totally out of control. I thought… I really thought he was going to kill me."

Indra took a breath.

"All of a sudden, he pushed me back, and I stumbled to the floor. Then he grabbed Becky by the arm and began dragging her, kicking and screaming, toward the door. Yelling back at me. 'You can't have her, you bitch! Becky's mine!'

"I just lost it. I grabbed a small table lamp that had been knocked to the floor and threw it at the back of his head, hoping to knock him out. Or smash his head in, I don't know. I didn't care. I couldn't let him take Becky. I—"

Indra's eyes closed, as though to shut out the memory.

"That's when it happened. I'd just thrown the lamp when Becky, still struggling in his grasp, looked back at me. Crying, terrified. 'Mommy! Help! Mommy!'

"That was the moment my heart stopped, and I don't know if it's ever started again. I'd underthrown the lamp. It didn't reach Billy's head. The hot bulb shattered against my poor baby's face." Whispered voice now thick with grief. "I swear, I'll never forget her scream. Never…

"Billy let go of Becky's arm and just stared at her. Horrified. Panicked. Maybe aware, even in his drunken state, of his own culpability. Or maybe just how it would look to the police. Breaking into the house, assaulting me. Our only child being injured in the conflict. Because suddenly, after a quick, wild-eyed glance at me, he ran out of the house…"

I reached across the table and covered her hands with mine.

"Indra…I'm so sorry. I can't even imagine…"

"No, you can't." She sniffed. "In my Becky's mind, from that moment until recently, she thought it was her father who'd injured her during his fight with me. And I…to my shame, I let her think that. It was the story I told the police. The doctors at the hospital. Everyone. Including Dr. Owens. And since Becky had no clear memory of what actually happened, she had no reason to believe otherwise."

Indra looked down at my hands still covering hers.

"I've lived with the shame of that deception my whole life. I even convinced myself it was better for Becky. After all, her father was gone. Out of her life. Why not let her blame him?"

"But that's just it, Indra. Billy *does* have an equal share of the responsibility. His actions certainly contributed to—"

"Nice try, Danny. But I swear I'm not looking for you—or anyone—to let me off the hook. I just felt that if you were going to treat Becky, you had a right to know the truth. Otherwise her desire to be with Billy wouldn't make any sense."

"But even if she agrees to see me, it's not my place to try to dissuade her from choosing to stay with her father. She has a right to make that decision for herself. Especially if her memory of that night is returning..."

"I know. It's unfair of me to ask anything of you that you can't ethically do. I guess I just wanted you to know what happened. From my side. But I really want you to help her, Danny. Because even though she says she hates me, and wants to go live with Billy, I know she feels guilty about hurting me. After all these years, I've been the only parent she's known."

"And, in her experience, the only parent who's loved her. Taken care of her. No wonder this is such a confusing time for her. And yet now she probably also feels bad for hating him all these years. For seeing him as a terrible man, a father who injured and then deserted her."

Indra slipped her hands from mine. Offered me a wan smile.

"Aren't you glad I called, Doctor? Instead of getting a nice, normal referral to a new patient, you also get the 'poor me' act from the patient's mother."

"I don't see it that way at all, Indra. It took courage to tell me what happened."

"Doesn't feel like courage. It feels like I'm trying to gain your sympathy. I…I even dressed in a way that I thought would hold your attention. How's *that* for lame?"

"Not lame. Maybe desperate. Worried for your daughter."

"Anyway, Danny, the only thing that matters to me is Becky. She's in turmoil and needs help. Your help. Even if it means she ends up deciding to live with her father… All I want is for her to be happy. To feel okay about herself, whatever she decides. Can you help her do that?"

It was then that a thought struck me.

"When you first contacted Billy's law firm, did you tell them you were planning to get Becky back into treatment?"

"Yes. With you, the noted trauma expert." Her lips tightened. "I figured they'd know who you were. And they did."

*And,* I thought, *were sure to tell their client.*

I knew Billy Reynolds wouldn't be thrilled to learn this. Like many parents in the middle of a custody dispute, he probably feared that Indra would use my work with Becky to try to influence his daughter's decision. Turn her against him.

Given his reputation for violence, he might even have decided to take steps to circumvent this. Warn me off.

Like taking potshots at me in a dark alley…

—

I was still turning this over in my mind when I heard an audible gasp from a nearby table. Indra and I turned at the same time. A man and woman were peering intently at the cell phone he held between them.

The news alert on my own cell pinged. At a questioning glance from Indra, I checked my phone.

Under the banner of a well-known crime-oriented blog, the video from the sniper that Gloria had shown me filled the small screen. The macabre grinning skull. Then the raspy, mocking voice, with its dire warning of more killings. Sounding tinny and mechanical from the cell's speaker.

More gasps and frantic, hushed conversations filled the restaurant. The cartoonish image of the exploding skull replicated on a dozen cell phones. The mad, staccato laugh reaching a crescendo as it echoed and re-echoed.

The panic in the room was palpable. The waitstaff froze where they stood. Silverware clattered from customers' fingers.

One young woman, hands to her face, began to sob.

Somehow, someway, the sniper's incendiary message to the authorities had been leaked.

# Chapter Sixteen

The city was on fire, the sniper's ominous video message having lit the match.

When I got back to my office, two of my early-afternoon patients had left messages, canceling their sessions that day. Having seen the video replayed numerous times on various news outlets, they were afraid to leave their homes.

I returned their calls and managed to convince them to keep their appointments via Zoom. I only insisted because each patient happened to be in the midst of a significant personal crisis. Despite their fears about the sniper, this was not the time for either of them to forgo psychological support.

Still, another last-minute cancellation meant my workday was over by three, so I called Indra Bishara's cell. After the disruption caused by the sniper's video, we hadn't been able to finish our conversation at the restaurant. Not as far as I was concerned, anyway. Getting her voicemail, I offered to speak further with her, if only by phone.

I also reaffirmed my willingness to treat her daughter, if Becky would consent to seeing me. After all, my suspicions about Billy having shot at me were just that—suspicions. I had no way of knowing for sure.

Before closing up the office, I checked my cell for the latest news. The mayor's office had released a statement sternly condemning the posting of the sniper's video. This was followed by a similar comment from Chief Logan decrying the distribution of such an inciting, frightening message from an obviously deranged individual. He went on to remind citizens that the video's authenticity had not been determined. That there was no way to confirm that it had actually been sent by the sniper.

I knew he was lying but understood the rationale for it. No use creating more anxiety than necessary.

Finally, in an effort to demonstrate some level of transparency about the ongoing investigation, the mayor, Chief Logan, and Assistant Director Clemmons of the FBI had scheduled a press conference for four o'clock this afternoon. It was to take place in the City Council chambers, with all members present. It would also be broadcast on TV and radio, as well as livestreamed, and the public was invited to attend.

So, as it turned out, was I.

I'd no sooner locked the outer door to my office than my cell rang. It was Sharon Cale, Sinclair's executive assistant.

"The district attorney wanted to make sure you'd be attending the press conference, Doctor. If you're available."

"Well, my day *has* ended earlier than usual. Still…"

As before, her voice was equal parts silky smooth and assuredly determined.

"That's great. I know Leland would really value your opinion afterward as to how it went."

Again, feeling I had little choice in the matter, I agreed.

—

By the time I made it from Oakland to downtown and the City Council building, the press conference was well underway. The spacious chamber was packed with journalists from all media, cameras and microphones aimed at the curved dais at which sat Chief Logan and about a dozen City Council members. Standing in front of them at a podium was a tall, well-built man with deep-set gray eyes behind horn-rimmed glasses. His balding pate gleamed under the room's powerful fluorescent lights.

Beyond the twin rows of media types he faced were at least forty or fifty clearly unhappy citizens, raising their hands—and sometimes their voices—in an effort to get the speaker's attention. Studiously ignoring them, he instead focused on answering questions from the reporters, which he did in the clipped, authoritative manner of a senior government official.

This, I realized, had to be Assistant FBI Director Tony Clemmons, sent up from Quantico. I'd seen his kind before.

I'd shouldered my way through the throng of people to take a spot at the back of the room. And found myself standing next to District Attorney Sinclair, his arms folded, his frosty eyes aimed at the front of the room.

He looked bored. I said so.

"I am, Doctor. Over the years, whenever there's a crisis along these lines, the press asks the authorities the same questions. What do they know so far? Any clues as to the identity of the sniper? What are the police and FBI doing to protect the public from further deaths?"

"Seems to me those are reasonable questions."

"Reasonable, perhaps. Answerable? Rarely."

I craned my neck to see past the noisy, unruly mass of people still waving their hands or shouting out questions.

"I don't see the mayor."

"His Honor has already spoken and departed, referring all questions about the sniper case to Chief Logan and Clemmons."

"Have you met him yet?"

"Clemmons? Yes, unfortunately. I don't know where the Bureau gets people like him. Real bureaucratic tight-ass."

"No wonder he and Stu Biegler hit it off."

Sinclair ignored that, gesturing with his chin at the dais. I had to admit, Clemmons was predictably expert in answering the press's questions in a vague, indirect way. He'd even perfected that look of pained exasperation when asked to disclose information that everybody—including the press members themselves—knew he'd be unwilling to share. Not when it could risk hampering the success of the investigation.

Chief Logan took to the podium next, fielding questions from the only folks who really mattered—the fickle, demanding public. As usual, when forced to speak before a group of people, the chief looked miserable.

"How safe are our streets?" A man in the crowd yelled out.

"Yeah, Chief," shouted another. "Can you guarantee our children's safety?"

Another: "Do we need to hire more cops?"

And another: "My mother's a widow, and she's afraid to leave her house. What am I supposed to tell her?"

As a therapist, I was struck not only by the sense of outrage and frustration in these raised voices, but the urgent, naked fear underlying them. More than simple panic, it was as though those assembled had regressed to a childlike state, needing the assurance of a parental entity to keep the terror at bay, to make the nightmare stop. Our leaders as Mommy and Daddy.

As the tension in the room escalated, many angry voices blending to create an undecipherable babble, Chief Logan grew visibly frustrated himself. At one point, he raised his hands, palms out, in a failed effort to bring the decibel level down.

Still at my side, Leland Sinclair gave a dry chuckle.

"I'm afraid, Doctor, things are about to go sideways."

I nodded, watching a number of City Council members shift uncomfortably in their seats or whisper in each other's ears, obviously in agreement with Sinclair.

Then I noticed something else. One of the council chairs was empty.

"Looks like one of our dedicated city fathers decided to skip the party," I said to Sinclair.

He shook his head. "No, that's Gary Landrew, Fifth District. He called my cell just before you got here and said he's running late. One of his constituents had him on the phone, and Gary couldn't get rid of the guy."

Meanwhile, Chief Logan was trying to quell the crowd's anger with the usual police party line.

"Please, all of you... It's important to remember that the best thing you can do for yourself and your family is to take reasonable precautions. Try not to go out at night unless absolutely necessary. Keep your eyes and ears open. Alert the police if you see anything—anything at all—that seems out of the ordinary. Strangers in your neighborhood, whatever. Frankly, folks, I'm just asking you to use common sense."

All this did was elicit a new round of angry shouts.

"Fuck common sense!" A heavyset man in the crowd cried out. "I'm gettin' me a goddamn gun!"

"Me, too!" yelled another, to a chorus of approving voices.

Sinclair sighed. "Second Amendment scholars, apparently."

"They're just scared, Lee. And with damn good reason."

He offered me a WASP's version of a scowl. "I'm afraid my empathy tank is on empty, Daniel. At least for tonight."

Then he began to sidle past some of the people near us, making his way for the rear exit.

Suddenly, a councilwoman rose from her seat and pointed toward the broad window at the left of the chamber. Whether from nerves or an inability to stop herself, she started laughing.

"Hey, look! It's Gary Landrew!"

"Late as usual," said another member, laughing, too, as he rose from his seat.

"Yeah." It was a third member. "Why should *he* get outta being on the hot seat?"

I swiveled where I stood and peered out the large window. Outside, the sunlit day had morphed into a chilly, pink-hued dusk, and the corner streetlamps had come on.

About fifty yards away on the street, weaving between and around parked cars, was a blond-haired man in an opened topcoat that flared like wings behind him. Gripping a briefcase, his face flushed, he was running wildly toward the building.

Something about his hapless attempt to get to the meeting brought an abrupt halt to the cacophony of angry voices. Joined by the amused journalists at the front of the room, most of the crowd turned to stare out the window at Landrew.

At the same time, the councilwoman—obviously relieved at the diversion—began a humorous chant.

"Run, Gary, run!"

The chant was repeated by a number of her fellow council members, standing and clapping in time.

*"Run, Gary, run!"*

By now, even people in the crowd had picked up the chant, laughing and clapping. Some moved to the window to get a better look, waving at the beleaguered councilman. Urging him on.

*"Run, Gary, run!"*

I could only marvel at this stunning example of crowd

dynamics. How a collective rage could so quickly reverse itself and turn silly, boisterous. As though the people assembled were themselves relieved to be delivered from their own anger.

Councilman Landrew was less than ten yards away, brow sheened with sweat even in the cold. At this distance, I could see that he was somewhere in his fifties, quite stout, and with a bushy mustache the same yellow color as his hair.

He was smiling now, aware of the row of faces pressed against the window. People cheering on his progress. Waving.

So he waved back.

Suddenly, the top of his head exploded like a blood-filled balloon. With an obscene, sickening pop.

Then, briefcase flying, he fell forward onto the concrete.

And everybody started screaming.

# Chapter Seventeen

"Well," said Leland Sinclair, "in legal terms, we have ourselves a real clusterfuck. A city councilman, no less, shot down in the street in front of fifty registered voters."

It was two hours later, and the DA, his jacket off and tie undone, was leaning back in his desk chair, nursing his third whiskey.

"Christ, the media is going to have a field day with this. The optics couldn't be worse, in terms of highlighting our inability to protect even one of our own. And the mayor's impromptu speech from his office afterward didn't help. You could tell he was just reading from the usual 'thoughts and prayers' template into the camera."

Outside Sinclair's office window, the cold, hardened darkness of a November night was the backdrop for a dozen light-bejeweled buildings ringing the city center.

I stood against the near wall in the opulent suite, gazing at my reflection in the double-paned glass, my own drink in hand. Across the room was Assistant Director Clemmons, FBI, sitting forward on the small leather couch, his eyes narrowed to dark points behind his glasses. Next to him, arms folded, his face the color of drying cement, was Captain Stu Biegler.

A fourth member of what had amounted to a debriefing meeting, our beleaguered Police Chief Logan, had just departed, on his way to be reamed out by the mayor.

Moments after Councilman Landrew was killed, Sinclair had taken my elbow and asked me to accompany him. He'd sequestered us in an empty room in the building as the machinery of an official investigation went into overdrive. Detectives and CSI units were on the scene, fanning out on the street. The dead man's body lay under a tarp, awaiting the coroner's wagon. Uniformed officers escorted the terrified council members out to their cars, leading them carefully around the blackening pool of blood spreading from beneath the body.

Meanwhile, additional police kept the equally terrified crowd of attendees together in the council chambers, allowing no one to leave until the detectives outside deemed the streets secure. As they exited, each person was stopped briefly to give a statement as to what he or she saw—or thought they saw—when the murder occurred.

By the time Sinclair and I were escorted from the council building to his office, a number of TV camera vans had arrived, and two news choppers were hovering overhead.

During all this, Sinclair made a series of urgent calls on his cell to various city department heads, his own ADAs still at their desks, and the mayor. Finally, giving me a wry look, he asked Sharon Cale to arrange for a cold supper to be delivered to his office.

In answer to a questioning look of my own, Sinclair merely smiled. "We have to eat, right?"

"I get the need for food, Lee. It's the 'we' I don't understand."

"It's as I said before, Daniel. I need someone I can trust, whose instincts I respect. To bring a qualified civilian's perspective to the task that lies ahead."

"Bullshit. You just don't want to sit alone in a room full of cops and Feds as they take turns protecting their turfs."

Logan and Clemmons immediately did just that from the moment we all assembled in Sinclair's office. Not even the bountiful trays of cold cuts—courtesy of the ever-efficient Ms. Cale—and numerous drinks from the wet bar could quell the animosity between the two law enforcement men. It only came to a halt when the chief was summoned away to his grilling by the mayor.

Now, after draining his glass, the DA sat forward, his manicured hands flat on his desk blotter. His eyes bored into those of Captain Biegler.

"I'm still waiting for the latest incident report, Stu."

Biegler held up his cell. "I just got a text from Sergeant Polk. He's on his way up."

Moments later, there was a hesitant knock on the door. Then, red-faced, either from drink or exertion, wrinkled jacket opened across his ample belly, Harry Polk came in, carrying a thick file folder. After a quick nod at Sinclair, then another at Clemmons, he sat on a chair across from his boss.

"Here's everything we got, Captain." He flipped open the folder and spread it across his knees.

"Just give us the main points, Sergeant," Sinclair said.

"We won't have the full autopsy results till mornin', but the ME got the bullet out right away and ballistics confirm it's a .338 Lapua Mag. So it's our guy."

"Presumably." Clemmons adjusted his glasses.

"Yeah. Also, CSU did a sweep o' the surroundin' buildings and figger the sniper took position across the street. From the roof o' the Continental Insurance Company."

"From the estimated trajectory of the bullet, correct?"

"And from some scuff marks and loosened slate tiles near the southwest corner o' the roof. They're still processin' the area around there, but they're not expectin' to find much."

"Not surprising." Sinclair clasped his hands behind his head. "Our perp has been annoyingly careful up till now. I don't expect him to suddenly get sloppy."

He turned to me. "You're still thinking military?"

"I told you, I'm not sure about that."

Clemmons stirred. "Well, my people *are* sure. Ex-military. Young, white. Possibly dishonorably discharged. That video he posted has the classic signs of a disaffected vet, turning his perceived grievances into revenge on society."

"Don't forget the jokey tone of the thing," said Biegler. "He's fucking with us. Having a laugh at our expense."

"Maybe," I said. "Or else that's the impression he wants to give. That whole video seemed overly theatrical to me. Something you'd see in a horror movie. Or crime thriller."

Sinclair waved a hand.

"Speculation is not helpful at the moment." He turned to Polk. "What do the detectives think about how it went down?"

The sergeant rubbed his nose.

"Well, sir, they figger the perp positioned himself up on the roof, waitin' for some bigwig to either come in or outta the City Council buildin'. The press conference was all over the news, so the killer knew when and where it would take place. It was the perfect opportunity to take out somebody important."

Clemmons grimaced. "For the shock value. Escalating the level of panic. The killer showing the public that even government officials weren't safe."

"Then Gary Landrew comes running across the street, toward the City Council chambers." Sinclair shook his head. "Grinning. Waving to the people inside. Carrying his briefcase."

"It would have been irresistible," Clemmons said.

"Made to order." Biegler nodded importantly.

The district attorney sighed. "Anything else, Sergeant?"

"A quick background check confirms Landrew had no obvious connection to any o' the other vics. But our techs are gonna do a deeper dive into the councilman's personal and professional life. Social media, all that shit—er, stuff."

"They won't find much," Sinclair said. "I knew Landrew slightly. Married, two kids. Conservative. Churchgoer. Coached his older son's Little League team. He checked off all the boxes for a civil servant looking to climb the proverbial ladder."

"So he had higher aspirations?" Clemmons asked.

Sinclair didn't even try to hide his annoyance. "You mean, like every other politician?"

*Yourself included,* I thought.

Clemmons merely shrugged. As I'd expected, the FBI man was too skilled a politician himself to show he'd taken any offense.

When Polk looked expectantly at his three superiors in the room and saw no sign that more was needed, he closed the file. Then Biegler held out his hand and Polk gave it over.

"I'll have the relevant intel digitalized and sent to everyone on my team." The captain flipped casually through the folder. "CSU report. Crime scene photos. Ballistics. And any forensics. All of which can be amended as more details emerge."

He turned to Clemmons. "And, of course, everything we have will be copied to your people."

"And vice versa." The Bureau man glanced at Sinclair. "I spoke to the director earlier, and he feels that the best way to imply full interagency cooperation is to form a special Task Force. We'll send out a joint FBI and Pittsburgh PD press notice to that effect first thing in the morning."

The DA nodded. "The phrase 'Task Force' is always good PR."

Meanwhile, Harry Polk had levered himself up to his feet.

"Ya need anythin' else from me, Lieutenant?"

Biegler shook his head. "Not at present, Sergeant. Maybe you should go on home. You don't look well."

"Just tired, sir. Long day."

"For all of us."

After Polk shuffled out of the room, Sinclair stood abruptly and slipped his jacket from the back of his chair. Apparently, the meeting was over.

"Thank you, Captain," he said. "And you, Director Clemmons. I trust you'll both keep me updated on any new developments..."

"One question, Leland." Biegler jerked a thumb in my direction. "What's Dr. Rinaldi doing here? He's a civilian, after all. And, frankly, a lot of us in the department got pretty mixed feelings about him."

"Come on, Stu." I smiled at him. "Your feelings aren't mixed. You hate my fucking guts. And, by the way, back atcha."

Sinclair was chuckling as he put on his jacket, enjoying this way too much.

"Let's at least pretend to be grown-ups, okay, guys?" His tone grew serious as he regarded Biegler. "Dr. Rinaldi is here at my invitation. I find his clinical acumen and instincts to be quite valuable. He's on the team, so to speak, but with enough distance from the department's bullshit posturing to offer some perspective. Not that I have to explain myself to you."

Biegler reddened but said nothing. Standing next him, Tony Clemmons did his best impression of a disinterested observer.

Sinclair next regarded him. "Did you have any problem with Dr. Rinaldi's presence here?"

Clemmons shrugged. "I don't have a dog in this fight, Lee. Frankly, I think we have other priorities at the moment."

"As do I." The DA was stuffing his tie in a jacket pocket. "Now, if you two will excuse the doctor and myself..."

Clemmons reached to shake Sinclair's hand and then headed for the door. After giving the DA a stiff nod, Biegler turned and followed the FBI man out of the room.

"Well," Sinclair said to me, "that was fun-and-a-half."

I shrugged. "I just hope you're right about the idea of a joint police and FBI Task Force sending a comforting message. You've got some pretty scared people out there."

He nodded distractedly. "I'm hoping it buys us maybe another day of public support. Goodwill. Until there's another murder. Then it starts to get nasty, no matter how we spin it."

I knew what he meant. Internet trolls, out for political blood. Twitter threads trumpeting conspiracy theories. Extremist groups who fear they've fallen off the cultural radar taking credit for the sniper attacks. The infernal, unthinking, and uninformed white noise of social media, volume cranked up high. Opinions presented as fact. Hatred disguised as argument. With enough opportunism to go around for everyone with an ax to grind. Which, nowadays, appeared to be literally everyone.

Heading for the door, Sinclair paused suddenly and gave me an uncharacteristically intense look.

"Do you believe what he said on that video, Daniel? That this is only the beginning?"

"No idea. What I *do* know is that he wants you—and everyone else—to believe it."

—

Though it was long past midnight, I knew that Gloria Reese would be up, working along with her fellow Bureau agents.

Regardless, I hoped to grab a few minutes with her on the

phone. Driving out from the Point, heading toward the Fort Pitt Bridge and home, I hit speed dial on my cell.

I got her outgoing message, so I left one of my own.

"It's me. Just checking in. I know you guys are in it up to your eyeballs. But if you get a minute, give me a call. It'd be nice to hear your voice."

As usual, my words were warm, friendly, and noncommittal. Just as her messages to me struck the same careful note. Other than flirty banter, our verbal interactions always walked that tightrope separating passion from romantic entanglement.

Someday one of us was going to have to figure out what both of us were so afraid of…

Suddenly, moments after I'd clicked off, my cell rang. I glanced at the display. It wasn't Gloria.

I picked up. It was Martin Hobbs, from Teasdale College. Calling at this hour? His words were so slurred, he had to identify himself twice.

To my surprise, the dean was quite drunk.

"What is it, Martin? Are you all right?"

His voice was thin, raspy. A whisper freighted with fear.

"Daniel? Dr. Rinaldi? I have something to tell you. It's important…"

"What is it? I can barely hear you."

"Not on the phone. Too dangerous."

"I don't understand, Martin."

"I have to see you. In person." A hacking cough, threaded with booze. "You have to come now. To my house. Please!"

"All right, I will. I promise. Where are you?"

He gave me his home address in Lockhart, and I punched it into my GPS. With scant traffic at this time of night, I'd get there in about a half hour.

"Hurry, please, Danny! Please!"

Then he clicked off.

As I wheeled the Mustang around and headed for the Parkway East on-ramp, a crowd of conflicting thoughts fought for my mind's attention. Though I barely knew Martin Hobbs, I knew fear in a man's voice when I heard it. In fact, he sounded so drunk I wondered if he'd needed the alcohol to screw up his courage to make the call. Unless it was the reverse: that his middle-of-the-night inebriation had fueled an unwarranted paranoia.

Racing along a near-empty highway to Lockhart, city lights receding as I headed into a deepening rural darkness, I heard Leland Sinclair's words in my mind from earlier tonight.

"Speculation is not helpful at the moment."

As it turned out, he was right.

# Chapter Eighteen

Martin Hobbs lived in a modest ranch-style house on an equally modest street just south of the Lockhart city limits.

There were few streetlamps, and none within a hundred yards of his place. The fact that no lights shone from any window in the house, nor was any porch lamp lit, caused the hairs of my forearms to rise as I pulled up to the curb.

Just to be sure, I used my cell to call the dean back at the number he'd used. After a few rings I got Hobbs' outgoing message, delivered in the insistently cheerful voice I recalled from my time with him at Teasdale College—so different from the drunken, desperate tones of his last call to me.

I clicked off, then got out from behind the wheel. Using my cell's light to guide me, I made my way up to the shadow-draped porch and knocked on the front door. No answer.

I knocked again, louder this time. Again, nothing.

Trying the knob, I found that the door was unlocked. Without taking the time to think about it, I pushed it open.

"Martin, it's me. Dan Rinaldi. Martin?"

No reply. Still standing in the opened doorway, I called out again, raising my voice slightly but keeping it as measured as possible.

Again, there was no response.

"I'm coming in, okay, Martin?"

Stepping carefully into the house, I had the sense of the night's icy darkness behind me flowing into a similar darkness within. The entrance hall was a blackened tunnel whose angled contours were only heightened by the erratic way my cell's light poked along its length.

As I walked slowly into the belly of the house, the only thing more unnerving than the darkness was the still, heavy silence, broken only by my muffled footsteps on the hardwood floor.

"Martin! Are you in here?"

I'd called out again so as not to alarm him or give the impression of an unwanted intruder invading his house. And, frankly, I needed to penetrate that implacable silence, if only with the sound of my own voice.

Turning my cell's light in a waist-high swivel, I sent its beam briefly into a couple rooms, their doors open, that led off from the hall. First was a small dining room, then what appeared to be a kind of den. I peered inside. Wood-paneled walls. Book-lined shelves, big-screen TV. Floor lamps and table lamps, none of the bulbs lit.

Though my eyes had become more accustomed to the dark, I needed my cell's light to guide me to the back of the house. My tread was still careful, measured.

Until, to my surprise, I noticed another light up ahead. Indistinct, flickering.

Hurrying my steps, I ventured toward it. And found myself in the kitchen, my cell's glow revealing the smooth linoleum floor and the dull gleam of modest appliances.

But it was what stood on the kitchen counter that riveted me. The source of that flickering light. A thick votive candle, whose flame danced from its wick above the small base below.

At the same time, I was aware of an odd, unnerving sound.

Not loud, but strikingly unexpected. Penetrating the yawning silence of the house.

It was coming from an open, closet-sized space just off the kitchen. A slow, rhythmic creaking, like that of a rocking chair going back and forth.

My heart lurched. As though my senses, my every nerve ending, knew before I did.

I turned toward the sound.

The candle threw just enough light for me to see what I was supposed to see. A built-in pantry, barely wide enough to hold the body hanging in it. Attached by a thick rope to a hook screwed into the ceiling.

It was Dean Hobbs, his face contorted in a grotesque mixture of shock and agony, the loop of rope cruelly buried in the flesh of his slender neck.

I stared, stunned. Heartsick.

Martin Hobbs swayed gently, almost unobtrusively, in the stark, guttering light cast by the candle. As inoffensive in death as the man himself had appeared to be in life.

—

Within a half hour, the kitchen was flooded with a very different light. Cold, unyielding. Twin halogen lamps on tripods were aimed into the narrow pantry, where the remainder of rope still dangled from the ceiling. The noose had been cut by a young CSU tech who happened to live nearby and, having gotten the call, was the first on the scene. Together, he and I had gently lowered the body of Martin Hobbs to the floor.

"Don't move him anymore," I'd said, "until the sheriff and the ME get here."

The tech nodded, then went out to his van to get the lamps

and his forensics bag. Within minutes, powered by extension cords leading from the vehicle's on-board generator, the entire kitchen was ablaze with light.

Though neither the tech nor I had touched it, the candle had long since gone out. Its spent wick sent wispy curls of black smoke into the still air.

Sheriff Roy Gibson and the medical examiner, Dr. Max Sable, arrived almost simultaneously, both men looking like they'd just been roused from bed.

The ME gave me a curt nod, then bent to examine the body on the floor. Behind him, his sturdy frame backlit by the halogens, Gibson could only stare down at Hobbs, his face stricken. Weary eyes glassy, pained.

Then, abruptly, he turned to me.

"You found him, Doctor?"

"Yes. This young man here helped me cut him down."

He considered this, jaw tightening.

"You wanna tell me what you were doing here at three in the morning?"

I told him everything, from Hobbs' drunken call to my discovery of the body.

"And there were no lights on in the house?"

"None. The only light came from that candle. I get the feeling I was supposed to see it in the darkness, that its purpose was to guide me here. To find the body."

Gibson looked doubtful. Before he could reply, we were both startled by a series of lights coming on. The overhead in the kitchen, a lamp light streaming from somewhere down the hall. Turning, I could even see that a faint light was visible coming from within the den.

At the same time, a uniformed officer strolled down the hall and into the kitchen, shaking his head at Gibson.

"Hey, Roy, you won't believe it. Know why there weren't no lights in the place? I was checkin' around out back and found the fuse box. All the switches been flipped off."

Gibson and I exchanged puzzled looks. Though the officer's news explained why no bulb had been lit in the house, it explained little else.

By now, Max Sable had risen with some difficulty to his feet. His efforts reminded me of the limp I'd noticed when we first met. Presumably from an injury during the Afghan war.

"On preliminary examination, I'd say it's suicide, Roy." His black skin looked older than when I'd seen him before. It was mottled beneath the unsparing halogen glow.

Gibson shook his head, almost vehemently.

"I don't buy it, Max. I've known Marty Hobbs a helluva long time. So have you. Do ya think he'd do something like that?"

Sable shrugged. "Hard to ever say for sure what a man will do. I learned that a long time ago."

"And why call me before doing it?" I looked from one of them to the other. "Remember, he said he had something important to tell me. Something he was afraid to discuss on the phone. Why tell me that, if he planned to kill himself before I even got here?"

"I was thinking the same thing," said Gibson. "The whole thing sounds crazy. And I don't care how drunk Marty was, he's never done a crazy thing in his life. Not that I've ever heard about, anyways."

He moved across the kitchen to stare down at the candle.

"It doesn't make any sense. I mean, do either of you really believe that Martin Hobbs would take the trouble to kill the lights in the house at the fuse box, then stumble back into the kitchen with only a lit candle to see by? Then, placing the candle on the counter, he somehow rigs up a noose and hangs himself?

Christ, there's no way the guy I know could even dream up something like that, let alone pull it off."

Dr. Sable nodded. "I *have* been wondering how he managed to do it. The only way I can think of is to put the noose around his neck first, then get up on a ladder or sturdy box and attach the rope to the hook in the ceiling. Then jump off."

As if sharing the same thought, we all three glanced into the pantry. A small wooden stool lay on its side in a corner.

"Nice touch." Gibson rubbed his beard stubble. "Laying the stool on its side, like it'd been kicked over when Marty jumped off."

Sable frowned. "What do you mean *nice touch*?"

"I mean, Max, that Marty Hobbs didn't hang himself, though that's what someone wants us to believe. He was murdered."

# Chapter Nineteen

No one spoke as one of Dr. Sable's assistants from the coroner's office zipped Martin Hobbs into a body bag. Then, as he was about to follow the deceased's gurney out to the waiting van, the ME looked back at Sheriff Gibson.

"I'll know more once I have poor Marty on the table, but I'm still not sold on your murder theory. I didn't see any defensive marks on his hands or under his nails. At least not at first glance."

"Well, let me know the autopsy results as soon as you can, will ya, Max? This is top priority for me."

Sable's eyes narrowed. "Not just for you, Roy. Marty Hobbs was *my* friend, too."

The tension between the two men was slight but palpable, broken only when Sable turned and left the room. As if to acknowledge this, the sheriff offered a wan smile.

"Case like this, when it's so personal...it's bound to get on everyone's nerves. Plus, Max can be a bit touchy."

"Like the rest of us, I guess."

"That said, we still got to follow protocol. I'll need you to come down to the station and give a formal statement."

I nodded. *Been there, done that*, I thought.

Leaving the lone CSU tech to finish his work on the scene, Gibson and I went out the front door to the street. The pink, predawn sky was accompanied by a crisp, bone-chilling frost.

At Gibson's insistence, we rode in his unmarked sedan down to the Lockhart sheriff's office. It was on the ground floor of a two-story brownstone building on the rural community's main street, flanked on either side by a boarded-up hardware store and a forlorn diner. As we pulled into the narrow alley leading to the open-air parking lot behind the office, I was struck again by the weary, half-hearted feel of the town. As though abandoned in the wake of a broken economy's inevitable retreat.

Gibson's office, where I gave my statement to a Mrs. Willoughby, the department's middle-aged stenographer, was a plain, plywood-paneled room with walls covered by fishing photos, various civic organization plaques, and a faded map of the surrounding area.

On the sheriff's desk was a snow globe in which stood a replica of the state capitol building in Harrisburg, alongside a huge mug with the former president's image on it and a framed family portrait. Roy Gibson, his sallow-faced wife, and two young daughters.

After I'd finished the official report, and Mrs. Willoughby had departed to her cubicle across the hall, the sheriff poured two Styrofoam cups of black coffee.

"Worst java in the county, but good and strong." He offered me a cup, from which I quickly and gratefully took a sip.

"Hot, too," I said, scalding my tongue.

He sat down in his desk chair, took a long swallow from his own cup, then locked eyes with mine.

"Look, you and me don't know each other, but I gotta ask. Since you were the one who found the body and called it in…"

"I'm a possible suspect, I know. Especially since you're convinced Hobbs was murdered. Which I believe, as well."

Gibson scratched at his trim mustache and said nothing.

"For the record, Sheriff, I didn't kill Martin Hobbs."

He stopped scratching. "Hell, I know that, Doc. Like I said, I gotta follow the book. The problem is, if it wasn't you, then who did it? And what was so important that Marty called you and asked you to come over right away?"

"I have no idea. I wish I did."

"Plus, about that thing you said before...that it felt like you'd been led to the back of the house. That you were supposed to find him hanging there. What do you make of that?"

"Again, not a clue. Besides, it's just a feeling I have. Maybe I'm wrong."

"Yeah, maybe." He shook his head. "You know, Marty kept pretty much to himself, but the people who did know him are gonna be devastated when it comes out. It's not the kind of thing that happens in Lockhart."

It was then that I had my first thought about Indra Bishara, and how she'd react when she heard about Hobbs. Though she didn't share the feelings he'd had for her, it was obvious the two of them were close.

So the last thing I wanted was for her to get the news from the papers, the internet, or from a casual colleague. Meaning, I realized dolefully, it should probably come from me.

—

After one of Gibson's officers drove me back to where I'd parked my Mustang in front of Hobbs' house, I got behind the wheel and immediately called Indra's cell.

Though it wasn't yet six a.m., she picked up.

As gently as I could, I told her that Martin Hobbs had died during the night. Without going into details, I also disclosed that it looked like he'd committed suicide.

At first, there was only a choked silence on her end.

Then, suddenly: "No! Not Martin!" Though laced with tears, her voice was strong, insistent. "I...I can't believe he's gone, but I *know* he wouldn't kill himself. He...he *couldn't*..."

"If it's any consolation, Indra, Sheriff Gibson doesn't believe it, either."

She sniffed. "I don't understand. What does that mean?"

"He thinks someone made it look like a suicide. That—"

"That Marty was killed?" Voice sharpening. "Murdered?"

"The sheriff thinks so, yes."

I could hear her taking some big breaths to calm herself.

"But what do *you* think, Danny?" she said at last.

"I think he's right."

A long pause. "It's...it's horrible if it's true. But I still prefer it to the idea that he killed himself. I just know he couldn't..."

Perhaps I was mistaken, but I wondered if the subtext of her words was her belief that Hobbs didn't have it in him to commit suicide. I remembered her description of him as weak.

But I didn't see the purpose in pursuing that thought with her.

"I know this is a terrible shock, Indra. But I didn't want you to find out later this morning..."

"No, I'm glad it was you who told me. I appreciate it."

"Are you going to be okay?"

"I don't have much choice. I'll have to get over to the college right away and start dealing with this. Martin's colleagues and friends will have probably heard about it on the news by then. Plus, the students, their parents." She sniffed again. "And this on top of the shooting on Saturday. We haven't even finished planning Lucas Hartley's memorial yet."

I was struck by the internal conflict going on within her between her grief about Hobbs and her sense of obligation to the Teasdale College community.

"If there's anything I can do to help..." I said quietly.

"No, thanks. I'll be all right." Another long breath. "Not that it matters at the moment, but I *did* talk to my daughter about seeing you for therapy. Becky said okay."

"Fine. We can deal with scheduling an appointment later. You have enough to do today. And, Indra...my condolences for your loss. Though I only knew Martin a short time, I liked him."

"Everybody did. Or at least I thought so..."

—

It was seven a.m. by the time I got home. As soon as I did, I checked the appointment schedule on my laptop and called each of the day's patients to cancel their sessions.

The shock of what happened during the night—my discovery of Hobbs' body, my statement to the sheriff, and my call with Indra—had left me both mentally and physically exhausted. And since one of the tools I urged on my traumatized patients was the practice of appropriate self-care, I figured that same remedy applied to me as well.

After making my calls and, just in case, following up with emails conveying the same message about canceling today's sessions, I went into the bathroom, stripped, and took a long, hot shower.

Then, swathed in a thirsty towel, skin tingling, I padded into the bedroom and collapsed on the bed.

And slept for most of the rest of the day.

—

It was late afternoon before I was roused from sleep by a loud, insistent pounding on my front door. Stepping into a pair of gym shorts on a chair next to my bed, I stumbled out into the front room. The half-opened drapes revealed the soft glaze of the last of the fall day's sunlight.

Blinking myself more fully awake, I reached for the door handle before whoever was on the other side smashed it in.

It was Harry Polk, looking as bad as I'd ever seen him. And that was saying something.

"Hey, you're home." His voice a harsh, liquor-soaked wheeze. His normally wrinkled clothes were even more disheveled.

"Harry? I thought someone was breaking the door down."

He looked with curiosity at his still-upraised fist. "Yeah, that was probably me."

"That was *my* first guess, too."

His eyes bloodshot, his face blotchy and red, Polk had to grab the doorframe suddenly to keep from swaying.

"Jesus, Harry, you didn't drive here in this condition?"

"Sure I did. Why the fuck not?"

"Never mind. Just come on in."

I put my arm around his thick waist and led him into the middle of the room, and then gently lowered him to the sofa.

He offered me a hurt, aggrieved look.

"Know why I'm here, Doc?"

"Nope. I'm just glad you're no longer behind the wheel."

"Well, I'll tell ya anyway. 'Cause I got nowhere else to go. And no*body* else, neither. Not even my old partner, Lowrey. While she's off takin' care o' her sister or some shit, who's got *my* back? Fuckin' nobody, that's who."

I sat beside him on the sofa. "What's going on, Harry?"

He leaned closer and squinted at me. "I told ya my Maddie's gettin' married again, right? Some rich, ugly scumbag."

"I remember, yes."

"So I can't go bawlin' to her no more, huh? Am I right?"

"You've never been more right, Harry."

"But I can't go back to my place. I just can't. It's too lonely there. Old an' broken down an' lonely." A broad, self-pitying grimace. "Like me, eh, Doc? Just like me."

"Come on, Harry, that's the liquor talking."

A lame comment, like something out of a movie, but it was the best I could come up with. I figured it was also true.

"I know, I know." He rubbed his beard stubble. "I'm actin' all wounded and pathetic, like one o' your loser patients, eh?"

I had an appropriate reply in mind but then changed course. "You still haven't told me what's happened."

His head came up, face tightened with boozy indignation. "Jerry Banks happened! That's what happened!"

"Your partner…?"

He and Polk had never clicked since Banks had been made Eleanor Lowrey's replacement while she was on sabbatical. The fact that he'd been promoted so quickly because he was the assistant chief's nephew also didn't exactly endear him to Polk.

"The stuck-up weasel complained to Biegler 'bout my drinkin' on duty. Said it was makin' it hard to work with me."

"He's a little shit, I agree, but he's got a point. I've been worried about you myself."

"Well, who fuckin' asked ya? The thing is, Banks's report was all the excuse Biegler needed to pull my ass off the sniper case. Startin' tomorrow, I'm ridin' a goddamn desk!"

"That sucks, all right. But maybe—"

"Ain't no maybe 'bout it. Thanks to Banks, I'm fucked."

Then, head swiveling to take in the room, he said, "Ya got anythin' to drink somewhere in here? All this pissin' and moanin' is makin' me thirsty."

I regarded him sternly. "I guess it wouldn't do any good to say you've had enough."

"Wouldn't do a damn bit o' good."

"Then I'll make a deal with you, Harry. You get your drunk, sloppy carcass into my bathroom and take a long shower. You can use one of my robes afterward. They're pretty big, and I figure they'll fit you."

He scowled. "Why the fuck would I wanna take a shower?"

"Because if you don't, my liquor cabinet stays locked."

"Are you just bein' a prick, or is this some kinda candy-ass, do-gooder therapist shit?"

"Probably a little of both. Deal?"

Polk gave a slow nod and, with my help, managed to get to his feet. Again, slipping my arm around his waist, I walked us down the hall toward the bathroom. Given his bulk, I almost tripped when he began to weave to one side.

I also knew—after I'd deposited him in the bathroom and shut the door—that once Polk sobered up, he'd barely remember my having to hold him upright going down the hall.

It was the only time I wished I had a surveillance camera set up in the house.

—

As soon as I heard the bathroom shower going full blast, I turned on the five o'clock news. The lead story, as expected, was the press conference at which the formation of the sniper Task Force was announced. Both the Pittsburgh Police and the FBI were well-represented before the cameras, including Chief Logan, Captain Stu Biegler, Tony Clemmons, and Hank Bowman, the federal agent I'd met earlier with Gloria Reese.

Also on the dais was Gloria herself, as well as a stoic black detective I didn't recognize, both of whom displayed the awkward solemnity of those unaccustomed to the public gaze.

After Logan and Clemmons made their prepared remarks,

primarily focused on their shock and sorrow at the murder of Councilman Gary Landrew, the event was opened to reporters' questions. The usual thrust and parry between the cautious officials and the probing journalists was as raucous and uninformative as ever, so I clicked off the TV.

On my way to the kitchen to put together something for dinner, I happened to glance down the hallway. There, bundled in the roomy robe I'd lent him and fast asleep on the hardwood floor, was Sergeant Harry Polk curled up in a fetal position and thunderously snoring.

Apparently he'd been making his way, post-shower, to my bedroom and had only gotten this far before collapsing into a deep sleep. Carefully stepping over him, I went into the bedroom myself and retrieved a thick blanket, as well as an extra pillow. Then I came back to where he lay, gently lifted his head for the pillow, and covered him with the blanket.

For a long moment, I just stood there, looking at him, feeling a surprising tenderness toward the foulmouthed, opinionated, and deeply unhappy man with whom I often jousted.

*Life's hard on everyone,* I thought. Not a particularly new or seminal insight, but one that came to mind as I watched him, oblivious, settle contentedly under the blanket.

Then, leaving him there to sleep it off, I headed back toward the kitchen.

—

I was sitting at my kitchen table, halfway through the ham-and-Swiss sandwich I'd made, and somewhat more than halfway through a bottle of Iron City Beer, when Gloria called.

"I got your message, Danny. I miss you, too."

"How's the case going?"

"It's not. I suppose you saw the press conference."

"Yep. You were never lovelier."

"Bite me. Meanwhile, right after the presser, we were led off to a conference call with Quantico and Harrisburg. The pricks with the tailored suits yelled at us for ten minutes, and then Logan and Clemmons begged for more resources for the Task Force. Primarily, more warm bodies on the ground and a shit-load of additional money."

"How did that go?"

"The suits promised more of both, then emphasized how badly the investigation was playing on the media. And how many heads would roll if we didn't make progress toward catching the sniper. Progress, in this case, being defined as actually *catching* the psycho bastard."

I waited as she took a well-deserved breath.

"At the risk of stating the obvious, Gloria, you sound pretty stressed out."

"Brilliant, Doctor. Also exhausted, pissed off, and horny."

"I might have a remedy for that."

I heard her warm laugh. "Emphasis on *exhausted,* in case you weren't paying attention. Sex I can always get. It's sleep that's hard to come by."

"Can you grab a few hours now?"

"Just a few. Then it's another twelve-hour shift. They've broken the Task Force up into teams. Fresh eyes to go over everything we have. Forensics, witness interviews, timelines.

"If this lunatic is willing to target a city councilman, who else is he willing to go after? The mayor? The chief? Maybe a juicy high-level Bureau agent?"

I considered this.

"I assume I can trust you to keep your own pretty head down?"

"I said 'high-level,' Danny. I'm more your middle-level federal grunt. Though with better legs than Clemmons, I'd bet."

"Couldn't say. I'll have to reserve judgment till I've seen the man's legs."

Again, her soft, warm laugh. Then we both fell silent. Until, after taking turns saying goodbye, we clicked off.

—

The night was dark as wet ink outside my kitchen bay window as I nursed a Jack Daniel's and scoured the news outlets on my laptop. Other than the usual outrage from pundits and politicians about the maddeningly elusive Steel City Sniper, there was nothing new. At least nothing the authorities were inclined to release to the public.

There was, of course, an onscreen interview with Gary Landrew's grieving widow. For once, the segment didn't seem to be a gratuitous exercise in ratings-grabbing. Probably because the distraught woman's dignity and sincerity were quite apparent.

I'd just switched off the laptop when my cell rang. It was Jason Graham, following up on my message about his making an appointment to see me for therapy.

"You still have that four o'clock time tomorrow, Doc?"

"Yes, it's still available, Jason."

"Then I'll be there. It'll be good to see you again. And this time, I promise I won't be some kinda basket case."

"Well, at least you've alerted me to one of the issues we'll need to work on. Your negative self-talk. For example, calling yourself a 'basket case.'"

A strange, awkward pause. Then:

"If you say so, Dr. Rinaldi. Anyway, see you tomorrow."

Though I'd tried to couch my remark in a warm, supportive manner, he'd seemed somewhat ruffled by it. And suddenly eager to get off the phone.

Before I had time to reflect further on this, I heard the sound of my front door quickly opening and closing.

Rising from my seat, I called out.

"Harry? Is that you?"

No answer, so I went out to the front room. There, in a heap on the sofa, was the robe I'd lent him, as well as the blanket and pillow.

I headed into the bathroom, where a quick glance revealed that he'd dressed in the same clothes he'd been wearing when he'd shown up at my door.

Back in the front room, I pulled aside the drapes just in time to see Polk's old, unmarked sedan driving away.

# Chapter Twenty

By mid-morning the next day, Pittsburgh was being pummeled by a torrential rain. Taking both its citizens and most weather forecasters by surprise, the sudden downpour meant gridlock on the streets and a relentless clattering at my office window.

As I'd assumed, I never heard from Harry Polk after his hurried departure the night before. Given his proud, stiff-necked attitude toward me—and life in general—his appearance at my door had betrayed a vulnerability that could only infuriate and embarrass him. This meant that the next time we met, the whole experience would go unmentioned. By either of us.

The last of my morning's patients had left, and I was unwrapping the Genoa salami sandwich I'd brought from home for lunch, when Sheriff Roy Gibson called my cell.

"I figured you'd want to know, Doctor. We just got the autopsy report on Martin Hobbs. And now even Max Sable agrees with me. It was murder."

"Based on what?"

"Max found traces of Rohypnol, the date-rape drug, in Marty's system. Enough to make him semiconscious. Pliable."

"And so a lot easier to maneuver into a noose. And then hang from that ceiling hook."

"Right. Also explains why there weren't any defensive wounds. Marty was too out of it to put up a fight."

"Any suspects?"

"Not a single one. We'll have to start with family and friends, though poor Marty didn't have many of either. Also gotta check his phone logs, bank accounts, internet searches. But I got a feeling we're not gonna find squat."

"I tend to agree. Not that I knew him well, but from all outward appearances I'd guess he led a fairly small, contained life. What there was of it was devoted to Teasdale College."

Gibson sighed heavily.

"Yeah, you pretty much got him pegged. Listen, if you want, I'll keep you updated on the case. Since you found him an' all."

"Thanks, Sheriff. I'd appreciate that."

---

The storm departed as quickly as it had arrived, leaving the slanted rays of the late afternoon sun glistening off rain-slicked windows and swirling street puddles. Water dripped in fat, desultory drops from every roof gutter and shop awning.

I was nearing the end of my scheduled session with Jason Graham. He'd shown up in jeans and a roomy sweater, both swallowed up by a voluminous, hoodless rain slicker. Although it was stiffened with moisture, and, to my mind, obviously stifling, Jason kept it on throughout the session.

*Metaphorical armor against whatever painful feelings might emerge?* I wondered. The presumed solace of being engulfed and safeguarded within the slicker's thick, unyielding bulk?

I quickly chastised myself. A neat interpretation—perhaps

a bit *too* neat—and therefore of little clinical use. So I kept the thought to myself.

As with most initial sessions, the majority of our time was taken up with family dynamics, childhood experiences, and medical history. The latter included his occasional bouts with what he now acknowledged were panic attacks.

"The worst part about them was the way my old man acted."

He slumped in his seat, eyes darting to the window. As though suddenly mesmerized by the thick rivulets of rainwater meandering down the glass.

"Can you say more about that, Jason?"

"He didn't yell at me or anything. Or beat the living shit outta me. All that stuff you hear about on the news. You know, uneducated, blue-collar guy in a wifebeater tank top, terrorizing his emotionally fragile kid. It wasn't like that at all."

"What *did* he do, then? Something he said to you?"

Straightening, he withdrew a handkerchief from somewhere under the slicker and began cleaning his rimless glasses.

"He didn't *say* anything. It was more how he looked at me. Like at first he couldn't understand, didn't get why I was so freaked out all the time. Then the look changed, and I knew..."

"Knew what?"

"That he was disappointed. Ashamed of me. Ashamed of his nutcase son."

I recalled then that when Jason was in the hospital, his father had requested that his Asian doctor, Jennifer Chang, be replaced by a white male physician. So the man wasn't merely unwilling or unable to empathize with his troubled son, but was seemingly a racist or xenophobe as well.

What had Jason called him? "Old school." Whatever you called it, he wasn't the best father for such a sensitive kid. Not that this would be news to his son.

"Okay, Jason, let's say you read his thoughts correctly. That you're right about what you saw in your father's look. If that was true, is it any wonder that now *you* feel the same way about yourself? The same shame?"

"What do you mean?"

He returned his glasses to his nose and peered intently at me.

"The phrases you use, like 'basket case,' and 'freaking out'... It's the self-recriminating language, the contemptuous self-talk, that I mentioned on the phone..."

"But why shouldn't I talk that way about myself? I mean, why the hell not? What do *I* got to be so panicked about?"

"Jason, just days ago someone shot another kid who was wearing the mascot outfit you usually wear. That would make anyone panic. In fact, I'm somewhat surprised—and impressed—that you're doing as well as you are now. So soon after."

He vehemently shook his head. "Maybe, but I'm talking about *before* that. Ever since my early teens. All these years. Why did this crazy feeling happen to me sometimes? Like I'm losing my shit. Like I'm gonna die? Nobody was shooting at me *then*!"

I leaned forward, permitting myself a careful smile.

"That's what we're going to try to find out, Jason. There are any number of underlying causes for panic attacks. Any number of possible associations in your mind, going all the way back to childhood. But I bet the two of us, working together, will get a handle on it."

It would be generous to call his returning look dubious, but at least he didn't refute my words. Instead, he rubbed his youthful chin stubble, as though considering the possibility.

Then, climbing to his feet, he glanced again at my office window, at the droplets of water glazed by the waning sun.

"Hey, the rain stopped." He shook himself, loose-limbed, under the tarp-like slicker. "Maybe that's a good omen."

—

As I was showing Jason out of the waiting room door, I offered to validate his parking ticket. But he explained that, due to the earlier heavy rainfall, my building's parking garage had been filled when he'd arrived. He'd had to park at the curb half a block down Forbes Avenue and around the corner.

He'd been my last patient for the day, so I went back to my office to gather my stuff for home. Though the rain had long since stopped, the sky outside my window was an expanse of dull, pouting purple, interlaced with feeble sunlight.

For some reason, I paused to look down at the street, at the pavement dark and slick with water. Among the thin stream of pedestrians stepping over puddles I caught sight of Jason, who'd just emerged from the lobby and was walking down Forbes.

Despite the cloud layer, there was enough sun to send light glinting off the windows of the many shops and buildings along the street. So much so that I had to shield my eyes as I peered at Jason's diminishing figure.

Until, suddenly, a flash of light got my attention. Squinting over at the squat, four-story building across the street, I could just make out something moving on the roof.

A rifle barrel, the pale sun gleaming off its length. The figure holding it obscured behind a roof cornice.

I froze where I stood. The rifle was moving, the shooter shifting position. Realigning his aim.

I risked tearing my gaze away from the roof long enough to register Jason, just about to turn into a side street off Forbes. Then I glanced across the street again at the shooter.

His rifle barrel was tracking the boy's movements. With dozens of other potential targets on the street below him, the shooter was clearly aiming at just one.

Jason.

I almost cried out, as though the boy could hear me, then bolted out of the room. My office was on the fifth floor, but I couldn't risk waiting for the elevator. Instead I pushed through the emergency exit, then started taking the stairs two at a time down to ground level.

By the time I raced from the lobby out onto the street, Jason had reached the end of the city block. Pausing at the corner. Probably trying to get his bearings. To remember where he'd parked.

My eyes flitting between his slender figure on the sidewalk and that of the shooter on the roof, I ran down the street after Jason. Weaving frantically through and around oblivious passersby, calling out at the top of my lungs.

"Jason! Get down! Jason!"

He didn't react. Hadn't heard me. I yelled again, jostling past stunned, annoyed pedestrians. Ignoring them.

Then it all happened at once.

I'd gotten within ten yards of Jason, just as he finally turned, surprised at the sound of my voice.

At the same time, I heard the muffled crack of the sniper's rifle. And saw, to my horror, a small plume of blood burst from Jason's chest.

He fell backward, arms flailing, sprawling onto the asphalt. I reached him in seconds, pulled off the rain slicker, and covered the gaping wound with both hands. Blood pulsed, bubbling darkly through my fingers.

By now, a dozen pedestrians had gathered around, shouting and screaming. I was about to ask for someone to call an ambulance when a uniformed cop pushed through the crowd, joining me at Jason's side.

"He's still alive," I said.

He nodded, already calling dispatch for an ambulance. My hands still pressed against Jason's chest, I glanced up and behind me at the rooftop across the street just in time to see the rifle withdraw from sight.

Meanwhile, a police cruiser had pulled to the curb, and another uniformed cop leapt out of the passenger door. A short but heavily built black man with steely eyes, wearing sergeant's stripes, shouldered his way through the excited onlookers.

"He's still up there!" I yelled. "The shooter!"

The cop attending to Jason looked up at his colleague, as did I. I noted his lapel tag: SGT. FRANKLIN, 2ND DIVISION.

"Stay with the kid," the sergeant said to the first cop.

Then, jaw tightening, Franklin turned and headed across the street toward the lobby of the building, his hand reaching for his service weapon as he did so.

Instinctively, I glanced again up at the roof. No sign of the sniper.

My mind raced. I knew that building. A campus dorm, with a pair of exits, either one of which the shooter could be using. Stairs led from each to the back alley. There was no way Franklin could cover them both.

Without thinking, I grabbed the hands of the cop at Jason's side and placed them on the gunshot wound. He looked at me in surprise. But I'd already climbed to my feet.

"Keep pressure on it till the ambulance gets here."

Before he could protest, I began threading my way through the semicircle of onlookers, some of whom were recording the scene with their cells. Narrowly avoiding a passing car, I raced across the street toward the building Franklin had entered.

I'd just crossed the lobby when I saw the sergeant charge through an open doorway that led to a series of steps. I figured he planned to intercept the shooter as he tried to escape via the adjoining stairs leading down to the rear exit door.

Except there were two stairwells up to the dorm floors. Since Franklin had taken the one to my right, I hurried to the one on the other side of the lobby.

And ran through the door.

*Just keep moving,* I told myself as I vaulted up this second stairwell. *Don't think. Just move.*

*Don't think about what might happen if I encounter the shooter. Don't think about the fact that I am unarmed, and he obviously isn't.*

*Don't think about how crazy this is.*

*Just…don't think.*

So I didn't. Instead I raced blindly up to the first landing, then continued climbing. The sound of my footsteps echoed hollowly off the concrete walls of the stairwell.

Until I heard a second set of footsteps.

Above me. Pounding down the stairs. Toward me.

Gasping, blood roaring in my ears, I kept heading up. Reaching the third floor landing.

The descending footsteps louder now. The clatter of boots on metal stairs.

I stood where I was on the landing, looking desperately around me for some kind of weapon. Trash can, fire extinguisher. Anything I could use.

There was nothing.

And then he was standing halfway up the stairs from the landing, looking down at me.

Panic seized me, and I found I couldn't move. Couldn't breathe. My vision suddenly blurred.

All I had was the impression of a tall, burly man. Black clothes, black ski mask. Black-gloved hands holding a rifle.

Aimed at my head.

I wanted to close my eyes but, inexplicably, couldn't.

I was going to die staring at that hidden face. At the cool, austere gray eyes that were the only feature revealed by the mask.

*Stupid,* I thought to myself. *You're so goddamn stupid…*

Then, for some reason, I said aloud, "Sorry, Barbara."

Saying goodbye to my late wife. Somehow, as a doomed man's last words, it seemed appropriate.

Finally, my brain's signals to my burning eyes reached their destination and I closed my lids.

And waited.

—

The single gunshot thundered, reverberating off the whitewashed concrete walls.

My eyes popped open, in time to see the shooter crumple on the stairs above me. His rifle clattered down the steps and skittered to a stop at my feet.

A half dozen steps higher up on the stairs, his gun held with both outstretched hands, was Sergeant Franklin. He offered me only a cursory glance, then stared down at the masked shooter.

He lay across the lower steps at a crooked angle, writhing in pain. Groaning. Hand gripping his right thigh, where he'd been shot. The blood spreading rapidly.

Franklin slowly descended the steps, until he stood over his wounded prisoner, regarding him with disdain.

"Shut the fuck up, or I'll let ya bleed out right here."

Then, without lifting his eyes from his prisoner, Franklin freed one of his hands to use his two-way radio.

"We'll need another bus, Dispatch. Got me the goddamn sniper… Yeah, ya heard me. And hurry up, he's a bleeder."

Clicking off, Franklin squatted next to the shooter and roughly removed his ski mask.

Revealing the face of a man I'd never seen before.

He was white, with a severe buzz cut crowning a set of surprisingly bland, nondescript features. Except for those deep-set gray eyes, tightened now in agony.

Finally, the sergeant looked over at me. "You okay, pal?"

I gave a weak nod. Still gathering myself. Breathing through my mouth.

"Who the hell *are* ya, anyway?" he said.

"My name's Rinaldi."

My legs like rubber beneath me, I reached for the near wall to steady myself.

Franklin frowned. "Shit, you're that shrink Polk told me about, right? The one who ain't on the job but acts like he is?"

"Afraid so."

I was about to add that I wasn't a shrink but a clinical psychologist, then thought better of it.

"By the way," I said instead, "thanks for saving my life."

"We both got lucky. I cleared the other stairwell, so I started down this second one." He scowled. "Though I don't know what ya were thinkin', goin' after this prick."

"Neither do I, Sergeant."

The wounded man sprawled between us moaned again, as much in anger now as in pain. Franklin ignored him, and instead favored me with a wry smile.

"Well, Harry told me you were fucked in the head. Guess he was right."

# Chapter Twenty-One

Three hours later, in the blinding glare of multiple camera lights, Chief Logan's doughy face shone with a mixture of pride and relief. Speaking from the front steps of City Hall, he was announcing to a hastily assembled group of print and broadcast reporters that the sniper's reign of terror was over.

Flanking him was a beaming troupe of local politicians, FBI agents Reese and Bowman, and assorted Pittsburgh PD brass. And, of course, the mayor himself.

"Thanks to the efforts of the joint Pittsburgh Police and Bureau Task Force," Logan said, "and particularly the bravery of one of our finest uniformed officers, the so-called Steel City Sniper has been apprehended."

As expected, the live press conference led the evening news, and I was watching it on my cell phone in an interrogation room in the Oakland precinct. I'd just given my statement about the pursuit and capture of the sniper suspect to a stern female officer, after which I was instructed to stay put.

Sitting in the hard-backed chair in the windowless room, I used my cell to check the other TV and online news outlets.

Thankfully, no report I found mentioned my name in connection with the story.

Nor was any other name revealed. When I clicked back to the press conference, Logan was explaining that the identities of both the sniper and his intended victim were being withheld for the purposes of the investigation.

"I can confirm that the suspect was wounded during the course of the arrest and is being treated at a local hospital. Also wounded was the suspect's latest target, though his injury is more grievous. He's currently undergoing emergency surgery, and his doctors have listed his condition as critical."

The chief concluded by acknowledging that, at present, the motive behind the suspect's horrific acts remained unknown.

I clicked off as a volley of questions erupted from the reporters at the scene.

It was another thirty minutes before the female officer returned, this time accompanied by an older, plainclothes cop. Stoop-shouldered and with a dour, splotchy face, he told me his name was Rizelli and that he was there to take me downtown.

And that he did, in his unmarked sedan, under an icy black sky indifferent to the affairs of we poor souls beneath it.

—

"Boy, did we get screwed!"

Denise Ramirez, to whom I'd been introduced after being led to the top-floor conference room at City Hall, gave a mirthless laugh. She was an attractive woman in her early thirties, her wiry energy at odds with the formal constraints of her pale blue power suit. She worked for Pittsburgh PD and, it was explained to me, headed up media relations.

Vigorously shaking my hand, she said, "Spin doctor. Flack catcher. Crisis manager. I answer to all of the above."

Ramirez wasn't the only unfamiliar figure I saw when I entered the large, wood-paneled room whose expanse was almost totally taken up by the oval conference table. Seated at various chairs around its polished surface were DA Sinclair, Stu Biegler, and Assistant FBI Director Tony Clemmons. But new to me were two others whose names I didn't catch. Not a problem, since neither of them—a man and a woman, both young and earnestly alert—said a single word throughout the meeting. As ordered, obviously.

In response to the media liaison's somewhat jarring words, Clemmons leaned forward, palms down on the table.

"What do you mean, Ms. Ramirez? Who got screwed?"

She offered a careful smile. "I mean no disrespect, Mr. Clemmons. But the fact is, soon after the joint police and FBI Task Force was announced, one of our own uniforms—a veteran street cop—captured the suspect."

Clemmons frowned. "I'm afraid I still don't follow."

Now it was Sinclair's turn to laugh.

"Bullshit, Tony. You know damned well what she means. You saw the press conference. Instead of just Logan up there, representing a win for the Pittsburgh Police, he had to share the stage with some Bureau agents. None of whom, let's be honest, had anything to do with nailing the perp."

The FBI man's face stiffened. "Are you and Ms. Ramirez forgetting the untold man-hours our agents spent working the case? Regardless of how the arrest went down, the investigation was a joint effort. Now that a suspect's been captured, you people want to grab all the glory."

Ramirez leveled her gaze on him. I had the feeling she was used to dealing with alpha males like Clemmons, who didn't like feeling excluded or marginalized. She was savvy enough to couch her remarks in a friendly, collegial way.

"No one's impugning the contribution of the Bureau, Tony—I assume I can call you 'Tony,' right?—but my job as media spokesperson is to guide the narrative so that it puts Pittsburgh PD in the best possible light."

"I'm aware of that, Ms. Ramirez. However—"

She went on, unfazed. "And here we have a uniformed cop—a black man, a family man—an officer who represents those basic, blue-collar values that the public treasures. The point is, it's a guy like him—and not some elite federal agent—who took down Public Enemy Number One. I mean, come on. From our perspective, the optics couldn't be better."

This tidy speech did little to mollify Clemmons. Not that I cared at this point. At first, I'd been content to watch the levers of power grind away, until the absurdity began to irritate me. Especially after what the past few days had been like for the people of this city. And for me.

In fact, I was about to ask those assembled why the hell I'd been summoned to this meeting when Lee Sinclair, obviously feeling as I did, stood up from his chair.

"I'm not going to dignify that petty exchange with a comment, other than to suggest we all get up to speed on where the investigation is at this stage."

Both Ramirez and Clemmons looked as though they wanted to respond, yet each had the good sense to reconsider. Ramirez probably because, though she worked for the department, she wasn't actually law enforcement. While Clemmons, I suspected, knew that his role as advisor to Pittsburgh PD had, because of today's events, been appreciatively diminished.

Meanwhile, Sinclair had turned to Stu Biegler, who was studying a laptop screen on the table in front of him.

"Bullet points, Captain," Sinclair said. "Status of the suspect first, then the victim."

Biegler nodded and typed a command onto the keyboard. At the far end of the room, a huge flat-screen monitor flickered to life. We all turned in our seats to watch.

The first image was a mug shot of the sniper, though obviously from some years back. Not only were his features younger than those of the man I'd seen, but he wore shoulder-length hair. In this photo, he looked to be in his late teens.

"The suspect is Randy Wells Porter." Biegler began reading from text on his laptop. "Caucasian, thirty-five, single. Born and raised in Cleveland. Busted for petty theft, dealing. Copped a plea, got some candy-ass judge to clear his sheet."

Another image appeared. Porter was older now, hair trimmed, and in a crisp dress uniform.

"Enlisted in the Army," said Biegler. "Trained as a sniper. Did two tours in Iraq. Forty-five confirmed kills. Dishonorably discharged after an altercation with a female superior officer."

Ramirez smirked. "Real charmer, this guy."

Biegler ignored her and tapped another key. The next photo was from an employee file. Porter sported a thick beard and an insolent smile.

"After the service, he worked as a trucker for an outfit in his hometown. Got his ass fired for behavior problems. Then, for reasons unknown, moved here to Pittsburgh."

There was a final image: Randy Wells Porter in a hospital bed, eyelids closed. Hooked up to an IV drip. He was swathed in sheets and a blanket except for his exposed right leg. Bandaged from knee to groin. With his clean-shaven face and buzz cut, he'd at last morphed into the man Sergeant Franklin had brought down.

Biegler looked up from his laptop.

"That was taken an hour ago. Prick's expected to make a full recovery. He got lucky. They say the bullet missed his femoral artery by inches. Otherwise, he'd have been dead before the ambulance got there."

"That's a lot of intel in such a short time," Sinclair said.

"Porter's prints are in the system, Lee. As are his service records. Still, once he moved here, there's no additional info. Workplace, residence. Known associates. Nothing."

"Well, like I said, it's pretty early on."

Clemmons cleared his throat. "I can help expedite some of what we need, Lee. And pass it on to Stu."

"Where is Porter now?" Sinclair asked. "Where was that last picture taken?"

"In a private hospital in Sewickley, under heavy guard. He's recuperating from the gunshot wound, lightly sedated but able to talk. Except he won't. Won't say one goddamn word other than that he wants an attorney. Bastard."

"Find out who's next up on the rotation at the public defender's office and get him or her assigned to Porter ASAP. I assume our suspect doesn't have the means to procure a private attorney."

"Probably not. No record of a bank account or credit cards."

Sinclair considered this. "So, after coming to our fair city, Porter just fell off the grid?"

"Looks that way."

"What's the deal with this private hospital?"

"Chief Logan contracted with them for times like this, when we need to keep a wounded suspect under wraps, hidden away from the press."

Clemmons stirred. "What we in the Bureau call a secure, undisclosed location."

"Don't worry, Tony," Sinclair said, somehow smiling only with his eyes. "I know you're still here."

The DA returned his attention to Biegler.

"What about Porter's weapon? Make and model?"

"A Mark V Tacmark. Classic sniper rifle. All identifying markers filed off. But ballistics matches it to the bullets taken from all the victims except Lucas Hartley."

"Yes, the kid in the tiger suit. He was shot by that rifle recovered in pieces at the scene, correct?"

Biegler sniffed importantly. "We call it a ghost gun."

"Whatever." Sinclair sighed heavily. "What about the intended victim? Jason Graham."

Biegler hit a few more keys and the boy's Teasdale College student photo appeared on the big screen across the room.

"Right before I got here, one of my people spoke to Jason's doctor and briefed me. The kid's still alive but in bad shape. The bullet missed his heart but punctured a lung, among other damage. What you'd expect from a high-velocity round. The doc said the surgery went okay, but to be safe they put Jason in an induced coma. Whatever the hell that means."

"It means we won't be talking to him anytime soon."

After once more taking his seat, Sinclair looked at me.

"That's a shame. I was hoping to use *you*, Doctor, to help us with him. He obviously has a connection with you, since his panic attack the day of the Lockhart shooting. Then earlier today he began therapy with you."

I nodded. "I'll get in touch with Jason's doctor when we're done here. I want to be there at his bedside as soon as possible once he's brought out of his coma."

Ramirez glanced up from her iPad.

"Why is that so urgent? We got the perp."

"Because of what Rinaldi here saw today," Biegler answered scornfully. "Of course, as usual, his actions were foolhardy and unwarranted, but..."

*"But,"* Sinclair broke in sharply, "the result of those actions has been invaluable. I scanned the doctor's official statement and the conclusion seems irrefutable."

Ramirez's gaze narrowed. "Which is?"

"That Jason Graham was the intended target," I said. "I saw the sniper on the roof, tracking Jason. Singling him out. Which, as far as I'm concerned, means that the sniper *did* think it was Jason in the Teasdale Tiger outfit last Saturday.

"It also explains today's shooting. If Porter's goal was to kill Jason Graham, and then soon afterward he learned that he'd killed someone else by mistake—"

"Lucas Hartley." Biegler pulled up another photo from his laptop. Displayed it. Obviously from a high school yearbook. "The kid who took Jason's place in the tiger suit."

"Yes. Once Porter realizes Jason is still alive, he's forced to make another attempt."

Tony Clemmons had been curiously quiet during this discussion, but suddenly spoke up. He looked intently across the table at me, almost accusingly.

"Odds are he's been following Jason the past day or two. Probably saw his chance when he spotted him going into your office building. Then all he had to do was take his position up on the roof opposite and wait for the kid to come out."

My eyes met his. "That's how I figure it, too."

Sinclair sighed. "If Jason was deliberately targeted, then it's likely his earlier victims were, too. Which suggests that all of them must be connected somehow."

Ramirez put her hands to her face. "Then you're saying that, like Jason, they'd been *chosen*..."

"Exactly." Clemmons folded his arms. "Which means the case is far from over...*Denise*. I assume I can call you that?"

# Chapter Twenty-Two

Clemmons had pronounced the woman's name with steely, undisguised contempt. I realized then that the rumors were true about the assistant director. He was a dick.

Nevertheless, his comment reduced everyone in the room to silence for a full minute. Because, despite what Chief Logan had told the media, and regardless of the relief the general public was doubtless feeling, Tony Clemmons was right.

Instinctively, I glanced over at Denise Ramirez, to find that she'd been pensively looking at me. If she'd been offended by Clemmons' tone of voice, she hid it well, though she'd obviously decided it was safer to direct her question at me.

"But how were the victims chosen? Why?"

"I think it's a reasonable assumption that they all share something in common."

"Not that we have any idea what that is," said Sinclair.

"It also confirms my suspicion that the video sent to the police and then leaked online was meant to throw us off," I added. "To reinforce the idea that the shooter was seriously unbalanced and that his victims merely random targets."

"Yet if he *was* serious when he said that this was only the beginning," Sinclair went on, "it makes me wonder how many more victims were on his list. If any."

"I was wondering the same thing," said Biegler. "Whoever they are, at least we can hope they're safe for the time being."

"Of course, that just leaves us with a whole new set of questions." Sinclair steepled his fingers. "Not only how Jason and the earlier victims were connected, but who was behind their murders? Because I seriously doubt that Porter was acting on his own. Nothing in his history indicates he has either the intelligence or the temperament to mastermind these attacks. He was either paid or in some other way induced to methodically track down and kill these people."

"That's how I see it, too." Clemmons nodded. "So maybe if we can figure out what connects all the victims, we'll have a better idea of why someone might want them dead."

"It might also give us a clue as to whether there're more potential victims. Maybe even some idea of who they are."

"Are you saying there might be more people in danger?"

It was Ramirez again, her eyes flitting from one of us to the other. The concern on her face was clearly genuine.

"Why not?" Biegler snorted, as though irritated by the question. "Whoever's behind these murders could always get himself another shooter. Maybe not a sniper, but..."

"Stu's right." Sinclair grimaced. "At this point, other than having Porter in custody, there's a hell of a lot we don't know. Still, if we're lucky, this is the end of the killings, and Jason was the last loose end the sniper's handler needed him to tie up."

"Too bad Porter won't talk," Biegler said sourly. "Save us all a shitload of trouble."

There was another long silence, after which Sinclair once again regarded Ramirez.

"As far as the public is concerned, Denise, the sniper's been caught. For now, let's allow them to believe that Porter's victims *were* chosen at random. That his actions were that of a severely disturbed individual. This way we can continue the investigation without undue scrutiny from the press."

"That won't last long," she said.

"Point taken. So, assuming we have a limited window of opportunity to stay under the media radar, let's try to red-ball this. Okay, people?"

Sinclair looked from Biegler to Clemmons, unable this time to keep the wry smile from his lips.

"Turns out, we're going to need the Task Force to stay in place and demonstrate that interagency cooperation we're always bragging about. Right?"

The two men nodded almost simultaneously.

"All right, then," Sinclair stood again. "Let's call it a night. We all have a lot of work to do."

As everyone began pushing back from the table and getting to their feet, I spoke up.

"I just want to add how much I appreciate that my name was left out of the media reports. Makes a nice change."

Biegler gave me his most truculent glare. "It wasn't outta the goodness of our hearts, Rinaldi. You takin' off after the sniper coulda gotten your ass killed."

Ramirez sighed. "That's right. Talk about a PR disaster. A civilian under contract with the department gets injured or worse while chasing the sniper. Then there's the financial liability. A good lawyer could argue that Dr. Rinaldi, as a paid consultant, was acting as an agent of the Pittsburgh Police. Which makes the department accountable for his actions."

She gave me a sidelong look. "Sorry, Doctor. Nothing personal. Just telling it like it is."

Which brought a dry chuckle from Sinclair. "I have to admit,

Daniel, your occasional attempts at heroics do make the police nervous. As they do me, sometimes."

I held up my palms. "Hey, all of you. I get it. Trust me, my friends and colleagues feel the same way. I admit it was foolish, but…"

Biegler's jaw literally tightened.

"It wasn't just foolish, Rinaldi. Like Ms. Ramirez says, it was potentially embarrassing to the department. As I explained to the commissioner as soon as I heard what you did today. Which sucks for you because he agreed with me."

"What the hell are you saying, Stu?"

"Remember what you said before, about how you had fans in the department? Well, you also have enemies. People who see it my way, that you're more trouble than you're worth. And guess what? The police commissioner is one of them."

By now, Lee Sinclair's patience had run out.

"Jesus, Stu, will you let it go? I'm sure you have better things to do than keep bitching about Danny here…"

"Yeah, I do. But before that…" He reached into his jacket pocket and brought out a long envelope. And gave it to me.

"It's official, Rinaldi. And I wanted to be the one to hand it to you personally."

"What is it?"

"A notarized letter signed by the commissioner himself. Your contract with the Pittsburgh Police is suspended, as of midnight tonight." He made a big show out of looking at his watch. "About an hour from now. Like they say, smart guy, your services are no longer required."

—

I had to admit, Stu Biegler got the reaction he'd obviously wanted. Sinclair, Clemmons, and Ramirez looked equally stunned. Even the two nameless Bureau agents looked embarrassed on my behalf.

As often happened in Biegler's presence, my first instinct was to lay him out. But I resisted, my hands clenching into fists at my side. Which, as before, I let him see.

Of course, I wasn't going to do anything. Couldn't. And Biegler knew it.

After all, we were all civilized people. More or less.

It was Leland Sinclair who finally spoke, puncturing the unremitting tension.

"Christ, Biegler, you had to pull this stunt here? To try to embarrass Dr. Rinaldi in front of his colleagues?" He shook his head. "You are one classless son of a bitch."

Biegler started. "But, Lee, you have to admit—"

"I don't have to admit anything." Sinclair's voice grew an edge. "Other than my disgust at your choosing an important case debriefing to display your personal animus to Rinaldi. Which you've been doing in one way or another for years."

Now it was my turn to be stunned. Why the hell was Sinclair defending me? Unless it was merely to display his own personal animus toward Biegler. Given what common knowledge it was, I suspected Lee was as annoyed as I was over Biegler's promotion.

Nevertheless, whatever was transpiring between the two men had no effect on the contents of that long envelope. I'd opened it by then, read the single paragraph letter signed by the commissioner of police, and pocketed it.

It was official, to use Biegler's words. My role as consultant to the Pittsburgh Police was suspended.

Indefinitely.

---

Ironically, it was almost exactly midnight when I pulled into my driveway. The meeting had broken up minutes after that exchange between Sinclair and Biegler, after which I'd been consoled privately out in the hallway by Denise Ramirez.

This had struck me as somewhat odd, since we were hardly acquainted, until I thought about it driving home. She was the department's PR flack, and, aware of my modest reputation in the public's mind, she was probably trying to ensure that I wouldn't go complaining about my suspension to the media.

She needn't have worried. Not my style.

After changing into sweats and a Penguins T-shirt, I went into the kitchen and fixed a drink. Jack Daniel's. Neat.

I sat at the kitchen table, nursing my drink, and reread the short letter of dismissal. While it occurred to me that a suspension wasn't a termination, the message to me was crystal clear. If there was even a chance of the suspension being lifted, I'd have to be a good boy. A very good boy.

Again, regrettably, not my style.

*Fuck it,* I thought, finishing my drink, although my real feelings were somewhat mixed. While I had little regard for the department brass, I'd grown to relish my role as a consultant. The opportunity to treat crime victims traumatized by their experience had become, over the years, both personally and professionally meaningful. I knew in my heart that I'd made a difference in people's lives.

And nothing in that bullshit letter could take that away.

Still, it took another couple drinks before the defensive argument roiling in my brain began to quiet. At least enough for me to haul myself to my feet, stumble into bed, and fall into a deep, dreamless sleep.

—

I got up early enough the next morning to, once again, cancel that day's patients. Claiming I'd come down with a bad cold, I avoided disclosing the real reason. I was just too damned hung-over to function.

Not my finest moment as a mental health professional, but there it was.

I went into the kitchen, where the bay window was glazed with wintry sunlight. I made a big pot of strong coffee and, after swallowing two ibuprofen tablets, sat drinking cup after cup.

My head had just ceased throbbing when my cell rang. It was Sam Weiss, calling from his office at the *Post-Gazette.*

"You're at work early, Sam."

"The news doesn't sleep, buddy, so why should I?"

"You mean about the capture of the sniper? Randy Porter?"

"Hell, Danny, that's yesterday's news. Literally. I'm calling to offer my condolences."

"About what?"

"The word just leaked that you got your ticket punched by the cops. The pricks suspended you."

"Oh, yeah."

"It's bullshit, Danny, and you know it. After you've hauled their asses out of the fire a bunch of times."

"And got my own ass handed to me by the brass an equal number of times. Frankly, I'm surprised it's taken them this long to get rid of me."

"Well, I, for one, think it's a crock."

"Thanks, man. I appreciate it. Funny thing, though. These last couple days I've been getting a lot of love from Leland Sinclair. And I can't for the life of me figure out why."

I heard Sam's easy laugh. "You mean you don't know?"

"Know what?"

"To absolutely no one's surprise, Sinclair's gonna take another run at the governorship next election."

"What does that have to do with me?"

"His team's already doing some discreet polling, gauging the public's awareness of and opinion about aspects of his tenure as district attorney. And your name was included in one of the questionnaires."

"Really? I have to admit, I'm surprised."

"You shouldn't be. You're quasi-famous in certain circles. And your numbers aren't bad. Among those polled who knew who you are, your favorables just beat your unfavorables."

"And this should make me happy?"

"Nobody cares about that, Danny. Least of all Sinclair. It just means that your association with law enforcement—and, by extension, the DA's office—isn't going to be a liability, should he decide to run again. In fact, it could be an asset."

I considered this. "At least it helps explain Sinclair's sudden buddy-buddy routine with me. I was beginning to wonder if he'd had a religious conversion or something."

"You want my advice, Doc? Enjoy it while you can. You know how the great unwashed are. Once they get wind that you've been suspended, it'll take some of the shine off you."

"Don't worry. I'm sure if that seems to be the case, Lee's people will conduct another poll."

"Count on it. Anyway, I gotta go. My editor is trying to arrange an interview with Porter through his public defender."

"He has one already?"

"Yeah. Guy named Shelton. Dave Shelton. Poor schmuck. Apparently, he's been on the job for two minutes and he gets handed this nightmare of a client."

"I don't envy him."

"Tell me about it. Take care, Danny. And don't worry about

that suspension. As my old Aunt Ethel used to say, 'Fuck 'em if they can't take a joke.'"

—

It was sometime past eleven when—after a quick workout in my basement gym and a long, hot shower—I started to feel like a human being again.

In fresh clothes, I was on the sofa in the front room, surfing the various news channels. Nothing other than the expected follow-up to Porter's arrest, including interviews with some family members of his victims.

However, it seemed the one interview everybody wanted—with sniper suspect Randy Porter—wasn't going to happen.

Apparently, as had been the case with Sam Weiss's editor, all requests for interviews with Porter had been denied by his lawyer from the public defender's office. Though the attorney's name wasn't mentioned, I remembered Sam telling me it was a guy called Dave Shelton.

Finally, a live report from Pittsburgh Memorial included a statement from one of Jason Graham's doctors. She explained that his surgery had gone well, but that he remained in an induced coma until his condition could be reassessed.

*Poor kid,* I thought. In his panicked state back at the motel, he'd been convinced that his life was still in danger.

And he'd been right.

—

No sooner had I turned off the TV when my cell rang again.

To my surprise, it was Jerry Banks, Polk's temporary partner. As usual, his tone was sharp and impatient.

"I know this is a long shot, Doc, but the captain said to call everyone who might know where he is."

"Where who is?"

"Sergeant Polk. Harry. He didn't report in for desk duty yesterday, and he hasn't shown up this morning, either."

"He's missing?"

"Looks like it. We even sent wheels to that hellhole he lives in in Wilkinsburg. Not there."

"Have you checked the Spent Cartridge? Or maybe even Noah's Ark? He's been frequenting that bar lately, too."

"Called 'em both, Doc. *Nada.* So I was hopin' you might know where he is?"

"I wish I did, Detective. Of course I'll let you know if he gets in touch, but..."

"Thanks. I figgered you were worth a shot. Shit, Biegler's gonna skin Polk alive when he finally turns up."

We hung up, and I sat looking at the phone in my hand, wondering who I might call regarding Polk's whereabouts. But other than his ex, Maddie, no one came to mind.

I looked up her number online and left a message on her voicemail. My gut told me she wouldn't know where he was, either. I remembered Harry saying he couldn't go to her seeking solace anymore.

I'd just clicked off when there was a knock on the door.

When I opened it, I was greeted by Special Agent Gloria Reese, in a sweater and jeans under a heavy coat.

"Are you gonna invite me in or what, Rinaldi? I'm freezing my butt off out here."

"Depends. What's on your mind, Agent Reese?"

With a knowing smile, she threw her arms around me.

"I was thinking about a nooner. How's that sound?"

"Sounds like just what the doctor ordered."

# Chapter Twenty-Three

I didn't know how or when she'd hidden the handcuffs, but at that precise moment I didn't care.

It was a nice surprise, since our lovemaking had begun slowly and languorously, with my head buried between her taut, lovely thighs. Taking my time until I heard her quick intake of breath and felt her deep, satisfying shudder.

As I got up on my elbows and somewhat smugly smiled, her hand slipped under the pillows and withdrew the pair of cuffs. Before I could register what was happening, I found myself on my back, my hands shackled to the bedposts on either side.

From that point, my thoughts shredded as she took me inside her mouth. My urgent erection intensely, exquisitely painful.

Then, abruptly, she was astride me, the wan sun from my bedroom windows burnishing her naked body. The small, perfect breasts. The smooth, finely muscled arms. Her slow, supple control as she rocked above me, accentuated by my restraints. So that the more I struggled against them, the deeper my thrusts inside her.

Until, finally, I gave it up and felt that sweet, propulsive release. Leaving us both gasping, laughing. Happy.

It was a rare feeling lately.

Then came the fun part, at least for her: negotiating my way out of the cuffs. My promises in exchange for release began with a champagne dinner at her favorite restaurant, then escalated by degrees to a week in Paris.

At last, still laughing, she undid my restraints.

"I'd better see some plane tickets, mister," she said as we settled together under the covers, our arms around each other. "And pretty damn soon."

"I'm a man of my word." I kissed her forehead, slick with sweat. "Even when it's exacted under duress."

A shadow suddenly fell over her eyes. "Hell, lately there's a lot of duress going around."

"Tell me about it." I didn't know what else to say.

As if to cling somehow to our previous feelings, I held her tighter, but the mood had shifted. The real world and its woes had already rushed back in, intruding on our postcoital solace.

—

When I finished showering, I went into the kitchen. Gloria, wearing only her sweater, was sprinkling salt on some steaks she'd found in the fridge. The aroma from the stove was intoxicating.

"Now that you've worked up an appetite," she said, adjusting the flame, "I figured you'd want something to eat."

I came up behind her and kissed her neck.

"You read my mind," I said.

She playfully shook me off and concentrated on her cooking.

As I watched her, I couldn't help but notice how comfortable she seemed in my kitchen.

This, unexpectedly, made me very *un*comfortable.

---

By three that afternoon, Gloria had dressed and left for work. After pouring myself a freshly brewed cup of coffee, I carried my cell out to the back deck and checked my office voicemail.

Other than a request from a colleague for a referral and a chiding from the editor of a clinical journal about an article I'd promised him, the only additional call was from Rebecca Bishara, Indra's daughter. In a hesitant, slightly tremulous voice, she said she was reaching out at her mother's urging to set up a therapy appointment.

I called back right away and left a message of my own, suggesting a couple of appointment times the following week.

I was struck by her outgoing message, which, rather than being voiced by Rebecca herself, was relayed in the flat, impersonal tones of a digital recording. Very unusual for a teenager.

Finishing my coffee, I leaned against the deck railing, replaying the image of Gloria standing at my kitchen counter, while beams of chilled sunlight skittered across the surface of the river waters below.

On the one hand, given all that had happened in the past few days, whatever confusion I had about my relationship with Gloria seemed beside the point. On the inevitable other hand, I wasn't sure how long she'd be satisfied with our "friends with benefits" situation. A phrase I disliked, and that didn't do justice to the feelings we had for each other.

Which begged the question: what did?

---

The temperature had fallen sharply, so I went back inside. Almost immediately, I heard a staccato knock at the front door.

Why was my house so popular, all of a sudden? And had everyone forgotten how to use the doorbell?

My first thought was of Harry Polk. Had the missing detective sergeant come stumbling up to my threshold again? I sure as hell hoped not. With a heavy, uncharitable sigh, I put down my mug and made my way through the front room to find out.

To my surprise, when I opened the door it was Sam Weiss who pressed past me and, without a word, invited himself in.

As always, the youthful, wiry energy of this married father of two belied his years as a veteran journalist. The same was true of his torn jeans, open-necked shirt collar, and thick Navy peacoat. He had the unruly hair of a much younger man as well, though his usual crooked smile was missing.

In its place was a set of firm, determined lips. Which matched his equally firm, determined gaze.

Then, finally: "I'm really pissed at you, Danny."

At a loss, I motioned to the sofa. "You want to sit down?"

"No, I won't be here long. Neither will you."

"I won't?"

"I mean, shit, after all I've done to hype your reputation in this town…"

"What the hell are you talking about, Sam?"

"I thought we were friends, that's what I'm talking about."

"We are. Aren't we?"

"Yeah? Then how come I just find out today from my source at Pittsburgh PD that you were present at two of the sniper attacks? The stadium and that lawyer in Shadyside. Not to mention when they took down the sniper."

I decided to take advantage of the sofa myself, sitting on one of its wide arms.

"Come on, Sam, you know how much I've tried to stay out of the press. Especially lately."

"Yeah, but you should've told me anyway. We could've discussed it. Made the call together."

"Maybe you're right..."

"Of course, I'm right! If nothing else, you could've given me some eyewitness stuff that nobody else had. I would've kept your name out of it, if that's what you wanted."

I was about to reply when he held up a warning finger.

"And while we're on the subject, what the hell's wrong with you, anyway? Why did you go running into that building to stop the sniper? You could've been killed."

"I know, but—"

"I hate to say this, Danny, but you won't make up for your wife's death by dying yourself."

His reddened cheeks told me he instantly regretted what he'd said. Frankly, so did I. But I kept my voice measured.

"That's not why I did it, Sam. I just couldn't imagine not helping catch the guy. Stopping the murders."

He shrugged, clearly unconvinced. "Hero complex. Death wish. Take your pick. One thing for sure, Doc—you can't help your patients, present and future, if you get your ass killed."

"I do know that. Believe me. And I'm sorry for keeping you in the dark this week."

I took a breath then. "But about your building up my reputation...hyping me...I never asked you to do that. I made damned good copy for your stories, and you knew it."

His face finally softened.

"Yeah, but I also *wanted* to do it. To pay you back for what you did for my sister. I figured I owed you. If nothing else, I could give you some positive ink. Help make your name."

"Which you did, and for which I was grateful for a long time. But lately...well, like I said, I want to keep a lower profile. At least for a while."

He nodded, then favored me with his trademark crooked grin.

"Okay, okay. I guess I'm gonna be a mensch about it and forgive you. But you still owe me. So get your damn coat."

"Where are we going?"

"I'll explain on the way. Now hurry up."

—

"You know the mistake the cops always make?" Sam asked. "Even therapists like you?"

"No. Enlighten me."

Sam was at the wheel of his late-model Toyota. We were driving across the Fort Pitt Bridge, the last of the day's sun glinting off the steel arches overhead, on our way to Sewickley. The wealthy borough was about a twenty-minute drive from town.

"People think guys like Randy Porter are just stone-cold killers," Sam said. "Which they are. But that's not *all* they are. They're also somebody's son, or maybe somebody's brother."

"Meaning...?"

"Meaning that I can relate to him on a very specific level. I did some research and found out he had one sibling. A younger sister, just like me. Her name's Julia."

The evening rush hour had just begun, slowing our progress. At which Sam's fingers tightened their grip on the steering wheel. Reflecting the usual Type-A personality's impatience.

"Through his lawyer, Dave Shelton, I sent Porter a letter saying that we each had baby sisters in common. Julia's even close to my Amy's age. She and Randy come from a broken home. Poverty, alcoholism, domestic abuse. The usual *Dateline* nightmare."

"I'm sorry to hear that, but..."

"Listen and learn, Doctor. If Randy Wells Porter, heartless killer and probable nutcase, has one redeeming quality, it's this: he adores his sister, Julia. Protected her the whole time they were growing up. Wants her to have a better life than he's had."

"He *does* sound like you. At least in terms of how much he cares about his sister."

Sam nodded. "All of which I emphasized in my letter. How we had this one crucial thing in common. It must have worked, since Porter has agreed to giving me an exclusive pretrial interview. My guess is, Porter thinks that his cooperation might help take away some of the shame Julia must be feeling as a result of his crimes."

I had to admit, I was impressed. "Jesus, you've managed to get the hottest interview in the tristate area. Nice job."

By now we'd moved across the river and had joined the line of sluggish traffic clogging the parkway.

"That just leaves one question," I said. "Why the hell am *I going* with you?"

"It's part of the deal I worked out with Porter. I told him that I wanted a mental health professional at my side during the interview. And then I insisted it be you."

*"Me?* Sam, he was just about to shoot me when Officer Franklin took him down. Why would I want to sit in on an interview with Porter? Hell, why would *he* go along with it?"

Sam laughed. "Yeah, I went over that with Shelton. And here's the funny part. When the lawyer told him that I wanted you to attend the interview, Porter said he had no problem with it. And I quote: 'I don't give a shit if he's there. Tell the headshrinker, don't be scared. I can't do nothin' to him now, anyways.'"

"And you really believe he's okay with my being there?"

"Why not? He's got nothing to lose. He knows he's looking at life in prison, if not the needle. I don't think he'd care if I brought the Kardashians to the interview."

"You've got a point there."

"I'm telling you, Danny, this guy's more complicated than you think. For example, the only remorse he's apparently expressed to Shelton since his arrest was about the death of Lucas Hartley. Porter feels badly that he killed the wrong kid. He says it's unprofessional to take out a collateral target and asked Shelton to extend his condolences to Lucas's family."

I considered this. But not for long.

"As much as I'm moved by his sniper's code of ethics, I'm still the one he was aiming that rifle at. So even if *he* doesn't have a problem with my attending the interview, I sure as hell do. To put it politely, fuck him."

"It's not about him, Danny. It was *my* idea to have you there. I want your clinical read on the guy. Things that I might miss that you could clue me in on later."

He gave me a sidelong look. "Besides, don't tell me you aren't curious about Porter. His background, what makes him tick. It's an opportunity to look inside the mind of a hit man. To be honest, I figured you'd jump at the chance."

I had to admit, he was right. Not that I'd let him know that. Instead, I gave him my best aggrieved sigh.

"And this bullshit is all because I didn't tell you about my involvement in this sniper case?"

"Like I said, Rinaldi, you owe me."

And there it was again. That crooked smile.

# Chapter Twenty-Four

Some snipers have all the luck.

As Biegler had noted, Randy Porter was recuperating at the city's expense in a private hospital. On the outskirts of Sewickley, it was a small, red-bricked, turreted building right out of the 1920s, set well back from the street. To reach the front entrance, you had to navigate a paved circular driveway and then park on a narrow gravel spit.

"Nice, eh?" said Sam. "Used to belong to some steel magnate. A private hospital for him and his family. When the last of his heirs died twenty years ago, it was sold to some Japanese investor. To treat local VIPs. The city's rich and almost famous. Real cash cow, from what I hear."

A cool dusk had settled over the stand of maples in which the venerable building was nestled, contributing to that sense of Pittsburgh's sepia-toned, industrial past—and the dozen or so robber barons who'd profited from it.

Sam pulled up to a spot next to where two police cruisers were parked. Adjacent to them was a shiny white ambulance, and lined up behind it were a BMW, a Porsche Turbo Carrera, and a sleek Jaguar. He whistled appreciatively as we headed over to the entrance.

A uniformed cop opened the double doors for us, and we stepped into an ornately decorated lobby manned by another officer. Built like a linebacker, he indicated the elevator with a curt nod.

It wasn't until we'd arrived at the third floor that I felt like we were in an actual hospital. The spacious hall boasted gleaming white walls, linoleum flooring, a series of fully equipped patient rooms, and a nurse's station.

The only jarring note was the presence of another massive uniformed cop standing behind the desk of the middle-aged duty nurse.

Sam and I showed our IDs to the cop, who pointed us to the room at the end of the hall. He needn't have bothered. It was the only room in front of which stood another, equally intimidating policeman. It was clear they were taking no chances with their prized suspect.

"Are there any other patients on this floor?" I asked.

"No, sir." It was the duty nurse who answered. "They've all been moved to rooms on the upper floors. For their own protection, according to the police."

The cop gestured again to the room fronted by his brother in blue. Sam and I got the hint and headed down the hallway.

As we approached Porter's room, I noticed that the door was closed. The cop guarding it stood with his back against it.

"Is he in there alone?" Sam asked him, after we'd once again had to explain who we were and why we were there.

"Naw." This second big cop chewed on a toothpick. "His lawyer's in there with him. Nice guy. Named Shelton. Too good for that asshole Porter, ya ask me."

"I understand he's new to the public defender's office," I said. "Tough break catching Porter so early out of the gate."

The cop laughed. "I think Shelton feels the same way. But at least it's nice here. Quiet. Tomorrow's a different story."

"What do you mean?"

"After the doc releases Porter in the mornin', the prick's gettin' shipped downtown. City jail. No more happy pills. No more pretty nurses."

The door had a small, square window, so I glanced inside. Randy Porter looked much the same as he had in the photo Biegler had shown us. Reclining on the hospital bed, hooked up to an IV, leg exposed and well-bandaged. Even under the heavy covers, I could see his chest rising and falling. The steady rhythm of his breathing.

His lawyer, Dave Shelton, sat at his bedside. He was a slender, slightly balding young man with a neatly trimmed beard and wearing an inexpensive but well-pressed suit. The overall effect was of a boy playing grown-up. Even the concerned look on the public defender's face as he leaned in to speak to his client betrayed a rookie earnestness.

I was still peering through the window when Shelton abruptly rose, gave his client's forearm a solicitous pat, and headed for the door. Before he could reach for the handle, I opened it for him.

Momentarily startled, his youthful face rearranged itself, and he grinned.

"Hiya." He shook hands with Sam and me. "I'm Dave Shelton. Which one of you is Sam?"

My friend nodded, then introduced me.

Shelton's smile widened. "You're that shrink sitting in on my client's interview. I think I've heard of you."

Sam winked at me. "You're welcome."

I ignored him, focusing on the lawyer.

"Will you be joining us for the interview, Mr. Shelton?"

For the first time, his features seemed to tighten.

"Of course." He cleared his throat. "If you must know, I've

repeatedly advised my client *not* to participate in this interview. But he's insistent. Nevertheless, he's still entitled to representation. So I have to be there. In case—"

"In case he might volunteer something he shouldn't?" Sam took a step closer to the lawyer. "Look, I understand you have a job to do, but so do I. I don't want you cramping my style."

Shelton looked unruffled. "No, sir, Mr. Weiss. I wouldn't want to do that."

"Good." Sam gestured at the cop, who'd stood silent and unmoving as a stone sentinel. With an uninterested shrug, the big officer moved aside.

Then Sam took hold of the door handle. "C'mon, let's get this party started."

But Shelton reached in his pocket for his cell phone.

"Just give me one minute, okay, guys? I've gotta call the office. Be right back."

With that, he tipped his cell at us, as though it were a cap, and then proceeded down the hall. I watched him nod at the duty nurse and the officer sharing her desk, then he went into a small lounge area I'd noticed when Sam and I had stepped from the elevator.

Meanwhile, Sam was glancing at his watch.

"It's nearing six. I promised the wife I wouldn't be home later than nine. Ten, at the outside."

The cop at our side grunted. "No worries, buddy. I figger Porter ain't got that much to say. Crappy family, victim of society. Ain't really his fault how he turned out. I've heard all that same bullshit before. Boo-fuckin'-hoo."

"Might be some truth to it," I said.

Which only got me another disgusted grunt. Sam and I exchanged looks, his more amused than mine.

Another minute passed. Then two.

"What's keeping him?" Sam said to the air.

For some reason, I turned again and looked through the door's window. Peering at Porter in his bed.

His eyes were closed. His body still.

His chest not rising and falling.

Randy Porter wasn't breathing.

—

Sam and I burst through the door to Porter's room while the big cop hurried down the hall to alert the duty nurse.

But it was too late.

Before I'd even reached Porter's bedside and checked his pulse, I knew the man was dead.

Leaning over the bed from the other side, Sam stared at me. "What the hell—?"

Suddenly an alarm bell sounded. Code Blue.

At the same time, the big cop, followed by the duty nurse and a slender man in hospital greens, came into the room. The latter quickly introduced himself as Dr. Singh.

I stepped out of his way so he could examine his patient. In moments, he turned back to the nurse.

"TOD at 6:02 p.m." His voice was terse. "Please alert the director and call police headquarters."

"What happened to him?" Sam asked.

"No idea, sir. Not till the autopsy."

But an idea was already stirring within me.

"Was this the first time Dave Shelton showed up here?" I asked the cop, whose face had gone ashen.

"Today, yeah."

"And you checked his ID?"

"Sure I did. Picture ID, in fact. What do ya think?"

I made a deliberate show of looking around the room.

"Then how come he's the only one not here?"

Sam had already headed for the door, and I followed as he raced to the end of the hallway. As I'd expected, Shelton wasn't in the lounge area. But one look at the exit door just beyond it told me where he'd gone.

"Son of a bitch," Sam said. "It was Shelton, wasn't it? He killed Porter. While we were standing around with our thumbs up our asses, waiting for him to come back, he made his escape."

"Yeah," I said. "Except I have a feeling that guy *wasn't* Dave Shelton."

The moment I uttered those words, a sudden fear sluiced like arctic water through my veins. Sam had already headed back to Porter's room, but I stayed in the lounge. Hurriedly using my cell to get online and call up the phone number of the public defender's office downtown.

I made the call. It took a few minutes, but after identifying myself and explaining the situation, I got Shelton's supervisor on the phone. Then had to explain things again.

"I don't understand," she said. "Dave called in this morning. Said he was sick and would be staying home."

"Are you sure it was him? Did you recognize his voice?"

"I didn't speak to him. Our operator took the call."

"Then can I have Shelton's home address?"

"Well, I don't know if I should—"

"Then I'll make it easy for you, lady. Yes, goddamn it, you should. This is official police business. Now what is it?"

I was being a bit careless with the truth, but there wasn't time to cajole the info out of the officious woman.

After getting the address, I went over to the nurse's station, where the officer there was on the phone to his superiors. As was true of the cop who'd guarded Porter's room, this one's face showed a mixture of anxiety and embarrassment.

As soon as he'd hung up, I barked out Shelton's home address to him. He merely looked at me, distracted. Perhaps still reeling from Porter's death and fearing the effect it might have on his career.

I slapped my palm down on the nurse's desk, trying to pierce the guy's mental fog.

"You've got to get a patrol car over there ASAP! Make the call, Officer. Now!"

Grabbing a pad and pen from the desk, I quickly wrote down the address for him and started back down to Porter's room.

I was met halfway there by Sam Weiss.

"Captain Biegler himself is on the way down now," he said. "And Clemmons from the Bureau. Meanwhile, the cops here just got the order to lock down the whole building."

"Then we better get going before they do. You're driving me to the South Side. To Shelton's place. Now."

Before he could protest, I grabbed his arm and we stepped into the elevator.

"I just hope we're not too late," I said.

—

We were.

Dave Shelton's apartment was on a narrow street off the main drag of the South Side. It was in one of those former industrial facilities that had been converted into a residential building, boasting a number of expensive lofts. Ultra-trendy apartments whose interiors were still factory brick-and-mortar, whose ceilings were crisscrossed with steel beams, and where no walls or doors separated the living spaces.

By the time Sam had us pulling up to the curb in front of

Shelton's building, I'd hoped to see a police cruiser already there. Blue lights flashing. But no such luck.

It took some persuading—and another series of half-truths—to get the super to let us into the young lawyer's place. As he unlocked the door, he explained that Shelton's was the cheapest loft in the building, and that he'd only been able to make the rent because his parents footed half the bill.

"Mr. Shelton?" The super called out as we entered. "Hey, Dave. You in here?"

No answer.

"Thanks," I said. "We can take it from here."

He looked concerned. "You sure that's okay?"

I showed him my Pittsburgh PD consultant's badge. Now, of course, invalid. Not that he needed to know that.

He peered at it for a long moment, then shrugged and departed, calling over his shoulder that we needed to make sure to lock the door on our way out.

Without exchanging a word, Sam and I moved carefully through the barely furnished apartment. No carpets. Few pictures on the exposed-brick walls. IKEA furniture. The open kitchen shared space with what could be called the living room, and a set of metal stairs led to the bedroom above.

Still maintaining an odd, wary silence, we climbed up the steps and looked around. The bed was unmade, the closet jammed with clothes, the wooden shelf along one bricked wall stuffed with books. The room certainly seemed lived in. And, to my mind, the only comfortable-looking area in the place.

"You could be wrong." Sam's were the first words either of us had uttered in at least five minutes. "It happens, you know."

"More times than I'd like," I said. "But if the Dave Shelton we met *was* bogus, then..."

Another thought occurred to me. There was probably only

one room in the loft with a door. The one room requiring privacy.

"I'm an idiot," I said aloud. Then turned and pounded down the metallic rungs of the staircase, the tinny sound echoing.

This time, it was Sam who was on my heels.

On the main floor again, I passed by the kitchen to an alcove, in which a closed door stood. The bathroom.

With Sam at my shoulder, and my breath held like stone in my chest, I opened the door.

He was on the floor, nestled as though napping against the glass shower stall. Knees up, arms across them, face tilted to one side.

The other side exposed to us.

The side with the neat bullet hole in the temple, and the coagulating blood painting the blanched, sunken cheek.

# Chapter Twenty-Five

The homicide detective was a stout woman with a shrewd face, whose wrinkled jacket and slacks suggested she was at the end of a long shift. Her name was Bennett, and she wore her dark hair in a short, no-nonsense bob.

The CSU techs were still on the scene in Shelton's loft, though the county's medical examiner had come and gone. He'd been followed out by two attendants carrying a litter on which lay the deceased, zipped up into a body bag.

Sergeant Bennett motioned for Sam Weiss and me to join her in the kitchen area, where she invited us to take our seats on the counter stools.

One of her officers had taken our statements, which she read carefully in front of us. Never saying a word, she flipped over some pages in the spiral notebook she'd been given, then flipped back as though to confirm something for herself.

Finally, she put down the notebook and regarded us.

"I know about what happened at the hospital," she said quietly. "But what made you come here to look for Shelton?"

"So, the dead man is the *real* Dave Shelton?" Sam said, though obviously knowing the answer. Getting confirmation for the story he was already formulating in his head.

The sergeant nodded. "Yes, that's Shelton. But it appears that one of you suspected he might be in danger. Is that true?"

"Yes," I said. "When it looked like the guy we thought was Shelton could have been an imposter, it occurred to me that harm might've come to the real one."

Sam leaned across the counter, eyes glittering. I realized he couldn't help it. His reporter's hunger was spiking.

"What can you tell us about Porter's death?"

Bennett laughed. "Like I'm going to tell you, Mr. Weiss. That investigation is just getting underway, and you know it. I'm sure the chief will make some statement to the press once it becomes public knowledge that Porter is dead."

I stirred. "Do they at least know the cause of death? I'm guessing something fatal injected into his bloodstream. Maybe through the IV tube. I saw where the fake lawyer was sitting. The tube was right next to him at the bedside."

The detective merely shrugged. "Couldn't say, Doctor, and I wouldn't tell you if I could."

Sam tried another tack, jerking his thumb in my direction.

"Don't you know who this is? He's Dan Rinaldi. Practically on the job himself. Believe me, Sergeant, if you don't tell him now, he'll probably find out from the brass before long."

This only brought another laugh from the detective.

"That might've been true before yesterday," she said, giving me an almost pitying look. "But now that he's had his contract suspended, I don't think he's gonna be kept in the loop the way he used to be. What do you think, Doctor?"

"I think you're right, Sergeant."

—

To Sam's dismay, he learned within an hour that he was not going to get to write about the Shelton murder. As his editor explained to him on the phone, Sam was himself part of the story, and therefore too personally involved to be allowed to report on it.

After being released from the scene by the police, Sam and I had gone back to his car. It was while he was driving me home that he'd gotten the bad news from his boss.

"I got screwed, Danny."

He'd just hung up, and now turned his full attention to his driving, which hadn't been the case while he was on the phone, arguing with his editor. Barreling across town in heavy night-time traffic, he'd twice almost clipped a car in the next lane.

"I hate to say it, Sam, but your boss is right. Hell, you and I might even be called as witnesses if Shelton's killer is caught and brought to trial."

"I know, but..."

We drove in silence for a few minutes. Then, without turning his eyes from the road, Sam spoke.

"I've seen a few dead bodies, but that was still tough. I can't get the image out of my mind. Poor guy."

"I've seen my share, too," I said quietly. "Just this week, in fact. I'm starting to feel like I'm cursed."

"Shit, now that you mention it...maybe you are."

I rubbed my tired eyes. "One thing for sure. Cursed or not, I'll never get used to it."

---

After Sam dropped me off at home, I found out some bad news of my own.

I'd opened an Iron City, taken a seat on my sofa, and clicked on the evening TV newscast. As I'd expected, the double murders of Randy Porter and Dave Shelton led the broadcast.

What I hadn't expected, and should have anticipated, was that my name would be all over the story. As one of the two people who'd discovered Shelton's body, whatever local notoriety I had made the mention of my name irresistible. Moreover, though it was unconfirmed by the police, the report went on to state that I was also rumored to have been at Porter's bedside when his sudden death was revealed.

So much for keeping a low profile.

I took a long pull of my beer, then sat back against the sofa cushions and closed my eyes.

And waited for the phones to ring.

There were at least a dozen messages on my landline answering machine, and an equal number of texts on my cell. Even my office voicemail was filled with calls. Not to mention emails.

All from friends, extended relations, and colleagues. All offering the familiar condolences, followed by the equally familiar admonitions about my once again getting mixed up in a criminal case.

Gloria's message on my cell was an exception.

"If you need to talk about it, Danny, I'm home. And don't try keeping it bottled up inside. You of all people should know that doesn't work."

She was right, of course, and I planned to return her call. But not just yet. Frankly, I wasn't in the mood to talk to anyone. Not even Gloria.

I stretched, then rose to get another beer. As I did so, I heard the click of yet another message being left on my home machine.

It was Angie Villanova, her voice still thin, halting. But as confrontational as ever.

"I knew it... Danny... Goddamn it... I knew it..."

That was all she said. And, smiling ruefully to myself, I realized it was all she needed to say.

—

Sergeant Bennett had been right. When it came to the details of the sniper investigation and its continuing evolution with the murders of Porter and Shelton, I was undeniably out of the loop.

Stripped of my consultant's role, and with no begrudging updates from Harry Polk or the out-of-commission Angie Villanova, I didn't have my usual insider's access to what was going on with Pittsburgh PD. Even Gloria had little to share, since she'd been assigned the deep dive into the sniper victims' lives. Which meant she was planted at her desk, eyes glued to her computer screen.

Until the next night.

I'd had a day full of patients and come home to a microwaved dinner of leftover rigatoni. After changing into sweats and a long-sleeved sweatshirt—it promised to be another cold night—I relaxed on the sofa, sipping a Scotch and listening to Coleman Hawkins on the CD player. Then my cell rang. Gloria.

"Hey, Danny." Her voice sounded thin, weary. "I finally got a pair of bolt cutters and unchained myself from my desk."

"Glad to hear it."

"Seriously, Clemmons and Biegler called a Task Force meeting to bring the team up to date."

"Sounds like fun."

"Yeah, a million laughs. Anyway, I figured you'd want to know where things stand with the Porter death."

"You sure have my number, Agent Reese."

She yawned. "Well, whatever turns you on, Doc. Anyway, you were right about the IV drip. Porter was killed by a massive amount of morphine injected into the tubing. Took a few minutes to do the job."

"Which was why the killer had us waiting outside Porter's room while he supposedly went to call his office."

"Right. He needed to make sure Porter would be beyond saving by the time anybody checked."

"Any idea who the guy was? Pretending to be Shelton?"

"Yeah. Got his prints from the hospital room. Which means the asshole was either stupid or incredibly careless."

"Or else maybe he planned to be long gone by the time the cops ID'd him. Maybe even out of the country."

"Maybe. You know the drill. We have people watching the airport and train stations."

"So who is he?"

"Known perp named Hubert Sedarki. Street name is Baby Huey, because of his youthful appearance. Got a rep for being brash, a wiseass. With a mouth on him. But he's a bad one, Danny. Done time for armed robbery, assault. Has a big-time sheet."

"His mother must be so proud."

"I don't think evil shits like him even have a mother. The point is, he's a known violent offender, but this is his first murder. That we know of, anyway."

"A paid job, I assume?"

She sighed, her exhaustion obvious. I decided I didn't want to keep her on the phone longer than necessary.

"We think the same thing you probably do, Danny. Whoever's behind the sniper's hits—we're calling him the Handler—got worried that Porter, despite how tight-lipped he's been since his arrest, might still be persuaded to talk. To make a deal with the DA. He names the guy who paid him in exchange for avoiding the needle. Life in prison is still...well...life."

"So the Handler gets himself another hit man. Some street thug with a record. And the gift of gab. But how would he know about a guy like Sedarki?"

"Well, if we knew who the Handler was, we could answer that question. But if our guy was savvy enough with computers to send out that bullshit video, he might be able to hack into ViCAP. Or any of the other law enforcement systems, some of which are surprisingly available. With the Freedom of Information Act, almost anyone can find out info about almost anyone else."

"That's true. Just ask any reporter."

"Or blogger. Or true crime nut. Everything's so goddamn porous nowadays..."

She yawned again. "Anyway, we figure Sedarki finds out where Dave Shelton lives—again, not hard to do online—and heads over there yesterday morning. Somehow, he talks himself in the door, kills Shelton. Next, he calls the public defender's office, pretending to be Shelton, and says he's too sick to come in to work. Then Baby Huey heads off to the hospital."

"But the cop on guard duty says he had ID."

"Again, not hard for Sedarki to fabricate. Or else maybe the Handler did it for him earlier. We won't know for sure till we catch Sedarki."

I paused. "Last question, Gloria, and I'll let you get some sleep. What do you think the chances are of finding this Baby Huey before he takes off? Like for someplace without an extradition treaty with us?"

"Not good. Though I was talking about it with Hank Bowman, and he thinks we will end up finding him. Just not alive."

"Yeah?"

"Hank figures the Handler, whoever he is, doesn't like loose ends. That's why he got rid of Porter, right? Why not do the same to Sedarki? Maybe even do the job himself."

"Good point. Though I've noticed that you and everyone else keeps calling the Handler 'he.' It could be a woman, you know."

"*Could be*? As far as I'm concerned, Danny, that's always been on the table."

—

I'd just finished the next day's sessions, and was closing down the office when a slow drizzle outside began fogging up my window. It was a few minutes after five p.m., and between the wintry darkness and the sheet of soft but insistent rain, I dreaded the drive home.

So instead of facing the hellish commute, I took the elevator down to the street, pulled my coat collar up around my throat, and walked briskly to the Starbucks on the corner.

Once inside, I ordered a grande, black, and took a seat near one of the windows. I knew the caffeine would make it harder to sleep, but I wasn't doing much of that lately anyway. Besides, I was chilled from my short sojourn in the rain and wanted to wrap my hands around a cup of something hot.

Unsurprisingly, the murders of both Porter and Shelton were still dominating the news, especially as new tidbits of information emerged. And while, as I'd guessed, the public seemed relieved that the sniper's activities had been halted, the media was unconvinced that the story itself was over.

And, this time, the media had it right.

The identity of the presumed killer of both men had been revealed earlier today by the police as one Hubert "Baby Huey" Sedarki. Yet as long as his whereabouts remained unknown, the press had enough to keep stoking the rumor machine. Which meant that Chief Logan, DA Leland Sinclair, and FBI Assistant Director Clemmons were pressured into releasing daily statements as to where the investigation stood.

Sipping my coffee, I clicked around on my cell until I came upon an unexpected piece of news. It was an interview that had taken place just an hour before on WTAE-TV, during which Captain Stu Biegler offered his opinion that Hubert Sedarki, when found, might ultimately prove to have been the man behind Randy Porter's deadly sniper attacks. And that with Sedarki's arrest, he believed, the entire investigation would come to a quick and satisfactory conclusion.

I finished my coffee but stayed seated, letting my thoughts drift as I watched the drizzle grow into a more serious, steady rain outside the window.

Regardless of Biegler's theory, the description that Gloria had given me of Hubert Sedarki didn't leave the impression of a criminal mastermind. Someone able to orchestrate a series of sniper attacks on a group of seemingly unconnected people who, despite initial appearances, must be connected in some way. Given the two attempts on Jason Graham's life, there didn't appear to be any alternative to the notion that these disparate victims had something—whatever it was—in common.

And until the thing linking all the victims could be revealed, this case would not arrive at Biegler's "quick and satisfactory conclusion."

Just then, my cell phone rang. I glanced at the display. Sheriff Roy Gibson, from Lockhart.

"What's up, Sheriff?"

"Two things, Dr. Rinaldi. First off, we might have a motive for Martin Hobbs' death."

"Which you're still treating as murder, right?"

"Oh, yeah. Fact is, Marty had a secret we've just uncovered. About his gambling."

"Hobbs was a gambler?"

"Big-time. Kept it from everyone who knew him. As it turns out, he owed a couple local guys a ton of money. Bookies, and the real bad boys they work for. Marty was into these people for over a hundred grand. And these are a nasty bunch of guys."

"I find it hard to believe, Sheriff. He seemed…"

"No one's more surprised than me, Doc. We'll keep digging, of course, but my feeling is that we're really onto something. If one of these guys got tired of waiting for their money…"

I finished his thought. "Then it might be a smart business move to make an example of Hobbs. In case there were other guys having a hard time paying what they owed…"

"Something like that. I don't want to jump to conclusions. But it's the line of thought we're pursuing. At least for now."

"But then why make it look like a suicide? Wouldn't his killers want to ensure that Hobbs' death was clearly known to be murder? As a message to others like Martin? Make them see what happens to people who don't pay up?"

"I had the same thought, Doc. But the gambling angle is the only one we've got. So far."

I let out a long breath, trying to reconfigure the image I'd had of Martin Hobbs.

"You said there were two things, Sheriff," I said at last.

"Yeah. There's a small funeral service planned for Marty on Saturday afternoon. Friends and colleagues. I thought—well, me and Max Sable thought it'd be nice if you could come. I guess we figure Marty would like it if you did."

"Of course. I'll be there."

I also suspected that Gibson and Sable feared that the turnout would be embarrassingly low, and they wanted to spare Marty's memory that.

After asking the sheriff to text me the details of the service, I clicked off.

---

Hank Bowman's hunch proved to be right on the money. Hubert "Baby Huey" Sedarki was indeed found, early the following morning. Dead, and in a clump of tall weeds behind the extended-stay parking lot at Pittsburgh International.

# Chapter Twenty-Six

Sedarki had been shot once, through the heart. The man's death, the coroner announced in a statement released to the press, had been instantaneous.

But the media, as expected, wanted more. As did, it seemed, the general public. Sedarki's murder, and where it fit in with those attributed to the Steel City Sniper, made the police investigation appear even less credible than before—leaving everyone, according to a pundit on MSNBC, wondering what unexpected outrage was coming next.

It was Friday night. I was in my kitchen, having a bowl of tomato soup and listening to the feeble last remnants of the previous day's downpour. I felt as if the rain itself was melancholy, exhausted by the week's horrendous series of events, and so unable to give today's storm much effort.

*Anthropomorphizing the weather*, I thought, chastising myself. I was either a poet trapped in the wrong job or totally losing my shit.

No doubt, it was this whole sniper business. In one way, as I'd said to Angie Villanova, it had nothing to do with me. Other than my concern for Jason Graham. But that was purely clinical.

However, as a criminal case, a police investigation, it also fell well outside my ostensible role. Even before I'd been suspended from my duties as a consultant to Pittsburgh PD.

So why was I so obsessed with it? Why did I feel as though everyone—the police, the FBI, me—why did I feel that we'd all missed something?

That we'd missed, from the very beginning, what this whole nightmare was really about?

—

I was still reflecting on this when Noah Frye called.

"Danny? It's your favorite schizophrenic."

"What is it, Noah? Are you okay?"

"Now that's the kind of existential question we just don't have time for, man. There are cognitive issues to contend with, let alone the phenomenological and the spiritual."

"Granted. Let me put it this way: what's happening?"

"Again, those are deep waters, metaphysically. But to cut to the chase, your cop buddy is here."

"You mean Harry Polk?"

"I sure hope you don't got more than *one* cop buddy. It's distressing enough that you hang out with *this* mindless tool of the dominant culture."

I swallowed my impatience. "When you say he's here…"

"I mean he's *here,* Danny. At my place. He's sleepin' off a hellacious bender on the floor behind the bar. I came out from the kitchen and almost tripped over him."

I glanced at my watch. Closing on eight p.m.

"I got payin' customers here, Danny boy. And it's the start of the weekend. So I can't have some drunk cop messin' with the Ark's cool vibe. I got a reputation to think about."

"Okay, okay. I'll be right there, Noah. How'd he get in there, anyway?"

"Like everyone else. Walked in the front door. One of the regulars here says Polk just came up to the bar, walked around it, and collapsed on the floor. Like I said, I was in the kitchen with Charlene. Only gone a goddamn minute and—"

"Got it. Look, if you can move him, do so. Put him back in the kitchen or someplace. If you can't—"

"I think we got some kinda produce cart out back. Maybe I can roll his fat ass onto it, and then—"

"Forget it, all right? Just leave him where he is. And try not to step on him while you're pouring drinks."

—

Even with the desultory rainfall, traffic was brutal, so it took almost an hour to get to Noah's Ark. As before, I had to park a block away, and then tread carefully on the slippery sidewalk till I reached the entrance.

Weaving through the boisterous Friday night crowd, I came up to the bar and was met by Noah's stony stare. Then, without a word, he pointed theatrically to the floor beneath him.

I leaned over the counter and saw Polk, looking remarkably similar to when I'd found him sleeping outside my bathroom. In the same quasi-fetal position and making the same thunderous snoring sounds. Though given how loud the jazz trio across the room was playing, Polk's staccato bleats were barely audible.

I hurried around the end of the bar and joined Noah behind it. I was about to ask his help in hauling Polk to his feet when I remembered the weakened condition Noah was still in. And especially how fragile his injured hands were.

Instead, I poured a glass of soda water from the bar's

dispenser, crouched by Polk's body, and dribbled it down on his face. In moments, he was sitting up, sputtering angrily, wiping the water from his eyes and cheeks.

"What the fuck—?"

Even his normally high-decibel bellow was drowned out by the music, though there was no mistaking the rage in his voice.

"I mean it, Rinaldi! Where the fuck am I?"

"Calm down, Harry." I reached to help him clamber to his feet. "You're at Noah's place. You kind of crashed the joint."

Polk looked around, bleary-eyed, disoriented. "I'm in that floatin' shithole o' his?"

Noah gave me a hard look. I spread my hands.

"He's drunk, Noah. Doesn't know what he's saying."

"Like hell I don't!" Polk roared, settling his red-eyed gaze on Noah's broad features.

"Better get him outta here, Danny." Noah folded his arms. "Or else I won't be responsible for my actions."

I laughed. "When have you ever been?"

He squinted, clearly pained. "Jesus, man, low blow. I expect better from you."

"Me, too, Noah. But it's been a rotten couple of days. Now let me take our friend the sergeant here over to a corner table and you can bring a vat of black coffee."

"Goes on your tab, right?"

"Of course. Doesn't everything?"

While he was considering this, I grabbed Polk's forearm and walked us both over to the table I'd seen when I first came in. Even with the place almost full, there were a few tables free. Most customers were either at the booths lining the walls or packed shoulder to shoulder on the bar stools.

I wedged Harry Polk into a seat at the small table and took

the chair opposite. He was still breathing heavily, as though coming out of sedation, and his eyelids fluttered. But he was sobering up.

Noah arrived with a large pot of black coffee and two huge mugs, then, scowling, departed without a word.

I got Polk to drink a whole mug of coffee, then poured him another. A sour wakefulness came over his florid features.

"How did I end up here, Rinaldi?"

"Beats me, Harry. The Department's been looking for you. They got Jerry Banks, of all people, calling around trying to find you. I hear Biegler's fit to be tied."

"Fuck him." Polk swallowed some more coffee, winced. "What is this, motor oil?"

"It's getting your engine running, Harry, and that's all I care about."

He rubbed his bulbous nose. "An' ya say Jerry Banks been callin' 'round after me? That little shit?"

"Afraid so." I took a sip of my own coffee. Jesus, it was strong. And bitter.

"Where the hell have you been?" I asked.

He shook his head mournfully. "No goddamn idea, Rinaldi. Just drove around, hit some bars… I think I slept in my unmarked down by the Tenth Street Bridge."

"If so, you're lucky you didn't get busted."

He laughed shortly. "I'd like to see some uniform try. I'd kick his ass to Philly and back."

"So, I'm guessing this is about Maddie's upcoming marriage to that bank exec?"

"No shit, Sherlock. I just can't… What is it you shrinks say? I guess I just can't cope with it."

"And, like a homing pigeon, you ended up crashing here. Your new favorite bar."

"It ain't my favorite, Rinaldi. I just found myself in the neighborhood."

"Whatever. Now all that matters is getting you home. Then, tomorrow morning, shaved and showered and in fresh clothes. You're going downtown to fix things with Biegler."

"Sounds like a lotta work. Do I hafta?"

"If you want to keep your job, yeah."

He let his head drop to his chest, avoiding my eyes and saying nothing for a long moment. Then, in a whisper:

"Nothin' I'm gonna do, no matter how bombed I get, or how much I trash my career…" Now his gaze came up to meet mine. "Nothin's gonna stop Maddie from gettin' married again, huh?"

"Nope. Nothing, Harry. She's not going to rescue you from your pain over this. It's not her responsibility to do so. And, deep down, you know it."

"I do?"

"Sure." I let my voice soften. "That's why, with all your running around, boozing and driving all over and sleeping in your car…with all that, you haven't bothered her. Haven't gone to her, castigating her about it. Wanting her to somehow fix it. You've been punishing yourself these last few days, Harry, but you haven't punished her."

He put down his mug and grew silent.

"Is that what I've been doin'?" he said at last.

"I think so. I can't know for sure, but I think so."

He nodded, as though slowly coming to terms with the idea. Then he sat back in his seat, a self-satisfied grin spreading on his face.

"Well, I'll be damned. Guess I'm copin' better than I thought. Thanks, Rinaldi. Let me buy ya a drink."

# Chapter Twenty-Seven

That didn't happen, of course. Instead, I got Polk into a Lyft with instructions to the driver to take the sergeant home. But not before I assured Harry that the department could send someone the following day to pick up his unmarked. I figured by then he'd remember where he'd parked it.

It was nearing ten, the rain had let up, and I was driving under a cloud-knitted sky down to Station Square. Gloria and I had made a date to meet for drinks at some trendy new bar she'd read about.

I found the place, which was tucked between an equally upscale restaurant and some kind of boutique store, and was looking for a parking spot, when she texted me: Sorry Danny. Bowman asked where I was going and then invited himself along.

I texted back: You two want to be alone?

Gloria: Hilarious. Get here ASAP. I need backup.

I finally found a place to park and made my way past the throng of nighttime revelers on the sidewalk to the bar's retro, neon-encircled entrance. Inside was crowded and atmospherically gloomy, the dimness relieved only by a series of overhead track lights. A typical watering hole for the self-consciously hip.

Gloria and Hank Bowman were seated at a corner table, half-empty drinks in front of them. I pulled up a chair, shook hands with the FBI man, and ordered another round for all of us.

I gave Gloria a subtle wink, which she returned with a silent, mouthed "thank you," and turned my attention to Bowman. He looked tired, as did Gloria, and, I suspected, everyone else who'd been involved in the sniper case.

"Gloria tells me the Bureau's pulling out tomorrow," I said to him. "That doesn't mean the case is over?"

Bowman took a sip of his drink. Whiskey.

"It's not over by a long shot," he said. "Soon as there're more developments—and there will be—the director will send us back up here. But for now, there are other cases to be worked, and the Bureau's manpower is at a premium."

Gloria nodded. "Hank and I agree that Hubert Sedarki's murder doesn't end things. If anything, it raises more questions than it answers."

"For one thing," Bowman went on, "if we're right, and neither Porter nor Sedarki was behind these murders, then the Handler is still at large. But there's a good chance we'll never run him down."

"What makes you say that?" I asked, as a pretty but sullen waitress brought our drinks and then, wordlessly, departed.

"Because I think we've seen the last of the murders." Bowman exchanged his old glass for a new one. "It's just a gut feeling, but I really believe that everyone on the Handler's list of victims has been crossed off."

"Based on what?"

"Think about it, Doctor. After a rapid series of sniper attacks, over a very short period of days, the only other murders were of the sniper himself, Randy Porter, and the fake lawyer the Handler used to silence *him*."

I wasn't convinced.

"The way I see it," I said, "there haven't been any more sniper attacks because Porter was in custody. But as we've seen since then, the Handler has other methods to get rid of people. How do we know that someone isn't being killed right now? Mugged on the street or something? And that this latest victim isn't just the next one on the Handler's list?"

"We don't," Bowman agreed. "But does that mean that every new murder is part of the guy's victim list? How can we know? Is the list endless? It's absurd."

He took another swallow of whiskey. "The one I feel sorry for is Dave Shelton. Poor kid. Talk about collateral damage."

"Agreed," I said.

We three grew quiet, which made me aware of the subtle hum of the other customers' voices. Intimate murmurs, soft laughter.

Then Gloria spoke up, turning to me. "I think what Hank said before was right, Danny. The case isn't over till we bring in the Handler, whoever he is. That's why I've been asked to stay on, to keep looking into the lives of the sniper's victims. To figure out what the connection is. Though we're getting a lot of pushback from some of the victims' families."

"You are?"

"Yes. A few have retained lawyers to fight us about the victims' tax records. Or having full access to their cell calls and online activity."

Bowman laughed. "Meaning some of these upright citizens might have a long porn history."

"Or are complicit in fraud or God knows what," said Gloria.

"Luckily, the Bureau has lawyers, too. Sooner or later you'll get to browse through these folks' dirty underwear."

Gloria frowned. "Thanks for the image, Hank."

The FBI man laughed again. "But I'm glad it's your

problem now, Gloria. I'm on vacation starting tomorrow. A week of golf in Seven Springs. In my opinion, the best resort in the state."

"I take it your wife isn't going along?"

"Christ, no. Me and a couple college buddies. Strictly stag." He leaned closer to her, which made her stiffen almost imperceptibly. "Unless *you* wanna tag along? I won't tell my better half, if you won't."

Gloria flushed, but managed a watery smile.

I changed the subject. "If you're taking off, Hank, and so are the other agents, does that leave Gloria in town alone?"

"Hell, no. We'll have our usual complement of local field agents posted here. Besides, Tony Clemmons is sticking around, too. Seems that Harrisburg wants him and Captain Biegler to put together a formal report on the case. For the State Police and other Pennsylvania agencies."

"Politics as usual," I said. "Figuring out who to blame and who to praise."

Hank Bowman finished his drink and pushed back from the table. The way it wobbled a bit, I could tell he'd had enough.

"Like I said, not my problem." He stood, then gave Gloria a chaste peck on the cheek. "In case you change your mind, Glo, I'll text you the address of the resort."

"Great. Soon as I get it, I'll be on the next bus."

The Bureau man laughed hoarsely, then ambled away, careful not to bump into other people's tables in the practiced way all experienced drinkers have perfected.

Gloria put her chin in her cupped hands.

"Christ," was all she said.

—

By mutual consent, fatigue won out over sexual desire, and we parted company outside the bar. Gloria had an early morning the next day, reexamining everything the Task Force had on the sniper case up till now.

My Saturday would start a bit later. I didn't keep office hours on the weekend, so no patients. But I did have to drive to Lockhart for Martin Hobbs' funeral.

Happily, the midnight skies were still free of rain, though the air was frigid as ever. Buttoning my coat to the top, I hurried down the wet sidewalk toward where I'd parked. Given the array of streetlamps, I had no trouble finding my way there.

As I neared my Mustang, I immediately noticed something different about it. Easily visible under one of the overhead lights, the car had acquired a new accessory.

It was a tall, sturdily built man in a windbreaker and jeans, casually leaning against the driver's side door. Maybe mid-thirties, dark hair and eyes. Handsome in that arrogant, self-assured way that usually made smart people nervous.

Or at least was making me nervous.

I got a better look at him as I approached. He seemed to be sizing me up, too, at the same time.

"You Dr. Rinaldi?"

His voice was sharp, more youthful than his years. As if life hadn't mellowed it. Chastened it.

I nodded. And took a guess.

"And you're William Reynolds the Third. Billy Three."

He cocked his head. "Only my friends call me that."

"I assume then that we're not going to be friends."

"Don't think so."

With that, he pushed off from the side of my car. Stood facing me with his feet planted apart. I recognized the stance.

He was planning on a fight.

I took a few more steps toward him, but stayed just out of range of those long, powerful-looking arms.

"Look, I think I know what this is about," I said.

"Good. Saves me the trouble of havin' to spell it out."

"It's obvious your lawyers told you that Indra planned to send her daughter to me for therapy."

"Becky's not just *her* daughter, dude. She's mine, too. *Mostly* mine."

"I don't know if the courts will see it that way, Billy."

"Don't matter, as long as Becky sees it that way. And she does. So nothin' you can say to her will change her mind."

"I hadn't planned to try to change her mind."

"Now that's good to hear."

"Just like you standing there pretending to be a badass isn't going to change my mind about treating her."

Billy Three grinned. It didn't add to his appeal.

"You're just achin' for a poundin', aren't ya, Doc?"

"Not if I can help it."

He affected that world-weary, tough-guy shake of his head. As though he didn't really want to do what he had to do. If only the other guy could listen to reason...

"I think you've seen one too many movies," I added quickly.

"What do ya mean?"

"I mean all this street punk attitude feels fake. A put-on. You can't hide that you're a product of fancy private schools. That you come from money. The fact that you're a bully who terrorizes women doesn't mean you're as tough as you think. In fact, in my experience, it means the opposite."

"I still don't get you, man."

I took another measured step toward him.

"Let me put it this way, Billy. You ever been in a fight? A real fight?"

"Sure. Plenty of times."

"I don't mean some schoolyard shit. I mean, out here. On the streets. Against some *real* badass guys."

"Fuck you, Rinaldi. You're just tryin' to distract me."

"Is it working?" I took another step closer.

His gaze, never having left mine, narrowed slightly. As though thinking hard. Planning a move.

That's when I realized my mistake. I'd been so busy talking trash, trying—as he'd guessed—to throw him off, I'd misjudged the distance between us. That I'd figured was beyond his reach.

Those two steps I'd taken. To crowd him. Back him off. They did just the opposite. While I was trying to read the intent behind those narrow, hooded eyes, he saw his opening.

And took it.

His right fist swung up, wildly, and connected with the side of my jaw. Amateur hour. All rage and no technique.

Still, the punch had plenty of muscle behind it. I stumbled backward, pain shooting up my face, arms pinwheeling to find my balance, my eyes burning.

With a guttural shout, Billy stepped inside, where I was now open, and threw an ungainly roundhouse. I managed to raise a forearm, deflecting most of its impact.

But not enough. I went down.

Gasping, standing over me with bloodlust gleaming in his eyes, Billy Three cranked up a dark grin. Though he was shaking his dangling right hand, no doubt needled with pain.

"You *feelin'* me, Rinaldi? Smart-ass fuck. You stay away from my kid, okay? No bullshit therapy sessions. No nothin'. You don't say one fuckin' word to her. *Got it?*"

I could barely form words, but I forced myself to make the effort. Getting gingerly up to my elbows on the wet concrete.

"If bullets didn't scare me off, Billy, what makes you think this'll do it?"

He squinted down at me, confused. "Bullets? What the hell are you talkin' about?"

"In that alley downtown."

"What goddamn alley?"

I was too groggy, struggling just to stay conscious, to argue with him.

"Look, asshole," he was saying, though I was having a hard time registering his words. "Just steer clear of my Becky. Otherwise, you and me gonna have another dance, and trust me, you don't want that."

Still with the gangster movie lingo. If my jaw wasn't throbbing with pain, I might've actually laughed.

Or at least would have tried to, if I hadn't blacked out.

# Chapter Twenty-Eight

By my watch, I'd only been unconscious for about twenty minutes. As I slowly levered myself to my feet, I automatically felt in my pants and jacket pockets. Wallet and keys still there. Somehow my prone body had gone unnoticed by some enterprising street person. Or a passing cop.

Head still spinning, I unlocked my Mustang and sank behind the wheel. Planning to sit there until I felt okay enough to make the drive up to Grandview Avenue and home.

Apparently, I drifted off a couple more times, because when I finally roused myself, the dashboard clock read two a.m.

But at least I was thinking more clearly. Replaying Billy's words in my mind. Trying to make sense of what I'd heard.

Unless I was wrong, he'd seemed genuinely surprised when I mentioned his shooting at me in the alley.

But if it hadn't been Billy Three, then who?

At a loss for an answer, I put the Mustang in gear and pulled away from the curb.

—

When I woke at ten the next morning, I was grateful that it was a Saturday and, more important, that the pain in my jaw had lessened. Still, it felt stiff and tender enough that I took more ibuprofen with my morning coffee.

As I sat in my kitchen, blinking against the sunlight streaming through the bay window, I thought about what had happened the night before. I wondered if I should call the police and make a complaint against Billy Three for assault.

Almost immediately, I realized I wasn't going to do that. For one thing, I couldn't imagine what good it would actually do. There hadn't been any witnesses, so it was essentially my word against his. Plus, Billy's high-priced law firm would shield him from any real consequences.

Besides, the last thing I wanted was to see my name in the papers again. Moreover, given his prominent family, Billy's identity would offer as much red meat to the media as mine. The whole thing could end up spiraling out of control. Fodder for talk shows and gossip blogs.

So Billy's sucker punch would remain our little secret.

---

It was almost noon by the time I'd finished breakfast, showered and dressed, and was back behind the wheel.

The previous days' rains had left the city glistening in the sun, which, added to the light Saturday traffic, made the drive across the river to the parkway more pleasant than usual.

However, as I traveled east, and reflected on the reason I was doing so, my mood quickly turned somber.

But not only because today was Martin Hobbs' funeral. I knew Indra Bishara would be there and would almost certainly notice my jaw's slight discoloration. If so, however,

I'd decided not to tell her about my encounter with her ex-husband.

Though, even now, as I neared the Lockhart city limits, I wasn't entirely sure why I wanted to keep it from her. To spare her the shock, perhaps? The unnecessary concern about me, in addition to all her other burdens? After all, she might even blame herself for having set Billy against me.

The funeral service was being held at a small chapel on the edge of the Teasdale College campus. Stepping inside the cool, marbled building, its stained-glass windows splashed by the bright noonday sun, I quickly spotted Indra sitting a few rows back from the altar.

Not hard to do, since she'd turned in her seat at the sound of my hushed, echoing footsteps. She offered me both a sad smile and a gesture inviting me to sit with her.

I walked down the aisle, a scattering of mourners on either side of me, till I arrived at Indra's shoulder. She wasn't alone, sharing the wooden pew with Sheriff Roy Gibson, Dr. Max Sable, and, at the far end, a teenage girl. Her head down, features shielded by her winter coat's upturned collar, I knew it could only be Indra's daughter Rebecca.

After acknowledging Gibson and Sable, I extended my hand toward the girl. When she didn't look up to acknowledge it, her mother, whispering, gently urged her to do so. In response, her eyes still aimed at the floor, Becky managed to say a barely audible "Hello."

When I took my seat next to Indra, she clutched my arm, as if to signal her apology for her daughter's behavior. I shook my head at her. No problem.

The service itself was brief. Though the turnout was as sparse as I'd expected, I did see what I assumed were other faculty members, as well as a few students. The saving grace was the pastor's remarks from the pulpit. Apparently, he'd known Martin Hobbs for many years, and spoke warmly and appreciatively about the college dean.

Following the funeral, I joined Indra and her daughter outside on the flagstone patio. Sheriff Gibson and Dr. Sable stood some distance away, speaking to the pastor. The remaining mourners went off in other directions, their obligation completed.

"Thanks for coming, Dr. Rinaldi." Indra was using my formal title, I suspected, for the sake of her daughter. Becky was mute and slump-shouldered at her side.

"I was glad to be invited." I turned to her daughter. "And I'm glad to finally meet you in person, Becky. I've heard a lot about you."

She brought her face up suddenly, at the same time flipping down her coat's collar. She glared at me, the jagged scar on her cheek accentuated by the brightness of the sun.

"Then you've heard about this." Pointing at her cheek. "It's all anybody talks about."

"Becky, honey..." Indra lightly touched her daughter's shoulder, but then quickly withdrew it as she saw Becky's hand come up to swat it away.

The girl's gaze remained steady, as though trying to read my face, glean something about me.

I returned the favor, noting her beautiful eyes and the richness of the coloring she'd inherited from her mother. As well as her hands placed on her hips to indicate her defiance.

"I only called for an appointment to please my mother," she said to me, making an effort to sound harsh. "No offense, but the last thing I need is to talk about my feelings. I did all that with Dr. Owens, but I'm still the same freak."

"It's okay. You don't have to see me if you don't want to."

"But you *promised*, Becky," Indra said wearily.

"Don't worry, Mom, I'll keep my promise." Turning back to me. "Just don't expect me to say anything."

"I won't," I said. "In fact, whenever I meet a new patient, I try not to have any expectations at all."

Becky made a grunt of annoyance, then turned her collar back up and stomped off.

"I'll wait for you in the car," she called back to her mother over her shoulder.

Indra let out a quiet groan. "Jesus, Daniel, I'm so sorry. She's having one of her bad days. The truth is, she really liked Marty. His death affected her more than she lets on."

"I was wondering about that. But I like her fierce spirit, Indra. Even her anger. I only wish she'd direct it at someone other than herself."

"Then you'll still help her?"

"I'll try. If she'll let me."

After a moment's hesitation, she brought her fingers up to my face.

"You're hurt."

"Fell in the shower."

She gave me a doubtful look, then obviously decided not to pursue it. Instead she smiled and nodded toward the parking lot. As we headed there together, she put her arm through mine.

"Roy Gibson told me about his investigation into Marty's personal life," she said carefully. "The gambling."

"Did you know about it?"

She nodded. "Though I think I was the only one Marty told."

"So the other day, when you said that Hobbs was weak..."

"It was unkind of me, and unfair. But, yes, that was... Well, I'm hardly someone to point out another person's flaws."

"We all have them, Indra."

We'd reached her car, a Honda hatchback, by then, so I held

the door while she got behind the wheel. Becky was in the passenger seat, eyes closed, nodding rhythmically to whatever was playing through her earbuds.

She didn't look up as I waved goodbye.

—

My Mustang was in a spot a few cars away from Indra's, and I'd just unlocked it when Dr. Max Sable came walking across the gravel lot toward me. Even with his pronounced limp, the older black man was moving at a good clip.

"Dr. Rinaldi!" He finally slowed, catching his breath.

"Please," I said. "Call me Dan. Or Danny."

"Thanks. Given the tragic events that have thrown us together, it *does* seem foolish to stand on ceremony."

Tilting his head, Sable peered with his shrewd eyes at the line of my jaw.

"Did you injure yourself? Looks like it smarts."

"Only when I talk. Or smile. Or breathe."

"I can prescribe something for the pain."

"No need. Hit myself opening an old cedar chest lid. I figure the pain is punishment for gross stupidity."

"Hah. You sound like my old man. He was a Southern Baptist preacher, and he used to say the Bible should've made stupidity a sin."

"Minus the piety, he sounds like *my* old man. By the way, anything new on Hobbs' death?"

"No. And while I agree with Roy that Martin was murdered, I wonder whether this whole gambling angle will pan out."

I smiled. "Not too many secrets here in Lockhart, eh?"

"Not many, no." A rueful sigh. "It's both the blessing and the curse of a small town. We're neighborly enough to know when someone needs our help and nosy enough so that keeping a secret to yourself is impossible."

"Are you also talking about Dr. Bishara?"

"Yeah, everyone knows her story. What happened when she divorced Billy. How he attacked her and scarred Becky."

"I'm surprised the town had much sympathy for her. Given how her family was treated when they moved here."

"Some folks felt bad for her, some didn't. Still the case, I guess."

I watched a shadow cross his eyes. A stirring of memory.

"How about you, Dr. Sable? Have you lived here long?"

He nodded. "Since I was a kid. My own family...well, let's just say I can empathize with what Indra and her folks went through. So-called Christian towns like Lockhart aren't exactly known for their racial tolerance. Or acceptance."

Sable pulled at his lips. "Still, I guess I've been luckier than most. It doesn't hurt that as the only ME in town, I'm needed. Papers over a lot of issues, if you know what I mean."

"I'm afraid I do."

A brief, awkward silence settled over us.

"Anyway," he said at last, "I didn't stop you to talk about *my* problems. It's about Indra Bishara. I'm worried about her. That Billy's a bad one, and I hear he's back, making trouble for her again. So when I saw you talking with her, I thought—"

The purring of a car's engine made us both stop and turn. It was Roy Gibson, behind the wheel of a Lockhart Sheriff's Department cruiser. He slowed as he approached us, put the vehicle in park, and rolled down the driver's side window.

Leaning his head out, he gave a curt nod to Max Sable, then regarded me.

"Glad I caught you before you left, Doc. We have a lead on one of the bookies that Marty used. If we can get him to name his boss, the guy Marty owed money to, we may have our killer."

"That's great, Sheriff."

"Yeah, Roy," said Sable. "I hope you nail the bastard."

"Me, too, Max. I feel like I owe it to Marty. And I'm getting closer. I can feel that, too."

Then he gave a little start, apparently noticing my jaw for the first time. And offering a smile.

"Hey, what happened, Doc? You run into a door?"

# Chapter Twenty-Nine

An hour later, I was standing at the reception desk at Pittsburgh Memorial, showing the pleasant-faced woman on duty my hospital privileges card. A brief elevator ride later, I was walking down the hall in the ICU.

When I arrived at Jason Graham's room, I found he already had visitors. A middle-aged couple I assumed were the boy's parents sat together on the near side of the bed.

Holding hands. Faces drawn. Sharing not a word.

Their son, still in an induced coma, lay under a tangle of wires and tubes, the gleaming machines on either side of him humming softly. Feeding him, monitoring his vitals.

Jason's parents both looked up at the sound of my step at the door and I hurriedly introduced myself. Sort of.

"My name's Daniel Rinaldi. I'm a friend of Jason's and just wanted to stop by. See how he's doing."

The woman smiled weakly. "I'm Muriel Graham, and this is my husband, Fred. And you needn't worry, Doctor, we both know who you are."

She was a sturdy-looking woman of medium height, with a kind but no-nonsense face. She wore loose-fitting jeans and a thick sweater, her coat hanging from the back of her chair.

Her husband, Fred, though slimmer and taller, had a forceful handshake and a more distressed cast to his features, as though the pain over his son's condition had cemented on his face the tracks of permanent sorrow.

"Jason told Muriel and me that he was coming to see you, Dr. Rinaldi." He indicated a chair on the other side of Jason's bed. "For therapy."

"He also told us what a big help you were at that motel," Muriel added. "With his panic attack. We can't thank you enough for all you've done for him."

I waved my hand dismissively as I took my seat, only to get back up a moment later when a woman in hospital scrubs under a white coat came into the room.

Still standing as well, Fred Graham turned to introduce us, his face brightening somewhat. Mournful eyes enlivened.

"Dr. Rinaldi, this is Dr. Nora Suzuki, who did Jason's surgery. They say she saved his life."

Dr. Suzuki flushed, reddening her handsome features. She couldn't have been more than five feet, dark-haired and dark-eyed, yet her handshake was as firm as Fred Graham's had been.

"Pleasure to meet you, Doctor," she said.

I said something along those same lines as Fred once more took his wife's hand. She joined him in smiling at Suzuki.

"We owe her so much," Muriel said warmly, tearing up.

"Please, both of you." Dr. Suzuki flushed again. "You'll give me a swelled head. My husband says I already have one."

We all chuckled politely, then Mr. and Mrs. Graham retook their seats. I remained standing while Dr. Suzuki quickly but thoroughly examined her patient and checked the various machines arrayed around him.

When she'd straightened again, I nodded to his unconscious form under the hospital sheets.

"How long will he stay in the coma, Dr. Suzuki?"

"We're confident we can bring him out of it soon."

Fred looked up. "And after he wakes up, he'll be okay...?"

She nodded. "We think he'll be fine. He'll need some outpatient care, and plenty of rest, but..."

Muriel spoke up, having taken a tissue from her purse to dab at her eyes. "Don't worry, Doctor. We'll see he gets it."

After Dr. Suzuki left, I sat quietly with the Grahams for another minute or so. Having remembered what Gloria had said the night before, I had a question for the couple.

"I assume you've talked to the authorities," I said.

"Oh, yes," Fred answered. "Both times. I've met cops before, but it was the first time I talked to an FBI agent."

"Yes, they're both working the case, as you know. Did they ask permission to take Jason's laptop? Or to check his cell phone history?"

"The FBI guy did. Named Bowman, I think."

"That would be him. And you were okay with it?"

"Of course." It was Muriel who answered then. "Why wouldn't we be? Jason's a good boy. He has nothing to hide."

"I'm sure he doesn't, Mrs. Graham. The Task Force just wants to see if there's anything connecting him with the sniper's other victims."

Fred Graham shook his head. "Well, if there is, I can't imagine what it could be."

The three of us lapsed into another silence. Watching the couple turn once more to look longingly at their son, I thought about their response to my questions and noted there was no mention of retaining a lawyer.

After what I felt was a reasonable interval, I rose and said my goodbyes.

"Thanks for coming." Fred stayed seated, reaching to shake my hand again. "We'll be sure to tell Jason when he wakes up."

—

I was just pulling out of the hospital parking lot when Sam Weiss called.

"You have dinner yet, Danny?"

"A bit early, isn't it?" I checked my watch, as well as the sun still floating stubbornly above the horizon. Hazy shards of autumn light streamed between the clean lines of the Point's towering buildings.

"Whatever. Listen, since I can't report on the Shelton murder, my editor is letting me do a 'think piece' on the sniper case as a whole. A long feature article covering everything from the investigation itself to the families of the victims. Even a look at how the media covered it, and why."

"Sounds fascinating."

"Try not to get too excited, okay? Anyway, I thought you and I could sit down and brainstorm a bit. It'd be a big help getting your perspective on all aspects of the case, as both a trauma expert and a consultant to the cops."

"Yeah, but there's one little problem. I just got booted from that job."

"Who cares? I'll just describe you as an anonymous source. An expert familiar with the case. No attribution, no quotes. Anyone with half a brain will be able to figure out it's you, but let them prove it…"

"I don't know, Sam. I'll have to think about it."

"Well, while you're reflecting, snowflake, I'll be doing a goddamn colonoscopy on each of the sniper's victims. The down-and-dirty insides of their personal lives. Ever since Randy Porter was captured, it feels like the cops—and the Feds—have kinda dropped the ball on that."

"Actually, you're wrong. I happen to know that one special

agent has been tasked with doing exactly that. Gloria Reese. She's taking a more thorough, in-depth look into the lives of the victims, to try to ferret out any connection between them. If their lawyers will let her, that is."

Sam whistled, a shrill metallic sound over the cell.

"No shit? Lawyers, eh? Pushback from those near and dear? Love it. Gives me a nice, snarky take on the grieving family members. Now I've got an angle. Thanks, man."

"I'm happy you're happy, Sam. Now if you don't mind, I have a few calls to make myself."

"Okay, Doc. I'll get back in touch about scheduling a get-together. And no worries. First round's on me."

After we hung up, I checked my office voicemail. Luckily, no patient messages. I was still feeling the effects of a long, brutal week, and the thought of a Saturday night by myself sounded pretty good.

Besides, Gloria had begged off on our seeing each other, since she felt the Bureau's patience with her background work on the sniper's victims would be short. Especially since, as Hank Bowman had pointed out, there were other urgent cases to work.

Ironically, talking about dinner with Sam had made me hungry, so I stopped in at Primanti Bros. The famed restaurant's dining area was already packed, even at this early hour, but I found a spot at the counter and ordered a steak sandwich and a beer. Absently checking the news on my cell, I made short work of my meal and asked for the check.

That's when it occurred to me that I'd never finished my conversation with Max Sable. The coroner had seemed eager to discuss Indra Bishara's new troubles with her ex-husband, but we'd been interrupted when the sheriff drove up.

Sable had given me his business card after Gibson had

departed, and now, checking it, I saw that he'd included his personal cell. I punched in the numbers.

"Danny? I wasn't expecting to hear from you."

"I'm sorry if I'm interrupting dinner."

"Not at all. Roast's still simmering in the pot."

"Good. Look, when we were talking after the funeral, you seemed like you wanted to say something about Dr. Bishara."

"Oh. Well, it wasn't anything too specific. It's just that I've noticed how she is around you. I can tell she trusts you."

"I hope she does, yes."

"Like we were saying, her family's had its issues with the town. And now, with this new thing with Billy Reynolds, I figure Indra needs all the friends she can get."

"Especially since he's hired some high-priced law firm to get full custody of Becky."

"Yeah, but the truth is, that's not what I'm worried about. I mean, everybody knows how violent that bastard can get."

*Including me,* I thought.

"In fact, years ago, after Billy broke into their house and tried to hurt her, I urged Indra to get a gun. I have one myself, and I—"

"Did she do it? Did she get one?"

I heard his baritone chuckle over the phone.

"It was classic. It took me forever to convince her, but she finally buys one. Then I suggest she practice a little at a gun range. Just to get a feel for the weapon. Next thing you know, she's at the damned range every weekend."

I felt my throat tighten.

"Does she still go there?"

"Sure, started right up again when she came back to town. I tagged along one time, to do some shooting with her. You know, just some friendly competition. I'm not ashamed to tell you, man, it was a lesson in humility. Indra's a crack shot."

# Chapter Thirty

I found her sitting on the red-bricked patio behind her house, smoking a filtered Gold Flake. Long and slender, the cigarette sent a wispy spiral of smoke up against the cold black immensity of night. An unremitting darkness that the feeble yellow light near the back door did little to dispel.

However, attached to the wall near where Indra sat, what it did manage to illuminate was the deep sorrow etched in her face.

"Becky told me you were out here." I took a chair opposite, a small glass table between us.

She acknowledged me with a brief, sad smile.

"Yes. I needed some space. Sheriff Gibson called an hour ago to say that they'd brought in some low-level crook who could know something about Marty's death."

I nodded. "He hopes this guy turns on his boss, the one who might've arranged Martin's murder. Sounds like a real lead."

"Maybe. But all it did was remind me how much I miss Marty. He was more than just a colleague. He was one of my few friends at Teasdale. I mean, real friends."

She tapped ash from the cigarette into a ceramic dish on the table.

"I didn't know you smoked," I said.

"I don't," she replied dryly.

Indra Bishara lived in one side of a modest duplex not five miles from Teasdale College. When I'd knocked on the front door, it was her daughter, Rebecca, who answered, and who sullenly directed me to go around to the rear of the house. After which she'd shut the door before I could say thanks.

"Or at least," Indra continued, after inhaling a deep drag, "I don't do it in the house. Becky hates it."

I took a long, deliberate pause.

"Well, on the plus side, once she's living full-time with Billy, you can smoke inside as much as you want."

She started, cigarette halfway to her lips. Eyes darkening.

"Christ, Danny, that was a shitty thing to say."

"I know. I get cranky around people who shoot at me in dark alleys."

Her jaw tightened. Then, with a forced, unhurried calm, she slowly stubbed out her cigarette in the dish.

When she turned her head to look at me again, her eyes had lost their momentary fierceness. In its place was resignation.

"How did you know?" she said quietly.

"I didn't. Not for sure. Until just now."

"Did you tell the police?"

"If I had, they would've been here already."

"Why didn't you?"

My face was now as hard, as unyielding, as my voice.

"I have no fucking idea."

She uttered a small, choked moan, then buried her face in her hands. With an unaccustomed disinterest, I watched her slender shoulders quiver.

"Do you hate me?" she said, between teary gasps.

"Again, no fucking idea. I'm still—as we therapists like to say—processing it."

Catching her breath, she roughly brushed the tears from her cheeks. Straightened. Then she looked away, out at the darkness blanketing the unseen patch of yard beyond.

"I have no excuse, Danny. I just thought... Hell, I don't know what I was thinking."

"Bullshit. Yes, you do."

A somber nod. "Yes. I do. I wanted you to assume it was Billy who shot at you, trying to warn you away from me. I guess I wanted to ensure that you'd help me."

"By hoping I'd think it was Billy? Which, I have to admit, was exactly what I *did* think. For a while."

"Yes. I figured if you did, and when you realized how dangerous he was, you'd be more on my side."

"And so more likely, if Becky *did* seek treatment with me, to try to sway her against leaving you. And going with him."

Another nod. "I read a lot about you before we met, Danny. Then, after poor Lucas was killed, I saw how you were with Marty. And later heard what you'd done for Jason Graham."

Now her gaze leveled itself at me again.

"You're a rescuer, Doctor. You can't help it. So I thought if you were worried about the lengths Billy could go to—"

"That I'd try to influence Becky's decision. Despite what I might feel about it ethically." I paused. "Well, now at least I know why the shooter didn't come out from behind the dumpster and kill me."

Indra stirred uncomfortably in her seat.

"Listen, Danny. Please. You *have* to understand. I know what I did was crazy. Maybe unforgivable. Yet you said yourself at the café that you could tell how desperate I was. And God knows I was. But I never intended to harm you. Never."

"I don't give a damn what you intended, I—"

"But it's true!" Her voice plaintive, beseeching. "I'd waited in that alley long enough before you arrived for my eyes to grow accustomed to the dark. Then, when you took cover behind the front of your car, I could see the glint of its grille in the ambient light from the street. A perfect target. Easy to hit. But to scare you, that's all."

"And, as I learned earlier, you're a crack shot."

"I qualify as expert." Offering me the smallest trace of a smile. "Believe me, you were never in any real danger."

"Yeah? It sure as hell *felt* like I was..."

A heavy silence. Then, tentatively, Indra reached across and put her hand on my forearm. I brusquely removed it.

"No." My tone hardening still. "No more playing on my empathy. My concern for you and Becky. This stops now."

She blanched, as though slapped. "What...what does that mean?"

"It means I'm so goddamn angry that I—"

At that moment, I didn't exactly know what I meant. All I knew was that I wanted to get the hell away from her. Away from her conflicting stories, apologies, excuses.

Feeling a searing rage building in my chest, I quickly got to my feet and stared down at her stricken face. I wanted to express my outrage, my stunned, wounded resentment.

But no words came. Instead, I merely turned and walked out of that dim circle of yellow light.

—

Driving up to Mt. Washington, it struck me that Indra Bishara and Billy Three had at least one thing in common.

They'd each attacked me, and yet neither assault would be reported to the police. Not if I wanted to avoid any further exposure to the media's voracious glare. Thankfully, I'd barely been mentioned in the most recent news updates about the sniper case, and I wanted to keep it that way.

Moreover, despite Indra's unconscionable act, making it known to the authorities would give her ex-husband powerful, damning evidence in the upcoming custody battle. And even now, that was something I was unwilling to do.

Why? I didn't really know. Maybe, after all she'd done, how she'd played me, I still felt sorry for her. Or maybe I was just being a fool. If so, it wouldn't be the first time.

It was nearing eleven when I made it home. Unmindful of the cold, I went out to my rear deck, beer in hand, and dully watched the lights from downtown reflected on the river below.

My guts still roiling from my encounter with Indra, my mind a jumble of conflicting thoughts, the hoped-for peace and solace of a night alone had long since fled. Now I found myself wishing that Gloria were here with me. I hungered for her company, for the balm of her playful insolence, the breeziness of her knowing, flirty comments.

Yet, if she *had* decided to be with me tonight, and perhaps registered the distress on my face, I wouldn't have been able to disclose what Indra had done. As a duly sworn federal agent, Gloria would then be obligated to report the shooting in the alley. Bringing down on Indra's head exactly the kind of trouble I was determined to spare her.

I finished my beer and went back inside. After taking a quick, hot shower, I collapsed on my bed. After such a long, difficult day, I needed to let myself unwind. To give my turbulent, unsettled mind the rest of the night off.

Sleep came soon afterward, though it wasn't to last. Sometime after one a.m., the cell on my bedside table rang.

It was Gloria Reese. Her voice was raw, agitated.

"Oh, Danny..."

"Jesus, what is it? What's happened?"

"It's Hank Bowman… They—they just found him. Danny, he's dead. He's been murdered."

# Chapter Thirty-One

It took me less than an hour to rouse myself, dress, and drive downtown to join Gloria in her temporary office in the FBI building.

When I first entered, the whole place seemed to be lit from within, aflame with outrage and incomprehension. Agents having been pulled from their beds all over town, they were being directed to specific detail offices, to various communications and tactical operations rooms. Meetings were hastily convened to collate any new information coming in. To try to separate rumor from fact, conjecture from data.

Hank Bowman, chief of the regional office, one of their own, had been murdered.

Naturally, I'd been grabbed the moment I came in the door. Even though vouched for by Gloria herself, I was frisked for weapons and questioned for twenty minutes by some junior agent. Finally, in frustration, she'd pulled rank on the poor guy and literally dragged me away.

Now, closing us inside her Spartan office, she turned and gave me a fierce, unaffected hug. I returned her embrace.

"Jesus, Danny, I can't believe it. We were just with Hank, and now..."

"I know. I'm stunned myself."

"I mean, it wasn't that I liked him, really...but I didn't *dis*like him, either. Even when he was a condescending ass. As bosses go, I could've done a helluva lot worse. And have..."

"You don't have to explain, Gloria. I get it."

We stood that way for a long moment, then she stepped back and took her seat behind the steel desk. Settling herself, she pushed her hair back, tying it behind her with a rubber band.

I could tell that the quick, practiced movements helped her compose herself and focus on the tasks ahead.

Then she gestured for me to wheel my own chair around and join her. I did.

"We have agents on the scene," she said, opening her laptop. "Working in conjunction with Pittsburgh PD and the State Police. Clemmons and Biegler are heading the investigation, of course. Putting their trip to Harrisburg on hold, at least for the time being."

"I'm not surprised. Hank Bowman was the top agent here."

"More than that. He was on the fast track to a high-level position at Quantico."

I paused. "Look, Gloria...I'm happy to be here for moral support and, as before, I don't want you to feel you have to tell me anything. Besides, this early in the investigation, I assume everything is on a need-to-know basis."

She gave me a frank look.

"It's more like an '*I* need you to know basis.' That's one of the reasons I called you. God knows, I'll take all the moral support I can get. But more than that, I trust your instincts. And this is no time to worry about protocol."

"Never been much for protocol myself. So, what can you tell me about what happened to Bowman?"

"He was found in his car, just before midnight, on the side of the highway. He'd been driving east on I-76."

I nodded. "Heading to Seven Springs. For his vacation. Was he in a rental?"

"No, it's his car. Registered to him, plus I've seen it before. Been in it myself. A Chevy sedan. Anyway, his car was in park, with the engine running. That's what caught the eye of a State Police trooper. He thought the driver might be in trouble. When he approached the driver's side window, he found it was open and Hank's body was still strapped in his seat belt. But at a strange angle. Leaning across, hand outstretched toward the passenger seat. Here, I'll show you."

She clicked a few buttons on the keyboard and a series of black-and-white crime scene photos were displayed. They all showed, though from different angles and perspectives, Hank Bowman's dead body. As Gloria had described, he was positioned reaching awkwardly to his right, the seat belt straining against his weight. Though none of the photos gave any indication of what he might have been trying to reach. The passenger seat, as well as the floor beneath it, were empty.

What was unmistakable, however, was the gaping, black-encrusted wound on the back of his neck. Congealed rivulets of blood spidered down the back of his white shirt. I didn't need a cop's badge to know that Bowman had been killed at close range, execution-style.

I turned away from the horrific image.

"Any idea what he was reaching for? If, in fact, that's what he was doing?"

Gloria shook her head. "We don't know. May never know."

"How about the glove compartment? Maybe going for his gun?"

"I doubt it. Most agents don't keep a weapon there. Too easy for a perp—or any passenger, for that matter—to get it."

She nodded at her laptop screen. "We also have video."

Gloria clicked a few more buttons on the keyboard.

"This video was taken by one of our agents at the scene. It's been shared with everyone on the Task Force, and it's being used in conjunction with the body cam footage recorded by the State Police trooper who found Hank."

"But it hasn't been released to the media?"

"No, we're trying to keep it under wraps. But who knows how long till it leaks? Here's what our agent shot, after the report of Hank's death was called in. Maybe a half hour later."

The video that appeared on screen showed a wide-angled view of the entire scene. Bowman's car on the side of the highway, his body still strapped inside. As the camera swiveled, I could see a State Police cruiser, two Pittsburgh PD units, and a number of unmarked cars. Orange cones had already been arrayed around the area, closing off the right lane.

The view shifted, and I could make out Tony Clemmons and Stu Biegler, conferring with a young man I took to be the trooper who'd discovered Bowman's body. I also saw a plainclothes woman I recognized as Detective Bennett, who'd taken statements from Sam Weiss and me after we found Dave Shelton.

From the way Bennett commandeered the scene, I assumed she was going to be the primary on the case. I was surprised to see Jerry Banks standing by her side. With Polk riding a desk downtown, it appeared that Banks had been assigned to partner with Bennett for the time being.

Abruptly, the video cut ahead to show the arrival of the CSU team and the ME's van, out of which stepped another familiar face. Dr. Max Sable. Given where Bowman's car was found, it was just inside the doctor's jurisdiction.

As Sable approached Bowman's car, Gloria spoke over the video image.

"From a preliminary examination at the scene, the ME says

Hank had been dead for at least two hours before his body was found. Death was instantaneous, from a single bullet to the back of the head."

"Did Sable ID the bullet?"

"Yes, but not till later, after this video was shot. Once Hank was on the table at the coroner's lab, the bullet was removed and transferred to ballistics. A .45 caliber, from a revolver. No shells found at the scene."

Gloria tapped another key and another video appeared.

"This is from the trooper's body cam."

Starting from within the trooper's point of view behind the wheel of his cruiser, the video recorded his movements opening his door, turning on his flashlight, and slowly approaching the Chevy. We're with him as he comes up to the driver's side door, its window open, the body slumped to the right. Almost bisected by the straining seat belt.

We see the trooper tap on the exterior door frame.

"Sir," says the trooper. "Are you okay? Have you been drinking?"

Then the trooper brings his flashlight up, illuminating the back of the man's head. And the horrible wound.

"Holy Jesus!" The trooper backsteps, almost stumbling on the gravel lining the highway. Then, regaining his balance, he peers once more into the car. Using a handkerchief, he slowly removes a wallet from the dead man's back pocket.

"Holy Jesus," he says again as he registers the victim's Bureau ID. Reaching for his shoulder mic, he starts calling Dispatch, voice quavering.

Gloria shut off the video and swung her chair around to face me.

"After the officer calls it in, he waits by the car for backup. Having relayed Hank's FBI creds to his superiors, the guy's smart enough to know this murder is way above his pay grade. In half an hour, the scene is swarming with agents, cops, and detectives, with Clemmons and Biegler arriving a few minutes later."

"So what happens now?" I asked.

"It'll be another joint investigation, the Bureau and Pittsburgh PD sharing forensics, manpower, and suspect leads."

"Any of the latter on the radar?"

"Not that I've heard. Clemmons, Biegler, and Chief Logan have convened a Task Force meeting here at six a.m." She glanced at her watch. "About three hours from now."

Neither of us spoke for another minute.

"You know," I said finally, "I've been thinking about something Hank said at dinner last night. Maybe it's nothing, but..."

She rubbed her weary eyes.

"I have a feeling we're both thinking the same thing. About Hank's belief that the Handler's string of murders had come to an end. That with the death of Porter and Hubert Sedarki, the Handler had finished tying up loose ends."

"But what if he hadn't? What if Hank himself had been on the Handler's list of victims? Maybe even the last one."

"But why would he be?"

"Why would all the *others* be on the list? Based on the second assault on Jason Graham, we've theorized that the sniper's victims had been connected in some way. If that's true, then Hank Bowman might share in that connection."

She shook her head. "But that's only *if*—and it's a *big* if—Hank's killer was the Handler. Or someone working for him. And we have no proof of that."

"Still...it's worth looking into."

"How?"

"Have you made any progress digging deeper into the sniper victims' personal lives?"

Gloria allowed herself a mirthless laugh. "Hardly at all. I'm doing as much as I can online, checking bank records, phone calls, etcetera. But without access to their personal computers, their home or work laptops…"

"The victims' families are still using legal firewalls to prevent that?"

"Oh, yeah. We've been barraged by shielding briefs from some of the biggest law firms in the state. Our legal team hasn't even finished examining all of them."

She leaned up from her chair and stretched.

"Besides, this idea that Hank's murder is connected to those sniper hits… I don't know, Danny. Remember, we're only guessing that the earlier victims had something in common. We haven't proved *that,* either."

"Well, I'm convinced it's true. Porter's second attempt on Jason Graham's life confirms it. Besides, Porter himself expressed regret to Dave Shelton for Lucas Hartley's death. He acknowledged that he'd killed the wrong person. Which proves, as far as I'm concerned, that the murders he carried out were *not* done at random. That his targets had been selected and the info about them provided to him beforehand by his handler."

Then another thought struck me.

"And what about that councilman, Gary Landrew? Remember, he'd told Leland Sinclair that he'd be late for the City Council meeting because a complaining constituent had kept him on the phone. What if this so-called constituent was the Handler?"

"What are you saying?"

"Look, the Handler keeps Landrew on the phone long enough so that the councilman has to rush to the meeting. Everybody in that room saw Landrew running, coat flapping, carrying his briefcase, toward the building. An obvious, easily spotted target for Porter, who's positioned across the street on the roof of that insurance building."

"If you're right, Danny, then Landrew was specifically targeted, too."

"Just as all the sniper's victims were."

I wheeled in my seat around to the other side of the desk and got to my feet.

"That still doesn't tell us what the connection among all these people is," Gloria said, frowning. "Including—though I think you're wrong—Hank Bowman. Goddamn lawyers. If only we could get a look at even *one* of the victims' computers..."

"We can," I said, smiling. "Jason Graham's parents never said anything about a lawyer..."

—

Nor, as we soon discovered, had Harriet Parr's family. We found both Mrs. Parr's laptop and that of Jason Graham in the evidence lockup, downstairs in the FBI building. Gloria quickly signed them out and we hurried back up to her office.

For the next two hours, while I watched—and sometimes paced—Gloria was hunched over Jason's laptop, using whatever personal information the Bureau already had on the college student to try to determine possible passcodes. She succeeded often enough to delve pretty deeply into the various realms of Jason's life, both personal and academic. Sports teams. Classwork. Music. Social media. A modest amount of porn.

"Nothing so far." She pushed back from the keyboard, stifling another yawn. She'd been doing that for quite some time. "Nothing out of the ordinary for a kid like Jason. And nothing I can see that ties him in with the other victims."

I'd left her side only once, moments before, to bring us each large Styrofoam cups of black coffee from the lobby vending machine. Handing one over, I took my seat across from her.

"Don't you think you should give it a rest, Gloria? You've been up forever."

She took a sizeable gulp of coffee. "I know, but the Task Force meeting is in less than an hour. If I put my head down now, I'll sleep right through it."

I reached across the desk and took hold of her free hand.

"Okay, but why don't you just wrap up with Jason's laptop and do Harriet Parr's later today? Or tonight."

Gloria managed a wry smile. "Are my eyes glazing over that much?"

"No, but mine are. It's tough hanging around, doing nothing, while you're working your ass off. It's taking a real toll on me."

Her smile widened, and, shoving the laptop aside, she leaned over the desk and kissed me. Soft, sweet, and long.

"When this is all over," she said quietly, "it'll be nice to get back to some *non*-crisis sex."

"Couldn't agree more." I got to my feet. "Now, do yourself a favor and set your watch alarm for one hour. This way you can grab a few winks and still make the meeting."

"You know, you can be downright bossy, Doctor."

"I'll add it to the list of my faults. It grows daily."

We kissed again, briefly this time, and then I headed for the door.

As I was driving across town for home, I wondered if the victims' laptops-—even if the Bureau's lawyers could negotiate access to the rest of them—would actually tell us anything. Reveal some kind of connection among the sniper's victims.

What I didn't know then was that, within twenty-four hours, the connection would in fact become very clear.

And very disturbing.

# Chapter Thirty-Two

Operating on as little sleep as Gloria, I, too, still had to go to work. I'd gotten home as the sun was rising, giving me just enough time to shower, change, and fill my travel thermos with strong, black coffee.

Fighting Monday morning traffic, I made my way to Oakland, pulled into my building's parking garage, and headed up to my office on the fifth floor, where a day full of therapy patients lay ahead of me.

On the drive to work, I'd heard the first vague reports on the radio about the suspicious death of a prominent FBI agent. The announcer explained that, until notification of the victim's next of kin, no further details would be forthcoming.

It was the first time since Gloria's call the night before that I remembered the wedding band I'd seen on Bowman's finger. As well as his dismissive mention of his wife when talking about his upcoming vacation. I also found myself wondering idly if the man had any children.

After my morning sessions, I watched the local TV news on my cell, but the report—while the leading story—offered no more information than that released before. For any number of reasons that were easy to guess, both the FBI and Pittsburgh Police were deliberately staying tight-lipped about the case.

Reported with much more detail were the funerals of three of the Steel City Sniper's victims. Footage showed Laura Steinman, Peter's widow, leaving a service accompanied by a host of family members, including her sister, Mary Anne North. As when she'd spoken to the press after her brother-in-law's murder, the woman's face revealed her disdain for the cameras intruding on the family's private sorrow.

The second story featured a similar, but smaller, gathering of friends and family, paying their last respects to Harriet Parr. As the mourners separated outside the church, I caught sight of Mrs. Parr's daughter, the Carnegie-Mellon grad student. Visibly shaking, she had to be helped to her car.

The last report actually showed footage of Dr. Francis Mapes' graveside service, attended as it was—in addition to his wife and children—by many prominent locals. Politicians, CEOs, and some well-known sports figures, as well as a representative from the UPMC hospital system were among the mourners. I recalled Gloria's description of Mapes as wealthy and well-connected, and saw now that she hadn't been exaggerating.

The news program ended with the announcer reminding listeners that the funeral of City Councilman Gary Landrew was scheduled for Friday, and that the ceremony would be carried live and online. The mayor himself was expected to speak.

That was about as much news as I could take, so I clicked it off. Sometimes I regretted the unceasing access to the world's troubles that today's cell phones granted...

I'd brown-bagged my lunch, so I unwrapped the capicola on rustic bread I'd made that morning and forced myself to take a few bites. Though my stomach had been growling all through my previous patient's session, now that my lunch hour was here, I barely had an appetite. Watching three murder victims laid to rest can do that to you.

I saw the remainder of the day's scheduled patients and began closing up shop. Yet I was still not used to the night falling so quickly and early. It was barely past five o'clock and Forbes Avenue below my window was blanketed by a frigid darkness broken only by a few streetlamps, the diffuse glow of restaurant windows, and the headlights of passing cars.

As I locked the outer door of my suite, I was aware before even seeing him of the presence of a powerfully built man. He stood a few feet away from me in the hall, the paunch that pushed against his jacket buttons doing nothing to dilute the intimidating impact of his broad chest and wide shoulders. His florid face was equally broad, with unfriendly eyes and a smile as insincere as an insurance salesman's.

It was obvious he was not here to sell me insurance.

"Evenin', Doc. Ya mind comin' with me?"

His voice was flat, atonal. As though he could have been from Anywhere, USA.

"Why should I do that?" I stepped away from my office door, facing him with what I hoped looked like self-assurance.

"There're some people who want to meet with ya," he said matter-of-factly. As if that were sufficient answer.

"Are you a cop?" I asked.

"Used to be. Then I got smart. You comin' or what?"

"Give me one reason I should."

With a weary, resigned sigh, he unbuttoned his coat jacket to reveal the automatic pistol in its holster at his side.

That put a damper on whatever bravado I'd managed so far. I spread my hands in surrender. The insurance salesman smile widened, then the guy rebuttoned his ill-fitting jacket and motioned for me to go ahead of him. Down the hall and toward the elevator.

I did.

—

The discreet brass plaque outside the polished double doors read Bruschi, Goldstein and Rhodes. I'd been driven by my dour, corpulent escort—whose name, in answer to my query, was Barton Kerns—to a new steel and glass tower at the Point, whose entire top floor was occupied by the prestigious law firm.

Without knocking, the big man opened the door and led me through a beautifully appointed, though empty, reception area, into a large, equally impressive office. Designer furniture surrounded a huge cherrywood desk. Soft unobtrusive lighting, Hockney prints on the walls.

No sounds came from what I assumed were other rooms in the suite, which suggested they were as empty as reception had been.

I glanced at my watch. Five-forty. Seemed as though even the secretaries and paralegals kept banker's hours.

I was still contemplating this when Kerns pointed at one of a pair of leather chairs facing the desk.

"Sit," he said.

I sat.

He backed away, shoes clicking on the polished hardwood, to lean against a massive bookcase whose shelves were lined with thick legal volumes.

Moments later, two men entered from an adjoining room, both wearing tailored, designer label suits. The older of the two, by at least thirty years, boasted obsessively combed white hair; dark brown, sharply intelligent eyes; and a prominent nose.

The other man was William Reynolds III. Billy Three.

I wasn't halfway out of my chair before I felt Kerns' catcher's-mitt-sized hand on my shoulder. He didn't exert much pressure. He didn't need to.

Meanwhile, the older man had taken a seat behind the desk. Billy Three slumped in the other leather chair facing it, not more than a foot separating the two of us. Offering me a lazy smile. I suspected that the expensive name-brand suit was meant to either intimidate me or legitimize him. If so, neither goal was accomplished.

The older man leaned forward now, hands palms-down on the desk blotter in front of him. Other than a few neatly stacked files and a framed portrait of what I presumed were his wife and children, the desktop was startlingly empty.

"Good evening, Dr. Rinaldi. My name is Arthur Bruschi. I'm a senior partner here in the firm."

Bruschi then nodded at the younger man.

"And this is William Reynolds, Doctor. My client."

Billy extended his hand. "Nice to meet ya, Doc. How ya doin'?"

I stared at his outstretched hand, then up at him.

"Not bad. Now that I can chew solid food again."

Billy laughed, and clapped his hands appreciatively as he sat back in his chair. Arthur Bruschi's brow tightened. He was obviously unaware of his client's former encounter with me. Though within seconds his features returned to their former, placid self-possession.

"Hey," Billy said abruptly, looking from one of us to the other. "Bruschi and Rinaldi. You guys are *paisans,* right? Fellow Eye-talians. Oughtta make this easier."

The older man gave Billy a brief, dismissive glance. It was obvious he didn't much care for his client. Which made me start liking him better already.

"Make what easier?" I asked.

"Come now, Doctor. It shouldn't be too hard to guess why I asked Mr. Kerns to escort you here."

Unnoticed by me, the big man had relinquished his grip on my shoulder and returned to his place at the bookcase.

"Mr. Kerns is a private investigator employed by the firm," Bruschi continued. "At present, he's doing surveillance on the home of Mr. Reynolds' ex-wife, Indra Bishara."

"Yeah," Billy piped up excitedly. "He's been watchin' her place night and day for a week now."

"As you no doubt know, Doctor," Bruschi continued, as though his client hadn't spoken, "Mr. Reynolds is seeking full legal and physical custody of their daughter, Rebecca. And as you've also been made aware, the girl is anxious to be reunited with her father."

"If you say so."

The lawyer shook his head gravely. "Please, Dr. Rinaldi. We know you've developed a relationship with Ms. Bishara, and that she's explained the situation. We also know she's managed to convince Rebecca to begin therapeutic treatment with you. And for the express purpose of dissuading Rebecca from choosing to be with her father."

"Not that I'd ever do that."

"Perhaps. I've been an attorney long enough to see how divorcing couples try to use therapists to twist the minds of their children in custody cases. Vulnerable young people come to rely on the therapist, to trust his or her judgment. Even, in extreme cases, to make choices solely in the belief that this would please the therapist. Anything to maintain the therapist's affection and support."

"You sound like you're making a summation to a jury."

"Perhaps I am, Doctor. To a jury of one. You, yourself. Who

I sincerely hope will see the wisdom in abiding by what Mr. Reynolds has asked me to convey."

"Which is?"

"Cease and desist any and all contact with either Ms. Bishara or her daughter. As of now."

"'Any and all contact' covers a lot of ground."

Bruschi shrugged. "As it's meant to, Doctor. And I suggest you accede to Mr. Reynolds' wishes."

"Or else?"

"Or else some facts—and video images—may come to light that could threaten your license to practice. Thanks to Mr. Kerns' diligence, we have evidence of malpractice, primarily a disturbing personal relationship with the mother of your new patient."

Billy Three couldn't contain himself, stirring exuberantly in his chair.

"Yeah, Kerns has footage of you going in and out of Indra's house last night. Doesn't take a private eye to figure you two are hookin' up. Doin' the nasty. Plus, I told him to check out the funeral of that Hobbs guy, since I knew how close he and Indra were. And guess what? Kerns got some sweet shots of you and my ex, walkin' arm in arm. Cozy as hell."

I turned to him. "Listen, Billy, I—"

Bruschi interrupted us both.

"Think about it, Doctor. Added to the recent suspension from the Pittsburgh PD, which the public is just becoming aware of, these new unsavory revelations will put both your professional and personal reputation in considerable jeopardy."

I returned his meaningful stare with one of my own.

"Believe me, Counselor, I've been there, done that."

"Even so," he replied calmly, "are you quite sure you want to take the risk? I've been assured by Mr. Kerns that if he looks hard enough, he can find even more damaging information about you. After all, even you have to admit that some of your past actions have been reckless, to say the least. Subject to many reprimands and warnings from the department."

"This present action seems pretty reckless, too," I said. "Abduction, intimidation, blackmail."

Bruschi permitted himself a smile.

"Hardly. The suite is empty. The only people on this entire floor are the four of us. None of whom, I assure you, will admit to this meeting having even taken place."

"I might find myself mentioning it. To the cops, for one thing. Or the press."

"Yet without substantiation, your accusation would be worthless. Perhaps even damaging to your position." Bruschi sighed. "Believe me, Dr. Rinaldi, the lines of communication between this firm and the police have been long established. We know your somewhat sketchy reputation with the department, and this recent suspension only reinforces it. Frankly, I doubt you'll find much support from that quarter."

Billy Three stood up from his chair to scowl down at me.

"Enough of this shit." He plucked impatiently at the knot in his tie. "So, Rinaldi, are ya gonna exit the scene—I mean, like disappear altogether—or do we have to trash your career? Fuck up your life forever?"

His lawyer raised a hand, as though a traffic cop trying to prevent a collision. His voice languid, almost soothing.

"Think of it this way, Dr. Rinaldi. Nothing is required of you. You just continue as before, treating patients, consulting with colleagues. All we insist upon is that you neither see nor have anything to do with, personally or professionally, Ms. Indra Bishara or her daughter. Ever again. Otherwise..."

Here the lawyer's eyes narrowed.

"Otherwise, Doctor, I'm afraid your life as you've known it is over."

# Chapter Thirty-Three

After declining Arthur Bruschi's offer to have Kerns drive me back to my office, I headed out of the room. But not before enduring a final, triumphant smirk from Billy Three.

In minutes, I found myself standing out on the curb of a busy street at the Point, the array of building lights glowing dully above. In the unquiet darkness, stung by bitter night air, I considered what had just happened.

It was blackmail, pure and simple, and with sufficient evidence to do real damage to my life and career. Especially now, in the wake of my suspension from Pittsburgh PD.

Of course, the irony was that, after learning of Indra's assault on me in that alley, I'd had no intention of involving myself further in her custody battle with her ex. However, now that I'd been threatened with severe consequences if I did so, my feelings on the matter had changed.

But why? I didn't understand it. After what she'd done, why was I still determined to help her in some way? Unless, of course, it had more to do with my animosity toward Billy Three.

Regardless, I didn't know exactly what it was I could do, anyway. Whatever help I might want to provide Indra or her daughter would have to fall outside the scope of my clinical license. Not as a result of what had just taken place in the lawyer's office, but rather because of my knowledge of Indra's assault on me in the alley. Given my obviously mixed feelings about that, as well as her need for me to be her personal advocate in changing Rebecca's mind, any unbiased therapeutic work with her daughter would be impossible.

Yet I bristled at the thought of Becky ending up with her father. Billy Three was a rich, entitled bully who I felt sure would try, over time, to turn his daughter against her mother.

Plus, I resented being threatened by the likes of him. Or, for that matter, by the smooth, patrician Arthur Bruschi.

*Paisans?* Hardly. Guys like Bruschi—to borrow a phrase a patient of mine once used—were "private plane rich." Which meant that they operated from a luxurious, privileged height totally independent of the rest of us, practiced at using their money, power, and position to get what they wanted.

I shoved my hands in my coat pockets and began aimlessly walking. I'd been subject to potential legal action before, including similar threats to my license. Not only the police but a fair number of my clinical colleagues had taken issue over the years with what they felt was my "maverick" approach with patients. Especially those who'd been victims of violent crimes, whose trauma continued to impose itself on their lives long after the events that had triggered it.

Yet, despite my suspension from Pittsburgh PD, I had to believe that I'd done more for them than if I'd acted otherwise.

Now, smiling grimly to myself, I realized I actually had no alternative to believing that. Otherwise, my whole mission as a therapist, as a survivor of crippling trauma myself, was meaningless.

—

Maybe an hour had passed. I was sitting at the bar of some downtown joint whose name I've forgotten, half-eaten roast beef sandwich in front of me, nursing my second beer. Trying to stoke the motivation to go outside again, grab a Lyft, and return to my office building to retrieve my car.

By the time I did, it was nearing nine p.m. I'd just pulled out of my parking garage and onto Forbes when my cell rang.

It was Gloria Reese. "Danny, are you free?"

"I guess you could say my day just ended."

"Like hell it has. Believe me, it's only beginning. Get over to my place. *Now!* And for Christ's sake, don't tell anyone where you're going."

—

Gloria's apartment was in a new building in Edgewood. Shrouded by spreading oaks and the uncompromising night, its features were practically indistinguishable from the similar structures on either side. The perfect, unassuming domestic arrangement for a local Bureau agent.

Her two-bedroom apartment was likewise. Sparsely furnished, it had only a few movie posters on the walls, a Pee-wee Herman doll on the sofa's end table, and a pair of wilting houseplants to give it individuality.

In answer to my knock, Gloria opened the door. She was barefoot, in jeans and a pullover sweater. She also looked beat.

I gave her a quick kiss. "Did you ever get any sleep?"

"I've had sleep. It's overrated."

Gloria led me across the modest living room to the smaller second bedroom, which she used as an office. As sparely furnished as the rest of her apartment, it held the requisite desk, chairs, filing cabinets, and wall-length corkboard. Plastered with photos and 3-by-5 cards, it looked exactly like you see on TV series about dedicated cops and lone-wolf CIA agents. We'd laughed about that the first time I'd seen the room.

Sitting at the desk, head bent over a laptop keyboard, was a slender young man, wearing jeans with suspenders, thick eyeglasses, and a black, unkempt beard. His equally slender fingers moved nimbly, with an almost obsessive rapidity, over the keys.

Gloria brought me over to stand next to him, after which she tapped him on the shoulder. Startled, he turned and peered up at me. Pale eyes blinking.

"Hermie, this is Dr. Daniel Rinaldi. The psychologist I told you about. Danny, meet Herman Gould."

"Hey." He offered me a languid, distracted hand.

Gloria turned to me. "I've known Hermie since he was a kid. Juvie hall for petty theft and dealing, then some serious time for hacking into corporate computer systems. Give him ten minutes and he'll have your credit card info, bank account passwords, and online dating history."

I smiled. "Nice skill set, Hermie."

"Thanks, man."

"Hermie's on parole," Gloria went on, "and really shouldn't be doing anything like what I'm asking him to do."

"Which is...?" I said.

She pointed at the laptop in front of the young man.

"That's Jason Graham's laptop, and since I got as far as I knew how, I called Hermie. He owes me for past favors. Isn't that right, Hermie?"

He raised his open, simple face. Maybe in his late twenties, he seemed as unschooled and callow as a boy. Someone you'd want to put a paternal arm around. And someone you'd never assumed had lived a life of crime, no matter how nonviolent.

"That's right, Glo. You ready to go?"

"Yes. Now that Dr. Rinaldi's here."

"Where are we going?" I said.

Hermie blinked at me again through his glasses. "Down the rabbit hole, Doc."

Then he swiveled in his seat and began striking the keys again. As furiously as before.

In answer to my puzzled look, Gloria smiled. "The Dark Web, Danny. That's where we're going. Hermie is some kind of tech genius—"

"Self-taught," Hermie added, without looking up.

"Apparently," Gloria agreed. "And according to him, the Dark Web is where it's all happening. That is, all the stuff that *shouldn't* be happening."

"That's right." Hermie nodded as he typed. "Heavy-duty porn. S&M. Snuff films. Pedophile chat rooms. Terrorist sites. Bomb-making instructions. Nazi stuff. Satanic shit."

He paused, his fingers trembling over the keyboard. Gave me a sidelong glance.

"You know the internet you use? For emails, social media, research? All the usual boring crap? Well, that's just the tip of the online iceberg. A lot of what goes on in cyberspace is on the Dark Web."

He resumed typing, and I peered over his shoulder.

"What are we looking for in Jason's laptop?" I asked.

"Whatever I couldn't find." Gloria bent to look at the screen over Hermie's other shoulder. "And that he probably wouldn't want us to see. Hell, the truth is, we could end up with nothing. Or we might find something that explains the connection between all the sniper's victims."

Two minutes later, Hermie sat back from the keyboard and indicated the screen.

"Ladies and gentlemen, we may have a winner."

Gloria and I leaned in for a closer look. On the screen was a brightly lit website page, its borders encircled with American flags. In the center was the familiar, profiled image of the bald eagle. In its talons, instead of branches, were hyperlinks.

There was a banner across the top of the page. It read:

THE DE GOBINEAU SOCIETY

"Never heard of it," Gloria said, glancing at me. I shook my head.

Meanwhile, Hermie was pointing with an excited forefinger. "See those links? Labeled 'Mission Statement,' 'Protocols,' 'Contacts,' and the rest? I clicked through on a couple and was sent to various portals whose data was encrypted."

Gloria said, "Could you decipher any of them?"

"Any of them? No. *All* of them? Fuck, yeah!"

He struck a number of keys and showed us the result.

"Here's one. Under 'Important Study Materials.' See, the site looks like it's some kind of educational institute, in case somebody almost as good as me hacked into it. But the so-called 'study materials' are encrypted *and* shielded by firewalls.

"Here's the beauty part: again, if somebody not as good as me tries to breach one of the firewalls, the whole site goes poof! Self-deletes. So only members of the society, given the right passcodes, can access these sections of the site."

"Got it," I said. "Now, what happens if someone as good as you *does* penetrate the site?"

"Then it's Christmas in November." Hermie folded his arms and nodded at the screen.

I looked closer and saw a list of what the society termed study materials.

Then felt my throat go dry. Heart clenching like a fist.

It was a series of book titles right out of a white supremacist's wish list.

"My God," Gloria said. "This is some kind of alt-right hate group. Look at this shit. *Mein Kampf. The Protocols of the Learned Elders of Zion. The Bell Curve. Might Is Right. Race, Evolution and Behavior. You Will Not Replace Us!* And this one. *Les Pleiades.* Jesus, in French."

"That's because de Gobineau was French," Hermie said. "You might wanna look him up. I just Googled the motherfucker."

I'd already taken out my cell phone to do just that.

"Joseph-Arthur de Gobineau was French, all right," I said, scanning an article I'd found. "And a count, to boot. He was also a big proponent of what was then called 'race science.' I'll be damned, look at this. He was the first to identify the 'Aryan' race as—I'm quoting here—'great, noble, and fruitful in the works of man on this earth.'"

Gloria scowled. "That's why they named the society after him. The patron saint of racist, anti-Semitic assholes."

Suddenly, Hermie raised his hand, like a bright student in a classroom trying to be teacher's pet.

"I just found something else." He squinted at the screen. "Check this out. If you successfully access the site, you're identified, acknowledged, and welcomed." He frowned. "Wait a minute, I thought this dude's name was Jason..."

"It is," said Gloria.

"But that's not who accessed this site. It's somebody named Fred Graham."

"What?"

I almost brushed Hermie off his seat as I stared at the name. Fredrick James Graham.

"You know what this means?" I said. "Jason's father is the member. Using his son's computer to access the portal."

Gloria straightened, rubbing her bloodshot eyes.

"Hold on, Danny. Let's say Fred Graham does belong to this hate group. How does this tie in with the sniper's attack on Jason?"

"I don't know."

"Exactly. Like we *also* don't know for sure that this site is a link among all the victims. Maybe it's just this guy Graham's dirty little secret. How do we know if any of the other victims are members of this thing?"

She bent again to look at the screen.

"Does it list any other member names, Hermie?"

"Nope. Just this guy. Maybe each member has his or her own passcode, so none of 'em know who the others are."

"If you're right," Gloria said, "it certainly reinforces site security. *And* maintains secrecy."

"One way to find out." I lifted a second laptop from its perch on the filing cabinet. It was labeled HARRIET PARR.

"Let's see if the well-respected bookkeeper, mother, and pet lover is a proud member of the de Gobineau Society."

She was.

---

As Hermie had guessed, it required a different set of codes to bypass the encryptions guarding access to the de Gobineau Society website on Harriet Parr's laptop.

One by one, he showed us the various portals displaying the group's mission statement, protocols, contacts, and study materials. This latter listed the same books we'd seen before.

"I guess whoever's running this thing wants everyone to be on the same page," said Gloria. "Literally."

I was absently glancing at the titles again when I was struck by something I hadn't noticed the first time.

"That book in French. *Les Pleiades.*"

"Yeah," Hermie said. "I checked that out, too. It's a novel this de Gobineau prick wrote."

Gloria searched my face. "What is it, Danny?"

I hesitated, but only for a moment.

"Gloria, do you have access to Hank Bowman's computer?"

"Hank's…? I'm sure Bureau forensics has it. It's evidence in his murder. Like his cell, laptop, any of his personal effects. Why?"

"Because I just remembered where I'd seen that French title before. It's one of the books on Bowman's bookshelf in his office at the Bureau building."

Her face, already pale and drawn from fatigue, seemed to lose even more color.

"Jesus, Danny, you're not saying…?"

"Yeah…" I let out a breath. "I think I am."

# Chapter Thirty-Four

When I left them at six a.m., Hermie was still trawling through Harriet Parr's history on the Dark Web and Gloria was on the phone, trying to track down Hank Bowman's laptop. She'd already told me that, given the importance of the FBI man's murder and the stultifying chain of command, it could take hours to get permission to requisition it. Even on a temporary basis.

I'd gone home, showered and changed, gnawed through a stale bagel, and was back on the road by seven thirty. The thermos propped up in the passenger seat was filled with strong coffee, and downtown commuter traffic crossing to Oakland was sluggish enough for me to gulp down healthy amounts at intersections.

I also had time to reflect on what Gloria and I had discovered about the connection between at least two of the sniper's victims.

Racism—supported and fomented by books like those listed on the website, whose pseudoscience failed to disguise their repugnant assumptions of white superiority. Even today, such racist beliefs remained a virulent national disease.

Even as I considered this painful reality, none of what we'd discovered about the de Gobineau Society shone any light on why Jason Graham and Harriet Parr had been targeted by the sniper. Nor did it help us understand why the remaining victims, should they also turn out to be members of the racist group, were killed as well.

I was still musing about this when my cell rang.

"Got a minute, Doc?" said Roy Gibson.

"Given the traffic, Sheriff, I have as long as you want."

"As promised, I'm keeping you in the loop about the Hobbs case. I know Marty's death hit you hard, finding him and all."

"Sure did. You still working with that bookie?"

"Yeah, he's still in the tank. He's lawyered up, of course, but is willing to do a deal in exchange for his sheet being cleared. Racketeering charges, bunco, the usual stuff."

"But he says he has info about Marty's killer?"

"He's being cagey, but he's hinting enough about it that I think the DA's gonna offer him the plea deal."

"I can tell you're not too happy about that."

I slowed at the upcoming intersection, clogged with traffic. Trucks idling noisily, car horns bleating.

"Happy? No, Doc, I'm not. But if it gives us a solid lead, I'll take it. I don't trust the guy, but he's all we got."

I thanked him for the update and we clicked off. By now, it was obvious that the traffic wasn't going to lessen any time soon, so I pulled out of the line and slipped onto a narrow, red-bricked side street.

My way took me between twin rows of weary, older buildings that blocked the dull morning sunlight. I vaguely remembered this street leading to an even narrower one, at the mouth of which I could make a left and connect with Fifth Avenue, and then angle over to Forbes.

I'd just turned into this second street when I saw, in my rearview mirror, a pair of headlights glowing in the shadowed space behind me. It was a sedan, whose make, model, and color were indistinguishable in the wintry morning dimness.

But what my rearview *did* reveal was that it was gathering speed, coming up fast behind me. The driver's face was obscured behind dark glasses and the lowered sun visor.

Given the narrowness of the brick-surfaced road, bracketed on either side by venerable, mid-last-century structures, I hesitated speeding up myself.

Then, suddenly, without warning—

The sedan closed the distance between us and rammed the back of my Mustang.

The hard jolt almost took the wind out of me, jostling me in my seat. My hands went white where they gripped the wheel.

I'd just craned my neck around to get a better look at the vehicle behind me when it slammed my rear bumper again. Harder.

Again, I felt the impact rattle my spine, and I struggled to maintain control of the car.

It was then, my eyes burning, peering ahead and squinting from the effort, that I saw it.

Another car. Parked at the side of the road up ahead. Not thirty yards away. Making the street too narrow to pass without sideswiping it. Or maybe wedging my Mustang in, braced against the wall opposite. Leaving me trapped.

I braked as quickly as I could, getting another jolt as the sedan behind me once more rammed into my bumper.

Then, when I slowed to a stop, so did it.

The street was deserted. A shadowed, empty tunnel.

I flung open my door and had stepped halfway out of the car when I saw the other driver climb out of his, coming quickly toward me, face red, glowering.

It was Barton Kerns, jacket unbuttoned, revealing both his considerable bulk and his empty side holster.

The gun that belonged there was in his hand.

I'd stood to my full height by the time he reached me, though I was still shaky from the multiple impacts. My back throbbed with pain. As I struggled to steady myself, he swung his gun up and clipped me under the chin.

I staggered back, then turned and grabbed the roof edge of my car to maintain my balance. Stunned, gasping.

With his free hand, he turned me back again, facing him, his voice so full of rage it almost quavered.

"Where the fuck *is* she, Rinaldi?"

Still trying to catch my breath. "Who?"

He pressed the nose of the gun to my left temple.

"Who the fuck ya think? The Bishara bitch."

"I don't know what you're—"

"She's gone, and she took her brat with her. The daughter."

"Gone?"

"Don't act stupid, okay, asshole? I don't like stupid. It offends me. I feel disrespected. I don't like that."

"But I don't know where she is."

"Bullshit! Just like ya didn't know she'd taken off…?"

"No, I didn't. Not till this moment."

I'd recovered somewhat and made myself straighten up.

"Look, Kerns, if Indra did take her daughter and go on the run, that's parental kidnapping. Did Billy call the cops? Surely his lawyer told him—"

My assailant shook his head, as though aggrieved, pressing the gun's barrel harder against the side of my head.

"There's that stupid thing again. Ya think Billy Reynolds wants that kind of publicity? His family's a big deal in that shithole town of his, and he don't want his private business spread around."

I let my gaze dart past his shoulder, flitting left and right down the narrow street. Not a single person, not one lone passerby. No help was coming.

I was alone with an angry man holding a gun at my head.

"Look, Kerns," I said, my voice as calm and measured as I could manage, "I have no idea where Indra went. In fact, I think she's making a foolish mistake. You'll find her sooner or later, and all this does is make her position worse in court."

He laughed shortly. "Shit, now ya sound like that rich dago Bruschi. Ya know, Billy was right about you two. Take away the nice suits and the fancy language, and you're just a couple of dirty wops from the neighborhood."

I could feel the pressure from the gun lessening. I also saw the intensity in his eyes receding. Despite himself, I realized, he was beginning to believe me.

He drew a heavy sigh. "If you ain't lyin', dirtbag, then I gotta do it the hard way. Her car's still in her driveway, but a neighbor says she saw the bitch and her kid get into the back of a black town car. That means I gotta track down the goddamn rental place she used and find out where the car took her."

I was barely listening, aware suddenly of the dull pain in my chin where he'd coldcocked me. Just when the ache in my jaw from Billy Three's sucker punch had started to subside.

Kerns took a step back, watching with a sudden, thuggish amusement as I rubbed my chin.

"I studied up on you, ya know, Rinaldi? You were some kinda boxer years ago, right?"

"Amateur. A long time ago."

"Well, you sure don't seem it now."

"Normally, it's not needed much in my current job."

He was still chuckling as he holstered his gun. "See what I

mean? Maybe that's why you shouldn't be stickin' your nose where it don't belong."

"I'll take that under advisement. By the way, Kerns, you ever done any boxing?"

"Me? Hell, no. That's why God invented guns."

"That's what I thought," I said, planting my feet and driving my fist as hard as I could into his solar plexus.

Kerns doubled up in agony, groaning as he fell to his knees on the rough bricks. I'd taken a few gut punches in my life, and I knew the shock to the system they delivered. Pain, nausea, a feeling of near paralysis.

"You…fuck…" he gasped, palms flat out on the hard surface, supporting his considerable bulk.

I got down on my haunches next to him, reaching inside his jacket for the gun. I slipped it into my own jacket pocket.

"You tell Billy Three and that slick bastard Bruschi not to send any more gorillas after me, okay? I still have a few friends on the force, and I'll make sure that trust fund kid gets more bad publicity than he'd ever imagine."

Kerns started slowly getting to his feet. I did the same and headed back to my car. Before getting in, I turned.

"And one more thing, Kerns. I don't know where Indra Bishara is, and I wouldn't tell you if I did. But I hope to Christ it's far enough away that you never find her."

Still barely able to stand, Kerns summoned the energy to offer me his middle finger.

I put the Mustang in gear and slowly went past the parked car in front of me. The narrow street opened onto Fifth Avenue, as I remembered, so I figured all I had to do to avoid damaging either vehicle was to take it nice and easy.

I made it by inches.

—

By the time I pulled into my spot in the parking garage at work, I realized two things.

First, that some old pugilistic instinct had made me turn my head slightly, deflecting much of the impact of Kerns' gun barrel. My chin hurt, but not as badly as I feared. A quick glance at my rearview mirror affirmed that the expected welt and surrounding redness were less pronounced, too. Still, they were prominent enough that I'd have to come up with a reasonable explanation when the day's patients commented on it.

As they undoubtably would. Most therapy patients are highly sensitive to any changes in the therapist's appearance. Weight loss or gain, a change in wardrobe, even a recent haircut.

But it was the second thing I realized that caused me concern. While it may have been momentarily satisfying to put Barton Kerns on the ground, it was a stupid mistake. I'd resented being harassed by the big man and was tired of having taken it on the chin—literally—since this whole thing started, but it was foolish nonetheless .

All I'd done was inflame an already dangerous situation with Billy Three and his lawyer. And made a serious enemy out of a man who worked for them.

I'd parked, but still sat behind the wheel, listening to the Mustang's engine ticking off. Luckily, enough coffee remained in my thermos to help me swallow a couple ibuprofen. I would've loved a stronger painkiller, but not when I faced a day full of therapy patients. OTC meds would have to do.

Then I remembered the loaded gun in my jacket pocket. I gingerly drew it out and locked it in the glove compartment.

Finally, I got out of the car and surveyed the damage to the rear fender—pretty severe. The impact from Kerns' vehicle crumpled the lower part of the trunk. Though drivable, my Mustang was no longer the cherry ride it had been the day before.

*Problem for another time,* I thought, as I headed toward the elevator, trying to shake the memory of my encounter with Kerns. I'd always been too quick to anger and, as more than one of my friends and colleagues had warned, someday it could be the end of me.

I was beginning to think they might be right.

# Chapter Thirty-Five

The first thing I did when I got to my office was call Indra to warn her about Kerns. I tried both her cell and her office number at Teasdale but had to be content with leaving her a message. Even though she was on the run, I hoped she'd check her voicemail.

Meanwhile, I still had to face my workday. As expected, a number of my morning patients inquired about my slightly swollen chin. I explained that I'd fallen in the bathroom, hitting the edge of the sink. Other than one particular patient, who tended to respond suspiciously to almost anything he was told, my ruse seemed to work.

It wasn't till my lunch hour, when I was about to go down to the street and pick up something to eat, that a question apparently nestled deep in my unconscious finally emerged.

How had Barton Kerns been able to track me so closely this morning that he ended up one car-length behind me? Unless he'd followed me when I left Gloria's apartment. But that would mean he'd been tailing me all night, which was unlikely. Especially since I had to assume that searching for Billy Three's missing ex-wife and daughter would be his first priority.

Then I remembered that Kerns was an ex-cop and probably

had access to equipment enabling him to track me via my GPS. So I went down to the garage, got into my car, and disconnected the device, hoping that would ensure some degree of security.

Unfortunately, I didn't have the skills to disable the comparable technology in my cell phone, which allowed it to be similarly tracked. It was a reminder that there's a limit to how safe you can be in this modern world…

Grabbing more coffee and a sandwich at a nearby deli on Forbes, it was with a rueful acceptance of this fact that I used my cell to check for the latest news.

The only story that interested me was the Task Force investigation of Hank Bowman's murder. According to a media spokeswoman, the authorities saw no connection between the FBI man's death and the earlier sniper attacks. Instead, the crime appeared to be personal in nature. As a result, law enforcement was checking the alibis of Bowman's friends, family, and work colleagues.

In a separate statement released to the news station, Assistant Director Anthony Clemmons emphasized that the slain Bureau station chief had been well-liked and respected by all of his peers.

I'd just clicked off the news when my cell rang. It was Gloria, her voice threaded with fatigue.

"Good news, Danny. Forensics is done with Hank Bowman's laptop. We can get it out of the Bureau's evidence lockup at three this afternoon."

"I'm surprised Pittsburgh PD doesn't want a crack at it."

"Normally they would. After all, it's a homicide within their jurisdiction. But as part of the joint Task Force, and as a goodwill gesture to the Bureau since the victim was one of our own, the department is letting Clemmons take the lead on the case."

"I thought a PPD detective named Bennett was the primary."

Gloria managed to chuckle through a stifled yawn.

"Let's just say, she is and she isn't. It's the usual interagency politics. And because Captain Biegler and Clemmons are besties..."

"Got it. After you pick up Bowman's laptop, where do I meet you? Back at your place?"

"No. I think taking it out of the Bureau station would look suspicious. Meet me at my office in the building."

I paused. "I realize you're taking a helluva risk on the basis of just a hunch. *My* hunch."

"Maybe, Danny, but I need to know the truth about Hank Bowman. I just don't know whether I want to prove that you're right or you're wrong."

—

My last therapy patient left at four p.m., after which I hurriedly locked my office, went down to my car, and headed across town to the FBI building.

Before I'd left Gloria's apartment at dawn, she'd given me a visitor's badge in case I'd need to get access to the field station again. Her foresight paid off, as I was quickly waved through the front entrance by a distracted junior agent. He looked as exhausted as every other Bureau operative I passed in the lobby, most of whom were still working double shifts due to Hank Bowman's murder.

When I opened the door to Gloria's temporary office, I found her once again standing at Hermie Gould's shoulder as the young man bent over a laptop keyboard. His face exhibited that same combination of youthful exuberance and obsessive focus.

I stepped over to join them, giving Gloria's arm a gentle squeeze. Her returning smile was weary but warm.

"Danny's here, Hermie," she said.

"Hey." As before, he hadn't even looked up.

I bent to watch as Hermie's fingers flew over the keys. Within minutes, the by-now familiar colors and design of the de Gobineau Society website appeared onscreen.

Gloria's shoulders fell. "Aw, shit..."

"I know," I said. "I'm sorry, Gloria."

She turned to me. "I just can't believe a Bureau agent...a station chief...would be a member of a white supremacy group."

Hermie, still without glancing up at either of us, gave a knowing laugh.

"I never figured you to be that naive, Agent Reese. You know how many cops, Feds, and Secret Service guys belong to groups like this? And not only on the Dark Web. If you know where and how to look, they're all over Facebook, too."

Gloria dug her strong fingers into the kid's shoulder. He winced in pain, huddling down in his chair.

"Jesus, Glo, I'm sorry. I take it back."

"I'm not naive, Hermie. Just...disappointed. I knew Hank Bowman and..." She let out a breath. "At least I *thought* I did."

Meanwhile, I was still peering at the computer screen. "How long till you decode the encryptions, Hermie? And break through the firewalls."

He gave his shoulder an exaggerated rub, then straightened and went back to work on the keyboard.

"It's just a variation of the same algorithms," he said. "It shouldn't take too long to..."

Hermie clicked a final series of buttons, then clapped his hands triumphantly.

"And...we're in! The same bullshit. 'Mission Statement,' 'Contacts,' 'Study Materials.'"

"And Hank is definitely identified?"

"Yep. And welcomed, like the other two assholes."

Suddenly, Hermie bent forward, squinting excitedly at the screen.

"Wait. There *is* something different. Look..." He sat back, inviting us to bend closer. "It's a whole list of names. Under the heading 'Patriots.'"

Gloria and I each scanned the list in a kind of shared, breathless silence.

Frederick James Graham
Harriet Louise Parr
Gary Joseph Landrew
Francis Herbert Mapes
Peter Isaac Steinman
Robert Anselm Conway

"It's the victims of the sniper," Gloria said. "All of them. Except for this Robert Conway."

"And Lucas Hartley, of course." I stroked my trim beard. "He was killed by accident."

Gloria frowned. "That's what I don't understand. If Jason Graham's father is the member, why was Jason himself targeted?"

I shook my head. "None of this makes sense. Was the guy who hired Porter to shoot these people—this man we've been calling the Handler—was he aware that they were members of this hate group? Was he exacting a perverse form of racial justice by arranging to have them killed?"

Hermie folded his arms. "You mean the guy behind the Steel City Sniper might be some kinda vigilante? Like Batman?"

"I doubt it," I said. "But as to what the Handler's motives are...or were...I have no idea."

"There's something else." Gloria rose stiffly, then turned to lean with her back against the wall. I had the feeling this was as much for emotional support as for any physical relief.

She looked from Hermie to me, her face pained. "If Hank had access to the whole list, and was the only one who did…"

"Then that means he knew who the sniper's victims were," I finished for her. "Once the killings started, and the victims' names became public, Hank knew who the next people on the hit list were likely to be…"

"And said nothing." Her lips tightened. "Alerted none of them of their potential danger. Nor did he provide this info to the Bureau. Or to the police. Even anonymously."

"Jesus," Hermie whispered. "That fucker deliberately let people die. Unless *he* was the Handler. Makes sense. He's the only one whose site lists all the names."

"That we *know* of," I said. "Because their lawyers are stonewalling, we don't have access to some of the other victims' computers. Though my gut says that Bowman's is the only site with all the names."

"I think so, too," Gloria said. "Besides, if Hank was the Handler, why was he himself killed? And by whom? Unless it *was* some personal thing. Unrelated to all this. He fell victim to an execution-style murder, remember. Not a sniper's bullet."

I shrugged. "At this point, there's still a lot we don't know. Though I'd guess there's probably going to be another murder. One we might have a chance to prevent." I pointed at the laptop screen. "Unless he's been killed already, and his body yet to be found, he's the last remaining name on the list. Robert Conway."

Gloria and I exchanged looks.

At which, Hermie jumped up from his seat, eyes wide behind his thick lenses.

"Jesus, you're sayin' this Conway dude could be next! So what the fuck are you waiting for?"

—

In ten minutes, Gloria and I were belted into my Mustang, racing along the parkway east to Edgewood. Somehow, we'd just skirted the heaviest of the end-of-day traffic out of the city, and were making surprisingly good time.

As I'd expected, we hadn't been on the road long before she asked me about the damage to the car. I told her.

"Jesus, Danny. Ever think about hiring a bodyguard?"

But she wasn't smiling. Then she promised to have her Bureau colleagues run down Kerns, though we both knew that could wait. We had more important matters at hand.

Before heading out, we'd tried calling Conway on all the numbers Hermie could find for him online. But at each number, business and personal, we had to contend with leaving a message on his voicemail. Gloria identified herself and managed to convey a sense of urgency while being somewhat vague. She'd even tried texting him, but it appeared his cell was turned off.

Now, as the sun sank to the horizon behind us, my mind churned over what we'd discovered so far. Meanwhile, Gloria had been on her cell phone again, this time to the FBI building. She'd gotten patched through to Tony Clemmons' office, but the assistant director's secretary told her that he and Captain Biegler had been called up to Harrisburg.

From what Gloria could glean from the woman's cryptic comments, the investigation into Hank Bowman's murder had stalled, and the governor, no longer willing to wait, required the two Task Force leaders to make their report. In person.

The conversation ended with Gloria telling the secretary to get in touch with her boss and inform him that a significant new lead in the sniper case had emerged.

"We can't afford to wait for backup," Gloria said to me.

I gave a brisk nod as I wove in and around the slowly clogging traffic on the approach to the Squirrel Hill Tunnel.

We'd caught one break back at Gloria's office. Given that Robert Conway had an unusual middle name—Anselm, probably in honor of some prominent family member from generations past—it was easy for Hermie to find him online. He was a medical supplies sales rep whose territory included much of Western Pennsylvania, but whose residence was in Edgewood. His house was in a cul-de-sac at the end of Willis Street.

I spotted the Edgewood exit on the far side of the tunnel and sped down the ramp. My every instinct told me that we needed to find Conway as soon as possible.

Unless, as I'd speculated, it was already too late, and his corpse was hidden behind an underpass somewhere.

As I drove down Willis Street, Gloria once more called Clemmons' secretary, who told her that she'd been unable to reach her boss, but she'd both texted and left a message on his cell voicemail.

Clicking off, Gloria's cheeks darkened. "I don't trust that bitch. Maybe it's getting close to quitting time, but she's way too casual about all this."

"Can't be a ton of fun having Clemmons for a boss."

"Point taken." Offering me the closest thing to a smile that I'd seen for some time.

I found where Willis Street curved into a small, tree-shrouded cul-de-sac, whose half-dozen houses were appropriately upscale for Edgewood. The darkness had descended like a thick blanket, blurring the features of the impressive homes, most of whose porch lamps and window lights had come on.

It was then that I saw him.

Robert Conway was hard to miss. The bald pate we'd seen

in his online photo shone under the streetlamp adjacent to his house. But it was the way he was frantically piling suitcases into the open trunk of his car, a Ford sedan idling noisily in his driveway, that caught our attention.

I pulled my car right up in front of his house, blocking the driveway. Hearing my brakes gripping asphalt, he whirled, eyes wide with fear. His face, even in the muted bowl of light thrown by the streetlamp overhead, was visibly contorted—riven with a desperate, unmediated anxiety.

As Gloria and I approached him from either side, he stepped away from the car trunk, hands upraised. Gloria had slipped her service weapon from her belt holster and was pointing it at him.

"Wait, please!" His voice a raspy croak. "*He* sent you, didn't he? The rotten bastard sent you!"

Conway was around fifty, with a flatiron face and a thin, wiry body. Though obviously expensive, his jacket, white shirt, and slacks had been sloppily thrown on.

"Nobody sent us, Mr. Conway." Gloria held up her Bureau ID in her free hand. "I'm Special Agent Reese, FBI."

"We know you're a member of the de Gobineau Society," I added. "We've seen the list and—"

Conway suddenly ran toward us, gripping both my arms.

"Thank Christ!" He stared wildly from me to Gloria. "You have to help me! He's going to kill me!"

"It's obvious you're trying to get away." Gloria holstered her gun. "But who's going to—?"

His words came in a breathless torrent. "The moment I saw on the news that Bowman had been killed, I knew I had to run. He was the only one who knew the names of all the rest of us."

"And you all knew his?" I asked.

"Yeah. He was the boss's mouthpiece."

"Your boss? The one behind all the sniper attacks?" I glanced at Gloria. "The Handler."

Conway gave a sharp, mirthless laugh. "Is that what you guys call him? Guess that's as good a name as any."

"You don't know who he is?"

"Nobody knew," Conway said, "except Bowman. He was the one who communicated with the rest of us. Gave us our instructions."

"Yet none of the rest of you knew each other's identities?"

"No. That's why I didn't figure out what was going on when the sniper attacks started. I assumed like everyone else that the killer was just some whack-job targeting people at random. Those victims were all strangers to me."

"Until Hank Bowman was killed. Then you knew..."

"Yeah! That he was wiping us all out! Even Bowman..."

Despite the night's growing chill, Conway swept dots of sweat from his brow with the back of his hand.

"But why?" Gloria pressed him. "Why would the Handler kill people who'd joined his website?"

Another hard, bitter laugh. Fear tinging it with hysteria.

"Website? Christ, lady! You think we're just some kinda chat room? *Don't you know who we are? What we do?*"

Before Gloria could respond, Conway abruptly pushed away from her, frantic gaze sweeping the surrounding houses and trees. All swathed in an ever-deepening darkness.

"Fuck this!" He turned his panicked eyes toward us again. "I'm not saying another word! Not till you get me outta here. If I keep standing here talking, I'm a dead man! Take me someplace safe. Now!"

Gloria hesitated only a moment, then strode up to Conway's sedan and slammed the trunk lid shut. Then she pointed to the passenger side door.

"Get in!" she commanded Conway, who raced to obey.

Picking up her cue, I'd already swung behind the wheel of my Mustang. I pulled a dozen yards down the street, far enough to let Gloria back the Ford out of the driveway.

As she turned and sped off up the street, I wheeled around and followed. Through the sedan's rear window, I could make out Conway slinking down low in the passenger seat.

# Chapter Thirty-Six

The bunker-like concrete walls in the motel's utility basement amplified the November cold seeping in from outside the broad, windowless room. One of the FBI's local safe houses, it was located in a dilapidated motor court in East Liberty.

Gloria had texted me the address, and by the time I arrived, she and Robert Conway were already inside. Per her instructions, I'd entered the empty lobby, gone through the steel door marked "Employees Only," and taken the stairs to the basement.

When I entered I saw, to my surprise, that our cooperative young felon Hermie was sitting with Gloria and Conway at a wide table in the middle of the room. I also noticed that the latter had regained much of his composure and was carefully withdrawing a laptop from a hard-shell silver case.

Gloria glanced up at me as I took a seat beside her.

"I called Hermie and asked him to meet us," she explained, "in case Mr. Conway here decided to jerk us around. By now, Hermie can access the website as quickly as he can."

"You don't gotta worry about me." Conway angled his opened laptop toward Hermie, who immediately began typing.

"Long as you keep my ass safe, I'll tell you everything I know. In exchange."

"For what?" said Gloria.

"Immunity from criminal charges."

"Not gonna happen, Conway. Besides, at this point you're just a person of interest. You're not under arrest."

He sat back to peer at his laptop screen, now displaying the familiar images of the society's opening web page.

"Nice job, kid," he said to Hermie. Then, casually, he turned back to Gloria. "Here's the thing, honey. We better make some kinda deal or I'm not telling you shit."

I gave Gloria a sidelong look, then reached past her to grip Conway's throat. Hard.

"I'm not a cop or a Fed, *honey*, so here's the deal *I'm* offering: tell us everything or I'll personally drive you back to Willis Street and dump your racist ass on your driveway."

"Hey, wait a minute—"

I leaned closer. "I figure your boss has gotten himself in position by now to have a clean shot at you. Maybe in that hedge in front of the house. Or behind one of those nice trees."

Conway's face lost its color as he turned again to Gloria.

"He can't do that, right, lady? I mean, Agent Reese. You can't let him do that!"

She shrugged. "Not my call. This isn't exactly an official Bureau investigation. We're so off the grid, protocol-wise, that bringing you here is probably a career-killer for me, anyway. So I've got nothing to lose. As far as I'm concerned, the Doc here can do whatever the hell he wants with you."

Conway's formerly restored composure was disappearing quickly as the reality of his position became clear to him.

"I wanted to be protected, not jammed up!" he said, new beads of sweat dotting his brow.

It was Gloria's turn to shrug. Adding a thin smile.

Two seats over, head bent, his fingers racing over the laptop keyboard, Hermie let out a low chuckle.

"Sorry, dude." Without bothering to glance over at the terrified man. "I think you're fucked."

I released Conway and sat back in my chair.

"Here's the only thing I *can* offer," Gloria said to Conway, who was making a big show of rubbing his neck where I'd gripped his throat. "Cooperate with us and I'll make sure my superiors know about it. Trust me, that'll go a long way toward helping you if charges are brought."

"And as an added bonus," I said, "you'll get to stay alive. It's a better deal than you'll get from the Handler."

Conway let out a heavy sigh of resignation. "Where do you want me to start?"

Gloria folded her arms. "You said we didn't know what the de Gobineau Society really is. Why don't you start there?"

A sudden change came over Conway. A sneer formed on his lips, and he affected a new, almost smug self-assurance. It wasn't hard for me to guess why. Robert Conway was what philosopher Eric Hoffer called a true believer. And now, despite the circumstances, he had the opportunity to school us poor, deluded souls in the righteousness of his cause.

"Look around you," he said with a sudden expansiveness. "Even *you* two have to admit that the natural order of things has been turned upside down. We got black hordes protesting, rioting in the streets. Destroying property. Attacking the foundations of proper society with violence."

"That's enough, Conway," I said, my anger rising.

But he ignored me, eyes gleaming. "Meanwhile, foolish, so-called civil rights activists—some of them even white—fall all over themselves defending them. The truth is, they're nothing but traitors to their own kind. Cowardly appeasers. Willing to let our cities burn, let the races intermarry, let our children be indoctrinated, our—"

"Spare us the usual racist garbage," I said bitterly. "Just answer Agent Reese's question. About the de Gobineau website."

He stiffened, the aggrieved truth-teller. Then, composing himself, he looked meaningfully at both Gloria and me.

"The society isn't just some group of like-minded people," Conway said importantly. "Though we all share the simple, scientifically proven belief in the superiority of the white race that is the cornerstone of our mission."

"And that mission is…?" Gloria asked.

"Each member is essentially a sleeper cell, an individual clearinghouse charged with collecting and distributing funds from wealthy donors around the country."

"For what purpose?"

"Why do you think, Agent Reese? Our job is to funnel money from those donors to fund various white power activities. We provide financial support to our fellow patriots, organized or not, underwriting everything from gun purchases and bombings to demonstrations on the street."

"Like Charlottesville?"

Conway smiled. "Our point was made, wasn't it?"

I felt my chest tighten, but I said nothing. The goal here was to get information.

"We also bankroll the majority of white power candidates," he went on. "There are more of them than you'd imagine, all of whom believe in the coming race war. And, believe me, no matter what blind fools like you think, it's coming. But it's a war we right-thinking people don't intend to lose."

"Who are these wealthy donors you siphon money from?"

He laughed quietly. "Let's just say they all belong to the same group, a group called Anonymous. Seriously, Agent Reese? Who do you *think* they are? CEOs, financial giants, celebrities from every field. Some whose names you might guess, though many of the names would surprise you. But as far as we were concerned, their names didn't matter. Only their money did."

I considered this. "You and the other members...Fred Graham, Dr. Mapes, and the rest...how were they all brought into the group?"

"As far as I know, Hank Bowman selected them," Conway said. "He told me once that the boss—excuse me, *the Handler*... love that name—anyway, Hank told me that he and the Handler chose the members through the internet."

"How?" Gloria asked.

"They had some kind of algorithm that identified people who'd been accessing right-wing and white supremacy sites. Who'd contributed to white power candidates and organizations. Who were privately and covertly in support of our cause, and probably felt isolated or estranged in their beliefs from family, friends, and coworkers."

"So it was Hank who recruited them? And you, as well?"

"Yes. And for security purposes, none of us knew the identities of the other members. Nor even how many of us there were in the society."

"And Bowman was the conduit between each member and the wealthy donors he or she was to contact?"

"Right again. And it's been working like a charm. Seen the news the past couple years?"

"Then something must've happened. Why did the Handler hire Randy Porter to start eliminating the society's members?"

Here, Conway's eyes lost their feigned serenity and went black with anger.

"Because someone betrayed us! The Justice Department has

begun a massive effort to expose and prosecute organizations like ours, and one of our members has been talking to them."

"How do you know this?" Gloria said.

"Because Hank Bowman told me that the Handler told *him*."

"Hank revealed this to you? I thought he only contacted each member to relay instructions for collecting funds."

"It started that way, yeah. Dealing with me like any one of the others. But we learned we had a few interests in common—"

"Child porn?" I suggested.

He gave me a disgusted look.

"Yeah, right. Fuck you, mister. Anyway, Hank and I had gotten friendly over the past years and he began to confide in me about stuff. Like the time the Handler mentioned to him offhandedly that if somebody in the society ever talked to the law, he'd 'clean house.' Kill all the members and form a new group."

"Wait a minute," I said. "Since Bowman had the complete list of members, he must've realized when their deaths were reported on the news that the Handler was purging the group. Why didn't he run, like you were trying to do?"

"Ego, Doc," said Conway. "I guess Hank figured since he was the Handler's right-hand man, he'd never be suspected of being a mole for the Feds. That the Handler would consider him too valuable and too loyal to be killed."

Gloria's voice lowered. "He thought he was safe."

"Yeah." Conway nodded. "But he thought wrong. None of us is safe. My guess is, since the Handler obviously doesn't know which of us talked to the Feds, the only safe thing to do is kill us all."

The three of us grew silent for a few moments, the only sound the clicking of the keys of Conway's laptop. Gloria and I had been so riveted by what the man was disclosing that we'd barely registered that Hermie was still working intently.

"What are you doing?" Gloria asked him with some annoyance.

"Research." Hermie kept his gaze on the screen. "Listening to all this crap, I decided to find out for myself what the hell's goin' on."

"Since when did you turn into a concerned citizen?"

"Hey, I happen to have many facets." He did his best to look offended, then turned his gaze back to the screen.

"Anyway, according to the Southern Poverty Law Center, white supremacist groups are on the rise all over the country. Especially in the past couple years. With an increase in hate crimes to prove it. Political action committees, well-armed militia groups, a coordinated system of racist and anti-Semitic organizations, many supported financially by both wealthy donors and regular, upright, God-fearing Americans."

Hermie grinned. "I added that last part myself."

"One thing's for sure," Gloria said grimly. "Their numbers are growing, as any Bureau agent could tell you. We've already arrested suspects linked to the white supremacist groups The Base and Atomwaffen Division. Two of the known hate groups advocating violence against minorities."

She peered at Conway. "Pretty heavyweight scumbags. So maybe your little band of 'patriots' isn't as special as you—or the Handler—think."

"Doesn't matter," he said coolly. "All that matters is the cause."

"Speaking of which," I said, "I'm curious about one of your members. Peter Steinman. I'm surprised he'd join such an anti-Semitic group. Why would he?"

"Who knows? Maybe he's one of those self-hating Jews you hear so much about." He offered me a dark smile. "Shit, I just wish there were more of them."

# Chapter Thirty-Seven

I drove out of East Liberty under a flowing darkness that seemed to seep from behind every building, large and small, challenged only by artificial lights. All that we'd come up with since medieval times to scare away the dark.

It was just after nine p.m., and I'd left Gloria and Hermie behind at the safe house with Robert Conway. I certainly wasn't needed at that point, and she'd explained that it would take her hours to record and try to verify much of what Conway had said.

To be honest, I also figured that son of a bitch had a better chance of keeping all his teeth if I took off.

Despite the frigid night air, I had my driver's side window open. I needed its bracing lash across my cheeks and brow to keep me focused on my driving, rather than letting my mind roil with outrage at what Conway—and people like him—represented.

Too wired to sleep and burning with curiosity about the last thing I heard Conway say, I was on a somewhat personal mission that I doubted I could really justify.

Because, frankly, it was none of my business. But the thing bothered me, puzzled me, and I was driven to find out the answer.

—

The Steinman house looked quite different at night. The huge expanse of manicured lawn lay under a carpet of darkness, while the structure itself was so set back from the tony Squirrel Hill street that it seemed less an impressive home than a somber keep.

On the other hand, my knowledge of what had happened to Peter Steinman no doubt influenced the way I experienced the place as I came up to the massive front porch and rang the bell.

The door was answered by a woman whose haggard expression didn't detract from her attractive, well-tended features.

"Yes?" Mary Anne North's voice still retained its wary tone, as well as its air of authority. "Who are you and what do you want? If you're a reporter, I swear I'll call the police..."

I shook my head. "Actually, Ms. North, I'm working *with* the police. My name's Daniel Rinaldi."

Once again, I brandished my police consultant's now-invalid ID badge, hoping that she was unaware of my suspension. Whether she was or not, she was clearly unimpressed.

I remembered her haughty manner from having seen her reaction to the press right after her brother-in-law's murder. So her response to my showing up at her sister's door wasn't much of a surprise.

"We've said everything we need to say to the police. And the FBI. As well as a parade of infuriating journalists."

"I'm sure you have," I said, as warmly as I could. "But I have a few follow-up questions for your sister Laura. It won't take much time, and—"

"At nine o'clock at night?"

"I realize it's late, but one of my jobs with Pittsburgh PD is to provide psychological support to crime victims. And their bereaved family members. Given my crowded schedule, it's taken me some time to get to Laura. I do apologize, but—"

Her face darkened. "I've been providing as much solace to my sister as I can since the tragedy. She needs family, not some overworked civil servant."

"I'm sure you're right. But if I could just have a few minutes with her..."

"I'm afraid that's impossible. I've just managed to get her to sleep, which she sorely needs. As you can imagine."

With that, Mary Anne North began to shut the door.

I stopped it with my foot. "Then, if I may, could I ask *you* a few questions? Just to clear up a few things for my report?" She eyed me suspiciously. And for good reason. The lateness of the hour, my unlikely request. I could almost see the wheels turning in her mind. Debating the best move.

Obviously attuned to the unwelcome intrusions of law enforcement, she probably figured that if she turned me away, I—or someone like me—would return with more foolish questions. And that a quick interview with me might be the better choice, and perhaps put an end to any future visits from outsiders.

"Well, if you must," she said at last, opening the door wider. "But I've only a few minutes to give you."

I thanked her and let her lead me down a gleaming, well-appointed hall to the opened doorway of a study. Wood-paneled and lined with bookshelves, it was furnished with plush leather chairs, beside each of which stood a Tiffany floor lamp. Or, at least, they seemed genuine to me. On the walls were two paintings, both in the neoclassical style, neither of which was a print.

It was a house created by, and meant to convey, great wealth. I had to admit, it succeeded.

Taking one of the chairs, she motioned me to another.

"First of all, Dr. Rinaldi, let me say I don't believe for a minute that you're here on police business."

"What makes you say that?"

"The time of night and the fact our lawyer has always alerted us to when the police or FBI wanted an interview. So while I don't know what your true purpose is in coming here, I must admit to a certain curiosity about it."

So much for my theory of how and why she'd assented to my visit. Which meant she was probably more on her guard than I'd even supposed.

"Well, then, Ms. North," I said, "I'll get right to the point. I do in fact work with the police, and we happen to know that Peter Steinman, your sister's husband, was a member of a secret society. A racist, anti-Semitic society."

"I'm sure I don't know what you're talking about. Why would Peter join such a vile organization?"

"That's what we're wondering, too. Especially since it ended up getting him killed."

She started, hand going to her mouth. That hand trembling.

"Wh-what do you mean? I don't understand."

Something about her response triggered a notion in the back of my mind. It seemed ludicrous, unbelievable, but…

I decided to reveal what we knew. It was a gamble but at this point I was going on pure instinct. Or adrenaline. I frankly didn't know which.

I sat forward in my chair.

"We think that whoever was behind the society decided to purge its members. That he hired the sniper—that man on the news, Randy Porter—to track down and murder each person affiliated with the group. And since Peter was a member…"

Mary Anne North gasped audibly, then rose from her chair.

Walking stiffly over to a near bookcase, she put out her hand to grasp one of the shelves. Steadying herself.

"It was a joke. A harmless..."

I stood now, too, and joined her.

"When did it start, Ms. North?"

She sniffed, struggling to maintain some of her usual proud demeanor.

"We...the family, I mean... Look, I'm not saying we go back to the *Mayflower*, any of that foolishness, but we have a proud lineage. Fine stock, if you will."

"You mean, WASPs..."

"If you must use that vulgar term. Anyway, when Laura told us she was marrying Steinman...that she intended to marry a Jew, despite our objections..."

Her voice caught. When she looked at me, as though trying to read my face, her eyes narrowed.

"I don't expect you to understand, Dr. Rinaldi. That's an Italian name, I believe?"

I nodded. "My ancestors came off a different kind of boat. About three generations back. At Ellis Island."

Her hand came away from the bookshelf. Touched her throat.

"The point is," she said, more calmly now, "we tried to accept the marriage. We all did. But it's always rankled me. Offended me. And so I...well, as a sort of private joke, I started visiting Aryan websites and blogs."

"Using your brother-in-law's name...an obviously Jewish name..."

"It was my little revenge on him for seducing my younger sister. Such a pure, beautiful girl. Now married to a kike."

Her lips tightened.

"The more I explored these anti-Semitic websites, the more I found. Hundreds of them. Fascinating, too, I must say. There was a lot of information I hadn't been aware of. About how Jews were taking over the banks. Everything."

"I don't want to hear any of that shit, you understand? I'm not interested."

I leaned in, deliberately crowding her space. Admittedly glad to see the fear leap up in her eyes.

"I just want to know what happened," I said. "How the hell Peter Steinman ended up a member of that Society."

She swallowed and tried to back away. I grabbed her wrist.

"Tell me!"

"I…a man named Bowman contacted me through the fake email address I'd created with Peter's name. He said we shared the same correct views, and then he invited me to join the group."

"And you did. Using Peter's name."

"Yes. I mean, what could it hurt? It just meant that Peter Steinman was a member of some white supremacist, anti-Semitic website. Like so many others on the internet."

She pulled away from my grasp and stood glaring at me.

"It was simply part of the joke. A private prank on that Jew who stole my dear Laura from me. From our family. How could it hurt? Don't you see? It was all just a joke."

"Yeah. A joke that got Peter killed. And the poor bastard—and especially Laura and *his* family—would never know why."

"But now I *do* know why!"

It was a shredded, anguished female voice, coming from the opened doorway.

Laura Steinman. Pale, drawn. Hand gripping the doorframe.

Her sister and I had turned at the sound of her voice, but Laura's gaze was riveted only on Mary Anne.

"I couldn't sleep," Laura said, "so I got out of bed…came down here when I heard voices…"

"Laura..." Mary Anne took a step toward her sister, hands twisting at her sides. Imploring. "You have to understand..."

But the widow's face had hardened to stone. Like white marble, with twin cold shards where her eyes should be.

"I *do* understand...!" As she stormed into the room. "You killed my husband! *I loved Peter and you got him killed!"*

With surprising speed for one so frail-looking, Laura was on her sister in mere seconds, sharp nails like claws as she went for Mary Anne's face.

"You bitch! You jealous bitch!"

Mary Anne tried to block the curved fingers but was too late. With an anguished howl, Laura raked both her cheeks.

"Please, Laura!" the other woman screamed, blood welling up in thin streaks on her face.

I managed to throw both my arms around Laura and pull her away from her sister. But nothing could stop her fury.

"Get out!" Laura yelled. "Get out of my house! I never want to see you again! *Ever!"*

Hands to her face, blood dripping between her slender fingers, Mary Anne sobbed. Her whole body shaking.

"Please, Laura! You don't mean that! It was just—for God's sake, I never thought it would—"

"I said, get the fuck out of my house!" Laura squirmed in my grasp, but I held fast. *"Now,* bitch! Get the fuck out now!"

Openly weeping, Mary Anne rushed past where Laura and I still struggled and ran out into the hall. In moments, I heard the front door open and the woman's receding footsteps.

It took some time—I lost track of the minutes—but I finally managed to calm Laura. At least enough for her to collapse on one of the leather chairs, hands to her face.

As her sister had done. Both pairs of hands were slender, expensively ringed, beautifully manicured. Both had blond hair worn in similar styles. I was struck by how much the two North siblings resembled each other.

And yet, in the end, how different they turned out to be.

# Chapter Thirty-Eight

Luckily, though she lived at the other side of the house, Laura Steinman's maid had heard the commotion coming from the study. I was still sitting with the distraught widow when the older Hispanic woman came through the door.

"Oh, Fernanda!" Laura cried, reaching out for the maid.

Sturdy, plain-faced, and confidently brusque, Fernanda immediately waved me away and took my place at her employer's side, holding her hand and murmuring softly into her ear.

"Do you want me to call anyone for you, Mrs. Steinman?" I said. "Your doctor? Your therapist, perhaps...?"

Her face streaked with tears, she merely shook her head. While the maid, still patting her hand, glared up at me.

"Therapist? You people, with your doctors and pills and foolish talk. All Missus Laura needs is love. The love of her husband. Can you call someone for that?"

"No," I said. "I can't."

Bidding Laura Steinman goodbye, I went quietly out of the room. And out of that harrowing, splendid house of sorrow.

---

I checked in with Gloria as I was driving across the bridge toward home and told her about how Mary Anne North had pretended to be Peter Steinman, a cruel joke that caused his death. She took a few moments to register this, then said that she had news as well.

"Tony Clemmons finally returned my call." Managing to sound both weary and excited. "He's still up in Harrisburg but was blown away by what I told him. About Conway and everything. He'll be back in town tomorrow but told me to put our favorite racist in the Bureau lockup."

"Which is where…?"

"Where I'm sitting, filing the paperwork. In the basement of the field office. I sent Hermie home from the safe house and brought Conway in myself. He's pretty pissed about spending the night in a cell and is screaming for a lawyer, but he'll keep."

"Works for me."

"Me, too. Meanwhile, I can tell that Clemmons can't wait to get a crack at him. He's so eager, he forgot to ream me out for going rogue."

"Why should he? You've been a beast on this thing."

"With a little help from my favorite psychologist."

"Aw, shucks, ma'am. So what's next on the agenda?"

"Clemmons arrives at three tomorrow, so I'm going to head home myself and sleep till then."

"Good. You deserve it. One last thing: can you give me Hermie's cell number?"

---

Finally back home and nursing a Jack Daniel's, I called Hermie Gould's cell. I got his voicemail, which meant that he'd either shut off the phone, wasn't answering, or was asleep. Or some combination of the three. So I left a message.

"Hermie, this is Daniel Rinaldi. Do me a favor, will you? A friend of mine named Indra Bishara needs a ride for herself and her daughter, so I was hoping you'd check out the main car rental places in the area. She'd like a town car, if possible. I'd really appreciate any help you could give me with this."

After I hung up, I took a deep swallow of my drink. I had to hope that Hermie would be able to decode my message. I was aware of how insecure cell communication could be, and the last thing I wanted to do was suggest anything on the young man's voicemail that would incriminate him.

Back at the Bureau building, while Hermie was working on Bowman's computer, I'd told Gloria about Indra Bishara's sudden disappearance. I could only hope that Hermie had overheard me, as he seemed to hear everything, even when absorbed at the keyboard. I had to trust that he understood my actual request, which is that he hack into the computer systems of the major auto rental places and find out which one had dispatched a town car to Indra Bishara's house, as well as the destination to which she'd asked to be driven.

By now, of course, it was possible that Barton Kerns had already tracked down the rental place and, in his usual subtle, sophisticated manner, had secured from some terrified employee the same information. Still, there was always the chance that he hadn't succeeded yet, so I tried her numbers again to warn her that he was on her trail. Again, all I got at each number was her voicemail.

Realizing there wasn't much else to do, I ended that long day by finishing my whiskey. Then I quickly stripped and climbed into bed.

In what seemed less than a few minutes, I'd fallen into a deep, dreamless sleep.

—

My cell rang before my bedside alarm clock did. It was Hermie Gould, calling at six a.m.

"Hey, Doc, you up?"

"I am now. But thanks for getting back to me, Hermie. Did you understand my message?"

"Didn't take a genius, though I happen to be one. Anyway, I found a great rental place for your friend. If she's still interested, a town car from Tri-State Rentals would be happy to drive her and her daughter to a cabin at Freeman Lake."

"That's about an hour northeast of here, right? Nice, sleepy wooded area."

"Sure looks like it, according to Google Maps. The car place even suggested one of the cabins rented by a former client. It's at a place called Lakeside Premium Cabins. The cabin number is 121."

"Great, Hermie. Thanks so much. I'll be sure to pass on the info to Indra."

"My pleasure. Just make sure you also tell our mutual friend, Gloria, about how helpful I've been. I could use all the brownie points I can get."

"Will do."

I quickly went into the kitchen, heated up some leftover coffee in the microwave, and called the Old County Building downtown. After identifying myself to the bored duty sergeant, who either didn't know or didn't care about my suspension, I was patched through to Harry Polk's cubicle on the detective floor.

I feared I might get an outgoing message, but, luckily, he answered the phone. Voice raw, resigned. Old.

"Sergeant Polk, Robbery/Homicide."

If he was here at this hour, it no doubt meant he was just

finishing up on the graveyard shift. Which also meant that Polk was still stuck on desk assignment.

"Harry, it's Dan Rinaldi."

"Jesus, like I don't got enough aggravation..."

"C'mon, it's urgent. At the moment, I don't have many friends in the department, so I figured I'd better call you."

"Since when are we friends, Rinaldi?"

"We can argue the complicated dynamics of our relationship later. Listen, you have to contact the local cops or State Police up near Freeman Lake. A place called Lakeside Cabins, specifically Cabin 121. There's a thug named Barton Kerns probably on his way there now, if he hasn't shown up already. He's after a woman named—"

Polk interrupted me with a hoarse laugh.

"You ain't seen the news this mornin', eh, Doc? There's a shitload o' cops up at that cabin already. It's a goddamn crime scene. Some rich kid named Reynolds got himself killed."

"What? Billy Reynolds is dead?"

"Yep. Shot through the heart by his fuckin' ex. Some Hindu broad. They got her in cuffs now."

"You mean Indra Bishara?"

"That's the name. She copped to the killing right away. Claims self-defense."

"What about Rebecca? Her daughter? Where is she?"

"Who the fuck knows? What am I, social services?"

I tried to think, my mind a jumble of disconnected thoughts.

"Tell me, Harry, where is she now?"

"The Bishara woman? In a cell in Split Acres. Godforsaken little town up near Freeman Lake. I think the station's got two cops, a coffeepot, and a Xerox machine."

"Call them for me, will you? Tell them I'm on my way up to see their prisoner."

"And why the hell should I do that?"

"Maybe so that I'm not tempted to spread the word about you sleeping off a drunk on my hallway floor."

"Shit! And you'd do it, too, wouldn't ya?"

"Hard to say. But it's been a rough week."

I heard his raspy, disgruntled sigh over the phone.

"All right," he said at last. "But if I do this, we're square, right? You'll keep your damn mouth shut about that?"

"Scout's honor."

"Fuck you. And what do I tell 'em up in Split Acres?"

"Say I'm Ms. Bishara's doctor, and that I'm worried for her state of mind."

Which wasn't far from the truth.

—

After hanging up with Polk, I threw back two mugs of yesterday's coffee and then called each of today's therapy patients, canceling their sessions. I wanted the day cleared for whatever might lie ahead.

Dressing quickly, I was in my car and on the road by seven, heading east and north out of the city, toward the timeless Appalachian Mountains.

Split Acres was a former mining town, now reduced to a handful of gun stores, marijuana dispensaries, and retail outlets. Its sole redeeming feature in the wake of the past decades' economic collapse was its proximity to Freeman Lake and the expanse of unsettled forest surrounding it. According to the posted signs as I approached the town via the lakeside highway, fishing and gaming were plentiful in the area and everybody was welcome.

That didn't do much to raise my spirits as I pulled to the curb in front of a squat, red-bricked building whose stenciled window read "Split Acres Police Station."

There was a sweet-looking teenaged girl manning the reception desk, talking animatedly to a cop who couldn't have been much older. He had an impressive set of shoulders and an easy smile. His name tag read "Larson, SAPD."

I'd seen his type in every small town in Pennsylvania. The local high school football star turned police officer.

I introduced myself to them both. The girl looked at her nails, disinterested. But Larson straightened right up.

"Yeah, Doc," he said. "We got word from Pittsburgh PD that you were comin' to see the prisoner."

With a courteous wave, he indicated a windowless side door and I followed him through. He led me down a small corridor, at whose end were two barred jail cells. Indra Bishara was sitting on a bench in the nearest one, her head bowed.

"Indra, it's me," I said, as Larson took out a ring of keys and unlocked the cell door.

She barely acknowledged me as I entered and took a seat next to her on the bench. At a nod from me, the young cop closed the door, relocked it, and headed back the way we'd come.

Indra spoke finally, her voice no more than a whisper.

"When I heard footsteps coming, I thought you'd be the lawyer." Now she looked up, offering me a sad smile. "I'm glad it's you instead."

"And I'm glad you're expecting a lawyer. I hope it's a good one."

"The best, according to Max Sable. He arranged for the man to see me for a reduced fee. Apparently, they're friends."

"Nice of him."

"He's also having Becky stay with him while I'm...well... here. She's known him for years, so it should be okay."

"How is she doing?"

"You mean, after seeing her mother shoot her father? She's doing *great*, Danny. What's another horrific trauma for a sensitive young girl?"

I let a long moment of silence pass between us. I had too much regard for Indra's intelligence to say anything. Or warn her of the difficult emotional journey that lay ahead for Becky.

"Are you able to tell me what happened?" I asked her. "If not, that's okay, too."

To my surprise, she took my hand in hers.

"No, I want you to know. I need you to understand."

"But that's just it, I don't. Why'd you run? Surely you know how serious parental kidnapping is. So why did you—"

She shook her head.

"I wasn't running away, Danny. And I wasn't kidnapping Becky. I just wanted to get out of Lockhart for a couple days. I'm still shocked by Marty's death, for one thing. I needed to get away from the college, and from the constant calls and emails from Billy's attorney. It was like I couldn't breathe."

"And Becky was willing to go with you?"

"Not at first, no. But I made a deal with her. Begged her, really. I asked her to give the two of us a couple of days away from everything, from everyone. Just some time so we could talk things over.

"I was her mother, after all. I'd loved and cared for her all these years and felt she owed me at least that much. I wanted the chance to explain why I'd misled her about how she'd been injured that night. If nothing else, I wanted to apologize. Finally, I told her that, after this time together, if she still wanted to go with Billy, I wouldn't fight it anymore."

"And she went along with that?"

"Begrudgingly. She was still Becky. Sullen, angry, and

distrustful. But, despite herself, I think she loves me as much as she hates me. So she agreed."

I paused, musing on what she'd said. "I understand now how you both ended up in the cabin. But then, last night..."

"I was in bed," she said softly, "when I heard sounds outside the cabin in the middle of the night. Around three or four a.m. I reached in the bedside table drawer for my gun..." Here, she gave me a quick look. "I brought it up with us. My .45 revolver. For protection."

I nodded and said nothing.

"Anyway, it wasn't till I'd gotten out of bed and gone to the front window that I realized Becky had followed me. We both saw Billy approaching. Looking big and scary, in a thick jacket and boots. Though I don't know how he found us..."

"Barton Kerns. Ex-cop who works for Billy's lawyer."

But she kept talking, oblivious. Lost in memory.

"I was terrified. Couldn't believe what was happening. It was like a nightmare. I grabbed Becky, tried to think of something to do, somewhere to hide. Then, suddenly, Billy ran up the cabin steps and kicked the door in. Becky and I both screamed and backed away. But he kept coming. I'd never seen him so angry before, so full of rage. Even worse than that awful night years ago. And then I..."

Tears dotted the edges of her dark, downcast eyes.

"It was so strange. All of a sudden I was aware of the gun in my hand. And Billy coming closer...and closer..."

She drew a long breath, then looked pointedly at me.

"You have to believe me. So do the police, everybody. They *have* to understand. I didn't *mean* to kill him."

Her grip on my hand tightened. Steely, convulsive.

"You of all people must know what I mean, right, Danny? You see it, don't you? The middle of the night, Billy breaking down the door. Coming right at us. I must have just...panicked."

# Chapter Thirty-Nine

On my way out of the station, I thanked Officer Larson for his cooperation.

"No worries, Doc." He walked me to the front door. "It's a big deal having a homicide in Split Acres. Not what we usually handle around here. I hate to say it, but it's kinda exciting."

"Believe me, I understand."

He stopped at the entrance, rubbed his hairless chin.

"Funny, though. About what happened. The victim was shot once, straight through the heart. Dead center. Not easy to do, backing away from a guy coming at you…"

I shrugged, thanked him again, and went out the door.

---

It was just before three and, as prearranged with Gloria, I met her in the FBI building parking lot. She'd arrived before I did and was leaning against her car, talking on her cell. Seeing me, she clicked off.

I pulled into the spot beside hers and opened my window.

"Hey," I called to her. "Somebody looks rested."

Smiling, she came over, leaned in the car, and kissed me.

"You mean I don't look like shit. But I'll still take it as a compliment."

Though the air was as frosty as ever, the sun was bright in a cloudless sky. The wintry light shone on her pretty face, now no longer drawn, her eyes undimmed by fatigue.

"I saw you on the phone," I said. "Anything important?"

"Only that Clemmons' flight was delayed. He won't be here till six this evening, at the earliest."

"Cool. Then maybe we can grab an early bite somewhere."

I was about to undo my seat belt when her expression changed. Grew serious.

"I forgot to ask you before, Danny, but what did you do with the gun you took from that Kerns prick?"

"I still have it," I said. "In the glove compartment."

"Are you crazy? If you got stopped and an officer found a gun not registered to you in there, you'd be toast."

"Good point."

"Give it to me, okay? I'll make sure it's buried somewhere in the Bureau evidence lockup."

I nodded and, still belted in, reached across the passenger seat and unlocked the glove compartment. Withdrawing the gun, I straightened and handed it to Gloria through the open window.

She'd taken a small zippered bag from her purse and, after carefully wiping the weapon with a handkerchief, put it in the bag and sealed it. Then dropped it in her purse.

But I'd barely paid attention to what she was doing.

An idea had formed in my mind. And then, as often happened when working with a patient in therapy, a series of associations began to emerge. Becoming clearer. Tumbling one after the other.

And if where they led was correct…

"Listen," I said firmly, which brought her gaze up to mine. "I think I know what happened to Hank Bowman."

—

"Can you get online and open up those crime scene photos from where Bowman's body was found?"

Gloria withdrew her laptop from her briefcase, set it on the desk between us, and booted up. She and I were back in her temporary office in the FBI building, sharing hot coffees from a vending machine. Our only stop before entering the small, featureless room and closing the door.

"The more I think about Hank's involvement with that racist group," she said as she typed, "the madder I get."

Which was evident in the way she was punishing the laptop keys. "To think that I wept when I heard he'd been killed. I feel like an idiot."

"Don't," I said. "He was someone you were close to who'd been murdered. I can't imagine how else you'd react. Besides, you didn't know about his hidden life… How could you?"

She nodded, unconvinced. "Maybe. But it doesn't help that he's not an isolated case."

"Unfortunately, no."

She sat back and indicated the screen. "I don't know what you're hoping to find, Danny, but there they are."

I leaned over her shoulder and saw once again the grim photos of the roadside crime scene. I swiped through the series of images until I found the one of Hank Bowman behind the wheel of his car. His body twisted awkwardly, its weight stretching the seat belt as he reached across the passenger seat.

I pointed it out to Gloria. "You see? When you asked me

to get Kerns' gun from my glove compartment, I had to reach across the passenger seat to open it. With my seat belt still fastened, I had to stretch in the same way Bowman is doing here."

"But I told you before, Danny. It's unlikely Hank would've kept his service weapon in the glove compartment."

"I know. But something occurred to me when I found myself making the same kind of move. Right after you'd warned me what might happen if a cop stopped me and found the gun. What if that's exactly what *did* happen to Hank?"

I turned to her, feeling a surge of excitement rising in my chest.

"Think about it. His car was on the side of the road. When found inside, his body was leaning to the right, reaching toward his glove compartment. What if he'd been pulled over and asked to provide his license and registration?"

"You mean…?"

I nodded. "I keep my Mustang's registration card in my glove compartment. What if Hank Bowman did, too? And that's what he was reaching for when he was shot in the back of the neck."

Gloria's eyes widened. "But if that's true, then…Jesus, Danny, are you saying Hank was killed by a cop?"

"Or maybe someone dressed like one," I said.

"But you don't think so, do you?"

"No, I don't."

She looked troubled. Clearly unconvinced.

"Just picture it," I went on, quickly. "Hank's driving along I-76, sees a patrol car behind him, lights flashing. It's a pain, inconvenient as hell, but he pulls over. In his mind, it's a routine traffic stop. Maybe he'll get a ticket, but he'll soon be back on his way up to Seven Springs. The cop comes up to the driver's side, Hank rolls down the window. The cop asks to see his license and registration, Hank's back is turned as he reaches across to the glove compartment..."

"And he's killed. Execution-style," Gloria said quietly.

"But with everything we've found out about Hank so far, that means his killer might be the Handler. Conway told us that Hank probably figured he was safe from the Handler's purge of the member list. He'd been the Handler's right-hand man."

"Yes, but that doesn't mean he'd ever *seen* the Handler. Maybe they only communicated by phone or email, even at the beginning. If so, Hank wouldn't have recognized the cop who'd pulled him over."

She took a careful sip of her steaming coffee, but I suspected she didn't taste it. It was just something to do while she tried to process what I'd suggested.

"There's more, Gloria," I said. "Remember that crazy video, with the cackling skull? Meant to convince us that the sniper was just some nutjob killing people at random."

"Of course, I do."

"It was sent to Chief Logan's office laptop by someone who must have had access to the interdepartmental system. It's used statewide, right, by every branch of law enforcement?"

"Again, something a cop could use."

"Just like a cop could access military records and find a disaffected veteran who'd been trained as a sniper."

"Randy Wells Porter." Gloria said evenly, her voice having lost its reluctant tone.

Now, despite herself, I could tell she'd begun forging her own set of links in the chain.

"And when Porter became a liability after his arrest," she said, "a cop could access ViCAP or search parole board records. To find someone who could make sure Porter wouldn't talk."

"That's right. The cop might even know some parole officers

and could ask about parolees. Looking for a violent offender who could talk the talk."

"Hubert Sedarki."

"Yes, whom the Handler instructed to eliminate Porter's public defender and then take his place at the hospital."

We fell silent for a long moment.

Finally, Gloria spoke. "This is all so incredible. And incredibly sad. The thought that the sniper's victims had all been secret participants in a racist group bankrolling hate crimes is horrible enough. But the idea that their boss might be a cop..."

"Yeah," I said. "Unless I'm wrong. About all of it. Let's face it, Gloria. Everything I've laid out is all guesswork. A gut feeling."

"And that's the problem. Your gut feeling isn't evidence. In fact, this whole scenario is just speculation."

I got up from my seat and leaned with my back against the door. The small room had suddenly become airless, stifling.

"I know there's no way to prove any of what I'm suggesting. I'm not a policeman, as a certain detective sergeant is always reminding me."

"You're not a Fed, either," Gloria said. "Like it or not,we have to do things a certain way. There are protocols. Rules of evidence gathering. All that boring procedural stuff that smart-ass guys like you ignore. We can't go by our gut."

Here she offered me a smile. "No offense."

"None taken."

"The point is," she added, rising herself, "even if I think you're right about most of it—and I think you are—we don't have enough to go to Clemmons and Biegler."

She bent and closed her laptop, slipped it once more into her briefcase, and headed for the door.

"Besides, I should get my notes ready for when Clemmons shows up. He wants me to ride shotgun when he grills Conway."

We shared a brief hug, and only a slightly longer kiss.

"And, hey, Rinaldi," she said. "I happen to like your gut."

She'd tried for a playful, intimate respite from where our discussion had led us. But her smile was small, rueful.

As was mine in return.

—

Left alone in the stuffy room, I was about to check my office voicemail for any patient calls when my cell rang.

The name on the ID screen was Leland Sinclair.

"Dr. Rinaldi?"

His voice sounded strange. Hurried, terse.

"Lee?"

"Are you alone?"

"As a matter of fact, yeah. What's—"

"Dan, you need to come to my office right away."

"Listen, are you all right? You sound—"

The strangled tone sharpened, rose.

*"Shut up and do what I say! Come to my office! Now!"*

"Okay, but—"

"*Now,* goddamn it! And alone. For God's sake, make sure you come alone! Or else he'll—"

The phone went dead in my hand.

# Chapter Forty

Commuter traffic heading out of town had dwindled, and the by-now familiar array of lights dotting the towers of modern Pittsburgh shone from the windows of empty offices.

As I approached the new, half-finished civic complex, enveloped in a cold, unremitting darkness, I felt an uncanny sense of dread. Although there were other cars on the streets, and pockets of pedestrians bundled into coats and scarves, I couldn't shake a sudden, intense experience of isolation. The impression that I was profoundly alone and moving willingly, but inexorably, into danger.

*But why? What am I doing?*

Polk was right, I'm not a cop. Nor anybody's idea of a hero. So why didn't I alert the police after getting Sinclair's frantic phone call?

Precisely *because* of that phone call. The terror in his voice when he begged me to come alone.

And my fears for what would happen to him if I didn't.

—

Sinclair's suite was one of the few completed offices in the building. The rest of the floors were deserted, the rooms untenanted. Under construction.

I parked at a corner adjacent to the building's entrance and hurried along the empty sidewalk. As I neared the front double doors, I looked up at the scaffolding hugging the walls.

And felt a chill having nothing to do with the icy air.

Illuminated by the cold glare of regularly spaced search lights, the hanging tarps, wooden platforms, and suspended metal buckets gave the entire structure a haunted, fragmented look. Like an unformed, motionless behemoth, all ribs and shredded flesh, being birthed out of the night.

Readying myself, I opened the heavy, steel-lined doors.

Unlike when I'd been here before, there was no guard at the reception desk. The lobby was completely empty, its overhead lights dimmed. And the only sound was the muffled echo of my footsteps as I made my way to the elevator.

I stepped off on Sinclair's floor and hurried down the equally ill-lit corridor to his suite. Though when I reached the polished doors, I hesitated.

But only for a moment. Spurred by the memory of Sinclair's choked, desperate voice on the phone, I pulled open the heavy doors and bolted in.

Again, the airy reception area was empty, and I went through it quickly. Found the door leading to the District district attorney's suite. Turned the knob.

The secretary's area was empty as well, and I was struck by the muffled silence of the small, carpeted room. Then, out of the corner of my eye, I noticed that the desk was standing at an odd angle. Somewhat askew, misaligned with the perfectly squared positions of the other furniture in the room.

Something, I realized, had pushed the desk aside. I went around to the back of the desk and saw what it was.

*Who* it was.

Sharon Cale, Sinclair's executive assistant, lay on her side on the floor, unmoving. Legs scissored, arms flung out.

An ugly red gash bled thickly from her forehead.

I bent and checked her pulse and her breathing. She was alive but unconscious. Blood splatter dotted her blond hair and silk blouse.

I reached for the scarf she was wearing and gently unspooled it from her neck. Then I pressed it against her wound to stanch the bleeding.

Still on my haunches, I glanced around the desktop, which was at eye level, and grabbed a heavy tape dispenser from the blotter. I used the tape to secure the makeshift bandage I'd applied to her forehead.

It wasn't pretty, but it would do. It would have to.

Rising to my feet, I came around to the front of the desk again and headed for the door leading to Sinclair's office. I paused before the polished wood, listening for any sounds from within.

Nothing.

I took a breath, trying to center myself. Focus.

It didn't help.

I pulled open the door and stepped inside.

And found Leland Sinclair sitting at his chair behind his desk. His handsome face dead white, eyes wide with fear.

With an automatic pistol pressed against his left temple.

"Well, glad you got here in time, Doc. I was just about to blow a hole in the DA's head."

Standing just behind and to the side of the district attorney, his smile as self-assured as his military-straight stance, was Sheriff Roy Gibson.

# Chapter Forty-One

*A cop,* I thought. *Or a sheriff.*

Everything that Gloria and I had surmised could just as easily have been done by the sheriff of Lockhart. All law enforcement personnel in the state had access to the same interagency computer system. And ViCAP. And military records.

And the car that had pulled over Hank Bowman could have been a Sheriff's Department vehicle. Like the one Gibson had driven up next to Max Sable and me at Marty Hobbs' funeral.

All these thoughts ran through my mind in seconds, even as I stood in the middle of Sinclair's office. Its ostentatious furnishings, oversized flags, and wall plaques formed an absurd backdrop to what was happening at that moment.

"Stay right where you're standing, Dr. Rinaldi."

Gibson let the smile melt from his face as he set his jaw. In his crisp uniform and leather jacket, with its insignia proclaiming his decade of service, he could have been the poster boy for law and order. Strong. Authoritative. Right-thinking.

The epitome of the white alpha male. At least in his own mind.

"You," I said stiffly. "You're the Handler."

He nodded. "Oh, yeah. That name the Task Force came up with for me. Gotta admit, it has a certain ring to it."

I ignored him and took a step forward.

"That's far enough, Doc," he said. "Just think of it as social distancing. You remember that, don't you?"

Meanwhile, a tinge of color had returned to Sinclair's cheeks. The anger and frustration at his helpless situation were waging a war with his fear.

"Are you all right, Lee?" I asked him.

"I'll live."

Gibson laughed. "That remains to be seen."

Sinclair swallowed air, still struggling to steady himself. "How's Sharon?"

"Unconscious, but alive." I risked another step toward his captor. "Jesus, Gibson, what do you want?"

"What all true patriots want," he said simply. "I want this country to return to its former glory. To embrace the undisputed truth of race science. To restore white supremacy and defend it against all attempts to sully or supplant it."

"In other words, to make America all white again—as though it ever was."

"See, that's the kind of attitude we're fighting against. Even in my own town. Lockhart's literally being defiled. We got Hispanics, Asians. Hell, I've even gotta work with a nigger coroner. Know what I call him in private? Max Sambo."

He gave me a wink, proud of his grim joke. Meanwhile, I was remembering the family portrait I'd seen on Gibson's desk.

"What about your wife and daughters?" I said. "Do they share your opinions?"

Gibson suddenly frowned. "That color-blind bitch of a wife turned my girls against me. Brainwashed them. When she left me, she took Evie and Jill with her."

"That must have hit you hard, Roy," I said carefully. "Otherwise, why keep the photo on your desk?"

He hesitated, angrily chewing his lip. Finally, he said, "It's there because, no matter what they think, I'm fighting for them, too. For all white Americans everywhere."

Despite the hollow tone of his words, and the rote dogma, he couldn't keep the pain out of his voice. He'd buried the grief of his loss under a blind, unreasoning hatred.

"You keep saying it's a fight. Sounds more like a war."

"It *is* a war. Against the darker breeds, the yellow races, the Jews. Real Americans know this. More and more of us are willing to stand up against them. Even die in the cause."

"I'm not so sure your band of merry racists, the other members of the de Gobineau Society, expected to die quite so quickly. Nor by their leader's own hand."

Gibson scowled. "One of them betrayed us. Sold us out to the Feds. Race traitors can't be tolerated."

"I get that. And since you didn't know which one was talking to the DOJ, you had Randy Porter take them all out."

"Yeah. The Steel City Sniper. Gotta give one thing to the liberal media, they're great with the snappy names. By the way, Porter was a talented sociopath but greedy as hell. No sense of mission at all, just wanted the cash. Our deal was half up front, the other half when all the targets were dead."

"Which you agreed to, since you knew he'd never be receiving the second half."

"Well, aren't you a smart guy? Got it all figured out."

"Not quite. I do know you set up Councilman Landrew as a target for Porter. I also know how you killed Hank Bowman. I'm guessing you tracked him using his car's GPS system. Your department would have the equipment to do so.

"I do have one question, though. That bookie you brought

in to interrogate. The one you said could finger who might've wanted Martin Hobbs dead. That was all bullshit, wasn't it?"

"Complete and total. I rousted a few local perps and sweated 'em, but it was all for show. Smoke and mirrors."

"Just like the trick *you* pulled. Insisting that Hobbs' death wasn't a suicide but murder. Even building the case for it. All to disguise the fact that it was *you* who killed him."

He shook his head gravely. "Now that was a damn shame. I kinda liked Marty. He was a bleedin' heart, like most of those college types, but harmless."

"Then why kill him?"

"It was just a fluke. He happened to come by my place and just strolled in. As you know, we don't lock our doors in sleepy little Lockhart. Anyway, he overheard me talking with Hank Bowman. Arranging a payment to one of the militia groups we fund. I was just hanging up when he came in, but we both knew he'd heard enough. Two minutes later, he mumbled some excuse about having to hurry on home."

"Where he got drunk to screw up his courage," I said. "But finally, he called me. Said he had to see me. In person."

Gibson sighed heavily. "Yeah, I didn't know what he would do, but I figured it wouldn't be good. So I went to his place to convince him he hadn't heard what he thought he heard."

"While you secretly dropped some Rohypnol into his drink."

"Made it a helluva lot easier to string him up. To make it look like a suicide." He laughed again. "Then, just as I'm heading out, who do I see comin' down the street? In that sweet, reconditioned Mustang? Couldn't be anybody else."

"So you decided to mess with my head."

"Sure. Why not give the famous trauma expert a dose of trauma himself? The brilliant police consultant, with the fancy-ass degree. I've hated pricks like you all my life. So-called progressives. One-worlders. American apologists."

His voice had risen sharply, and he made an effort to control its rancor. Hand wiping his brow.

"So, anyway, I ran back inside the house, lit the candle near where Marty hung like a skinny side of beef, then went behind the house and killed the lights."

"Leading me right to his body. And you had all the time you needed, since I sat parked in front of the house for a minute or two. Trying Marty again on his phone."

A slow, satisfied nod. "I just wish I coulda seen the look on your face when you found him."

I didn't reply, but instead glanced over to see how Leland was doing. His breathing was shallow but regular, the fear in his eyes replaced by a seething awareness of his impotence. Not a feeling the district attorney was accustomed to.

So he did something stupid.

Looking up at Roy Gibson with undisguised contempt, he muttered, "Just a common killer, you piece of shit…"

Gibson's face darkened. Then he raised his gun and raked it down hard across the side of Sinclair's head.

With a garbled cry of pain, Sinclair pitched forward in his chair, a splotch of blood sprouting above his left ear.

"For Christ's sake, Gibson!" I yelled.

I rushed forward, pressing my pocket handkerchief against Sinclair's bloody temple. I realized just then that, shocked at the sight of Sharon Cale lying injured, I'd forgotten I could've used it on her wound.

It took the DA a few moments to recover from the shock, but then he replaced my hand with his, holding the wadded cloth against the pulpy wound. Crouched low in his chair, in obvious agony, Lee Sinclair had lost whatever prideful defiance he'd been able to muster.

When I straightened up, I found myself looking at the barrel of Gibson's automatic pistol, which was now trained on me.

"That's enough, Doc. Now back up. Back to where you were."

I did as he instructed.

"You took a helluva chance, rushing over to help," he said easily. "If you weren't a wrongheaded traitor to your own kind, I'd say you had some balls."

He offered Sinclair a disdainful glance. "More than our renowned district attorney, at least. Who's turned out to be another empty suit created by the media."

I felt my jaw tighten. I'd had enough.

"I'm sick of your shit, Gibson. What's this all about, anyway? Why the fuck are we here?"

He paused for a moment, a strange, intense rigidity coming over his features. His eyes shrinking to black dots. Then, slowly, he bent down and picked something up from behind the desk. A thick canvas backpack.

Its pockets bulged, and a pair of twisted wires looped out from the top. They were connected to some kind of switch plate, its red light blinking dully.

A bomb.

"Why are we here, Doc? Simple." Gibson hoisted the backpack onto his shoulder. "We're all here to die."

# Chapter Forty-Two

I had my arm around Sinclair's waist, and he kept the blood-soaked handkerchief pressed against the side of his head. His legs could barely support his weight as we went down the corridor to the building's one working elevator.

Behind us, his gun jammed into my back, was Roy Gibson.

Moments before, as he'd instructed, Sinclair and I had preceded him out of the DA's office and passed through the reception area. Out of the corner of my eye I noticed that Sharon Cale lay where I'd left her but was still breathing. And from the look of my makeshift bandage on her head, at least the bleeding had stopped.

Now, at Gibson's direction, we three entered the elevator. With the backpack still slung over one shoulder, he sent us down. All the way down to the basement, the service level.

It was a dimly lit, concrete-walled, cavernous expanse. Low-ceilinged and crisscrossed with deep shadows, the entire room was crowded with construction equipment, great coils of thick wire, and stacks of boxes.

A bitter cold seeped through the walls and up from the asphalt floor, as though we'd descended to a frozen hell.

"Move," Gibson said.

Sinclair and I did as he ordered, the district attorney groaning as I urged him to quicken the pace. I could feel Gibson's growing impatience behind me, the way his gun barrel kept grinding into my back.

We hadn't gone more than a hundred feet when Gibson ordered us to stop.

I craned my neck around, but all I saw in the scalloped shadows were the blurred shapes of hand trucks, wheelbarrows, and scattered building materials.

"Okay, you two." Gibson had come around to stand in front of us, the gun waist-high, swiveling from Sinclair to me. "I figure this will do."

"For what?" I said. "I still don't understand. Why are you doing this?"

He gave a wry chuckle. "Turns out, Hank Bowman was smarter than I gave him credit for. He and I never met face-to-face, but he knew who I was. So at some point he got his lawyer to keep all the details of our group, including my identity, in a safe in the guy's office."

"I think I've seen that movie. If Bowman was killed, the lawyer was instructed to release the information to the cops."

"Exactly."

"But how did you find out about this?"

"A fellow patriot is an officer in the Pittsburgh Police. Though not a member of the society, he knew about us. As do many others on the Dark Web. He warned me that incriminating evidence about me and the group had just been delivered to the cops and that my arrest was imminent."

By now, Lee Sinclair had let himself sink to the cold concrete floor, his head down, weakened by his wound. His patrician features and designer-label suit were absurdly out of place down here, in striking contrast to the dingy, dust-covered tools and machinery all around us.

Gibson peered down at the district attorney and gave a resigned sigh.

"I knew right away what I had to do. I wasn't going to let myself be arrested. Charged by the likes of him. Sent to some prison filled with the rest of the country's filth."

"So you came here. To martyr yourself for the cause."

"Call it whatever you want. But can you think of a better altar to sacrifice myself on? A brand-new civic complex, a proud symbol of the jackbooted government."

"Like what Timothy McVeigh did in Oklahoma."

He shook his head. "No, I want more. What people like you don't understand is that there are many thousands of my fellow patriots throughout the country, all connected on the Dark Web. Before coming here, I alerted as many of them as I could about what was to happen. An explosion that would light up the civic center, before bringing it crashing down."

His eyes gleamed now with pride and purpose. The true believer, caught up in his own madness.

"It will be the opening volley of the race war," he said. "A flaming torch against the night sky, marking the beginning of the struggle of the white race to reclaim its heritage."

At this, Sinclair raised his head. Voice thin, reedy.

"You're insane, you know that, right? A lunatic."

Gibson merely laughed, then put his backpack on the floor. Still with his gun in hand, aimed in my general direction.

"You two should consider yourselves lucky," he said, his free hand doing something to the switch plate attached to the backpack. "Your names will go down in history, *if* they find enough of what's left of you to make the IDs."

He straightened again and waved me back a few feet with his

gun hand. Though my gaze was riveted on a timer next to the switch plate. Its illuminated face showing five minutes.

And counting down.

Gibson indicated the backpack, smiling contentedly. "Know what's in there, Rinaldi? Enough C-4 to blow up this whole goddamn place. Especially set off down here."

I couldn't stop myself from staring at the timer's display.

Four minutes, thirty seconds...

My mind raced. If I could somehow get past Gibson, I could pull out one of those wires. Or both of them.

I knew nothing about bombs or how to disarm them. But even if I pulled the wrong wires and set it off, what difference would it make? The bomb was still going to explode anyway.

In four minutes.

How had thirty seconds passed so quickly?

Seemingly unmindful of his wound, Leland Sinclair now gave me a stricken look. Panic gleamed in his eyes.

But when I turned again to Gibson, it was the look in *his* eyes that struck me. His previous anger, that assured intensity, had been replaced by a kind of serenity. As though his entire life until now had been a journey to this exact moment. A journey marked with a strange, silent hush that enveloped this area of the basement like a shroud. The three of us, pretty much immobilized, waiting for the end.

Then, suddenly, a sound filtered through the thick concrete walls. The wail of a siren, far off in the distance, but growing steadily louder.

*Sharon Cale,* I thought. She'd roused herself enough to reach for the desk phone. And call the cops.

Roy Gibson had started at the sound, like a sleepwalker pulled from his trance. With the instincts born from his years in law enforcement, he turned toward the direction of the sirens.

Gun up, in a two-handed grip. Ready for whatever was about to come charging toward him.

With his body half-turned to me, I saw my chance. Without thinking, I ran toward him and lunged for the gun. Shouting in outrage, Gibson tried to push me away, but I held fast, my hands covering his where they gripped the gun.

We wrestled awkwardly that way, gasping and cursing, fighting for control of the automatic, until I managed to slam our locked hands against the near wall.

With a strangled cry, he let loose of the gun, and it skittered across the concrete floor, stopping right in front of where Lee Sinclair sat.

Freeing myself of Gibson's grasp, I turned toward the backpack. My eyes darted to the timer.

Three minutes.

*Those wires,* I told myself. It was the only thing I could think of. Pull those wires. If that set off the bomb—

*Fuck it.* We were going to die either way.

I'd no sooner had that thought when Gibson roared in outrage and shoved me aside. Then he bent, scooped up the backpack, and began running back in the direction we'd come.

Suddenly, a shot rang out, echoing dully in the room, reverberating off the concrete walls and floor. I whirled around and saw that Sinclair, holding Gibson's gun, had fired at the running man.

"No!" I shouted. "If you hit the bomb—"

At the same time, I heard a guttural cry and turned again.

It was Roy Gibson, the backpack slung over one shoulder. He had his hand grasped to his other shoulder, and even in the dimness I could see that blood was oozing between his fingers.

"I got the bastard, didn't I?" said Sinclair, lowering the gun to his side.

I didn't answer but instead took off after Gibson as his bent, wounded figure disappeared into the cold, shadowed expanse of the basement.

# Chapter Forty-Three

In the flickering light of the fluorescents buzzing overhead, all I had to guide me was the sound of Gibson's shuffling footsteps.

Still, every few moments I'd catch sight of his shadowy figure flitting between massive piles of bricks or stacks of Sheetrock. But it was mostly his labored breathing, the wheeze of a seriously injured man, or the stutter step of his shoes on concrete, that kept me on his track.

Though my time in the basement had accustomed my eyes to the dim lighting and hulking building materials strewn haphazardly about, I continually found myself bumping into sharp, unseen edges or stumbling over tools.

But the clock in my head kept me going as fast as I could manage. My silent mental count had the timer at somewhere near two minutes. Not good.

I was moving so quickly, powered by fear and adrenaline, that I pushed from my mind the fact that—should I wrest the backpack from Gibson—I had no idea what to do then.

Except pull those fucking wires.

Another thirty or so seconds must have passed, and I found myself nearing the same elevator we'd taken to the basement.

But there was no sign of Gibson.

Until I reached the elevator door and saw a smear of something wet and black on the wall beside it. I touched it. Smelled it.

Blood.

He'd taken the elevator. So I pushed the button and entered it as well. Inside, I found a bloody mark—from one of his fingers—on the fourth-floor button. The top floor.

I pressed it and ascended.

Maybe ninety seconds left? In my haste, I'd lost count in my head.

I got out on the fourth floor and ran down the dark, empty hallway. Most of the rooms were unfinished, with hanging plastic sheets draping whole areas still under construction. And more building materials dotting the length of the hall.

But no Gibson.

Finally, at the end of the hall, I came upon a steel exit door. Another streak of blood on the handle.

I pulled the door open and raced up the short flight of stairs, at the end of which stood another door.

Pushing through it, I stepped out onto the flat, slate-covered roof of the building. Loose gravel crunched under my feet as I peered anxiously around the roof.

It was a clear night, and the stars shone coldly above. Their lights mirrored by those of the surrounding buildings did not lessen the oppressive darkness, nor the shrill voice that suddenly pierced it.

"Rinaldi!"

Standing not a dozen yards away from me on the roof was Roy Gibson, the backpack looped around his good shoulder. His opposite arm, drenched in blood, hanging uselessly at his side.

But the hand holding his gun was steady as he aimed it at me. The barrel glinted in the feeble ambient light.

For an instant, I was thrown by the sight of his gun. Didn't Sinclair have it? Then I recalled my father telling me once that most cops have a second weapon strapped to their ankles. "The smart ones, anyway," he'd added.

"I haven't checked the timer," Gibson was saying, wincing with pain, "but I'd say we have about thirty seconds left. Maybe less."

"Thanks for the bulletin. But we both know that bomb will do a lot less damage from up here on the roof."

He managed a weak smile. "Yeah, but it'll still light up the sky. And take these upper floors with it. So either way, Rinaldi, you're a dead man."

*Either way*, I thought. He was right. There was nothing to lose.

So, hellbent, I ran right at him. Even as he backed away, bracing his gun hand with the other. Taking a bead on me.

I was only a few feet from him, my hands outstretched.

Instinctively, Gibson backed up another few steps. Was about to fire—

Then, suddenly, the back of his heel hit the low cement rise encircling the roof. His body jerked, his gun hand flew up, firing into the sky—

And he tumbled backward over the roof. Screaming.

My own momentum took me to the roof's edge, just in time to peer over it and see him fall. The backpack clutched with both hands in front of him.

It detonated in midair.

—

Gibson had been right. The bomb lit up the night sky.

But its impact was negligible, falling as it did in mostly empty space. Yet the percussive power of the C-4 shattered a dozen windows of the civic center, as well as some of those on the building to the other side.

On the street below, people screamed and scattered as glass shards rained down from above, along with plaster, jagged bits of concrete, and other debris.

I stood as if frozen, unable to draw my gaze away from the chaos below, as police cruisers braked to a stop on the street. Officers leapt from the cars to attend to those injured by the falling glass. Finally, as my view became obscured by smoke drifting up from where the bomb had exploded, I turned away.

After stepping back from the roof edge, I stood shaking, nearly unable to breathe.

I don't know how long I stayed there, alone on that roof under a black, star-pocked, uncaring sky. Until suddenly I was moving again, walking stiffly back toward the roof access door.

When I reached for the knob, I had to concentrate to make my fingers grip it and turn as my hand trembled uncontrollably.

And I knew at that moment what form my nightmares would take in the days and weeks ahead...

—

In the hours that followed, Lee Sinclair, Sharon Cale, and I were each bundled into ambulances and taken to Pittsburgh Memorial. Though I was ostensibly uninjured, the EMTs knew a potential case of shock when they saw one and insisted that I go to the hospital as well.

Meanwhile, as I learned later, a team of uniforms scoured the building, going room to room in search of other occupants. But except for the lobby guard—who was found bound but alive in a service closet—the entire structure had been empty. His description of his assailant matched that of Roy Gibson.

When released from care the next morning, I was met with a crowd of reporters as I exited the hospital. Though it was obvious that some of the details of the previous night were known by now, they wanted my personal reflections on what one of them called my "obviously terrifying experience."

I answered that, yes, I was obviously terrified. But mostly I was just grateful that both District Attorney Sinclair and Ms. Sharon Cale were alive and expected to make full recoveries from their injuries.

Unfortunately, I'd no sooner escaped from the upraised mics and intrusive cameras of the media than Detective Jerry Banks was at my elbow.

"You're with me, Doc," he said flatly.

Dragging me brusquely to his waiting unmarked, he informed me that I was needed at the precinct. To give my statement.

I spent most of the rest of the morning doing just that, in front of an impressive audience that included Stu Biegler, Tony Clemmons, and Chief Logan.

To my surprise, even Denise Ramirez, the PR flack, had shown up at the halfway point. Though her presence at such an interview was unusual, apparently she was there at the chief's request. When the official inquisition finally ended, she closed her iPad and turned to Biegler and Logan.

"If half of what he says is true," she said, "and I bet Sinclair will confirm it, the doc here's going to come out of this looking like a hero."

Biegler scowled. "Which means what…?"

"It means we better get his suspension lifted and his contract reinstated. And soon. Remember, gentlemen, it's all about the optics."

# Chapter Forty-Four

In the days that followed, the lead news story both locally and nationwide focused on the shocking death of Sheriff Roy Gibson. The explosion of a bomb in midtown Pittsburgh wasn't something the authorities could cover up. However, it gave Task Force spokesmen Stu Biegler and Tony Clemmons the opportunity to spin the event in the way they wanted. While acknowledging the painful fact that the mastermind behind the sniper attacks was a member of law enforcement, they once again allowed the public to believe these murders were the result of Gibson's unhinged mind. And that at some point he decided to commit suicide by exploding a bomb at the new city complex, taking as many innocent lives as possible with him.

As I watched the succession of news conferences from the comfort of my sofa, I tried to understand the authorities' decision. My best guess was that the Task Force, in consultation with the Justice Department, had decided to withhold the fact that the sniper's victims were members of a racist group for two reasons.

First, law enforcement didn't want to get embroiled at this point in legal battles with lawyers representing the victims' families. Plus, there weren't going to be any arrests. Other than Conway, the members were all dead, so revealing their names would only cause additional pain and, most likely, public shame and harsh recriminations to people still struggling with their grief.

Secondly, Gibson's actions had revealed to the authorities a number of similar racist groups on the Dark Web, many of which were now being exposed due to his having contacted them online about his plans for that night. Rooting out these dangerous white supremacist cadres would be easier if done without the media's interference. Revealing that the sniper's victims had been involved in such a group would only bring renewed journalistic focus on what I'm sure law enforcement saw as an unnecessary and exploitative side issue.

So, as far as the public was concerned, the Steel City Sniper's actions would be forever seen as the product of a disturbed mind, seeking his victims for reasons unknown. Moreover, I knew that as the weeks passed, and new horrific crimes grabbed the nation's attention, the loose ends of the case would be of interest only to a few suspicious reporters or bestselling true-crime authors.

I wished them well.

—

Though my name was all over the Gibson story, I refused to grant any interviews. But, admittedly, my goal of keeping a low media profile from now on had blown up. Literally.

Also, given how crucial her role had been in exposing Roy Gibson, Special Agent Gloria Reese was intricately involved in the follow-up investigations. Carving out any time for us to get together was going to be difficult.

Though neither of us said it so many words, this time apart would also give us some space to reflect on our relationship. Specifically, what was it? And where would we go from here?

The one piece of good news that week arrived in the mail. It was another notarized letter from the Police Commissioner, this one ending my suspension and reinstating my consultant's contract with Pittsburgh PD.

Looked like I was back in business.

—

I got a call from Max Sable that Saturday afternoon, as I was leaning against the railing on my back deck, sipping an Iron City. The mid-November chill seeped through my Pitt sweatshirt, but the day was so clear and bright that I didn't mind.

"Dan?" Sable's voice on the phone was tight.

"Is everything okay, Max?"

"More or less. The good news is that Indra and the attorney I referred to her seem to be working together well."

"Are they still going with a self-defense plea?"

"Yes. Or justifiable homicide. Whichever gets them a deal with the DA up there and keeps Indra out of a courtroom."

"What about her daughter? Is she okay?"

"That's the bad news, I'm afraid. She's still staying here with us, but swears she'll never go back to living with her mother. She's having terrible nightmares about seeing Indra shoot her father."

"I can imagine. So what are her plans? Does she say?"

"Apparently, there's some money left to her in Billy's will. A great deal of it."

"Giving her a degree of freedom."

"Which she wants. Badly. In fact, regardless of what happens to her mother, Becky's going to court to apply for legal emancipation. Then use some of Daddy's money to bum around Europe for a while."

The sorrowful tone of his voice made me sad as well.

"Not the happy ending I was hoping for," I said. "For either of them."

"Nope. On the other hand, aren't guys like us too old now to wish for one? By the way, Danny, I always knew what that bastard Gibson used to call me behind my back. Max Sambo."

"So he told me. How could you keep working with him then?"

"Because it's my job," he said simply.

After we hung up, I wondered whether Indra Bishara would ever be brought to trial. If so, and in the event I'd be called as a character witness, I also wondered what I would say.

—

I didn't have long to wait to find out.

On Monday morning, as I was coming down the corridor to my office, I spotted a slim figure, bundled in a heavy coat, leaning against the door. It was Rebecca Reynolds, Indra's daughter.

As I approached, she glanced up at me with sad, troubled eyes.

"Hello, Dr. Rinaldi. Is it okay I came here? I thought if it was early enough—"

"It's fine, Becky. My first patient isn't due for fifteen minutes." I took out my office keys. "Let's go inside."

She merely nodded, then followed me into the suite. I turned on a couple lights and led her into my consulting room. Becky let herself sink into the chair opposite mine.

"I'm not here for therapy or anything," she said as I took my accustomed seat across from her. "I guess…well, I guess I just needed to talk to you. About Mom."

"I'm glad you did," I said. "I've been thinking about you… and her."

She permitted herself a small smile. "I know you like her, Doctor. She sure likes you."

"How is she doing?"

"Okay, I guess. She likes the lawyer Dr. Sable got for her. He's young and handsome, so of course Mom's doing her best to wrap him around her finger."

I noted the caustic tone in her voice but didn't respond.

"They're working out some kind of deal with the district attorney," Becky went on. "Self-defense. So the charges will probably be dropped. The cops don't have any evidence to contradict her story, and they have an eyewitness to the shooting. Me."

She looked down at her hands on her lap. When she did so, the pale morning sun glazing my office window cast her facial scar in deep relief.

"They had me meet with Mom and her lawyer in the district attorney's office, where I was asked to repeat what I'd told the detectives. That my father was about to attack us in the cabin and Mom just reacted out of panic and shot him in self-defense. To protect me."

I nodded. "She told me the same thing. With Billy about to assault the two of you—"

Her eyes came up then, shining. Fierce.

"But's it's not true. It's a lie."

I sat up straighter in my chair. "A lie?"

"Dad was standing there, in the doorway. He looked upset, yeah. Angry. But he didn't attack us. He didn't even move…and then Mom…" Her voice broke. "Then Mom just raised her gun with both hands and shot him."

A somber silence grew thick in the space between us.

"She...killed my father..." Becky took a deep, anguished breath. "I saw it. I saw what really happened. And I lied. To the police, to the district attorney. To Mom's lawyer."

She offered me another sad smile. "Just like my Mom lied to me all those years ago about how I got this scar. Like mother, like daughter, eh, Doctor? Lying must be in my genes."

"It sounds like you were trying to protect her. Keep her out of prison."

"Yeah. I figured I'd already lost my dad, what good would it do if..." Now her voice hardened again. "But I think I did it as much for me as for her. All that publicity if she went on trial for murder. Reporters, TV cameras in my face. I sure as shit didn't want *that*."

Becky reflexively touched her scarred cheek.

"Anyway," she said after a moment, "I'm getting out of town. Out of the country as soon as my own lawyer gets me emancipated. I'm done being anyone's poor, unhappy daughter, hers *or* my father's."

"I can understand how you feel, Becky. But what I don't understand is why you're telling all this to me."

"It's because I know you cared about Mom...and me, too, I guess. Tried to help us. I figured you at least deserved to know the truth."

I nodded again. Then, just as I was about to speak, she abruptly rose to her feet.

"That's all I wanted to say, Dr. Rinaldi. Thanks for listening to me."

With that, she turned and headed out of the office. I followed her out through the waiting room, to the suite's exit door. I stood at the threshold with her.

"If you'd like, Becky... I mean, I know you plan to leave as soon as possible, but I also know you might need emotional support. Even on a temporary basis, and I'd be happy to—"

She shook her head.

"You don't give up, do you, Doctor? But, no...no thanks. You won't be seeing me and my freak face again."

As she went out the door, she looked back at me over her shoulder.

"And neither will anyone else. At least, not around here."

She was true to her word. I'd learn later that Becky had indeed gotten her legal freedom and departed for somewhere in Europe.

All I could do was wish her luck.

—

Later that day I got a call from Sam Weiss. For the purposes of the feature article he'd been asked to write, he was doing in-depth interviews with the families of the sniper's victims.

He'd also checked in on the one person who'd survived.

"That's why I'm calling, Danny," he said. "I figured you'd want to know that Jason Graham is out of the coma and on the mend, according to his doctors."

"Have you interviewed him yet?"

"They won't let me do so till he's released from the hospital. I think today's his last day there."

"Thanks for the update, Sam."

I abruptly clicked off, wanting to get over to Pittsburgh Memorial before Jason was released.

I still had one last question that needed to be answered.

# Chapter Forty-Five

Jason Graham smiled as I entered his hospital room, looking a lot better than the last time I'd seen him. Bright-eyed and alert, he was also finally unencumbered by the array of tubes and wires.

He was sitting up in bed, his finished breakfast tray on the side table, and motioned me to the chair beside him.

"Hey, Doc, it's good to see you! They tell me I've been in the Twilight Zone for the past week or so."

"Pretty much. How are you feeling, Jason?"

"Okay. Everything hurts like hell, but the word is I'll come out of here in one piece."

"Great. Where are your parents?"

"They were just here. Been here all morning, so I sent them down to the cafeteria. With Dad's blood sugar, he can't go skipping meals."

He smiled again, his eyes cool and steady behind the wire rims. His pink cheeks made him seem younger than his years.

"I do have a question, Jason. If you feel up to it."

"Why not? I figure I owe you for savin' my ass. Twice."

"Not me," I said. "Your doctors. First, Dr. Chang after you

were brought in for your panic attack. Then it was Dr. Suzuki's surgical skill after you'd been shot."

"Yeah." His voice dipped. "I guess."

"Of course, you didn't stay Dr. Chang's patient for very long, did you? She was replaced by Dr. Rogers."

"That was my dad, remember, because—"

I interrupted him, sliding my chair closer to the bedrails.

"See, Jason, that's what I don't understand. When I came here to visit you after the shooting, while you were in the induced coma, I spoke with your father about Dr. Suzuki. He was effusive in his praise of her and deeply grateful that she had probably saved your life."

"What are you saying, Doc?"

"I'm saying that it makes me wonder. About your father. And about you."

He stirred uncomfortably under the bedsheets, his face losing some of its boyish cast.

What I didn't tell him—couldn't—was that lately I'd been thinking about Mary Anne North and how she'd used her hated brother-in-law's name when joining the de Gobineau Society. To her it had been a joke, a gesture of her anti-Semitism to have the Jewish Peter Steinman associated with such a hate group.

Which got me thinking about Jason's father, Fred Graham. Though he was also listed as a group member, his gratitude to his son's Japanese doctor didn't gibe with his reported need to have Jason's previous doctor, a Chinese woman, replaced by a white male. What had Jason called his dad at the time? "Old school?"

I rose from my chair and stared down at him.

"It was you, wasn't it, who asked that Dr. Chang be replaced by a white doctor? Your father wasn't in the room, so it was convenient to put the blame on him."

The young man didn't answer. Merely glared at me with mounting resentment.

"Which was why, to protect your own identity, you joined the de Gobineau Society using your father's name. So that if the group were ever exposed, or criminal charges ever brought, it would be your father who'd be arrested. Not you."

Jason didn't answer for a long time. Then, as I'd seen with Robert Conway and Roy Gibson, a change came over his features.

A placid calmness. Remarkably serene.

"My father is weak," he said flatly. "And weak-minded. He's even worse than my weeping willow of a mother. Hell, he's always been an embarrassment to me. He doesn't see what's happening to the white race when it's right in front of his eyes."

"And you do?"

"All right-thinking people do. You know, when they brought me out of the coma and I heard that some yellow-skinned bitch had done my surgery, I almost threw up."

He folded his arms contentedly.

"It's kinda like a metaphor, or whatever it's called. While I slept, a Jap snuck in and cut me. Same thing's happening all over. While America sleeps, the lesser breeds grow in numbers and power. Until they'll one day supplant us. Replace us."

"Jesus Christ, Jason, you can't really believe—"

"Don't pull that naive shit with me. Anyone with a brain knows that a race war is coming. That's why we whites have to organize, get our weapons stocked and ready. Why we have to infiltrate social media and support patriotic political candidates. Why we have to resist every attempt to appease the niggers and spics and anyone else whose very existence is a threat to white people everywhere."

"Nice speech, Jason. You get it off the net?"

"Fuck you, Doctor. Since I was younger, practically a kid, I could see the signs. I could see what was happening in this country. Everything going in the wrong direction. I knew that if things didn't change, the only people who belonged here—people like me—would be left with nothing. No pride, no power."

My heart had begun to sink as he spoke, and I could feel the intensity in my gaze weaken. What would my self-righteous anger accomplish? Did I think it would shame him? Change his mind? Soften his hatred?

Jason and so many others like him were simply picking up the banner from those who'd gone before, who'd seeded their hatred and fear of displacement in the minds of those now coming to maturity.

And so the cycle continued. The cancer spread.

"Can you answer one last question for me?" I said, though by now I really didn't care much about the answer.

"Hey, I'm happy to school you all day long, Doc."

"Given the two attempts on your life, you were obviously on the Handler's list of members needing to be silenced. Yet why were you—Jason—the target? Why not your father? *His* was the name listed on the society website."

Jason managed a knowing smile. "Because Gibson wasn't as clever as he thought he was. I could negotiate the Dark Web much better than an old fart like him. I mean, I respected him and the mission. But I didn't want him to think I was like the others he'd enlisted. So, just to let him know who he was dealing with, I hacked his own portal and told him who I was. That I'd used my father's name for my own protection, and that if he was smart he'd give me more responsibility in the group."

"Turns out," I said, "that wasn't so smart on your end. Now that he knew who you really were, you were a target the moment he decided to purge the group. A victim like everybody else."

His voice rose in anger.

"I'm *not* like everybody else! You'll see, Rinaldi. Everyone will see. When this country splits apart, and the true patriots rise, you'll see what I can offer. How I'll lead!"

I shook my head.

"Let me know when that happens, Napoleon. Till then, I think I'll leave you to your white power fantasies and make my exit."

I affected a thoughtful pause.

"Though I now have a clearer clinical understanding of your panic attacks. The symptoms of which you've suffered since your teens. They fall right in line with your paranoia about the potential decline of the white race. It's a tidy circle. The paranoia feeds your racism and your racism feeds the paranoia."

"I'm not paranoid. Just look around you…"

"Yeah, I've heard that speech, too. I do look around me. And despite the chaos and uncertainty, I like what I see."

I headed for the door, then stopped.

"By the way, Jason," I said, "I still hope you get treated for your panic symptoms. I can make a referral if you'd like."

"Yeah, right. Fuck you again, Rinaldi."

I shrugged and opened the door. But before I could leave, Jason called after me.

"Hey, Doc!"

I turned. His arm had raised, hand outstretched, palm down. The Nazi power salute.

—

I spent the rest of the day off the grid. No social media, no news programs, and with my emails, professional or otherwise, unanswered. Just rambled around my house, listening to my favorite jazz standards and drinking more than I should.

Finally, as night fell, I was once again on my back deck, whiskey in hand and watching the Three Rivers. Their ceaseless flow, the way they merged at the Point, reminded me that nature's quiet determination to endure was a good lesson for the rest of us. That, like these broad rivers, we should embrace the simple, undeniable fact of our own merging.

Of course, that requires justice, compassion, and hope, none of which seem to be in ample supply nowadays. But as a therapist, citizen, and human being, I have to believe there's enough of each to sustain us. Even to prevail.

And, all evidence to the contrary, I do.

# ACKNOWLEDGMENTS

This is a list that grows by the year, but my sincere thanks:

To my editors at Sourcebooks/Poisoned Pen Press, Diane DiBiase and Beth Deveny, whose thoughtful notes and suggestions made this a better book;

To my friend and literary manager, Ken Atchity;

To my friends, clinical colleagues, and fellow mystery authors—while too numerous to mention, I'm grateful to each and every one;

And, finally, to the people and city of Pittsburgh, my hometown and a constant source of both inspiration and fond memories.

# ABOUT THE AUTHOR

Formerly a Hollywood screenwriter (*My Favorite Year* and *Welcome Back, Kotter*, etc.), Dennis Palumbo is now a licensed psychotherapist in private practice and author. His mystery fiction has appeared in *Ellery Queen's Mystery Magazine, The Strand, Written By,* and elsewhere, and is collected in *From Crime to Crime* (Tallfellow Press). His latest short story, "Steel City Blues," appeared in *Coast to Coast Noir,* named Best Anthology of 2020 by *Suspense Magazine.* His acclaimed series of mystery thrillers, *Mirror Image, Fever Dream, Night Terrors, Phantom Limb,* and *Head Wounds* (all from Poisoned Pen Press), features a psychologist who consults with the Pittsburgh Police. For more information, visit dennispalumbo.com.